W9-BEU-866

To John,

Hope you enjoy The Spanish back-drop for this crazy tale.

THE MINOAN CIPHER

PAUL KEMPRECOS

SUSPENSE PUBLISHING

Best wishes,

Paul Kemprecos

THE MINOAN CIPHER
by
Paul Kemprecos

PAPERBACK EDITION
* * * * *
PUBLISHED BY:
Suspense Publishing

Paul Kemprecos
COPYRIGHT
2016 Paul Kemprecos

PUBLISHING HISTORY:
Suspense Publishing, Paperback and Digital Copy, August 16, 2016

Cover Design: Shannon Raab
Cover Photographer: iStockphoto.com/Roberto A Sanchez
Cover Photographer: iStockphoto.com/Adam Smigielski
Cover Photographer: iStockphoto.com/freestylephoto

ISBN-13: 978-1536866070
ISBN-10: 1536866075

All rights reserved. Without limiting the rights under copyright reserved above, no part of this publication may be reproduced, stored in or introduced into a retrieval system, or transmitted, in any form, or by any means (electronic, mechanical, photocopying, recording, or otherwise) without the prior written permission of both the copyright owner and the above publisher of this book.

This is a work of fiction. Names, characters, places, brands, media, and incidents are either the product of the author's imagination or are used fictitiously. The author acknowledges the trademarked status and trademark owners of various products referenced in this work of fiction, which have been used without permission. The publication/use of these trademarks.

DEDICATION

In memory of my pal Wayne Valero, collector extraordinaire, writer and friend of writers, a natural-born editor, lover of adventure and all-round good guy, who left this world far too soon.

ACKNOWLEDGEMENTS

The internet has made a universe of information available at the touch of a keyboard, but it is in physical books that an author searches for nuggets to stir the imagination of the reader. The Santorini eruption used as a backdrop in the Prologue is exhaustively examined in "Fire in the Sea" by Walter L. Friedrich. Two books, "Minoans" and "The Knossos Labyrinth," both by Rodney Castleden, provided fascinating insights into work of Sir Arthur Evans and the art, architecture and mysterious religion of the long-lost civilization he discovered. The remarkable accomplishments of the linguistic genius Michael Ventris are described in "The Man Who Deciphered Linear B" by Andrew Robinson and "The Decipherment of Linear B" by John Chadwick. Ventris actually died in an auto accident at the age of thirty-four. While the fanciful account of that tragic event in "The Minoan Cipher" is purely speculative, if any one could have translated Linear A, it would have been Michael Ventris.

PRAISE FOR
PAUL KEMPRECOS

" "The Emerald Scepter" just might be the perfect speculative thriller, offering up a seasoned blend of legend and folklore mixed brilliantly with actual historical fact. James Rollins and Clive Cussler have nothing on Paul Kemprecos who has been and continues to be a master of the form and then some. This is everything a great read should be, a riveting, tried-and -true tale of quests and daring-do, of great heroes and equally contemptuous villains. There's a reason why Kemprecos is a #1 *New York Times* bestselling author and it's all on display here."
—Jon Land, *USA Today* Bestselling Author

"A brilliant mystery that combines suspense with exciting adventure. Intriguing plot twists from beginning to end, shrouded under genuine history."
—Clive Cussler, *New York Times* Bestselling Author

"Kemprecos...writes sharp, readable prose."
—*Booklist*

"Absorbing...Soc is an appealing, witty protagonist...and the Cape Cod locale is rendered with panache in this fast-paced enjoyable yarn."
—*Publisher's Weekly*

"Former newsman Kemprecos delivers the where, why, what, when, and finally who in a whodunit strengthened by gritty dialogue and assured depictions of suspenseful dives."
—*Boston Herald*

THE MINOAN CIPHER

PAUL KEMPRECOS

PROLOGUE
PART I-CATACLYSM

The Aegean Sea, Circa 1600 B.C.

The gods were angry. There could be no other explanation for the quaking ground and the fire that rained down from the heavens on the hapless inhabitants of Kalliste, a small volcanic island located one-hundred-twenty miles north of Crete.

The island's high cliffs formed an open ring that enclosed a deep lagoon big enough for dozens of ships. The protective bay and the island's strategic location on the trade routes attracted cargo vessels from all around the Mediterranean. The island had prospered. The fruits of those riches could be seen in the thriving settlements that lined the harbor. The islanders celebrated the bounty of the sea in their art and architecture. Graceful frescoes of dolphins and flying fish decorated the interior walls of the two- and three-story houses that lined the bay.

The riches came with a price. Kalliste was home to restless volcanoes, below and above the sea, which occasionally triggered earthquakes and blanketed the island with choking ash. The islanders had become used to what they saw as divine temper tantrums. After each disturbance, there would follow a flurry of sacrifices and ceremonies to soothe the gods. When things quieted down, the islanders swept the pumice dust from their thresholds and rebuilt the houses that had collapsed. Commerce was restored and life went on. But the impending calamity about to hit the island would be greater than anything in memory. The natural forces soon to be unleashed from deep in the earth were more powerful than even the gods could have imagined.

Kalliste's fate had been preordained millions of years earlier. The island sat astride what geologists today call the South Aegean volcanic arc. The volcanic chain extends from Turkey to Greece, forming a line where the continents of Africa and Europe come together as they drift on a sea of molten rock known as magma. Where continents collide, cracks form in the earth's crust and volcanoes are born. The massive magma chamber under Kalliste was like a gigantic pressure cooker. When the molten forces fractured the rock above, the blast that followed was one of the most violent natural explosions in recorded history.

A black plume churned more than twenty miles into the stratosphere, causing dramatic colors in the sky and climate changes around the world. Super-heated air flowed over the rim of the caldera with a fury hotter than a thousand blast furnaces. The turbulent cloud of ash and dust rolled horizontally across the sea at more than sixty miles an hour. The fiery shock wave pummeled ships standing in its way.

The increasingly violent tremors leading up to the eruption had made the island practically uninhabitable. Fleets of ships had carried most of the population to Crete. Many refugees settled in or around Knossos, the bustling town on the north coast that was the home port to the far-flung Minoan empire.

The day the world ended for Knossos had been filled with bountiful promise. Sweating longshoremen toiled on docks piled high with trade goods. Pedestrian traffic streamed past the boat sheds, construction yards, warehouses, cafés, taverns and brothels that served the needs of ships and the crews that manned them.

From the balconies of the houses built into the hill behind the harbor, wealthy merchants could look out on a forest of masts sprouting from scores of wide-beamed sailing galleys. Some ships were more than a hundred feet long. More vessels were anchored to the east and west of the port or clustered in the natural harbors and bays that indented the island's one-hundred-sixty-mile-long coastline.

Ships sailing out of the island ports traveled to Africa, Asia and Europe, even beyond the Pillars of Hercules into the Atlantic Ocean. The merchant fleet carried the staples of a thriving civilization: olives, wine, and fine crafted goods to trade for copper used in the manufacture of bronze. Knossos was at the peak of its wealth, power and affluence. But in an instant, all that was about to change.

Along the waterfront, eyes turned to the north at the rumble of distant thunder. Refugees who'd fled Kalliste recognized the sound of a volcanic eruption. Some heaved a sigh of relief at their escape from their doomed island. But their destiny was only delayed. The volcanic eruption created an earthquake that in turn spawned a tsunami. And Crete lay directly in the path of the deadly wave.

The tsunami raced across open water in the form of a heaving sea, but when it encountered land, the wave released its full destructive force. It clawed the water out of the harbor, exposing the muddy bottom, then reared up in a moving brown wall more than twenty-five-feet high. Millions of tons of roiling seawater inundated Knossos and branched out in death-dealing tributaries that carried bodies and debris miles from the harbor.

The watery destruction swept several miles inland and finally ebbed at the foot of the sprawling palace that was the heart of the Minoan empire. When the wave receded, a muddy curve of shoreline was all that remained of the great commercial port of Knossos. All was silent. The only sound was the whisper coming from the blizzard of gray pumice flakes falling softly from the sky.

PART II-THE LABYRINTH

The squat-bodied man sat on a rock at the top of the hill, the dark wide-set eyes in his bovine face fixed on the horizon in a tight squint. He was dressed simply in a blue kilt; his muscular chest was bare. A bandanna protected his shaven scalp from the intense rays of the mid-day sun. He had come to this place every morning for the past few days, ever since he'd awakened after a sleepless night with the feeling that something was wrong. He didn't know what it was, but he had learned from his many years as a soldier to heed his instincts.

From his hard perch he had a good view of the harbor and the sea beyond. The nauseous stench of rotting corpses and dead fish still poisoned the air several weeks after the giant wave had wiped out the port, but the curtain of dust no longer blotted out the sun. Tides had thinned the gray blanket of pumice to reveal patches of violet-hued water.

The feeling of unease was stronger than ever when his chariot passed through the palace gates earlier that day. He traveled to his rock perch along the remnants of a paved road that was matted with seaweed and covered with ash. The morning was uneventful. Then, shortly after noon, a speck appeared on the horizon. The object moved closer until he could make out a striped red-and-white sail of the design favored by Mycenaean shipbuilders. It was exactly what he had dreaded. A scout ship from the mainland.

Since the day of the disaster, the few ships that had ventured to Knossos were Minoan, returning from voyages to distant places. Unable to navigate the wreckage and pumice clogging their home ports along the northern coast, the ships had sailed around to the south side of Crete which had escaped the full force of the volcano. The black-hulled vessel approached Knossos harbor and made a lazy pass along the outer edge of the pumice line. The observers on board must have seen enough, because the ship turned and headed out to sea. Oars sprouted from the sides, the vessel picked up speed and soon became lost in the sea mist.

A cold sense of foreboding flowed through the man's thick body. The mainland inhabitants had long chafed under Cretan rule. They paid tribute and accepted the onerous trading conditions enforced by the invincible Minoan navy. News of the destruction of Knossos would have spread to the mainland. The ship had been sent to assess the damage. An invasion would follow. As commander of the palace guard, known as the Followers, it would be up to him to stop the invaders.

The commander rose from the rock and climbed into the wicker chariot. He flicked the reins of the two piebald ponies, urging the pair to a gallop.

The chariot quickly covered the five-mile distance to the gates of the sprawling palace. The wheels clattered on a spacious stone-paved plaza where the commander then turned the reins over to a waiting guard. As he stepped out of the chariot he heard the sound of flutes, the musical prelude to a sacrifice.

The flute players flanked a procession moving across the plaza, headed by a half dozen young priestesses. They were leading two goats chosen for sacrifice to an altar in front of the massive sculpture known as the Horns of Consecration. At least a hundred people had joined the parade.

The commander frowned in disapproval. The crowds attending the ritual blood lettings were growing in size. The piping of the flutes faded as he strode between massive rectangular stone columns into the cool interior of the palace. He descended a stairwell several floors to a passageway. In the flickering light of sconces that lined the walls he saw two people step from a doorway and walk in his direction. He recognized the high priestess of the Mother Goddess sanctuary, and her brother. The priestess wore a long flounced skirt and a blouse with an open bodice that bared her breasts. On her head sat a tall, layered hat. She carried a clay urn that held the gold-hilted sacrificial dagger.

The commander stood with his back to the wall. The priestess brushed past the commander, her skirt swishing in the quiet passageway. The fragrance of oil made from flower petals filled his nostrils. Her eyes were fixed in a stony gaze. She was under the influence of a narcotic intoxicant used to heighten the sacrificial experience and paid no attention to the commander.

He had known the priestess when she was an alluring young woman of breathtaking beauty. Her physical and mental transformation began after she became emissary to the Mother Goddess. Her shoulder-length raven hair was streaked now with silver. Seductive eyes that had been inviting warm pools in her youth now burned with the intensity of smoldering coal.

Although she was barely thirty, her once soft features were as hard as marble. Her lush lips had thinned to a tight line. Hours spent away from the sun in dark temples and cave shrines had imparted a bloodless pallor to her face. The heavy use of kohl on her eyelids emphasized the whiteness of her skin. Her power rested on her success in dealing with the whims of a capricious deity. She allowed herself no life beyond the rituals.

The commander was a tough and fearless soldier, but the priestess made him nervous. He had seen her dance with poisonous snakes in her hands. He had witnessed sacrifices where she had slashed the throat of a two-thousand-pound auroch bull that stood more than six feet high at the shoulders.

The brother was tall and willowy like his sister, but where her face was beautiful his was feral, with a pointed chin, aquiline nose and yellow, almond-shaped eyes. His scalp had been shaved and painted blue, as was the fashion with elite Minoan males. He wore a jeweled girdle that thinned his waist to an unnatural size that emphasized his chest.

He shot the commander a glance that brimmed with hatred. The commander was used to hostile looks from the brother, knowing he resented his authority as second in command to the king. But this time the man's frown turned to a smile. Almost as if he was keeping a secret behind his yellow eyes.

The stunning architectural complexity of the palace had earned the building its name: The Labyrinth. The commander was one of only a few people who could navigate the maze-like passageways. He quickened his pace. Something was going on and he wanted to know what it was. He followed the passageway to an exit that took him out to the palace gardens. The sound of a child's laughter came from a pavilion built in the shade of tall palm trees.

The source of the laughter was a young girl. She bounced on the knees of her father, King Minos, who sat on a carved wooden stool. He was bare-chested, his lower body covered with a white kilt. The symbols of his power came in the form of the double-headed axe design embroidered on the hem of his kilt and the plumed headdress covering dark hair that hung over his left shoulder in a long braid. His daughter's linen dress was edged with a similar axe pattern, indicating her own royal status.

The little girl stopped bouncing and grinned when she saw the commander. She was a true princess; imperious, quick-tempered and fearless. She had become even more spoiled by the king since her mother had fallen ill and died. She was not put off by the commander's physical appearance like some in the court who referred to him behind his back as the Minotaur, a monster that was half-man and half-bull.

The king's daughter smiled and reached up to play with her father's crown. The king untied a blue ribbon in the girl's auburn tresses and replaced it with his headdress, which slid down over her eyes. Her fingers went to pinch her father's aristocratic nose. He groaned with exaggerated pain and handed the giggling child off to a nanny with instructions to take her to the nursery. The king gestured at the commander to take a seat on a stone bench. The smile on his face vanished.

"Did you encounter the high priestess and her brother?" he said.

The commander nodded. "They were on their way to make another sacrifice."

"I know. She came to tell me that the Mother Goddess is angry at the meagerness of our sacrificial offerings."

"There are goats and bulls for sacrifice to be found in the interior villages."

The king's lips tightened in a bleak smile.

"The priestess says animals are not *sufficient* gifts. She says that the Mother Goddess speaks through the mouths of the serpents who whisper in her ear the mother's wish for greater sacrifices." He paused. "As was done in the old days."

The commander had heard the dark tales of the barbaric rituals the priestesses had practiced when the empire was young.

"Human sacrifice?"

The king nodded. "I have tried to discourage this idea. The priestess reminds me that my power comes from the Mother Goddess. *She* who must be pleased." Lowering his voice, he added, "I am told that as the king, I must offer the greatest sacrifice a man can make."

He held up the blue ribbon he had taken from his daughter's hair.

The commander's eyes blazed like hot coals. "The priestess must be mad from the potions she ingests."

"Perhaps. But I believe she wants to replace me on the throne with her brother."

"The people would never allow that."

"The people still mourn their dead. Even in the villages, the thick dust makes it difficult to plant the fields. My subjects will remove me as king if she can convince them that I am to blame for their continuing misfortune by my refusal to give up my daughter. The priestess stokes their fears. She prays for another calamity to light the fire of rage within them."

"Then her prayers have been answered," the commander said. He told the king about the Mycenaean ship.

"How long before an invasion?"

"Once the ship reaches the mainland, a matter of days—an armada will be assembled. They can place five hundred warriors on shore within weeks. More will follow. They are fierce fighters and will be thirsting for blood and booty."

The king weighed the commander's words.

"News of the scout ship's visit will spread to our cities and villages," he said after a thoughtful pause. "The priestess will offer the people a way to save themselves. She will profess, 'if the king makes his sacrifice, the Mother Goddess will repel the Mycenaeans.' If I refuse, the people will storm the palace. Some of the marines will join them."

"The governors of the other cities will stand by you."

"My governors, even those close to me, will have no choice but to turn against me."

"My men will fight to the death to defend you."

The king waved his long fingers in the air. "I have other work for them. The priestess and her brother can't be allowed to gain control of the treasury. It must be moved out tonight, as soon as darkness falls, while they lay in a trance after the sacrifices."

"So soon?"

"No better time. I have prepared for this day. I will join you in the gardens after darkness falls. Now *go!*"

The commander followed a pathway that ran through an olive grove bordering the elaborate gardens behind the palace, to the barracks and stables used by the Followers. Couriers instructed the men scattered around the palace to assemble in the gardens as soon as the sun rested. Horses were brought in and a handful of sentries were posted in the gardens.

The commander led two dozen of his strongest men into the palace along a corridor that was high and wide enough for the horses to pass through.

The passageway ended in a wall decorated with a fresco that showed a school of fish in exuberant flight. The commander pushed with the tip of his sword against the third fish eye from the left. A lock clicked and the wall swiveled open to reveal a wide doorway. He and his men stepped into a huge vault and used their guttering torches to light wall lamps. The smoke escaped through an ingenious ventilation system.

The Minoans had amassed vast wealth, but most of that treasure was invested in the fleet of warships and merchant vessels, often one in the same, and in the buildings and infrastructure that were the hallmarks of a great empire. The jewels and gold accrued from commerce were scattered among the prosperous port cities. Aware that the delicate balance of power between the king and high priestess could be upended at any moment, Minos had secretly diverted the finest gems and precious metals to his own treasury secluded deep in the bowels of the Labyrinth.

The treasure was contained in dozens of bronze chests stacked on wagons that were ready to be hitched to the horses. Some chests were empty, in anticipation of riches yet to come. If any of the men thought it odd that the commander ordered them to hitch the wagons with both the empty and full coffers, they kept their questions to themselves.

One-by-one the wagons were pulled through the passageway to the gardens. Shortly after darkness fell, the king emerged from the olive grove. He wore a hooded cloak and carried his sleeping daughter over his shoulder. The nanny trailed behind them.

"All is well, I trust," he said in a low voice.

"The treasure is ready to be transported at your word," the commander said.

"Good. I want you to go to the south coast where a great ship will be waiting. Sail to Egypt and use the treasure to build a new navy. Each chest has more than enough for a great ship, its crew and contingent of marines. I will stay here."

The commander scowled in disbelief. "You must leave with us, sire. It is too dangerous."

Minos rose to his full regal height and pushed the hood away. "I am still the king. I will reason with the people."

"The priestess has whipped them into a fury. They are *beyond* reason."

"I am not the first King Minos, nor will I be the last. At the very least, if I stay, you will gain time to escape with my daughter." He slipped the sleeping girl from his shoulder and held her body cradled in both arms. "I entrust you with my *greatest* treasure. On your life, keep her from harm's way!"

The words came not from the monarch of a wealthy empire, but from the mouth of a stricken father saying farewell to his child forever.

"As you wish, sire," the commander said.

He lifted the slumbering girl into his brawny arms.

The king removed a leather pouch from under his cloak and looped the strap around the commander's thick neck. "Fill this scroll with your words. Write every day. If you or I are lost, it will show those that follow the way to the treasure. It must never fall into the wrong hands. Promise me!"

"I give you my promise, sire."

The king lifted the hood back onto his head and vanished into the shadows.

The commander stared into the darkness until he became aware of the heat of the girl resting in his arms. He told the nanny to get into a supply wagon, then handed the girl up to her. With a heaviness in his heart, he ordered his men to move out.

PART III-FLIGHT

The commander and his men marched under the stars, following a road that ran between rugged mountain ranges and across plains covered with agricultural fields. At dawn, he ordered the group to stop and rest in the shade of some hearty trees so his men could dine on bread, cheese and water.

The march continued under the blistering sun and well into the evening. Spurring him on to even greater urgency were the pinpoints of light moving along the royal road from the direction of Knossos. His instincts told him that the high priestess had recovered from her drug daze and rallied her followers much faster than he'd expected. The commander had lived through many battles by thinking far ahead of the enemy. His orders from the king were what the high priestess would expect him to do, so he did what he had prepared for when he ordered his men to transport empty chests from the treasury along with the full.

He split his men into two groups. One group would take some wagons and continue on to the coast. The nanny and the child would go with them. The commander led another contingent of men, horses and wagons onto a dry river bed through the rugged hills.

When the commander caught up with the procession the next morning, the weary faces of his men were smeared with sweat and dirt. The string of horses they led no longer hauled wagons. The commander spurred his men along the coastal road which gradually rose, passed through a narrow gorge and descended a series of switchbacks to a small harbor.

Tied up to a stone quay were four vessels. The largest, a cargo ship, had a narrow stern and an upturned prow carved into the head of a bird. The vessel had a graceful crescent profile. Towers at each end were designed to provide archers defending the ship with elevated battle stations.

The wagons were wheeled up a gangway onto the ship. The bronze chests were slid down ramps into the hold. Stalls were set up on deck for a few horses while the rest were given to a nearby village. The chariot was taken apart and stored in the hold.

The commander pondered the fate of the other vessels. Two were mid-sized trading craft. The last was less than a third the length of the great ship and its narrow white hull was painted with images of leaping blue dolphins. He recognized the king's yacht which had been on its way back from a competition in Egypt. The yacht had stopped at the southern harbor and the crew headed north on foot after learning their home port had been destroyed.

With its out-sized sail of red wool, and wave-cutting hull design, there was nothing on the water that could touch the yacht for speed. The commander ordered the yacht towed behind the ship. It would slow them, but he could never allow the king's boat to fall into enemy hands.

Dusk was settling. The wise course would be to torch the other vessels, but the commander hesitated. Every Minoan ship was precious. By the time he had reluctantly decided to destroy the ships, it was too late.

Someone yelled and pointed to the hill overlooking the harbor. A light crested the ridge. Then another and another. The lights flowed down the road leading to the harbor, moving back and forth along the steep switchbacks.

The commander ordered the captain to get underway. The crew cast off the dock lines and unfurled the sail. The pursuers swarmed along the quay. A hail of arrows from shore fell short of the departing vessel. In the light of the gathering torches, the commander saw a man wearing a plumed headdress. In his confusion, the commander thought that the king had succeeded in winning over the people.

Then the man removed the feathered crown to reveal his shaved blue scalp. The priestess stepped up beside her brother. The commander couldn't see her features in the waning light but he could sense her anger.

As soon as the ship cleared the harbor, the commander found a cabin for the king's daughter and her nanny. The girl threw a fit of anger when the commander said that the king was busy and would come later in another ship. The noisy tirade was short, thankfully, and she soon fell asleep.

The commander curled up under a cloak on the stern deck. He awoke at first light, rose to his feet, and cursed himself for not moving faster to torch the other ships.

Two sails followed in their wake.

Minoan ship designers had sacrificed the space needed to quarter a crew of rowers to gain more cargo room. The great ships relied on a highly efficient sail that allowed the ship to run close to the wind, but it was still slower than a fully rowed vessel with sail.

The captain suggested cutting the yacht loose. The commander told him to wait.

The pursuers had halved the distance by the end of the day. The captain estimated that they would catch up the following morning. With their superior maneuverability, the smaller ships would run rings around them. Archers posted on the fighting towers could keep them at bay, but only for a while.

The commander's jaw hardened in determination. The priestess would assume that he planned to seek safe haven in Egypt, long a friendly port of call for Minoan ships. Again, he would do the opposite of her expectations. As soon as darkness had fallen, he told the captain to change course.

The captain relayed the order to the helmsman. The ship swung around, and the bird figurehead pointed its beak toward the place where the sun had set. When the sun rose the next morning there wasn't a sail in sight. The commander brought out the vellum scroll the king had given him and dutifully summarized the flight from the island. Over the next several days he kept a running log of the voyage to the western end of the Mediterranean and around the coast of what one day would be a country known as Spain. The commander wanted to put distance between his ship and Crete.

They might have escaped if the wind hadn't died. With no rowing capacity, the ship lay almost motionless in the water. By the time the wind freshened, it was too late. A sail was sighted behind them. The high priestess must have figured out that the commander had detoured. She would have sent one ship to Egypt while the other headed west. Powered by a full crew of rowers, her ship grew closer.

The commander ordered his men to take defensive positions, but they could do little as the smaller, faster boat dashed in and shot off a barrage of fiery arrows. With its sail ablaze, the great ship came to a halt. The smaller vessel drew closer in preparation for boarding.

The cargo vessel's captain rushed up to the commander, and said, "You must take the girl and abandon ship."

The suggestion went against every molecule in the commander's body. "I can't leave you or my men."

"You must. We will stay and fight. The king ordered you to keep his daughter safe."

A second flight of arrows landed on the deck and the ardent flames quickly spread. The ship was doomed. The commander dashed below, scooped up the girl in his arms, and told the nanny to follow him back onto the deck. The captain was at the stern, where his men had hauled the yacht alongside. The commander climbed down a rope ladder into the yacht. The girl was tossed down to him. Then the nanny followed.

He cast off, raised the sail and took the tiller. The fast yacht was well away when the commander looked back and saw that the attacking ship had edged close to the flames. Both ships were enveloped in a billowing black cloud. A puff of wind cleared the air for a second or two, and in that brief instant the commander saw the high priestess at the rail.

Her mouth was open wide in an inaudible scream. Her clenched fists were raised high in the air, held in the same position he had seen when she did the serpent dance. The demonic expression on her face was seared into his memory. He turned his eyes away and looked at the girl in the arms of the nanny. *Keep her from harm's way*, the king had pleaded, but she wouldn't be completely safe until she was beyond the clutches of the priestess forever.

He took a final look back and saw only a thick curtain of smoke. Then he brought the yacht's sharp bow around and sailed toward the unknown.

CHAPTER ONE

London, England, September, 1956

Professor Howard Robsham rooted through the stacks of paper on his desk, like the foraging badger he resembled. He found the packet containing his train and ship tickets, and was stuffing it into a bulging briefcase when the doorbell's ring interrupted his labors.

"What the deuce," he muttered.

A visitor was the bloody *last* thing he needed. He snapped the briefcase shut, carried it out to the vestibule and set it down next to a couple of well-worn leather suitcases.

The doorbell rang a second time. Robsham scurried to the entrance of his King's Road townhouse and threw open the door, prepared to send the unwelcome caller on his way. Light from inside the house illuminated the face of the firm-jawed man in his thirties who stood on the landing.

"Michael!" Robsham said, the frown leaving his lips. "What a wonderful surprise."

"Sorry to be a bother." The man hoisted the portfolio case in his hand. "I know it's late, but this couldn't wait until tomorrow."

"Dear me! I'm about to depart for a conference of the World Philological Society in Athens. Leaving momentarily for Victoria Station to catch a sleeper heading to Venice, then onto a steamship bound for Piraeus. Didn't you get my note?"

The man looked crestfallen. "I haven't opened correspondence for weeks. I've been cloistered like a monk with my work."

"Designing a new building project?"

"I'm afraid my architectural career has suffered from my other preoccupations."

"Well…come in, come in. I'm all packed as you can see. A cab is due in twenty minutes. I'll pour us a quick brandy and we'll have a short but proper chinwag."

"Quite all right, Professor. That's all the time I need."

Robsham led the way into the study and motioned for his friend to take a seat. From a crystal decanter on a low table, he poured two fat fingers of Armagnac into a pair of snifters. Then he settled into a stuffed leather chair.

"Since time is short, I'll do this the way I deal with my more prolix students," he said. "State your premise in twenty words or less."

"I only need five words." The man smiled, "I have done it again."

"I don't—"

"The second script. I've unlocked its secret."

"What?" Robsham set his snifter down on the table. "Are you saying you've deciphered Linear A?"

His friend nodded.

"I'm speechless, Michael. This is stupendous. No, it's *beyond* that. Please don't hold back, young man. Tell me how you succeeded where others failed. Did you use the grid approach that worked with Linear B?"

"I tried that method, but this script is in a class by itself."

"How, then?"

"I had the help of the Rosetta Stone. Partial, imperfect and incomplete, but it held the key to my findings."

Even someone without Robsham's scholarly credentials would know the Rosetta Stone was the artifact inscribed with a message in three different languages that had allowed the decipherment of Egyptian hieroglyphics.

"If what you say is true, the translation of Linear A could tear away the curtain of secrecy that has hid so much of the marvelous Minoan civilization. Finally, we would be able to know everything about those amazing people. Not just through their ruined palaces. Their words would tell us what they were thinking. I've got to cancel my trip."

"No need to cancel, Professor. You can do far more to advance my research in Greece than here in London."

Robsham saw the unwavering determination in the calm eyes that gazed out from under the arching brow and wide forehead. He glanced at the clock. "Very well. You have ten minutes."

"I will take you on a shortened version of my linguistic adventure," Michael said. He unzipped the portfolio and extracted two photocopies. He moved the brandy snifters aside and placed the first copy on the coffee table. "I enlarged these with my architectural camera. What do you make of them?"

Robsham read a few paragraphs. "My Spanish is rusty, but this appears to involve the transfer of property belonging to a heretic. Something to do with the Inquisition?"

"Exactly. Now this."

Michael Ventris set two more pages covered with pictographs next to the first. Robsham tapped a page with his finger. "Linear A. What does this writing have to do with the Spanish pages?"

"They are one and the same, Professor. I've used the few Linear A symbols that have been deciphered, along with some that I have analyzed. They gave me enough traction to know that both texts are talking about the identical subject."

The professor felt as if the room were spinning. He gulped down his brandy to steady his nerves and glanced at the clock. Five minutes before the taxi arrived. Damn. He had told the driver to be prompt.

"Despite my excitement, I must be frank with my scholarly skepticism. This document would mean that someone knew, and used, Linear A script, thousands of years after it had vanished from all knowledge."

"My conclusion as well."

"Impossible, but there it is, right in front of us. Where did you find this material?"

"I was exhausted after my Linear B translation, but the problem of the second script still intrigued me. I engaged a book agent who was instructed to ferret out examples of the ancient script. I wanted a library in place, for me or other scholars who might take up the translation. The agent found a Spanish dealer in antique documents who had discovered the script clipped to legal papers involving a transfer of real estate property under the auspices of the Inquisition."

"But Michael, the juxtaposition of these two documents simply doesn't make sense. The Minoan civilization disappeared thousands of years ago. No one even knew the blasted Minoans existed until Evans started poking around."

"That's why I have put aside the question of *how* until I deal with *what*. I will use the documents to establish a lexicon. Then I can decipher this fully and perhaps it will tell us *who*."

"Have you told anyone else about this?"

"I corresponded with a historian at the University of Seville who is an expert on the Minoan colonization of Spain. I wondered whether there was a linguistic link, similar to the way Greek had become the basis for a Minoan script. He encouraged me to continue my research and I've kept him up-to-date."

The honk of a car horn interrupted their conversation.

"Blast it," the professor said. "Cab is right on time. Quickly now, tell me what I can do."

"Your trip to Greece must be the handiwork of the gods. The photocopies are for you to keep, but I need more examples of Linear A script to provide context for my translation. You have contacts in Athens and Heraklion."

"And I'll be happy to use them to get what you need." The professor stood and braced his friend by the shoulders. "The professional naysayers in academia will resist your findings as they did before. You know how they howl when amateurs like us beat them at their own game. But if you succeed, young man, this will far eclipse your debut."

"I'm aware of that, which is why I have been nervous and depressed even on the verge of success."

The horn honked again.

"The cab driver is getting impatient," the professor said.

They carried the bags out to the curb. While the driver packed the boot, the two men shook hands and the professor said he would call his friend after the conference. He got in the back seat and flashed his friend a Winston Churchill victory sign as the cab drove off. Michael smiled and returned the 'V.'

Robsham sat back in his seat and pondered the implications of his brief conversation. If there was one person on earth who could translate a script that had, thus far, defied all attempts at decipherment it was Michael Ventris. Once he set his mind, he pursued his goal to the end. There was no disputing the man's brilliance.

Ventris had been only fourteen years old when he went to a lecture given in London at the 50th anniversary of the British School of Archaeology. The speaker was Arthur Evans, the amateur archaeologist who had excavated the palace at Knossos, discovering the long-lost Minoan civilization that once ruled the eastern Mediterranean before slipping into oblivion.

Evans had talked about his unsuccessful attempts to decipher two different Minoan scripts, which he had labeled Linear A and Linear B. Ventris was a prodigy who possessed a photographic memory and would become fluent in several languages. As he sat, spellbound in the auditorium at Burlington House, the teenaged Ventris vowed that he would one day decipher a Minoan script.

He went on to become an architect, and was a Royal Air Force bomber navigator over Germany during World War II.

After the war he'd resumed his architectural career, but had devoted most of his energy to deciphering the ancient script. He brought cryptographic techniques to his work and gathered together a work group that corresponded on their findings. He drew heavily upon the notes of Alice Kober and Emmett Bennett, Jr.

Sixteen years after hearing Evans, he announced his controversial finding. The script known as Linear B was a Greek dialect, apparently used mainly for keeping trade records.

It was the archeological discovery of the century.

Robsham chuckled with amazement. Now three years later, the young genius was poised to do it again.

CHAPTER TWO

Ventris was ebullient after his talk with Robsham.

The professor was one of the few people who had kept in touch after Ventris went into a funk following his decipherment of Linear B.

The daunting task of decoding a language more than four thousand years old had taken its toll on him mentally and physically. He was proud of his accomplishment, but disappointed at the contents of the script he worked on. The text subjects were mundane and dealt mostly with commerce. They revealed little about the Minoan culture and why it had vanished.

Ventris would not have been comfortable being in the public eye, even if critics had not questioned his findings. When he produced evidence refuting their criticisms, they sniped at the unspectacular nature of the scripts.

He withdrew from the limelight and seldom appeared in public after that. As his energy gradually returned, he thought about delving into a study of Etruscan, another mysterious language used by a mysterious culture. The library collection had started off as a passive way to get back to his studies without having to throw himself into them.

The Spanish papers had changed all that.

He drove along, deep in thought, a dreamy expression on his handsome face. He hardly noticed that the brakes had an increasing squishy feeling when he stopped at a couple of traffic lights. He snapped to alertness at one stop. The pedal had gone almost halfway to the floorboards. He kept a light foot on the gas pedal and slowed the car to twenty miles per hour.

He was nearing home when the blinding reflection of headlights appeared in his car's rearview mirror. He squinted against the glare and pulled over to the left to give the car room to pass.

The obnoxious vehicle on his tail drew back several car lengths, then sped up to come within inches of the rear bumper before falling back again.

Ventris tried to keep his speed a steady forty miles per hour, hoping this would encourage the other driver to go by him. Instead, the car fell back. When it closed on Ventris again, it tapped the rear bumper.

Crying out in surprise, he regained control of the wheel, only to be bumped again.

His foot instinctively hit the gas pedal. The car sped up to forty-five.

He left his pursuer behind for a moment, then the car closed on him and once more tapped the bumper. Harder this time.

Ventris responded with greater speed, and his car surged up to more than fifty miles per hour. He was on the Barnet By-Pass. He'd soon be home, and away from this lunatic.

The pursuer moved in again.

Ventris got his car up to fifty-five. This was as fast as he dared or wanted to go given the state of his brakes.

As the car moved in again his eyes automatically went to the mirror. He was temporarily blinded by the high beams and didn't see the truck pull out of a side road until it turned directly in front of him.

He jammed his brake pedal. This time it went all the way to the floor. The car slammed into the rear of the truck.

The impact pushed the truck forward and the driver could barely keep control of the steering wheel, but he managed to bring his lorry to a halt. He grabbed an electric torch from its dashboard bracket, got out of the cab and staggered around to the rear of the truck.

The car looked like a large metal accordion. He flashed the torch at the body slumped behind the twisted steering wheel.

There was another car behind the wreck. Its headlights silhouetted a tall, slender figure moved toward the crushed car. At the side of the stranger was a huge four-legged creature.

The driver pointed the torch at the newcomers. The man was dressed entirely in a snug-fitting black once-piece suit that emphasized his barrel chest and narrow waist. He wore sunglasses and a short-brimmed hat that set low on his forehead. The driver realized he was shining the light in the man's face and lowered the beam, which fell on the body of the animal.

"Good God!" he muttered.

This was a dog like no other he had ever seen. Its bony white face resembled a skull that was vaguely human. But it was satanic in form, long and narrow, with the chin pointed. Red eyes blazed in their sockets like hot coals. The creature opened its mouth to display long curved fangs.

"The light makes my pet nervous. Give me the torch." The voice was quiet, like the rustling of a snake slithering over dry autumn leaves.

The stranger stepped forward and took the torch from the lorry driver's trembling fingers, then went over to the wrecked car. He reached in and placed his hand on the man's neck.

"Is he dead?" the lorry driver said.

"Very dead," the man said.

"Slammed right into me. Poor bloke never had a chance," the driver said. "We need help."

"I'll see what I can do," the stranger said. He tossed the torch back, said something to the dog and opened the back door of his car for the creature to get in. Then he got behind the wheel and accelerated quickly, flying past the site of the wreck.

A police car arrived minutes later. The lorry driver was surprised to see it come from the direction opposite from the one the stranger had gone, but with two police officers walking his way, he had other things to think about.

The stranger drove back to Robsham's house. He didn't know

whether the brief visit he'd witnessed earlier had concerned the discovery, but he could take no chances. He had flown to London as soon as the call came from the Seville informant. With the newfound data, he had followed Ventris that night and disabled his car brakes, allowing them to leak fluid.

The house on King's Road was dark. Leaving the Daemon curled up in the back of his Jaguar, he broke in through a window.

Heading into the study, he ransacked the desk drawers and found nothing that even mentioned the ancient script. Receipts on the desktop identified the occupant of the house as a Professor Robsham. Next to the papers were annotated train and ship schedules, which he stuck into his pocket. The stranger explored the rest of the house, including the bedroom closet. A number of hangers stood empty.

Leaving the home, he got back into his car and drove to the airport where a private plane awaited his arrival. Boarding the plane with the canine-like creature, he gave the pilot new instructions. First he would fly to Seville to visit the university professor who'd sounded the alarm. The professor had served his purpose and had to be dealt with. When that task was accomplished, he'd fly to Greece. The added travel was unanticipated, but it was all part of his lifetime mission. He had sworn on the altar of the Horns of Consecration an oath that required him to carry out his sacred work. He must eliminate anybody who unlocked the sacred script and threatened the Way of the Axe.

CHAPTER THREE

Woods Hole, Massachusetts, Present Day

Matt Hawkins pedaled his high-performance lightweight bicycle along the edge of Vineyard Sound, ignoring the twinge that reminded him, with each downward stroke, of the metal pins holding the bones of his left leg together. The lava black eyes behind the wrap-around sunglasses were tightly focused on the tarmac strip ahead of him. His muscular thighs pumped the pedals at a steady fifteen miles per hour pace. Sweat beaded a face that looked as if it had been carved from an oak tree.

Hawkins had rolled out of bed at dawn, downed a mug of black Jamaican coffee and grunted through a half hour of Navy SEAL exercises. After his workout, he had pulled on his biking shorts and jersey and grabbed his helmet. Before heading to the front door, he stopped in the kitchen and threw some dog munchies into a bowl for Quisset, the female golden retriever he had adopted from the animal rescue league. Her name meant Star of the Sea in the language of Cape Cod's Wampanoag Indian tribe.

He plunked the helmet over his salt-and-pepper mane of hair and buckled the chin strap. "Be back in a while," he said. Quisset barely lifted her nose from her dish. "Okay, be that way, doll. Good thing for you that I've got a weakness for blondes."

He wheeled his bike from the front porch of his Victorian-era house to the street where he pushed off and rode through the quiet neighborhood. He pedaled along the harbor past the Marine Biological Laboratory and the Georgian-style brick buildings of the Woods Hole Oceanographic Institution, the academic powerhouse that had transformed the old fishing village into a world-renowned center for oceanic research. Cars and trucks were lining up in the island ferry parking lot for the morning run to Martha's Vineyard.

Hawkins rode on to the Shining Sea bike path and picked up speed. He swept past Nobska Light hill and along expanses of turquoise water and velvety marshes cloaked in sea mist. He braked to a stop at the end of the path after covering more than ten miles, downed a deep swallow from his water bottle, and set off on the return stretch. By the time he reached the ferry terminal he had accomplished his two-fold mission.

He had beefed up the muscles of the leg that had been shattered by an improvised explosive device on a Navy SEAL operation in Afghanistan. And the cool breeze in his face had blown away the mental fog shrouding his brain. Thoughts fluttered around his head like butterflies, making him eager to get back to work before they flew away.

The Water Street drawbridge was being raised for a sailboat heading out of Eel Pond. He almost made it across the short span but had to skid to a stop when the gate dropped in place. He cursed a bit too loudly for some tourists, who moved away, allowing Hawkins to be the first across when the bridge came down. A couple of hundred yards past the bridge, Hawkins turned off Water Street and rode to the oceanographic institution's south dock. He leaned his bike against the twenty-foot-long metal shipping container that served his field office, opened the door and stepped inside.

Slipping his helmet off, he settled into a swivel chair, then powered up his laptop. The file he'd abandoned appeared on the screen. Late the previous night his frustration had peaked. Slamming the cover down on the computer, he'd walked across the street to the Captain Kidd bar, grabbed a beer and sat under the mural of pirates burying a treasure chest. After downing his second beer, he'd decided that an early morning bike ride might stimulate his sluggish mind.

He had hit the wall that stood between him and the completion of a big job for the Navy. His contract required him to design a new generation of ocean gliders. The torpedo-shaped drones were the 'sexy new thing' in undersea technology. Operating on its own, an ocean glider could swoop into the depths of the sea to gather data on water temperatures and currents, then rise to the surface to broadcast its findings.

Navy strategists envisioned fleets of gliders surveying ocean weather and integrating the data with satellites, radar stations, research buoys and other gliders. Ensuring smooth communication had been a major challenge, even for Hawkins, who was one of Woods Hole's leading robotics engineers.

After his final tour of Afghanistan, and months of physical therapy, Hawkins had enrolled at the Massachusetts Institute of Technology, specializing in the undersea application of robotics science. He excelled as a student and, after wrapping up his studies, he moved to Woods Hole and formed the SeaBot Corporation. He bought a forty-two-foot fishing trawler to use for sea tests and hired its former owner, a veteran fisherman named Howard Snow, to run the *Osprey* for him.

Except for Snowy he worked alone, but the Navy job was complex and he had assembled a group of the best engineers in Woods Hole. The SEALs had trained him to work closely with others on dangerous operations. He was kicked out of the Navy when he started asking questions about the ambush that had maimed him, and since then he found it difficult to trust anyone but himself.

He had recovered physically except for a slight limp. With his six-foot-two height and sturdy frame, he was an imposing figure. But he'd slapped a Band-Aid on an emotional wound that needed surgery. The scientific community around Woods Hole considered Hawkins a brilliant loner. His only real friend was Snowy, who used a dry Yankee sense of humor and a shrug of the shoulders to deal with the Hawkins temperament.

Working with a team again had been an opportunity to polish his image. He had had to dull the sharp edges of his personality and put a lid on his impatience. It seemed to have worked. No new friends, but at least he didn't frighten people with a hair-trigger temper and alienate them with his barbed tongue. So far, so good.

The bike ride had improved his mental clarity. An hour after he sat down at his computer, the pieces of the puzzle came together. He checked his computations. Air-tight. With a click of the computer mouse, he sent the file to the other team engineers, and then he brewed a cup of coffee to reward himself. As he raised the mug to his lips he heard the computer chirp. Someone was Skyping him.

That was fast.

The face on the monitor was not one of his project teammates. The woman peering out at him over metal-rimmed glasses had a high-bridged nose, and the skin on her prominent cheekbones was burnished to a healthy pink glow. Her reddish-blonde hair was gathered back from violet-hued eyes.

"Hello, Matt," she said. "Remember me?"

Hawkins smiled. "All the gods on Olympus could not make me forget you, Kalliste. You look terrific."

Kalliste Kalchis was a nautical archaeologist with the Greek government. Hawkins had helped her two years earlier with an underwater survey of the Santorini caldera. She was in her early fifties, but projected the vitality of a woman twenty years younger.

Speaking with a British accent she had picked up while studying at Oxford, she said, "When did you become Greek, Matt?"

"I'm not aware that I had. I'm still the half-Yankee, half-Micmac Indian from Maine that you knew."

"Only a Greek could flatter a woman with such silver-tongued skill."

"*Now* who's doing the flattering?" Hawkins said.

Kalliste laughed. "Guilty as charged. How are you?"

"Wonderful, Kalliste. Working with you and your colleagues was a turning point for me. I have many fond memories of that time."

Kalliste's husband had died of cancer only a year before the expedition; it had been her first time out in the field since his death. She and Matt spent hours under the stars, talking about their lives. Their discussions put things in perspective for him. As she pointed out, Hawkins had lost the full use of a leg, but she had lost a whole man.

"I'm happy to hear that, Matt. How would you like the opportunity to make even *more* fond memories? I'm organizing an expedition and would love to have you aboard."

"Glad to help, Kalliste. When is it?"

"We'll be on site in about a week. I apologize for the short notice, but it's a complicated situation."

Hawkins glanced at the note-covered notes scattered on his desktop.

"That could be a problem," he said with a slow shake of his head. "I'm trying to wrap up a big Navy contract here."

Kalliste put her forefinger to her lips, like a school teacher silencing a talkative pupil. "Before you say no, let me send you a quick e-mail. Then we'll talk again."

Her face vanished. The computer chirped. Hawkins clicked on the e-mail attachment and the ghostly green sonar image of a ship popped up on the screen. Hawkins printed the picture and studied the long tapered bow and stern of the vessel. In addition to SeaBot, he ran a non-profit shipwreck foundation called Sea Search and had surveyed a number of shipwrecks off New England's coast, but none were older than the 18th century. The lines of this vessel were unfamiliar, but he guessed that it was very old. Googling 'Ancient Ships,' dozens of files popped up. An Egyptian craft had similar lines. But the vessel in Kalliste's attachment was broader amidships and more substantial-looking in general.

He scrolled through the images and stopped at an artist's rendering based on contemporary descriptions. The illustration showed kilted crewmen working on a square-rigged vessel. He held the printed image next to the screen. The ships were almost identical.

Hawkins sat back in his chair, folded his hands behind his head, and stared at the screen for a few seconds before he clicked the Skype symbol. Kalliste's face re-appeared immediately. She raised an eyebrow.

"I knew you wouldn't be long."

He held the picture up to the camera lens. "I did some research on this ship."

"And what did your research tell you?"
"That I'd be a fool not to join your expedition."

CHAPTER FOUR

Kalliste clapped her hands with joy. "*Megala epharisto*, Matt. Thank you so much. You won't be sorry."

Hawkins raised his palm. "I didn't say I was actually *joining* the expedition. I'm still involved in my ocean glider project."

"But Matt—"

Softening his tone, he said, "This Navy project is a big deal for me. It goes back to that stuff we talked about. Putting the past behind us."

"I understand, Matt. It was rude to pressure you."

"Not at all, Kalliste. I owe you. Look, I'm waiting for word from my team. If it's a go, we'll submit our package to the Navy to study. That should give me a window of time to join your project. We don't have to sit on our hands. The Oceanographic Institution would jump at the chance to sponsor your expedition."

Kalliste jerked her head back and clicked her tongue in the Greek gesture for an emphatic no. "Later, maybe. If word gets out now, the site could be contaminated by unauthorized salvage groups."

"Good point, Kalliste. I'll keep my mouth zipped. How can I help?"

"I'd like you to do a preliminary survey. Once we make a positive ID, we can move to a big-budget project that includes security."

"Sounds doable. What can you tell me about the wreck?"

"It's about thirty miles off the coast of Spain, near Cadiz, in two-hundred-fifty feet of water."

Kalliste explained how the wreck was discovered. A fishing boat had snagged its net on an unmarked obstruction. The captain was aware that the ocean floor was littered with the ghosts of war. More than one fisherman had been killed trying to haul in a load that turned out to be a live mine or artillery shell. He cut the net free, marked the GPS position and called the authorities. A Spanish coast guard cutter ran a sonar survey. The image was relayed to an expert in ancient ships at the University of Madrid.

"He made a tentative identification," Kalliste said. "Then he sent the picture to my boss at the antiquities department in Athens, who passed it on to me. I confirmed the Spaniard's initial evaluation."

"That the ship is Minoan."

She clapped her hands again. "I love smart men."

"I don't deserve the Nobel prize for this one, Kalliste. I compared your photo to ships online. If you're right, this would be the first discovery of an intact Minoan ship. Very big deal."

"Exactly. A *very* big deal, as my boss and the Spaniard ship expert told their respective governments. They asked for money to fund a joint expedition. The governments told them *ohi.*"

Hawkins knew from his time in Greece that *ohi* meant an unequivocal *no.*

"That doesn't make sense. Someone in the government must have realized this is a major find."

"Don't you read the papers or watch TV, Matt? Greece and Spain are the beggars of Europe. If people see their leaders throwing money in the water, they will throw their leaders in the water as well."

"That's an interesting picture, Kalliste. But if the governments said no, where did you dig up the money for this expedition?"

"The professor in Madrid suggested that I talk to Hidden History. It's an American television history channel. They agreed to fund an initial survey. If that project produces evidence confirming the initial identification, they will open their pocketbooks for a full expedition. They're offering a bare-bones budget, just enough to cover the cost of the survey boat. It's not much, Matt. I can't pay you for your time or travel."

Hawkins remembered the sweet honey pastry he had enjoyed on the Santorini expedition. "No problem, Kalliste. You can pay me in *baklava*."

Her eyes lit up. "I'll make it myself."

"Even better. You've got a deal."

"Thank you, Matt. Your involvement was crucial to move this project forward. The Spaniards initially refused a permit. They changed their minds only after I told them a respected Woods Hole scientist was joining the expedition."

"You took a chance. I might have said *ohi*."

Kalliste made a dismissive flick with her fingers. "I saw your excitement when you worked on the Kolumbo crater project."

"Got me pegged, Kalliste." He liked designing undersea vehicles, but he got his biggest kick by using them to probe the mysteries of the deep. "Glad I could help with the permit."

"It wasn't a clear cut approval. Even with you on board they imposed conditions," she said. "The wreck is in Spanish territorial waters, and they didn't want the Greeks to get all the glory. I will be the sole Greek representative. The site cannot be disturbed in any way. Findings must be kept confidential until they give the word. Also, they want a Spanish observer on board."

"I can live with that if you can, Kalliste."

"Wonderful. When can you join us?"

"If the Navy gives me the preliminary go-ahead, I'll join you in a few days. Send me your schedule and I'll get back to you with my travel arrangements."

She blew him an air kiss, and the Skype image disappeared.

Hawkins pondered the implications of the discovery. A Minoan ship intact was the Holy Grail of nautical archaeology. The contents in the ship's hold would tell where the ship traded, and with whom. This discovery had the potential to rip the cover off mysteries the world didn't even know existed.

The ding of an e-mail brought him back to reality. Good news. The team had approved his computations. The Navy would want simulated dives, then actual field tests, but that was in the future. He'd have plenty of time to zip across the Atlantic.

Hawkins shut down his computer and left his office. He went around to the other side of the research vessel dock where the Oceanographic stored some of its larger hardware.

Housed in a shed was the *Deepwater Challenger*, the amazing submersible that *Titanic* movie director James Cameron used in a record-breaking dive to the bottom of the Mariana Trench. Nearby, was the passenger sphere from the Challenger and the titanium globe from the original deep-diving vehicle known as, *Alvin*.

He strolled over to a vehicle that looked like globs of Play-Doh wrapped around a fish bowl. He called the manned submersible he'd designed, *Falstaff*, after the rotund Shakespearean character.

The vehicle was seven feet long, six feet tall and wide. Cylindrical thrusters sprouted from each side. A smaller section containing the motors sat on the battery compartment. All this was wrapped around a transparent globe that served as the cockpit for the pilot and passenger. A hatch on top of the sphere provided access. Printed on the battery compartment was the name: SeaBot.

When he'd built the submersible, Hawkins hadn't gone the usual Woods Hole route of seeking Navy financing. He didn't want to deal with the government red tape. Congress had cut back on Navy research and the competition for money was fierce. And there was his lack of trust in the government, going back to Afghanistan. He had pulled together a package of loans, mortgaged himself to the hilt, and intended to pay for the expensive investment by farming *Falstaff* out for high-paying expeditions. He had at least one dive scheduled with the institution's Deep Submergence Laboratory.

Problem one. How to get *Falstaff* to Spain. Air-freighting the two-passenger vehicle to Cadiz could be complicated and expensive.

Hawkins locked up his office and biked back to his house. Climbing the stairs to the second floor office, he sat behind his desk, surrounded by his collection of antique dive gear and diving history books. He picked up the phone and punched out a number he hadn't used for months.

A woman's voice answered. "How do you do it, Matt?"

"Do what?" he said.

"Not call in months, only to snag me at the precise moment Global Logistics Technologies is in full freak-out mode."

"Sorry, Abby. I can call back later."

The crisp tone melted. "For heaven's sakes, Matt, don't be sorry. You're an island of sanity in a sea of crazy."

Hawkins was glad his ex-wife couldn't see his smile. His erratic behavior after he left the Navy with a psychiatric discharge had pushed their marriage over the brink.

"What's going on with GLT?"

"Landed a huge contract with Department of Defense, so I'm busier than a one-armed juggler. Pay no attention to my whining, it's all good, Matt. Okay, I'm through. Your turn to vent."

"No complaints here, Abby. I'm wrapping up the ocean glider project for the Navy."

"I've been reading about it on the WHOI website. Congratulations. Let me know when you can take a break. Maybe we can do something together."

"I'd like that Abby, but I'm jumping onto a project in Spain. Which is why I called. I need your help to move the submersible to Cadiz."

If Abby had been disappointed by his failure to follow up on her indirect invitation, she didn't show it.

"Let me check," she said, returning to business-mode. He could hear the clicking of a computer keyboard. "You're in luck, Matt. There's a cargo 747 leaving New York tomorrow night for Frankfurt. I can arrange an air freight transfer to Cadiz from there. Can you and the sub get to JFK by tomorrow afternoon?"

"That shouldn't be a problem. I'll call a trucking company I've worked with before."

"Done. Why are you going to Spain?"

"Can't say, Abby. I've promised to keep the details secret for now."

"You know I can weasel it out of you. You're easy. I can get you to tell me everything in less time than a coffee break lasts."

"Idle threats don't scare me, Abby."

"You know I don't make idle threats, Matt."

"Don't I ever. Okay, here's what I can tell you. I'm going off to find the Holy Grail of archaeology."

"Damn you, Hawkins! Now you've *really* got my curiosity up."

"Sorry, but here's the deal. The scientist I'm working for is worried about site contamination. She asked me to keep this close to my vest."

"She?"

"Kalliste Kalchis. A highly-respected archeologist I worked with in Greece a couple of years ago. That's all I can say."

"That's all the information I need. Someone will call you. Got to tend to business. Bye."

Hawkins clicked off the phone, then walked to the picture window that took up one wall of his home office. He gazed out at the harbor, thinking about his turbulent relationship with Abby, picturing her lovely face framed by hair the color of claret. She was one of the most elegant and graceful women he had ever met. Her Annapolis training and Navy service had given her a wealth of self-assurance and confidence, qualities that made her an effective CEO.

By contrast, in his Navy days Hawkins had been impulsive and dashing, traits that she loved. Then he came back from Afghanistan with a head full of crazy thoughts. Since then they had managed to set aside some of the misunderstandings that had plagued them after their messy divorce. Several months earlier, they even had a fling off Matinicus, the rugged Maine island that was his namesake. The encounter had been pleasant, but it confused rather than clarified their relationship.

His head would start spinning if he thought about Abby for too long. So he was glad when his phone chirped and the male voice on the other end spoke, "I'm with GLT. I understand we're moving a big load to Spain."

CHAPTER FIVE

Cadiz, Spain, One Day Later

The office that took up the entire top floor of the thirty-six story Auroch Industries tower was a unique space. Instead of tinted glass windows offering a spectacular view of the city and the river Manzanares below, the walls were solid. Every square inch was covered with a wrap-around panoramic photograph of soaring earthen terraces. Anyone sitting in the office would have the uneasy feeling of being stuck at the bottom of an open-pit mining operation.

The effect was exactly what Viktor Salazar had intended. As Auroch's Chief Executive Officer, Salazar wanted subordinates and visitors who entered his domain to be reminded that the company's wealth and power rested on its ability to remove vast amounts of solid and liquid material from the untouched locations on Earth. Auroch had grown into a conglomerate that made it one of the biggest players in the fossil fuel industry, but the company's roots were in mining.

Photographs from one Auroch mining operation were spread out on his large steel-top desk. The photos, taken from different angles—at ground level and from the air—showed a village, or what was left of it. Most of the corrugated metal houses were at the bottom of an enormous sink hole. Twenty-three people had been killed when the mining operation had weakened the ground under the village to the point of collapse.

Salazar was on the phone with Jared Spaulding, chairman of a consortium of environmental and humanitarian groups that had banded together, forming an international organization after a series of highly-publicized disasters near Auroch mines. The corporate public relations department had folded under the weight of wide-spread criticism. Auroch had come under increased media scrutiny. No such company with a worldwide reach can remain invisible, but Salazar preferred a low profile. When the coalition's president asked to talk to him directly, he agreed.

The conversation had been one-sided, with Salazar listening to Spaulding lay out in detail the damage done to people and planet from Auroch's undertakings.

"I understand your concern," Salazar said when Spaulding had paused for a breath. With his large bald head and wide shoulders, Salazar looked like a Turkish wrestler, but he spoke in a mellifluous alto voice that was surprisingly high for a man of his size. "I take full responsibility for everything, good and bad, that this company does."

"That's certainly a refreshing admission of culpability," Spaulding remarked.

"We are painfully aware of the unfortunate side effects that come with providing fuel for power plants that benefit millions of people, and minerals for our machines and electronic devices."

"Those villagers might object to being labeled as unfortunate side effects, Mr. Salazar."

"Of course, which is why we have provided restitution to the villagers and will help them rebuild their houses. Furthermore," Salazar said, "if you have suggestions as to anything else Auroch can do to make amends and prevent further disasters, I'd be glad to listen."

Spaulding presented Salazar with a list.

Salazar's reaction was amiable. "Nothing you have asked for is unreasonable," he said. "A huge corporation is always in danger of being unmindful of the hazardous, but unintended consequences of its work. If you present your points in writing, I will attend to them personally and assign staff to carry out my wishes. You can be assured of that."

Spaulding said, "Also, we'd like your cooperation in providing access to information about your mining operations."

It was a clever strategy, even if somewhat disingenuous, Salazar thought. They would make sure his acquiescence went public, thereby putting pressure on him. "Yes, of course. Anything else?"

"That's it for now." Spaulding chuckled. "You're not exactly what I had expected."

"And what did you expect?"

"That you'd deny having anything to do with the disaster. Instead, you've been quite accommodating. More like someone's uncle than a callous businessman."

"I am happy to have broken the stereotype. Please give my assistant all the contact information we will need. We'll get in touch with you in, say, a week. If you have any problem, you will have a direct line to me. The advantage of being head of a large corporation means that, while you are blamed when things go wrong, you also possess the tools to put the pieces back together. Let's talk again."

He hung up. As his gaze fell on the photographic walls, the genial smile faded from his lips. The greenish-yellow eyes under the prominent brow glowed with anger. The muscles hidden under the dark blue suit seemed to ripple as he picked up the photos and tore them to shreds.

"Fool," he muttered.

He would keep his promise. The company staff would carry out his wishes. There would be no restitution or cooperation. He had another plan for the coalition that had already been set in motion.

The phone on Salazar's desk blinked; he picked up the handset.

"You had a call while you were in conference," a voice said. "It's from our friend in the government. He said his superiors are going to allow the expedition to proceed."

"Impossible! He told us that the government had denied the permit."

"They changed their minds at the higher level after they learned that the American had agreed to join the project."

"What American?"

"A scientist from the Woods Hole Oceanographic Institution.

His name is Matt Hawkins."

Salazar's thick fingers clutched the phone as if to crush it. Sweat beaded on his bald head. "Find out everything you can about this Hawkins and get it to me within the hour."

"Yes, sir."

Salazar slammed the handset down in its cradle. He was furious at the change of heart. When the ancient vessel was first found, he'd used his influence in the government to make sure no permit was issued. After that, it seemed as if the whole thing would simply go away. Then this blasted Greek woman appeared on the scene. And now an American.

Taking a moment, he breathed through the anger. In a way, he mused, the government turn-around had made his job easier. Rather than depend on unreliable government sources, he would see that his wishes were carried out directly. He reached for his phone again and called the number that would be the first step in stopping the shipwreck survey and permanently ending further interference from the troublesome Greek and her American friend.

CHAPTER SIX

Leonidas had been stoned out of his mind for three days when he got the call from Salazar. With no work on his plate, he'd moved into a fancy hotel suite and entertained himself with booze, marijuana and expensive prostitutes, like the young woman lying in the bed.

"There's been a new development," Salazar said. "The job that's been on hold is active again."

Doing his best not to slur his words, Leonidas said, "I thought the whole thing had been canceled."

"The Spanish government issued a permit when they learned that an American scientist named Hawkins agreed to join the project. He will arrive in Cadiz in a few days."

"No big deal. I'll take care of it. Means a bigger body count, so I'll have to charge you extra."

Leonidas would never have joked with Salazar if he'd been straight, but the high potency weed had loosened his tongue. Salazar took the comment seriously.

"I don't pay you by the body, Leonidas. Reimbursement will be as agreed upon. It will be deposited in your bank account when the job is finished to my satisfaction."

Salazar clicked off without another word. Leonidas took a drag from his joint and spread his lips in a lazy smile. The call couldn't have come at a better time. It had been months since his last job. A Russian mining magnate had run afoul of Salazar who'd instructed

Leonidas to eliminate him.

The man had been well-guarded, however, Leonidas learned that surveillance was lax when the target wasn't on his yacht. He approached the yacht from the water one night, climbed aboard to plant several explosive devices and triggered a time-delayed switch to activate when the yacht left port on a voyage to the Black Sea.

He'd returned to Spain at the behest of Salazar, who said he had another job for him— stopping a Greek and Spanish archaeological expedition. But when that assignment had been canceled, he stayed in Cadiz. He liked the Spanish women and had no place else to go.

"Carlos!"

The prostitute called from the bedroom, using the phony name he had given her. He went back into the room and saw that the young woman had risen from the bed while he was on the phone. Her name was Isabel and she was barely out of her teens. Her charming innocence was combined with a willingness to please, and he had hired her night after night.

She had a sheet wrapped around her slim body and was bending over a black leather case that lay open on the bed. Instead of being embarrassed at being caught going through his luggage, she shot him a languid smile, reached into the case and pulled out a white wig and a bushy white false mustache.

"What's all this?" she said, widening her bright red lips in a drunken grin.

"You really shouldn't have done that, hon." He talked as if he were lecturing a naughty child.

She replied with a giggle, placed the white wig at a cock-eyed angle on her pretty head, and reached back into the case. This time she came out with what looked like a nose. She held it in the palm of her hand.

"Ugh," she said. "Is this real?"

"It only looks real," he said. "I'm an actor."

Still looking a bit disgusted by her find, she gingerly dropped the prosthetic and the wig back into the case, then came over to Leonidas. She stood close, undid the tie on his white terrycloth robe and kissed his naked chest.

"That's all right. The rest of you is *very* real."

She reached playfully for his hair and pulled. The brown wig slid off in her hand and she let out a loud gasp. His face ended at the top of his forehead as cleanly as if it had been cut away with a scalpel. Above the line of flesh, the bone-white dome of his head was covered with scar tissue. He removed the wig from her hand and placed it back on his head.

"What happened to you?" she said.

"I was in a bad accident years ago," he said.

The prostitute had said nothing when she'd seen the scar tissue on his body, but a sad look came into her eyes. "I'm sorry," she said. "I was surprised. Many of my clients have injuries. It's nothing." She pecked him on the lips. "Now I have to go. You make me tired."

She held her hand out for payment.

"Sure, hon. But first, you gotta give me a real goodbye."

"That will cost you extra," she said, giggling. Reaching up, she put her hands on each side of his head as if she were about to kiss him. He did the same, conscious that he could break her skinny neck with one violent twist. There would be a muffled snap, her eyes would roll back into her head and her body would go limp. Instead, ignoring the craving to kill, he let his fingers run through her long, dark hair as he stared at the beautiful face before him.

Tucking a wad of bills into her bosom, he gave her a light slap on the backside, and said, "Get your butt out of here, darlin."

"You got my number?"

"Oh yeah, babe. I got your number."

He proceeded to push her out of the room. Maybe it had been a mistake not killing her. The young woman had opened a small door to his secrets and, thus, should not be allowed to live. But Isabel was the only one he'd ever met who hadn't been turned off by his disfigurement. Besides, he wanted to enjoy her services again. He'd have to be careful, though. The last thing he wanted was for her to make him feel human again. That would be bad for business.

He picked up the leather case and carried it to the bathroom. Standing in front of the mirror, he removed the wig and peeled off the olive skin. His face was a featureless mass of white scar tissue that looked as if it had melted and re-frozen in place. There were only nostrils where his nose should be. His ears were mere stubs.

His lips non-existent. When he saw photos of his old self, it was like looking at a stranger. The hot-shot surfer dude, and later, the warrior in the Special Ops uniform, had been movie star handsome.

He had been an exceptional soldier, excelling at languages, marksmanship and martial arts. At that time, classes at the UCLA acting school and marriage to his honey-blonde girlfriend were still in his future. So was an improvised explosive device in Iraq. The IED that exploded under his Humvee had killed everyone else in his squad. Goggles had saved his sight, but the blast of flames had completely eradicated his facial features.

Later, while recuperating in a room at Walter Reed Hospital, he learned that the Hummer was one of the models that came with insufficient armor, one of many that had been thrown into the battle in the early days of the war. When his fiancée then came to visit him, he learned as well, after seeing the horrified expression on her face, that there were limits to love.

The Army discharged him with his face swathed in bandages, like the Invisible Man in the H.G. Wells story. His face was a patchwork surgery job that used skin from his body as an attempt to fill in the holes. With nothing else available to him, he went back to what the Army had trained him to do. Kill people.

He returned to Iraq as a mercenary. He only lasted a few months before being fired for drug abuse. Returning home, he was drawn to his old surfing beach. From a distance he watched the young surfers skimming the waves like sea gods. He projected himself into their handsome bodies and the germ of an idea began to form.

Returning to acting school, concentrating on the field of make-up and disguise, he'd learned the craft of fashioning facial features out of artificial skin. During his studies he came across the phrase, *Man of a Thousand Faces*, used to describe the film actor Lon Chaney, known as a master of make-up. He even adopted the actor's real name, Leonidas Frank.

He circulated his resume, stressing his chameleon-like ability to get close to a target. A client hired him for an assassination. The target was a heavily-guarded competitor of Auroch. Easily disguising himself as a bodyguard, he'd carried out the assignment with ridiculous ease. After the kill, Salazar had met with him personally and Leonidas accepted a job as a security consultant for special assignments.

Leaving the memories behind, Leonidas snapped back to reality. It was time to get moving on the new job. A cold shower cleared away some of fog in his mind. Then he applied a fleshy fake nose and a weathered olive skin to his ruined face. He replaced the wig with one that had streaks of gray and gained years of wisdom in only a few seconds. He was employed again, thanks to Hawkins. Too bad he wouldn't have the chance to thank the guy before he killed him.

CHAPTER SEVEN

Cadiz, Spain, One Day Later

Thanks to Abby's machine-like efficiency, the move from Woods Hole to Cadiz had gone off without a hitch. Before he left town Hawkins had dropped Quisset off at Howard Snow's house, given her a pat on the head and told her to have fun with Uncle Snowy. He hitched a ride on the truck transporting *Falstaff* from Woods Hole to JFK airport where the submersible was loaded onto a 747 cargo plane. He climbed aboard the plane for the flight from New York to Frankfurt, then on to Cadiz.

He slept for most of the Atlantic crossing and felt refreshed when the plane arrived in Spain. Abby had thought of everything. A crane truck was waiting at the airport to move *Falstaff* to the harbor. The submersible was lifted from the truck onto the deck of the *Sancho Panza*, the forty-eight-foot salvage boat Kalliste had hired for the survey. Hawkins had asked Kalliste to line up a boat that was large and sturdy enough to accommodate *Falstaff*'s weight. She greeted Hawkins on board with a hug. She said the boat was the best she could find on a limited budget, and the captain had a sterling reputation around the port.

Hawkins grew up on the Maine coast, son of a lobster fisherman. He had explored his father's boat from the time he could crawl. He knew that a ship-shape vessel was the secret to a long life at sea.

The *Sancho Panza*'s hull had welds and patches, but it was freshly painted. The winches that powered the arm-like cranes on both sides of the deck were free of rust. Every cable or coil of line looked brand new. When the captain introduced himself, Hawkins complimented him on the condition of the boat. The captain beamed at the praise and said he'd been strict with maintenance because the boat had been built in the 1960s. Together, they supervised the job of moving *Falstaff* onto the stern deck.

Hawkins soon learned why the boat had been named for the sidekick of Don Quixote. The skipper, Captain Alejandro Santiago, was a fanatic admirer of Cervantes, even naming his son Miguel after the famous Spanish author. Over a hearty dinner cooked by Miguel, the captain regaled them with stories of Don Quixote's creator. He would have gone on all night, but Hawkins politely suggested that they turn in early. The next morning, the *Sancho Panza* eased from its slip in the gray light of dawn and chugged through the steamy mists rising from the Bay of Cadiz, trailing a creamy wake in the mirror-flat waters. As the boat cleared the harbor Captain Santiago goosed the throttle, ramped up the speed to a steady twenty knots and pointed the bow southwesterly into the Atlantic.

The soft pinkish-gold light from the rising sun fell on the flags fluttering from the mast. Topmost was the horizontally-striped red and orange banner of Spain. Hanging below the Spanish pennant was the blue and white flag of Greece, dominated by its white cross. On the bottom was the familiar Stars and Stripes.

Hawkins wore a Woods Hole Oceanographic Institution T-shirt emblazoned with the picture of a sailing ship, a WHOI baseball cap, tan cargo shorts and high-topped work boots. Hawkins called the look, "Woods Hole chic," because it was the standard uniform around the world-famous ocean studies center. Kalliste had on white shorts and a sky-blue T-shirt that had a drawing on the front of an ancient square-rigged ship and the word, *AEGEO*, the name of a Greek research vessel she had worked on.

Nearing the destination, it was easy to spot the buoy that the Spanish coast guard had used to mark the wreck. The captain used the GPS to hone in on the orange foam sphere bobbing in the waves.

Cutting power, the boat plowed to a halt and the anchor splashed into the dark green water with a rattle of chain.

"Right on target," the captain said. "The rest is up to you, my friends."

Hawkins said, "Thanks, Captain Santiago. We can start as soon as Dr. Kalchis gives the word."

"We can start immediately as far as I'm concerned," Kalliste said. "But we are guests in Spanish waters, and it is Senor Rodriguez, as his country's official observer, who has the final say."

Rodriguez had been standing behind the captain, a mug of coffee in his hand. He was a short, pudgy man with several receding chins and a completely bald head partially covered by an ill-fitting toupee. He was dressed in a shiny dark suit and tie. He smiled and in a soft voice, said, "I am here as a colleague who wishes to help, not hinder." Setting the mug down, he pulled a notebook and pen out of his jacket pocket. "Since I am also the official government record keeper, could you tell me what your survey will entail?"

"Dr. Kalchis and I will dive together in the manned submersible, take a look at what's on the bottom and try to confirm the initial Coast Guard assessment," Hawkins said.

Rodriguez repeated what he had made clear a number of times since boarding the boat that morning. "My main job on this expedition is to guarantee that the wreck is not disturbed, and to make sure no artifacts are removed."

Hawkins nodded. "We'll hover at a safe distance. The only thing we plan on taking is video and photographs to study later."

Rodriguez licked his lips. "It is my job to see that protocol is followed. If you don't mind, I will have to make a call to ask for final permission."

"We hope that will not take long," Kalliste said. "Your government has given me permission for this survey. You must know, as a fellow archaeologist, that I would hardly risk damaging my reputation by allowing a physical inspection of an ancient site without first carefully mapping every detail."

"I am aware of that, Dr. Kalchis, but I must follow my instructions to the letter."

He jotted something down in his notebook and strolled off.

"Sanctimonious self-important little piglet," Kalliste said. "It drives me crazy the way he wets his lips with his tongue. Ugh."

Hawkins smiled, but his narrowed eyes watched Rodriguez go to the stern where he stopped to take out a phone and turned his back to them. Three tours of duty as a Navy SEAL in Afghanistan had honed Hawkins's observational skills. Something wasn't quite right. The guy was as slippery as an eel. Hawkins knew a number of marine archaeologists and none of them dressed for a shipwreck survey in a suit. Even odder, Rodriguez had shown no interest in the potential archaeological importance of the shipwreck other than to say it could not be disturbed.

Hawkins gave a mental shrug. Maybe he was reading too much into his first impression. Then again, maybe not.

When Rodriguez returned, he paused for a second, obviously enjoying the drama, and dabbed his lips with his tongue before he announced:

"I have secured you permission to make your dive."

"Very good," Matt said. "Dr. Kalchis and I will discuss the launch and retrieval procedures with the captain and his son."

After he was left alone, Rodriguez lit up a cigarette and took a deep drag. He had to watch himself, but the job had been easier than he thought it would be. He had expected to have to use all his considerable experience as a con man. But these scientists were as gullible as the usual victims of his cons.

When he was working a scam, he dispensed with the toupee. He was aware that with his bald head, watery blue eyes, pink face, and negligible chins, he resembled a very large baby. He capitalized on his innocent appearance, offering free counsel to elderly women who willingly turned over their money for investments that never panned out. But he had made a big mistake recently, conning a frail widow who just happened to have been related to a mobster. Which is how he ended up on this junky old scow in the first place.

He had lost all her money gambling. He knew that it was only a matter of time before the mobster sent some thugs to break his legs, so he'd chosen to lay low in his apartment, but after a few days ventured out to buy cigarettes. As he walked back from the kiosk to his apartment he lit up a cigarette and didn't see the limo until it was too late. The car pulled up to the sidewalk and two husky men muscled Rodriguez into the back seat where the mobster sat. As the limo pulled away from the curb with a screech of tires, Rodriquez knew his life was about to end. Unexpectedly, the mobster had put his arm around his shoulders.

"I've been looking for you, Rodriquez," he said; his breath held a heavy dose of garlic.

"I can pay the old woman back. I just need more time."

"Don't worry about that. I need you to do a favor for a friend."

He shoved a phone in Rodriquez's face.

The man on the other end of the line had a job offer. Speaking in a smooth-toned voice, he said he wanted Rodriguez to impersonate an archaeology professor working for the government. The job would only take one day. In return, the man would pay him a large sum of money. Rodriguez had agreed. The widow could go to hell. He had already decided to use the money he made from the job to leave town in search of other fertile hunting grounds full of vulnerable women.

Now, as instructed, he had reported the ship's discovery to his anonymous employer, who said, "Good. Tell them to dive."

The voice clicked off. Rodriguez shrugged. He didn't have the faintest clue what this crazy job was about. He didn't care. He just wanted to get back to Cadiz, then leave town faster than a mobster could shoot.

Which might have come to pass, if not for one simple thing.

By making the phone call, he had just signed his own death warrant.

CHAPTER EIGHT

After Leonidas had followed the *Sancho Panza* to the wreck site, he moved to within two miles of the anchored boat, the maximum distance that would allow him to make his kill with ease and accuracy. He stood on the deck of the leased forty-three-foot Spanish-built *Astrodona* and studied the vessel through powerful binoculars.

He had removed his disguise. He knew that he now looked like a giant slug but there was no one to see the scar tissue that had replaced his face. He'd smoked a joint on the way out. High-octane weed. He stretched his lipless mouth in a ragged grin. With an eye patch, he thought, he'd fit right in with the fishy crew of Davy Jones in the *Pirates of the Caribbean* movie.

The *Astrodona*'s twin 330 horsepower Volvo Penta engines rumbling under his feet could kick the boat up to a maximum speed of 35 mph. He'd finish this job and be back in Cadiz in time for dinner. A Galician fish stew would be nice, paired with a 2005 Lusco wine. Isabel would be his dessert.

Opening a storage compartment, Leonidas lifted out the king-size backpack that he'd bought in a wilderness equipment supply shop. He set the bag down on the deck, unzipped the top and pulled out a narrow cylinder around two feet long and slightly more than two inches in diameter.

At one end of the cylinder was a set of fins; at the other end was the plastic housing protecting a camera lens. He placed the Spike missile on the deck and pulled out three more projectiles, which he laid beside the first. When he'd first been hired to deal with the survey ship he intended to plant timed explosives on board as he'd done with the earlier assignment. But Salazar had insisted that nothing be left to chance, so he'd acquired the four missiles from his armaments supplier in Amsterdam.

The U.S. Navy had developed the 5.5-pound shoulder-launched Spike to pick off swarming attack boats that might leak through standard defenses. The missile could hit a target moving at sixty miles per hour. Nailing a stationary object like the *Sancho Panza* would be a piece of cake. He removed a launcher from another bag and placed it next to the missiles.

A camera in the missile's nose could transmit a real-time picture along a fiber optics connector. It was like taking a photo with a cell phone. The shooter puts a box around the target and BANG! That was it.

The one-pound warhead was a firecracker compared to bigger missiles, but the Spike had a focused explosion that packed a punch. Even better, the shooter could put the missile exactly where it would do the most damage. It was fast, too. The missile attained a velocity of six hundred miles per hour within 1.5 seconds of launch. The Spike had a reduced smoke motor, making it invisible as it flew toward the target. Missiles fired in a tight cluster would blast a huge hole in the hull. The boat would sink to the bottom within minutes.

He raised the binoculars again and saw activity on deck. A man and a woman were climbing through a hatch down into what looked like a giant bubble. The round vehicle was lifted off the deck and lowered into the water where it disappeared below the surface. He guessed that the man was Hawkins. Didn't matter who the woman was. For her, it was simply bad luck. The IED had blasted away his capacity for empathy along with his face.

However, Leonidas hadn't planned on Hawkins leaving the boat so soon. If he shot now, he'd miss two people. Salazar had been adamant. Everyone on the boat must go. No big deal. He had nothing else to do, so he'd wait. Lighting up another joint, he took a deep drag of the intoxicating fumes and blew the smoke out the twin nostril holes.

CHAPTER NINE

Color drained from the world outside the transparent passenger sphere as the submersible sank into the ocean's depths. The red and orange glow filtering through the sea sparkle disappeared first. Then the rest of the spectrum was absorbed. Violet light faded into blue and black.

Hawkins switched on the floodlights. A school of silver-scaled fish were caught in the twin cones of brilliance that penetrated the darkness.

"Meet the welcoming committee," Hawkins said. "Are you comfortable with the temperature?"

The interior of the cabin was cool, but Hawkins and Kalliste had changed into jeans and windbreakers before entering the sphere.

"I'm fine, thanks. Let's go make history."

"Aye, aye, and down she goes."

Hawkins put *Falstaff* into a slow, descending spiral around the marker buoy line.

Kalliste gazed with wonder through the wall of the transparent sphere. "I can't believe we're making this dive," she said. "Thank you so much for doing this, Matt."

"I'm the one who should be thanking you, Kalliste. I'd be in my office back in Woods Hole instead of being here on the brink of a great discovery."

She glanced around at the encroaching ocean. "I'm getting very nervous."

"Don't be. You're as safe here as on your living room sofa."

"It's not the dive," she said. "I feel perfectly comfortable with you. It's the ship. What if it's *not* Minoan?"

"We'll know soon enough. We're almost on the bottom."

The submersible set down close to where the buoys anchor flukes were embedded in the sand.

"Almost no vegetation," Hawkins said. "That's a good sign. The temperature at this depth discourages the growth of marine organisms that feed on wood."

Hawkins powered the vertical thrusters. *Falstaff* rose around six feet, coming to a hover. He put the submersible into a slow spin. The floodlights stroked the darkness like beams from a shore beacon. He was flicking on the video camera when he heard Kalliste say, "Oh!"

He looked up from the control panel. Directly in front of the submersible was a tall pillar that had a knob on top. The shape was indistinct because of an uneven covering of concretion, but the knob had the vague shape of a bird, with the beak pointing directly at them.

Kalliste murmured something in Greek. "*Omorphi. Poly Omorphi.*"

"Don't know what you said, but I wholeheartedly agree," Hawkins said.

"I said it was very beautiful. In more ways than one. You see how it looks vaguely like the head of a bird? This may be important. The bird motif was a common bow feature on Minoan vessels. Can we take a look at the stern section?"

Hawkins reached for the controls that would move *Falstaff* vertically. They rose several feet higher than the knob, and he angled the submersible into a forward tilt, piloting *Falstaff* slowly over the wreck. Although the deck was covered in sand they glimpsed some of the ship's ribs and amorphous lumps here and there.

Kalliste dug a cellphone out of a waterproof neck pouch and put it on video mode.

"I know the submersible has cameras," she said. "But I want something I can get back to the Hidden History channel as soon as we come out of the water."

The submersible traveled around a hundred feet. The floodlights fell on a section of fish net draped around the high stern.

Kalliste leaned forward, her eyes narrowing. "That's where the fisherman's net snagged the wreck. See that long plank projecting from the stern right about where water level would ordinarily be? We call vessels with that feature 'frying pans,' because that's what they look like."

"What's its purpose?"

"Some people think it was a stabilizer that lengthened the waterline without elongating the hull. Others say it would be a drag on the ship, like having a ladder down the side, and would tend to draw the ship's stern to the wind."

"That could be dangerous with high waves and a following sea," Hawkins said.

"That's why there's scholarly disagreement. But the stern projection tells us something. Like the bow, it is a design used by Minoan shipwrights."

"Are you ready to make a positive ID, then?"

She shook her head. "It makes no difference how ready I am. Any theory I present will be subject to scathing review from my colleagues and peers. It must be airtight. But evidence of Minoan shipbuilding techniques could help bolster our case."

"Cargo specimens would help even more."

"Without a doubt, Minoan artifacts would seal the deal. You forget that our pig-faced Spanish friend has forbidden us from touching the wreck. It's a shame, because I can't get funding from the television people without hard evidence."

"If I set *Falstaff* down within inches of the deck, the thrusters might *accidentally* blow sand off and uncover cargo. Technically speaking, we wouldn't touch the wreck."

Looking over at him, she smiled. "Who am I to argue with a respected Woods Hole scientist?"

Hawkins moved *Falstaff* back over the stern, then brought the submersible down to less than a yard above the deck and blasted away with the vertical thrusters. The submersible shot up above the billowing cloud of sand. He set *Falstaff* down again, several feet ahead, hopscotching to the bow. *Falstaff* pivoted to point back to the deck and, suddenly, its lights illuminated patches of newly exposed planking and ribs.

"Look at that blackened wood. There was a fire on board," Hawkins said. "Probably what sent her to the bottom."

"Maybe someone knocked over an oil lantern."

"Or the ship was sunk during a battle. We'll make another pass."

As *Falstaff* retraced its route, objects could be seen nestled on and between the planks.

"I see amphorae!" Kalliste said, practically jumping out of her seat.

Hawkins was more restrained but he shared her excitement. The clay jugs that carried wine and oil could be vital clues in identifying the wreck. As he scanned the deck his attention was diverted by another object, still partially covered with sand that was larger than the others. It was located on the starboard side, around midships. Something about it looked vaguely familiar.

Before he could move in for a closer look, he heard a muffled thud come from above. A vibration passed through the passenger sphere.

Kalliste lifted her eyes toward the surface. "What was that?"

Hawkins knew from his SEAL days exactly what it was. An explosion. He searched the blackness beyond the floodlights. Then, after a short pause, he heard a second explosion. "Hold on, Kalliste," he said. "We're going up."

Falstaff rose in a straight vertical line instead of the corkscrew path it had followed on the descent.

At the thud of a third explosion, Hawkins brought the submersible to a hover. They listened, but heard only the sound of their nervous breathing against the hum of the motors. He reached out for the throttle control and resumed the ascent, slower and with more caution.

The changing color spectrum was the reverse of the descent, shifting to violet, then blue tinged with yellow and orange.

Hawkins kept his eyes glued to the fathometer.

Two hundred feet. One-fifty. One hundred.

Kalliste had been tight-lipped during the ascent, but she suddenly pointed up. "Dear God!"

A huge fish-like shape was silhouetted against the sparkle of surface light. It rapidly expanded in size as it gained speed. Hawkins knew in an instant what was coming down from the surface.

The *Sancho Panza*.

And it was about to squash *Falstaff* under its keel.

CHAPTER TEN

Hawkins messed up Leonidas by getting in the water so quickly. He waited and kept watch through his binoculars…and got stoned. The dope he'd smoked was like brain dynamite. The passage of time was exaggerated under the effects of the cannabis. Seemed like days had gone by. Maybe years. Screw it, he thought. He'd waited long enough. Maybe if he made enough of a ruckus Hawkins would come up to see what was going on.

He clicked a missile into the launcher. The first Spike would take out the pilot house so no one would call in a Mayday. He sighted just below the window and squeezed the trigger. The Spike whooshed out of the launcher and blew a hole in the side of the pilot house.

As the structure was engulfed in a ball of flame, he loaded a second missile into the launcher and aimed it at the hull a few inches above the waterline. He squeezed the trigger a second time. The Spike hurtled to its target at six hundred miles per hour. The camera in the nose of the missile sent a picture of a man running back and forth on the stern deck. He must have been panicked by the first missile strike. Little bald guy in a suit. Leonidas cackled. Reminded him of a duck in a shooting gallery. He enclosed the man in the white square that defined the target.

The missile passed through the man as if he weren't there, scattering a shower of blood and body parts in a hundred different directions, then kept going and splashed into the ocean.

Leonidas experienced a moment of clarity. He cursed himself for the dumb stunt he just pulled. He'd wasted a damned missile that should have been used on the boat.

Crap. Things cost a fortune. He reloaded the launcher and fired the third Spike into the hull, intending to send the boat to the bottom. Nothing happened except for a lot of smoke and fire. He picked up the last Spike, the one he'd been saving to use on Hawkins, and sent it off after the others.

More smoke and flames. It seemed forever before the boat slowly listed at a forty-five degree angle. Water poured into the hull. The bow sank lower. The stern rose in the air at a sharp angle, as the boat slid into the sea leaving behind nothing more than foam and bubbles.

Leonidas snatched up a pair of binoculars and surveyed the debris and oil slick created from ruptured fuel tanks. The thick cloud of smoke swirling above the water hampered visibility.

Still no sign of Hawkins.

He squinted at the sky. Sheets of ashy clouds were moving in to blot out the sun. The wind had freshened and was whipping the greasy waves into whitecaps. The job had taken longer than he expected. The dope was making him fidgety. With stiff winds and rain on its way, it was doubtful Hawkins would last the night after he came to the surface. Leonidas was eager to get paid. He was hungry and the high was wearing off. To him, all of these facts together made the job complete.

Starting the engine, he set off for Cadiz at top speed. As he entered the harbor, he recited the alphabet. Then he counted to ten, putting an exaggerated crispness into his voice. Hardly any slurring. Not bad. All those acting lessons came in handy. He punched in a number on his phone.

Salazar answered right away. "Go ahead," said the unmistakable mellifluous voice.

"It's done."

"Details."

"The boat is at the bottom of the sea with everyone on it."

"You're 100 percent certain of that? *Everyone.*"

"There's nothing left of the ship except for floating debris. Guess that seals our deal, Mr. Salazar."

"Not quite. You'll be paid your fee as soon as the authorities confirm the loss of the boat and its passengers."

Salazar hung up. Leonidas held the phone to his ear and listened to the dial tone for a few seconds before he clicked off. He always stuck around after a hit, even when it was dangerous, to make sure his targets were dead. He hadn't in this case and that nagged at him. Finally, looking forward to a nice evening of lust with Isabel, Leonidas shrugged his shoulders. He was 99 percent certain Hawkins was dead, and that would have to do, but he couldn't shake the feeling that something had gone horribly wrong.

CHAPTER ELEVEN

Falstaff wasn't designed to peel off like a fighter plane breaking out of attack formation. But that's what Hawkins was asking it to do. He yanked the joystick over and gave the right vertical thruster all the power he could.

The submersible rolled into a forty-five degree angle. Hawkins hoped the move would get them out of the way of the *Sancho Panza*, but the boat clipped *Falstaff*—a glancing blow, before continuing its plunge to the bottom.

Falstaff bounced off the hull like a ping-pong ball off a paddle. Hawkins struggled to control the yaw. The vehicle rolled to the left, catapulting him out of the pilot's seat. His shoulder slammed against the inside wall of the sphere. The submersible swung violently the other way. He was about to land on Kalliste, who'd been similarly tossed about. Swiveling his body to the side in an attempt to avoid crushing her, he was thrown against the sphere once again.

Falstaff went into a tumbling free fall, rolled two more times then hit bottom. The soft sand absorbed some of the impact. The submersible bounced once more, then abruptly came to rest almost right-side-up against the hull of the ancient ship.

Hawkins and Kalliste lay in a heap in the darkened globe. As soon as he caught his breath, he wiggled his fingers and toes, disentangled himself and called her name. She groaned in response.

"Try to move," he said.

He heard a rustling, and mutterings that sounded more like anger than pain.

"Everything works," Kalliste said. "What about you?"

"Shoulder got banged up. Nothing broken."

He groped under the pilot seat for a flashlight and switched it on, keeping the beam low to avoid blinding Kalliste. Her face was about a foot from his. She brushed the hair away from her eyes and looked around. "What the hell happened?"

"The *Sancho Panza* sank and hit us on its way down."

She snapped out of her daze. "The shadow coming from above? My God! The captain and his son. Rodriguez. They must have been killed. How could this have happened?" She paused.

"Those loud thuds we heard were explosions."

"The boat couldn't—wait, did you say *explosions*?"

"The ship must have been attacked. We can't do anything about that. We have to help ourselves."

He cupped his hands around the light to minimize reflection and held it close to the cabin wall. After moving the light back and forth several times, he sat down again.

"Remember that trouble we had finding the wreck? Well, it found *us* this time. We're leaning up against the hull."

"Will we be able to get back to the surface?"

"Looks that way. The lights in the control panel are glowing. We still have power. The fathometer dial shows us at two-hundred-forty-seven feet. Both lateral thrusters work. The one on the left side seems okay. The right must have been knocked off in the collision. Pumps that regulate the pontoons are in working order, though. I could eject water from them and give *Falstaff* the buoyancy needed to make the ascent, and then level off using the remaining thruster."

"But that presents another problem. We won't have a support ship."

"Got that covered. Remember the fishing boats we passed on the way in? We'll call for help."

He rummaged in a gear bag and pulled out what looked like a hand radio. The device would broadcast an SOS and their position. He handed the transmitter and flashlight to Kalliste and began to work the controls. The hum of the pontoon pumps was like music to his ears. Even more encouraging was the submersible's slight rocking motion as it gained buoyancy and lifted off the bottom.

Falstaff rose a few feet and came to a thumping stop under the ship's overhang. Using alternate bursts from the lateral thrusters, he wriggled the submersible free. He ran the good thruster in reverse to balance off the loss of the other, and *Falstaff* began a wobbling ascent.

"Hang in there. We're going to be okay," he said.

"I'm not so sure about that," Kalliste said.

She pointed the flashlight at their feet. The beam reflected off sparkling ripples. Hawkins leaned over and stuck his hand into frigid water that was only a couple of inches deep, but flowing in fast. He had designed *Falstaff* to be as watertight as humanly possible. His computations never took into account being T-boned by a salvage ship.

"The impact must have cracked a seal," he said.

"What can we do?"

"Keep moving. Try to stay ahead of the leak."

"I don't mean to be pessimistic, but even if we get to the surface the submersible will sink under us."

"I'll blow the pontoons. There should be enough buoyancy to keep us afloat until help arrives."

It would be a tight squeeze. The cold water was lapping at their shins by the time the fathometer marked them at the one-hundred-fifty-foot mark. He gritted his chattering teeth and kept his eyes glued to the dial.

One hundred feet.

Kalliste was using every ounce of stubbornness in her body, but the cold was eating away at her resolve. Hypothermia was setting in. Hawkins was shivering, and her teeth were clacking.

"Matt, the water is at my knees." Her voice held a panicked edge.

"Promise me something, Kalliste."

"Yes. Anything," she said through chattering lips.

"That we'll have dinner together back in Cadiz."

She turned to Hawkins in the pale light, incredulous at his calm grin even with the prospect of death staring him in the face.

"I can't believe I'm here with a crazy man. Yes, of course we'll have dinner." She brushed the hair out of her face again. "But I will have to look better than I look now."

Hawkins placed his arm around her shoulders.

"You look like a Greek goddess."

"Oh!" she said.

Her startled reaction had nothing to do with his attention. *Falstaff* had popped to the surface where it was lifted high by a swell and dropped back down between the angry waves.

By then, the water was at waist-level.

And all around them was darkness.

CHAPTER TWELVE

Hawkins had switched on the Mayday transmitter but he knew that help could be hours, possibly days, away.

Falstaff bobbed in two-foot-high seas and the sphere was half-full of seawater causing a shift in the center of gravity. The submersible was inherently unstable on the surface because of the weight of the batteries behind the passenger space. The rocking motion created even more waves inside the sphere, making it look like wine being swished around in a glass.

Seconds after the pontoons emptied, the submersible tilted over backwards. The control panel lights blinked out. The water was under their chins. The choices were stark.

They could drown now, or crawl out of the submersible and drown in minutes. Hawkins figured he had been living on borrowed time since the explosion in Afghanistan that had nearly ended his life. But he felt bad for Kalliste, whose only offense against the sea was to uncover one of its long-held secrets.

"We've got to get out of here," he said.

"Out to *where*?" Kalliste said.

"I'll tell you when we get there."

Doing his best to stand up in the small, curved space, Hawkins undid the clasps holding the hatch in place and boosted Kalliste through the opening. Crawling out beside her, they clung to the battery housing as the sea sloshed through the hatch opening and the submersible's angle grew more pronounced.

"I'm slipping off!" Kalliste shouted.

Hawkins held onto the housing with one hand and reached down with the other. He could barely bend his cold fingers, but he managed to grab her wrist, stopping her descent into the ocean. The waves pulled at her feet. He didn't have the strength to haul her back up onto the sphere. His arm was being yanked from its socket, but he ignored the pain and summoned his last reserve of strength.

"Climb!" he yelled.

"Wha—?"

"Climb out of the water or we're gonna have to postpone that dinner."

She managed a garbled reply. "You're crazy!" Given the insanity of their situation he probably would have agreed. Especially after he heard a voice in the darkness shouting their names.

"Matt! Kalliste!" They were suddenly bathed in light. The voice called out again. "Hold on! For God sakes, don't let go!"

The light become brighter as it moved closer and was within a couple of feet of the rolling sphere when Hawkins lost his hold on the housing. He and Kalliste slid off into the sea and went under the waves. Hawkins still had his fingers locked around Kalliste's wrist in a death grip. Using a combination of kicks, and wild thrashing with his free arm, he got her back to the surface.

The voice again. Nearer this time.

"Swim! Swim!"

Another voice joined in.

"Over here! Come!"

Kalliste started to slip below the surface. Hawkins grabbed her around the waist and flailed in a clumsy attempt to swim.

Hands reached down, grabbed Kalliste under the arms and lifted her into the darkness behind the blinding light. He heard his name called again. He reached out. As he felt the strong grip around his wrists, Hawkins rose from the sea, his body slithering over a rubbery wet surface. There was the sound of a zipper being closed.

Hawkins lay next to Kalliste inside an enclosed life raft. He wiped water from his eyes and in the light of an electric torch, the faces of Captain Santiago and his son Miguel came into focus.

"You're okay now," the captain said.

Kalliste accepted Miguel's offer of a jacket and wrapped it around her shoulders. The jacket was wet, but it at least offered some insulation.

"How did you find us?" she said through clacking teeth.

The captain said, "We are floating around inside the life raft when I hear voices. Someone talking about dinner. So I open the door and shine the light. There you are on the big bubble."

"I thought you had gone down with the boat," Hawkins said.

"Close," Miguel said. Fear danced in his eyes.

His father nodded. "We'd be dead if we were in the pilot house. Miguel called me down to the deck to help him. We launched the life raft before the *Panza* went down."

"What happened to Rodriguez?"

"He disappeared," the captain said. "One second he is running back and forth on the stern. The next, he is gone. Lots of blood."

Hawkins remembered the suspicious call Rodriguez had made before they were hit.

"Too bad," he said. "I would have liked to talk to him. I'm sorry for the loss of your boat, Captain."

"Thank you. As the great Cervantes said, 'Those who play with cats must expect to be scratched.' I have worked on the sea for many years without a scratch. It was inevitable that the ocean would show her claws one day."

"I turned on my Mayday broadcaster," Hawkins said. "Help should be here in a while."

The son cocked his hand behind his ear. Audible above the slosh of waves against the raft was the low grumble of engines. Then the raft was bathed in the glare of a floodlight.

A grin came to Santiago's lips. "No, Mr. Hawkins," he said. "Help is here now."

CHAPTER THIRTEEN

The Spanish Coast Guard cutter plucked the survivors from the life raft a few minutes later. The refugees from the *Sancho Panza* each enjoyed long, scalding showers before heating their insides with hot soup. Wearing jeans and shirts on loan from the friendly crew, they climbed into a shuttle van back in Cadiz. The vehicle drove the captain and his son home and dropped Matt and Kalliste at a hotel where she had reserved rooms for them to use as a base. They crawled into her king-size bed with their clothes on and slept soundly until they were awakened by the telephone.

It was Captain Santiago calling. The cutter's captain had radioed his superiors, reporting that a government official named Rodriguez was missing and presumed dead. A police officer named Garcia had called Santiago asking to speak with everyone who'd been on the boat. Santiago had suggested the hotel for the meeting.

Kalliste had kept her suitcase in the room and had fresh clothes to change into. Hawkins had lost his bag when the salvage boat sank. He was still in his borrowed Coast Guard clothes and hadn't shaved, when he and Kalliste joined the Santiago's to, hopefully, find out more information about what on earth had happened the night before.

Sergeant Garcia signaled with a wave of a hand for them to take their seats. The sergeant was a big man, with most of his bulk centered in his substantial girth, a product of too many stakeouts and not enough exercise. He was tall as well, more than six feet in height. Simply sitting at the table in the hotel conference room, he presented an imposing figure. He often used his formidable physique to intimidate those he interrogated. With others, he took the opposite tact, beguiling them with his sympathetic tone and large brown eyes. He wasn't sure how he would proceed with this group.

The father and son were Spaniards. They were respectful in answering his questions, although the older man's deference seemed less than sincere. The American scientist had not been the timid academic Garcia expected. He was built like a longshoreman. His level gaze had an unnerving hardness that didn't match the smile he wore on his unshaven face.

The Greek woman was attractively middle-aged. In another setting, he would have flirted as well as questioned her. But she had displayed a quick temper after he'd asked for her version of events the third time. It was a routine police procedure; have a witness repeat his or her story and look for discrepancies, but her patience had run out.

She crossed her arms in front of her. "We have told you the story twice already."

"But you may have missed something."

She looked him straight in the eye. "Sergeant Garcia, you have two…ears, and I think there is a brain resting somewhere between them, so you have heard what I have to say and presumably have understood me by now."

Garcia had been embarrassed since childhood by his prominent ears and wore his black hair long to disguise them. He wagged his forefinger at the Greek.

"This is a serious matter."

Lowering her head like a charging bull, she wagged back.

"Then I suggest you bring in someone who does not need stories repeated again and again like an idiot child."

Which was when Hawkins intervened. Speaking in a quiet voice, he said, "Excuse me, Sergeant Garcia. May I make a suggestion?"

The raised fingers remained poised. Eyes were locked.

"What sort of suggestion?"

"We've gone through an exhausting ordeal and may not be as calm and patient as we normally would be. Maybe you could just ask questions about areas that concern you."

Garcia wasn't about to yield. And neither was the stubborn Greek. Hawkins must have seen the need for dramatic intervention because he turned to the captain. "To quote the great Cervantes…." He raised his eyebrows as a cue.

Captain Santiago smiled. Spreading his arms wide, he declared, "As the great Cervantes said, 'honesty is the best policy.' "

Kalliste and Garcia stared at the beatific smile on the captain's face, then slowly lowered their fingers.

"I would be the last person to argue with Cervantes," the sergeant said. "To be perfectly honest, some of what I have heard is very hard to believe." He consulted his notepad. "You told me you wished to examine an old ship on the bottom of the sea. Senora Kalchis and Senor Hawkins go down into the sea in a submarine. You find the ship. You hear noises. Then a boat almost…falls on you."

"*My* boat," the captain reminded him. "The *Sancho Panza*, a name from the great Cervantes."

The sergeant sighed. "Yes, Cervantes. Tell me again why your boat sinks, young man."

Garcia had hoped to take advantage of Miguel's youthful lack of guile. Miguel glanced at his father, who nodded, then said, "The boat explodes. First the pilot house, then the hull."

"Was the boat carrying any explosives?"

Kalliste broke in. "This was an archaeological project. We had a permit from your government to look at a ship. Why would we carry explosives?" she spoke with slightly veiled contempt.

"To blow up the ship. Maybe you're looking for gold?"

Kalliste smiled seductively. The sergeant took her reaction as a gesture of personal interest.

He didn't know Kalliste well enough to realize that she was actually looking for an unflattering physical attribute she could use as a cudgel to distribute a whack to his ego.

Hawkins cut in. "No explosives on board. I think the boat was hit by missiles."

"But you heard no missile launch?"

"That means nothing. They could have come from a distance. Or their rocket motors might have been muffled."

Garcia saw the opening and dove in. "And you are an expert in explosives?"

"Yes. I was with the U.S. Navy SEALs in Afghanistan."

"Huh. Well. Let's forget the explosives for now. There was an observer from the Spanish government on board. Senor Rodriguez."

"That's correct," Hawkins said.

The sergeant opened a manila folder and placed a photograph face up on the table. Unlike the pig-faced Rodriguez, the man in the picture had a lean jaw and a beard. Judging from his glassy stare and fish belly pallor, he was very dead.

"Do any of you recognize this person?" Hearing no answer in the affirmative, he said, "This is Senor Rodriguez, the government observer. He is an accountant, the brother-in-law of a high government official who recommended him for the job."

"That man was never on the boat," Kalliste said.

Garcia's thick lips widened in a triumphant grin. "No surprise," he said, tapping the photo with his forefinger. "Because this man is dead. His body was found in the harbor two days ago. Several relatives have come forward and identified him."

"If what you say is true," Hawkins said. "The guy on our boat was an imposter. What was the cause of death for the man in the photo?"

"Still being investigated."

"Are you charging us with his murder?" Kalliste asked.

"I'm not charging you with anything. I—"

Kalliste's dueling finger rose up once again. "In that case, I suggest that we end this discussion. Whether you believe us or not, we have all gone through a harrowing experience. This is all very fascinating, but if I don't get rest soon I will fall asleep."

Garcia liked this woman. She was not only attractive, but spirited as well.

"I understand completely," he soothed. "We will talk later. I'm sorry to have put you through this discomfort. Particularly you, *senora*."

Kalliste fluttered her eyelashes. "You are only doing your job. It's a shame we are not in a more informal setting. You must have many colorful policeman stories to tell about Cadiz."

"A policeman goes to many hidden places. I would love to tell you about them." He closed his notebook. "We'll continue this discussion after you have had some rest. In the meantime, I must insist that you not leave the country, and that you make yourself available for further questioning."

Hawkins burst into laughter after Garcia left the room. He mimicked Kalliste's eye flutters, and said, "You most have many poleezman storees to tell about Cadeez."

"A policeman goes to many hidden places," she responded in a basso voice. A look of disgust came to her face. "The dirty old cop was trying to offer me a proposal."

"A proposal is for marriage. He was making a proposition, which is something else."

"I'll *bet* it is," Kalliste said. "I need some coffee."

Hawkins turned to the captain and his son. "Care to join us?"

"Thank you, no, *senor*. My wife will be worrying about us."

"I understand. Again, please know how sorry I am for the loss of your boat, Captain."

Santiago shrugged. "The *Sancho Panza* was old. I would have retired her soon anyhow. I have good insurance. Please call me again if you have need of my services."

Kalliste gave the Santiago men each a hug and a double-cheek kiss.

She and Hawkins were heading through the lobby to the cafeteria when someone called Kalliste's name. A young woman who'd been standing at the reception desk was walking briskly in their direction. She wore a fashionably snug black leather jacket and a short russet colored leather skirt that clung tightly to her slim body. She was a statuesque woman and the black knee-high boots with heels made her even taller. Her hair, tied in a French twist, was the reddish blonde color that might be found in a Titian painting.

"Lily, what are you doing here?" Kalliste said in astonishment.

The woman gave Kalliste a bear hug. "Have you forgotten so soon? I'm your producer."

"I'm sorry, Lily. I never expected to see you here in Cadiz. The last time we talked you were in New York."

"After that I flew to Paris where I've been doing a story on werewolves. Cadiz was only a short hop so I thought I'd fly in and surprise you."

Hawkins couldn't resist. "Excuse me. Did you say werewolves?"

Lily turned and gave Hawkins a warm smile. "That's right. In the sewers. Yes, I know. Crazy stuff, but the viewers can't get enough of it." She extended her hand. "My name is Lily Porter. I work for the television channel Hidden History. We've been backing Kalliste's shipwreck project."

They shook hands. "Matt Hawkins. I came over from Woods Hole to help her with the technical aspects of the survey."

"Mr. Hawkins. I'm so pleased to meet you. Kalliste said you were the reason the Spanish government came through with the permit." She glanced around the lobby and lowered her voice. "Well, Kalliste. Is it or isn't it?"

"It is a Minoan ship, most definitely in my opinion."

"Wonderful! I'll go to the channel's money guys and request full funding as soon as I have the evidence in hand."

"You might want to wait, Ms. Porter," Hawkins said. "Maybe we can talk about it over a cup of coffee."

"Good idea, Matt. I'll buy."

The hour fell between breakfast and lunch which meant the cafeteria was practically empty. They sat at a table and, over coffee and pastry, Kalliste told Lily about the attack, the loss of the submersible and their close brush with death.

"That's an incredible story," Lily said. "I am so grateful that you're all right, Kalliste. You too, Mr. Hawkins. Wow! This is even bigger than we thought. It's every bit as dramatic as a James Bond movie. The money guys will be falling over themselves to fund production."

"I appreciate all you've done for me, Lily, but I'd prefer to wait until we know what we're dealing with." Kalliste glanced at Hawkins, who backed her up.

"Putting a production crew out there now will be dangerous," he said.

"You're right," Lily said with a sigh of disappointment. "I'd never forgive myself if someone was hurt." She seemed to brighten. "Why don't I start the paperwork shuffling along. I'll wrap up the werewolves piece and get back to you within a day or so."

"That would be fine, Lily. I'll look forward to hearing from you after I talk to my bosses in Greece."

Lily thanked them both and headed for the door where she paused and threw a kiss over her shoulder before stepping out into the lobby.

Kalliste reached across the table and put her hand on Hawkins's arm. "Please accept my apologies, Matt. I should never have dragged you into this project."

His throat was raw from the seawater he'd swallowed. His shoulder and the side of his face were sore from the hits he'd taken inside the submersible. "Not your fault, Kalliste. It was lots of fun until the boat fell on our heads."

"That's what I don't understand, Matt. This was to be nothing but a scientific inquiry. Who would want to sabotage our expedition?"

"The same person or persons who killed the real Rodriguez and placed an imposter on board the *Sancho Panza*. Beyond that, I don't have a clue. Maybe Sergeant Garcia can find out."

"Wait until he learns I have gone back to Greece."

"When are you leaving?"

She yawned. "After my nap. Will you be going back to Woods Hole?"

Hawkins pictured himself back home, sitting at a meeting of the Deep Submergence Laboratory, explaining that the submersible he planned to lease for their expedition was lying on the bottom of the sea.

"Think I'll stick around for a while. First, I'll buy some new clothes to replace the ones that went down with the survey boat. Then I want to see if *Falstaff* can be salvaged. Captain Santiago said he'd help, so I may take him up on it."

She put her hand on his arm. "A No Trespassing sign has been placed around the wreck site. Please promise that you'll be careful,

Matt."

"I promise. Don't forget we have a dinner date."

"I'll take you up on your invitation soon as I get back."

Kalliste gave him a goodbye hug and kiss and told him to keep in touch. Hawkins ordered another coffee, called Santiago's cell phone, and said he wanted to locate his submersible for possible salvage. Santiago asked when he wanted to make the survey.

"Tomorrow, if possible."

"I think I know of a boat that may be available. I'm anxious to locate the *Sancho Panza* as well. I'll make a few calls and get back to you."

Santiago sounded optimistic about the chances of procuring a boat, but Hawkins was determined not to be a sitting duck this time around. Whatever it was that he'd fallen into was big. Very big. He would need someone to watch his back. And there was only one person he would trust to do it.

CHAPTER FOURTEEN

Calvin Hayes perched in the elevated seat of the fifteen-foot-long fiberglass Hurricane Aircat as the flat-bottom boat skimmed over the waters of the Louisiana bayou at more than fifty miles per hour. His left hand gripped the rudder stick, the mangroves were a slurry green blur on both sides, and the kick-ass roar of the air-cooled power plant was like music to his ears.

His lips were stretched in a wide grin. Calvin was within seconds of winning the air boat race. He could almost taste the cold beer the loser had to buy the winner. He put the boat into a banking slalom turn through the last of the mangroves into open water, hunched his powerful shoulder muscles, leaned forward in his seat, and squinted through his goggles at the mile of straightaway that marked the final stretch of the race.

He'd gotten off to a jackrabbit start and maintained a slight lead. The race had been tight. He'd kept a lead of a hundred feet or so ahead of the other custom-built air-boat. Like his, it had a souped-up airplane engine as a power plant. He hoped that the modifications he had built into his own engine housed in the conical safety screen behind his head would give him the winning edge. His eyes searched for the flag marking the finish. A sliver of red. Coming up fast. He narrowed his concentration, excluding the rest of the world, willing the boat to go faster, although it was practically ready to go airborne.

That's when he felt the vibration over his heart. Damned cell phone. The distraction was brief, but it allowed the other boat to draw neck-and-neck with his. They pounded down the home stretch in a dead heat. Hayes might still have won if not for the branch floating in the water directly ahead.

He swerved the boat to the right of the mangrove limb then back on course. The diversion put him a second behind, which is where he was when his boat blew past the pennant floating on a square of styrofoam.

Hayes let out a mighty curse. He reduced the power and pulled alongside the winner. The man on the other boat cut the engine, and Hayes could hear him shout:

"You'all almost had me, Calvin! Why'd'ja slow down?"

The man was built like a haystack. He was dressed in jeans and a black T-shirt with the sleeves cut off, exposing thick arms that were colored blue with tattoo ink. His chin was buried in a thick blond beard.

Hayes could have told him about the phone call and the floating branch. But in the *mano a mano* world of air boat racing, that would have sounded like whining.

He grinned. "Just testing my brakes, Junior."

The man's laughter almost shook the Spanish moss off the trees. He rubbed his ample gut with one hand and mimicked drinking with the other. Then he powered up the engine, and headed back into the mangroves. They followed the winding five-mile course back to their starting point—a beat-up shack that was combination general store and bar-restaurant. They tied up at the gas dock.

"You go on ahead," Hayes told his friend. "Order up a tub of crawfish and I'll join you in a couple of minutes."

He reached for his phone, thinking he might have to deal with company business before the drinking began. "I'll be damned," Hayes muttered.

The caller ID photo was a picture of a much younger Hawkins and Hayes from their Navy SEAL days. Hayes hadn't started shaving his scalp back then, and both men sported buzz cuts. They had grins on their faces and matching camo do-rags around their heads. The sun-blasted skin on Hawkins's face was almost as dark as Calvin's natural dark brown complexion.

He hit the call button. Hawkins answered immediately.

"Hi, Calvin. How're you doing?" Hawkins said.

"Havin' more fun than a crawfish swimmin' in a bowl of gumbo, Hawk. Just finished up an air boat race with a gator hunter."

"How'd you make out?"

"Came in second place. Course, there were only two of us. Nice to hear your voice. Get your emails from time to time, but it's been awhile since we talked."

"Glad we could connect. Figured you might be busy fighting Somali pirates."

"Secure Ocean Services is changing our business model. Still keeping the pressure on the pirates with our on-board teams, but we're more into systems now. Port security, figuring out where the leaks are, putting personnel to stop them. Phasing out the cowboy stuff."

"Does that mean they're phasing out the cowboys?"

"Got that right, pal. I'm still majority stockholder. The directors pretty much run the show. That's why I got time to go bayou racing with my pal Junior."

"Junior?"

"Cajun guy. Gator hunter who made a killin' on reality TV. Drives an old pick-up, but that's for show. Lives in a trophy house and got a couple of Bentleys in his garage."

"What are you driving, Cal?"

"Ford pick-up." He paused. "And a Bentley Cabrio convert in the garage of my trophy house. Does two-hundred plus, but it can't pass a gas station. You still designing those Jules Verne gadgets at Woods Hole?"

"Taking a break from the scientific stuff, actually. I'm in Spain on a shipwreck expedition."

"Nothin' wrong with that," Calvin said.

"Actually, old pal, there's a *lot* wrong with it. You got a minute?"

"Hold on." Hayes went inside the shack which was filled with the succulent fragrance of boiling crawfish. He told Junior to go ahead without him.

He put a bottle of Dixie beer on the tab and walked out to a bench on the end of the fuel dock. "Okay, Hawk. What's got you riled up?"

"It's a complicated story. I'll give you the CliffsNotes version."

Hawkins told him about Kalliste and the invitation to survey what could be a history-making shipwreck. Calvin set his beer aside and listened intently as Hawkins laid out the details of the attack and sinking.

Calvin had an encyclopedic knowledge of weaponry. "From what you said, it sounds like you got hit by Spike missiles. Anything bigger could have sent you to the bottom with one shot."

"I've been out of the war game. Not familiar with the brand."

"Developed to slow down swarm-type attacks. Couple of feet long and a few inches wide. Highly portable. They pack a heck of a wallop, but nothing like the big hardware that's available. Interesting what you said about a missile blowing up the guy on deck."

"What's your take on that?"

"Coulda been intentional. Spikes are pretty accurate. He never knew what hit him. Still a tough way to go."

"It probably saved my ass. The captain and his son had time to get a life boat in the water."

"Glad you're all okay. Where do you go from here?"

"I want to see if my submersible is salvageable. I'll need someone to ride shotgun."

"I'm in. If I can scare up an executive jet, I'll be there tomorrow."

"Abby's company always has planes in the air. That's how I got over here."

"Good idea. I'll give her a call."

"Thanks, Cal. I knew I could count on you. I'm staying at the Hotel Cadiz. One more favor. I'm wondering if you can pick something up for me on the way."

Hayes listened to the request and said it would be no problem. Hanging up, he stared off at the mangroves. He was picturing mud huts set against the rugged landscape of Afghanistan. The SEALs mission was supposed to be routine, but the drug lord they'd been sent to capture knew they were coming and had ringed his compound with explosive devices. A fellow SEAL had triggered the

IED and was blown to pieces. Hawkins was close by, and his leg caught some of the fragments that would have killed Hayes. He still felt guilty about not having Matt's back when the Navy dumped him.

"Cal-vin!"

Junior's klaxon voice echoed throughout the swamp. The mountains and mud hut vanished. Hayes was transported back to the bayou. He picked up his beer bottle and headed to the shack to dig into some crawfish. He was looking forward to seeing Hawkins again. But, first things first.

CHAPTER FIFTEEN

Bend, Oregon

"When the bird flies over your head, don't reach up or it will think your hand is something to eat."

The warning provoked nervous giggles from the audience. At least half of those sitting in the rows of folding chairs were children. The speaker was a slightly plump, pretty woman in her twenties. Her name was Molly Sutherland. A brown-feathered falcon clutched her padded wrist guard with its talons.

At the back of the room was a wooden rectangle attached to a vertical support. A young female assistant standing next to the pedestal scattered food pellets on the platform and tapped the wood with her forefinger to get the bird's attention.

Sutherland lifted her arm and launched the bird into the air. The falcon spread its wings and flew to the back, passing inches above the heads of the audience. Some people ducked, but the children issued a multitude of *oohs* and *aahs*.

The bird fluttered to a landing on the pedestal and gobbled down the pellets of food. A third assistant enticed it back to the front of the room where it re-settled on Sutherland's wrist. She pointed out the forward-facing eyes, the sharp talons and the hooked beak designed for tearing. All raptor characteristics. She repeated the routine with a great horned owl, explaining how the soft fringe feathers made the owl's flight over the audience practically soundless.

The birds were returned to their cages. Sutherland introduced the assistants and thanked the audience for supporting the museum. As people filed out of the room, a naturalist on the museum's payroll came over and put her hand on Sutherland's shoulder.

"Nice going, Molly. Everyone enjoyed the show."

Sutherland once would have flinched at the physical contact. Instead, she removed her black-framed circular glasses to reveal remarkable orchid-colored eyes, and wiped her forehead with the back of her hand.

"Everyone but *me*," Sutherland replied. "I was a-sweating bullets." In her nervousness, she slipped back into her West Virginia accent.

"It's hard to stand up in front of a group of strangers under any circumstance. And you never know what the birds will do. Don't sell yourself short, Molly. You have a talent. Those raptors were perfectly at ease with you."

Sutherland replaced the glasses and coaxed a half-smile from her lips. "Don't know if there's much call for a hawk-whisperer. But thanks anyway. Means a lot coming from you."

"See you tomorrow?"

"You bet."

Sutherland headed for the parking lot and swung a leg over the saddle of her customized, low-profile Forty-Eight model Harley-Davidson. She swapped her prescription glasses for a pair of wrap-around shades, started the 1203 cc V-twin engine and rode past the High Desert Museum sign. She cruised along the meandering road enjoying the guttural rumble of the exhaust in her ears, the cool dry air against her face, and reflected on the journey that had taken her to central Oregon.

After leaving the Army, she had settled in Tubac, Arizona. Building a house in the hills, she'd taken up oil painting. She loved the desert light and the abundance of birds—hummingbirds, in particular. She had little contact with the outside world until Matt Hawkins, a fellow soldier who was pretty much her only friend, asked her to put her computer skills to work providing intelligence for a secret project he was involved in. Neither she nor Matt had any idea that they'd been drawn into a Byzantine plot that would have worldwide impact. Her computer probes triggered an assassination squad who burned her house, her paintings, and sent her running for her life.

Thanks to Sutherland, the plot had unraveled.

With her house and paintings reduced to ashes, Sutherland hit the road. She bought a tent and sleeping bag and headed West. In Salt Lake City, she got up one morning and decided she wanted to see the Pacific Ocean. California didn't appeal to her, so she headed to the Pacific Northwest and tarried a few days in Portland, Oregon. She'd liked the city's quirkiness but not the traffic and crowds, so she kept on moving.

She arrived in the town of Bend late one afternoon and pulled her bike up to the walking path that ran along the banks of the Deschutes River. When Sutherland chose to stretch her legs with a stroll, three strangers along the path had smiled and said hello. That night she stayed in a motel and the very next day she contacted a real estate office.

The agent showed her a rental house outside town that offered a view of the mountains. She had vowed never to paint again, but she still liked birds. She switched to photography. Unlike a painting, a photo could be stored in a computer, or in the cloud, or sent off to places where it would be safe from harm.

Sutherland invested in a high-end Canon digital single-lens reflex camera. The infinite patience that had made her a computer whiz allowed her to sit for hours waiting for the right shot. She became fascinated with raptors. During a visit to the museum, she showed the staff pictures she had taken of a Golden eagle's nest. The museum asked to see more, and ended up mounting an exhibition of her photographic work.

She started volunteering a couple of days a week. When the museum created the program that introduced raptors to the public, she joined the team. Sutherland was uncomfortable around other people, but enjoyed working with the birds and seeing the amazed expressions on the faces of the children. She spent more time in the field, and when she did go to her computer, it was only to download photos.

Her major talent was the ability to worm her way into other computers, leaving no trail behind. Since moving to Bend, she had used her talents only once, after she'd seen a newspaper headline in the local supermarket:

Congress Debates Bill
Curbing Sexual Abuse
In the Armed Services

Molly had narrowed her eyes in a Clint Eastwood squint. Pictures flashed in her head.... Staring up at the stars, savoring the quiet desert beauty of an Iraq night; rough hands grabbing her by the shoulders, slamming her to the ground and ripping her uniform off. The rape was a painful blur. Even more awful was the stony face of the officer who'd listened to her story, then recommended a psychiatric discharge and counseling.

In the days after she'd seen the newspaper headline, thousands of phantom e-mail letters in support of the bill went out to recalcitrant congressmen. The names of some senders came off lists of Civil War veterans. The modified bill was approved. Not perfect, but it was something. She felt like the token retired gunslinger who comes out of retirement to shoot up a town full of bad guys. As soon as she got home from the museum, she powered up her computer to download photos she had taken near Mt. Bachelor. She saw that she had an e-mail from Matt Hawkins. It was the same message he sent every couple of months.

HI MOLLY. R U OK?

She sent the same answer she always did.

YUP. THX.

Matt was the closest thing she had to a friend. They'd both been abandoned by their commanding officers. Matt's wounds were mostly physical; hers, mental, but the hurt was the same. But in trusting Matt, she believed there might be a chance to one day trust others. Molly had a long way to go before she was at that point. Maybe she'd never be there. Right now, all she could handle were her birds.

Matt usually ended the conversation by saying he was glad to hear she was okay. But this time the message was different.

NEED UR HELP MOLLY.

Her finger hesitated for a moment above the keyboard. She stared at the blinking cursor. Then she typed:

?

SOMEONE TRIED TO KILL ME.

?

??

The double question marks meant he didn't know the answer.

TALKED TO CALVIN?

HE'S ON BOARD.

If Calvin Hayes had joined Hawkins, it must be serious.

ABBY?

HOPE SO. R U 2?

Molly's mind raced. She was enjoying her new life taking photos and talking about raptors. The last time she helped him, she's lost her house and her art, but she didn't want to disappoint Matt. She typed: NOTHING OPERATIONAL. JUST INTEL.

OK. NEED INFO ON SPIKE MISSILES. SELLERS? BUYERS IN THE LAST SIX MONTHS.

The answer was quick in coming.

WILL GET TO IT DIRECTLY.

Hawkins thanked Molly, sent her a summary of the events leading up to his request for help and promised to keep her in the loop with daily reports. He leaned back in his chair and stared at the computer screen.

Sutherland had the ability to mess up things and people she didn't like, and that was a long list. The gods must have had a big laugh when they stoked the emotion of smoldering anger, mixed it with the potential for creating havoc, and poured the brew into a pudgy young woman with the meekness of a lamb. He needed her if he wanted to find out who sent the salvage boat and submersible to the bottom, but he was aware of a simple fact: Sutherland couldn't be any more controlled than a bolt of lightning.

The cell phone rang. It was Captain Santiago. "I'll meet you at the hotel in half an hour. I have found us a boat."

CHAPTER SIXTEEN

Leonidas had called Isabel as soon as he returned the boat to the lease company. They celebrated his impending payday with dinner at an expensive restaurant, followed by hours of bar hopping before they returned to the hotel for a wild night of drug-powered sex. At least, he thought that's what happened, but wasn't sure. They had gotten so blasted that he remembered little after they stepped into the hotel room.

When they woke up well into the next day, Isabel said he had asked her to marry him, which may have been true. He said they'd discuss it after a few more hours of sleep. His brain felt slightly less like scrambled eggs when he awoke the second time. Isabel was snoring beside him. He still had on the clothes from the night before and surmised that they had been too stoned-out to have sex. Just as well. The romp might have triggered the sock pistol tied to his ankle.

He stared at the clock with blurry vision. It was late afternoon. He got up and went into the kitchenette. His mouth felt like the Mohave Desert. After he re-hydrated by guzzling a gallon of ice water he felt better. He was thinking that life with a reformed prostitute might not be all that bad—it would certainly never be dull—when Salazar called and rained on his parade.

There were no preliminaries. He simply said, "You lied to me."

"Huh—?"

"You said you sank the boat."

"No lie there, Mr. Salazar. I saw it sink."

"Then consider this. I have learned from my government informant that the Coast Guard rescued Hawkins and the Greek woman. The captain and his son also escaped. The deal called for no boat *and* no witnesses."

"Damn, Mr. Salazar. Okay, I screwed up," Leonidas said. "I'll make it good. Hawkins and the others will be dead by this time tomorrow."

"Plans have changed. I'll deal with this problem in another way."

"Sorry about this, Mr. Salazar. I don't blame you for firing me."

"On the contrary, I'm not firing you," Salazar said, chuckling, his mellow voice warming slightly. "You've always come through for me before, so I'd like to keep you on retainer. It's helpful to be able to call on someone with no ties to me. Since you didn't accomplish your assignment, I won't be paying you the second half of your retainer. But I understand that you had certain expenses, such as the missiles, so I'll allow the first half. Does that seem fair?"

"More than fair, Mr. Salazar. I'm still available if you need me to take care of Hawkins."

"Forget Hawkins for now. That situation will soon be resolved."

"Whatever you say, Mr. Salazar. Thanks for being so understanding."

"Of course. Then you'll understand that with this situation being slightly more delicate than before, it might not be safe to put your payment in your Swiss account, with the potential for traceability."

"Whatever you say, Mr. Salazar."

"I don't like to drag things out. I'll send someone over to deliver the cash, if that's all right with you."

Even better, Leonidas thought. "Thanks, Mr. Salazar. I'll be waiting."

The phone went dead. The smile Leonidas had pasted on his lips disappeared. He threw the phone across the room. He had only himself to blame. He cursed himself for getting so stoned on the job that he'd imagined he was shooting ducks in a gallery.

He liberated a bottle of single malt whiskey from the liquor cabinet and poured himself a stiff shot. The smooth liquid fire trickling down his throat washed away his mental cobwebs. He picked up his cell phone and Googled Matt Hawkins. At least a dozen articles popped up having to do with Hawkins's robotics work at Woods Hole.

He learned that the man's first name was Matinicus. He was born in Maine and named after Matinicus Island. His father was a lobster fisherman and his mother an ornithologist who worked for the state. He read deeper into the biography and discovered that Hawkins was not an ordinary ocean engineer.

Hawkins had been a Navy SEAL. That explained his resilience. Like Leonidas, Hawkins had been injured by an IED. There was a big difference, however. The photos showed that Hawkins still had his handsome features.

Leonidas heard someone stirring. A moment later, Isabel appeared in the living room. She was wearing his Malibu T-shirt. Her long hair was straggling over her face. She stared at the glass in his hand, and croaked, "I need a drink."

Yessiree, Leonidas thought. Life with Isabel would never be dull.

He poured her half a glass of whiskey, and said, "I stink like a monkey. Want to take a shower with me?"

She sipped her whiskey and gave him a lazy smile. "You go ahead. I'll come in after I finish my breakfast."

Leonidas gave her kiss. "I'm expecting an important delivery. Call me if someone comes."

She waved her hand, then settled into a chair with her drink. Leonidas let his eyes linger on her face. As debauched as Isabel appeared, she was still beautiful. He went into the bathroom to shower, not knowing that it was the last time he would ever see her alive. If he'd not been so wasted, he would have seen through Salazar's fake charm.

As he washed away the sweat and grit, his mind regained some of its sharpness and he began to lay out plans on what to do with his money. It wouldn't be as much as he wanted, but still a substantial sum. He might have to give up the luxury hotel suites until he got more work. Hell, maybe he'd even retire from the killing business altogether. Since he knew all the tricks, he might be able to make a living protecting people from assassins like himself.

He got out of the shower, thinking that a cottage by the sea in

Majorca might be a nice place to set up a business. He was toweling off his body when he heard a strange noise, through the half-open door, that set off alarms in his head. It was a distinct *thut*, and he knew exactly what it was. The muffled shot made by a pistol armed with a silencer.

He edged to one side and peered through the crack between the doorjamb. Two men were standing in the room. They were big guys, both dressed in dark sport jackets over black T-shirts. Sunglasses hid their eyes but their mouths had the cold-blooded hardness of the men he'd worked with in Special Ops.

They both held pistols with extended barrels. One man had his weapon pointed down at Isabel's bloody body lying on the floor. Leonidas reconstructed what had happened. Isabel had gone to the door so she could proudly present him with the delivery. She wanted to please him. That's all she wanted to do. The strangers had stepped inside, closed the door behind them, and taken care of Isabel with a single shot.

He picked up the sock holster hanging on a chair with his slacks, eased the gun out, turned the shower back on, and called, "Be out in a minute, darling." The bathroom began to fill with steam. The man stepped through the door and aimed his gun at the shower curtain. Standing with his shoulders against the wall, Leonidas placed the .22 caliber muzzle on the back of the man's head, and kept it there for a second. He wanted the stranger to know exactly how he was going to die.

The shower noise drowned out the snap of the gunshot. The man crumpled to the floor. Still wearing the towel wrapped around his waist, Leonidas stepped over the body and into the living room, pistol raised. The other man saw him and could have gotten off a shot with the gun in his hand, but he became locked as he stared at the monstrous ruin of Leonidas's face. His hesitation was fatal. Leonidas aimed for the man's Adam's apple and squeezed the trigger.

The man grabbed at his throat with both hands and crashed to the floor. Leonidas let Isabel's killer choke on the bloody froth for a minute before he shot him in the heart. Walking over to Isabel, who lay face down, he turned her onto her back. She'd been shot in the forehead. The T-shirt was so drenched with blood the word

"Malibu" was now unreadable.

Leonidas felt something akin to sorrow, but that was quickly replaced by an icy anger. Salazar had set this up. The bastard intended to pay him, but not with money. He thought about Hawkins again. Salazar had wanted the man dead and would try again. If he stuck close to Hawkins, he might get to Salazar. The woman, who he now knew was named Kalliste, had been required to submit every detail of her project to the Spanish government, including hotel arrangements made for her and Hawkins. Salazar's government informant had sent Leonidas the information. Digging it out, he called the same hotel to reserve a room, using a phony credit card he'd bought on the black market. The name on the card was Fred Healy.

"A friend of mine is staying at the hotel," he told the clerk. "His name is Matt Hawkins. I wondered if you had a room close to his."

"I can give you room 311, Mr. Healy. Your friend is in room 308. That's the best I can do."

"That would be fine. Please don't let him know I called. I'd like to surprise him."

"I understand, sir."

He booked the room and thanked the clerk, then went into his bedroom. He made up a face with the features of a man in his sixties. The gray wig was in need of a trim. He dressed in tan slacks, a blue Oxford shirt under a navy blazer. Standing in front of the mirror, he practiced a slight hunch of the shoulders. Not bad. Middle-aged men were practically invisible.

Leonidas took a small, flat, plastic box from his suitcase and tucked it into his jacket pocket, then he wiped down the .22 pistol and placed it in Isabel's hand. He carried a spare pistol to replace the one from the holster. The police would ID her as a prostitute. Maybe they'd figure the dead guys were her pimps. It was a thin story but might just keep the cops occupied for a while.

He blew Isabel a kiss and slipped out of the room. Minutes later, he was in a cab heading for the hotel.

The clerk remembered his call. "You're in luck, Mr. Healy. Your friend just returned and is in the lounge."

Leonidas bought a *Financial Times* and walked into the lounge.

He sat at a table against a wall, ordered a club soda with lime, and unfolded the pink newspaper pages. Hawkins was sitting at the bar, head bent over an electronic tablet, when a couple entered the lounge.

The man with the shaved head was slightly less than six feet tall, although the muscular shoulders that bulged against the seams of his olive suit made him seem even bigger. He moved with an easy confidence in his step. Leonidas sized him up. Military. Probably seen combat. The attractive auburn-haired woman by his side was dressed in a black business suit. Leonidas thought at first that she was corporate, but there was an assertiveness in her slender body suggesting she also had military training on her resume.

The couple walked to the bar, and the man said, "Hey, Hawk. Brought you a surprise."

Hawkins swiveled on his stool. Leonidas would have been dead long ago if he couldn't read people from a distance. The oak-carved face of the American engineer displayed a mixture of amazement and pleasure. A stare. A hike of the brows, and a wide grin.

Leonidas placed his cell phone on the table in front of him and stuck a set of ear buds into his ears. An app allowed the phone to be used as a directional receiver. Keeping his eyes on the newspaper, he adjusted the volume.

This was going to be interesting.

CHAPTER SEVENTEEN

Hawkins slid off his stool and wrapped his arms around his ex-wife.

"You never cease to amaze me, Abby."

She pecked him on the lips. "Where's your Greek friend? The stuffy old archaeologist."

"I never said Kalliste was stuffy," Hawkins said. "I said she was highly-respected. Too bad you can't meet her. She went back to Greece."

"Good thing. I looked her up on the internet. She's quite attractive for a middle-aged woman. Actually, for *any* age."

"C'mon, Abby. You flew across the Atlantic because you were jealous?"

"Don't flatter yourself, Hawkins. I came to Spain because I heard you'd gotten yourself into a pile of trouble."

Hawkins gave Calvin a look. "It was no big deal."

"I'd say having a boat shot out from under you and almost drowning is a big deal."

His friend shrugged. "The lady is very persuasive."

"Don't blame Calvin," Abby said. "You and I were only married a short while, Matt, but long enough for me to know when you're being disingenuous with that cavalier attitude of yours. I would have worn Calvin down eventually and wormed the story out of him. I'm glad you weren't seriously hurt."

"I've got some bumps and bruises. That's nothing compared to my new submersible. Tough seeing a multi-million dollar piece of equipment sink under your feet."

Abby put her hand on his arm. "What can I do to help, Matt?"

Hawkins glanced at the entrance to the lounge. "I can tell you more in detail after we talk to these gentlemen."

He waved Captain Santiago and Miguel over, made the introductions and suggested they all move to a table, which put them beyond the range of the smart phone amplifier Leonidas was using to eavesdrop. He could have edged closer, but he didn't want to attract attention. He put some cash down, unplugged the ear buds, and went to the reception desk for his room key.

Back in the lounge, Hawkins began, "Captain Santiago owned the *Sancho Panza*, the salvage boat that sank during our survey. If it weren't for the captain and his son, I wouldn't be here talking to you. Could you tell my friends what happened before the boat went under, Captain Santiago?"

After the Spaniard repeated the story he had told the police, Abby said, "I don't get it. Who would want to stop you from diving to simply *look* at the wreck?"

"Maybe the ship was carrying treasure," Calvin drawled. "Folks figured you were poaching on their stash."

"That's possible, Cal. But how many treasure hunters would have Spike missiles in their back pockets?"

"Yeah, I catch your drift. Hardware's available on the black market, but the shooters would need intel about what you were doing, and where you'd be doing it. Takes money and contacts. That suggests a tight organization. Maybe a government."

"The big question is still, *why?*" Abby said.

"I don't know," Hawkins said. "I'm hoping I can find that out when I make another run at the site. Cal's going to handle security."

"Is this a no-girls-allowed boy's club adventure?" Abby said. "Just sayin."

"Molly has already agreed to help with research. I'd love to have you on board, but the last time we talked, you were barely holding your company together."

"Women are better multi-taskers than men, Matt. Besides, my

transports and executive jets will come in handy."

Hawkins knew that Abby had gone through Navy weapons training, kept herself in top-notch physical condition and had a quick mind that almost always made the right decision. But he hesitated. "You sure you want to do this? Things could get complicated," he said.

Abby folded her hands, looked him straight in the eye and in a level voice, said, "When have things *not* been complicated between us?"

Hawkins smiled. "Just sayin'."

"When do we start?"

"Tomorrow morning. The captain has arranged for a boat. He and his son will take us out to the site. I see this as a three-fold mission. First, find *Falstaff* and assess salvage possibilities. Second, Cal, I'd like you to make a forensic inspection of the captain's boat."

"I can do that. What's the third fold, Hawk?" Calvin said.

Hawkins powered up the tablet. The screen showed a shaky, greenish-gray image of the bones of the wreck illuminated in *Falstaff*'s floodlights.

"Kalliste took this video with her cell phone. The quality could be better, but she was shooting through the passenger sphere. The picture gets cloudy where we used the thrusters to blow sand off the wreck. It will clear after a second. Here."

He froze the image and zoomed in on the tapering, conical object partially buried under the sand.

Abby leaned forward. "What is that thing, Matt?"

He tapped on the tablet. An album of black-and-white prints appeared on the screen. The pictures showed different views of an object that looked like an inverted bucket suspended in the sea by ropes or chains. The final image showed a man in the bucket, which was being lowered into the water using pulleys and gears attached to a heavy framework.

"Damn," Calvin said. "It's a diving bell."

"A real old one from the looks of it," Hawkins said. "Diving bells go back to Alexander the Great, but they didn't become technically feasible until Dr. Edmund Halley improved on earlier models. This is Halley's bell design." He called up another image. "The model in the video looks even more sophisticated than that."

"Does this mean what I think it means?" Abby said.

"We'll know better once we get a vehicle down for a closer look. But the implication is pretty clear. Kalliste and I weren't the first divers to make it down to this wreck."

After he left the lounge, Leonidas had gone to his room and taken a miniature recorder from his suitcase. He switched it on and propped it up against a desk lamp. He made sure that the corridor was deserted. Then he went to room 308, slipped a plastic case from his pocket and took out a thin metal card. He ran the card through the door lock to pick up the combination and used it as a master key. Slipping into the room, he placed one electronic bug in the living room area and another in the bedroom.

Using a miniature battery-powered tool he drilled holes in the walls for the tiny microphone transmitters. Each cylinder was smaller in diameter than a thumbtack. He placed a ballpoint pen containing a micro-transmitter on the writing desk. The pen actually wrote.

He stood in the middle of the room and in a low voice, said, "Testing. Testing."

Leonidas returned to his own room and hit the play button on the recorder. His test came through loud and clear.

When he re-entered the lounge, he saw that Hawkins and his friends were wrapping up their business with handshakes. As Hawkins gave the woman a quick embrace he happened to look in Leonidas's direction. They locked gazes. Leonidas smiled and nodded, playing the part of an old man approving of young love.

Leonidas watched Hawkins and his friends leave the lounge and silently scolded himself. Hawkins had noticed him staring, and it had stirred a defensive curiosity. Leonidas should have known better. Hawkins had served in Afghanistan, where interest from a stranger was often the precursor to an attack. Sloppy move on his part. It was a strong reminder of what he should have learned by now. Not to underestimate Matt Hawkins.

CHAPTER EIGHTEEN

The fishing boat *Santa Maria* plowed through the mounding sea under a clear blue sky. The well-maintained wooden-hulled craft was about two-thirds the length of the *Sancho Panza*. Captain Santiago had leased the boat from a fisherman who had been laid up with a back injury and was glad to get the money.

Abby was with the captain in the wheelhouse. They were deep into the subject of Cervantes.

Hawkins stood at the bow, arms crossed, his gaze fixed on the sea. He was thinking about the diving bell on the old wreck. As a Navy SEAL, Hawkins had dropped into the ocean from a helicopter, wearing full combat and dive gear, rolled off a speeding boat into the surf, and assaulted a shore position in the belly of a miniature submarine. Yet he was finding it difficult to imagine how it must have been to descend to the wreck in a claustrophobic contraption shaped like an upside-down beer mug.

"How're you doing, Hawk?" said Calvin, who had come down from the pilot house.

"Fine, thanks," Hawkins replied. "Just wondering why anyone would make a suicide dive in that bell. The divers must really have wanted to get down to that ship. You saw the video. What do you think?"

Calvin spread his arms wide. "Thinking about how great it is to be out here with you and Abby. Especially Abby."

"Don't blame you there, Cal. Abby is pretty special."

"Well?" Calvin drawled the word out into two syllables. *Way-all.* "What's going on with you and the lady?"

"We haven't talked to each other in months, so you can assume not much is going on."

Calvin grinned. "I've known you both too long to fall for that line."

"Dang. Shoulda known you'd be onto me. But like Abby said, it's complicated. Maybe I should write Ann Landers for advice."

"She'd probably tell you that you're both worrying too much about getting burned again."

Hawkins felt the boat slowing under his feet and was glad to change the subject. "Looks like we're coming up on the site, Cal. Let's get Minnie prepped for the dive."

The storm that had swept in after the first dive had left clear weather in its wake. Low seas, cloudless skies, a light breeze.

Hawkins and Cal went to the stern deck where Miguel stood next to a heavy-duty plastic container, roughly the size of a large shipping carton that sat under a crane used to haul in fishnets. Hawkins unlatched the box and pushed the cover back on its hinges. Nestled in a contoured foam bed was a remote-operated vehicle around four feet long and almost as wide, with runners like those found on an old sled.

Hawkins had named the vehicle Minnie, after Mickey Mouse's girlfriend. It was a wordplay on the ROV's compact size, but also because the twin spotlights on top of the vehicle looked like mouse ears. Turbines on both sides of the battery housing powered the vehicle.

It was not unusual in ROV design to have one or more mechanical arms called manipulators. Hawkins had wanted this model to be a workhorse. Instead of jointed manipulators, he built it with two sturdy arms that could extend from the main body and lift heavy loads into a basket under the camera.

Following his conversation with Cal, he had called Howard Snow back in Woods Hole, checked on his dog and asked Snowy to put the ROV on a truck to Boston. Calvin picked Minnie up at Logan Airport during a stop-off on his trip to Spain.

They connected it to a 500-foot-long fiber-optic emergency cable coiled onto a drum. Next they set up the control console. Hawkins linked the units and placed the control and thirteen-inch TV monitor on a wooden workbench under the shade of a canvas canopy.

Hawkins asked Miguel to be the ROV tender. His job would be to stand on deck, watch the ROV and signal his father when to move the boat. The job normally required experience, but Miguel seemed quick-witted and eager, and he had good rapport with his father. He and the captain ran the boat with hardly a word exchanged between them. Hawkins attached the winch cable's quick-release hook to an eye-bolt on the top of the ROV frame and gave a thumb's up to Miguel who stood at the winch controls.

The winch motor growled, the cable went taut and the vehicle lifted out of its container trailing the tether as it unwound from the drum. The crane swung out until the vehicle was hanging over the water. The boat lurched to one side. The ROV was a light load compared to a net full of fish and the vessel took the weight easily. Hawkins crooked his thumb and forefinger in an OK sign and pointed downward with his other hand.

Minnie swayed at the end of the cable as Miguel lowered the vehicle under the waves. When the ROV had reached the depth of a few feet, Hawkins asked Miguel to stop the winch. He tested the video camera and controls. Then he instructed Miguel to release the cable hook from the eye-bolt. The ROV had neutral buoyancy, meaning it would neither sink, nor bob back to the surface.

The trick to operating an ROV is for the operator to act like a miniature pilot actually riding in the vehicle. Hawkins moved the joystick to point the front of the vehicle down and increased power to the turbines. Minnie's lights cut through the deepening darkness. The monitor displayed depth and speed. Hawkins tracked the vehicle until the image of grayish-brown sand filled the screen. He called for the vehicle to hover several feet above the bottom. There was no sign of the wreck.

"We'll mow the lawn," Hawkins said, using the term for a common search technique.

The vehicle began to move back and forth in a series of parallel underwater rows that covered a large rectangular area. The first pass failed to uncover any sign of the shipwreck. After a few minutes, the camera picked up a dark shape on the bottom.

"It's Captain Santiago's boat," Hawkins said.

The *Sancho Panza* lay at a forty-five degree angle. A big chunk of the pilot house was missing. Hawkins maneuvered Minnie until the vehicle was at right angles to the elevated side. As the ROV hovered, its lights picked out a ragged hole in the metal hull.

Calvin let out a low whistle.

"Nasty," he said. "Spike was designed to penetrate plate armor. Missile would have gone through regular ship-building steel like it was cardboard."

Hawkins pivoted the vehicle and sent it along the hull a few feet, where it stopped like a pointer dog in front of a hole that was an exact twin of the first.

Calvin squinted at the screen. "Run that attack sequence by me again, Hawk."

"There was one explosion, then a pause followed by two in rapid succession."

"Based on your recollection, I'd say the first missile was intended to disable the pilot house. After the pause, two more missiles were launched at the hull to sink the boat. Let's work our way backwards."

Hawkins elevated the ROV above the angled hull, then sent it over the stern deck.

"The captain said this was where Rodriguez, the bogus government observer, was standing when he was hit. The missile would have passed through his body into the sea, thus the lack of an audible explosion from the second Spike. That would have been the pause that I noticed."

"Like I said, that was no accident," Calvin said.

"Maybe a wave lifted the shooter's boat as he was taking a bead on the hull."

"Can't say for sure because I wasn't there, but he had time to correct his shot. With Spike missiles you hit what you aim for."

"Then the only conclusion is that the shooter must have been aiming for that poor bastard."

"That's my take on it. Don't know why he'd waste a shot if the goal was to sink the boat. Missiles like those don't come cheap."

"Maybe it tells us something about the shooter," Hawkins mused. "Sending the *Sancho Panza* and everyone on it to the bottom wasn't enough for him. He likes to kill people."

Hawkins pulled the ROV back and moved it around the ship in an ever-increasing spiral. The camera picked up *Falstaff* sitting on the bottom around fifty feet from the salvage boat. Abby had been standing behind Hawkins watching the monitor. She gave his shoulder a hard squeeze when the submersible appeared.

"You and your friend were damned lucky to get out of that thing. And please don't tell me it was no big deal."

Hawkins felt a dryness in his throat as he imagined being trapped with Kalliste in the water-filled sphere. "Okay, Abby. This was a *very* big deal. *Falstaff* is in bad shape, but may be salvageable."

Calvin returned from talking to the captain. "We've got two blips on radar, both beyond the effective range of a Spike," he reported. "No aggressive movement from either one. The captain hailed them on the radio. Both are fishing boats that he knows. I'm going back to the pilot house and keep watch in case someone starts moving in on our perimeter. How long will it take if we have to get the ROV on board in a big hurry?"

"Around five minutes if nothing goes wrong."

"That might work if I'm right about the shooter using a Spike. We'll see him moving in on us."

"And if you're not right?" Abby said. "What if they used something with greater range than a Spike?"

"We'll never know what hit us." Calvin flashed a wide grin and walked away.

"Sometimes I wonder about Calvin," Abby said with a shake of her head.

"Navy SEAL humor. If you say things may go wrong they'll always go right."

"I hope so," Abby said, sounding unconvinced.

Hawkins pointed to the screen. The ROV had stopped in front of the bow.

"What is that?" Abby said.

"A carved figurehead. Kalliste said the bird was a common motif on Minoan ships."

"Wow! Damn it, Matt, this ship *is* the Holy Grail you talked about."

"Only thing better would be if she's carrying the *real* Holy Grail."

He moved the ROV up and over the figurehead, then brought it down to within a few feet of the deck, moving the vehicle from bow to stern. He wanted to give Abby a sense of how large the ship was. He wheeled Minnie around at the upturned stern, then moved the vehicle back to hover above the large tapered object he'd seen on the first dive.

The object was partially covered with sand, which he blasted away using the vehicle's turbines like twin leaf blowers. He made a number of passes, bringing the ROV down again and again in swooping dives. It was a tricky maneuver, but after a few minutes enough sand was cleared to reveal the entire object.

"Hooyah," Hawkins said, uttering the SEAL war cry. "We got ourselves an old-fashioned diving bell."

Abby tapped the screen with her fingernail. "Can you get closer to that section?"

Hawkins brought the ROV to within a few inches of where the bottom flared out of the bell's curved surface.

"I can see writing," Abby said. She read the words engraved in the metal band that ringed the bottom. "It's French. *Dernier and Fils.* Does that mean anything?"

He shook his head. "It gives us something to go on, though. The guys who built something this sophisticated must have had a substantial operation going."

Abby pointed to a dark mound about a foot from what would have been the bottom of the bell.

"Is that an amphora?"

"Let's take a look." He ran the vehicle in circles until the twin thrusters had excavated a channel around the perimeter of the diving bell to reveal several more objects.

Hawkins stared at the screen. "Those aren't amphora."

"Then what are they?"

Hawkins struggled with a way to explain to Abby that the objects visible in the ROV's lights were diving helmets and suits, and their design suggested that they spanned hundreds of years.

"Abby, you are not going to believe this."

Calvin had a case of jangly nerves. He walked around the deck and scanned the horizon in every direction. Seeing nothing, he went back to the pilot house and asked the captain if radar was still picking up the fishing boats.

"Good news," Captain Santiago said. "They're moving away."

"Anything headed in our direction?"

"Nothing closer than twenty miles."

He went on the deck. Miguel was doing a good job as ROV tender. Everything seemed to be going as planned, but his gut was telling him that the sooner they got out of there the better he'd feel.

CHAPTER NINETEEN

Hawkins recognized the metal globe studded with small circles as an old dive helmet. A few feet away lay an enclosed cylinder rounded at one end. Next to the primitive dive apparatus was a bulbous dive suit that resembled the out-sized armor built for King Henry VIII.

The metal Michelin man was a Neufeldt and Kuhnke diving-suit. The predecessor of the modern-day atmospheric diving suit that'd been used successfully between World War I and the 1940s. The equipment lying between the ribs of the ship had been state-of-the-art, and the best underwater technology of its day had met its match at the bottom of the sea.

Abby was a trained diver. She knew exactly what she was seeing on the monitor.

Speaking in almost a whisper, she said, "It's a graveyard, isn't it?"

"I'd guess at least a dozen divers made it down and stayed down."

He moved the ROV from suit to suit.

"That helmet probably dates back to the 1700s. The most recent piece I see was used in the 1940s. The other stuff comes from centuries in between the two."

"If that's the case, people dove on this wreck over a period of two hundred years," Abby said.

"Right about that, Ab. The first level of equipment dates to the dawn of deep diving technology."

Abby frowned. "Why did the dives stop as the technology was getting better and safer?"

"My guess is that World War II got in the way. Cruising in the war zone would have been a high-risk proposition. Paper deteriorates if it's been exposed to conditions at sea. Maybe the charts marking the position crumbled away."

"That's possible, but the intensity during the dive period is impressive. They tried and tried again, even after losing divers."

Hawkins nodded. "With every significant advance in equipment, someone gave it a try and died."

"But why make this dangerous dive over and over?"

"Wish I could answer that question. We'll go over the video later. Calvin's pacing the deck. Something's bothering him. His instincts are usually on target. I'd better get Minnie topside."

Abby pointed to the screen.

"What's that?"

The rectangular object lay a few yards from the jumble of dive suits.

Hawkins brought Minnie around to the boxy object—its surface was covered with dark encrustation.

The twin arms on the front of the submersible extended like a forklift. Hawkins moved the ROV forward until the tips of the arms were under the box, then powered the thrusters. The arms slid under the box, raised it off the bottom then tilted back at an angle. The box tumbled into the collection basket and Minnie began its ascent to the surface.

When the attack came, it was by air. Calvin squinted through his binoculars at three helicopters headed straight for the salvage boat.

He shouted at Hawkins. "Choppers. Eleven o'clock. Bring Minnie up now!"

Hawkins responded with a command to the ROV to increase speed, then called out to Miguel to be ready with the crane.

Moving with a surreal calmness, Calvin unsnapped the cover to a large suitcase he had muscled aboard the fishing boat that morning. Inside were two mainstays of the SEAL armory; a CAR-15 and a shotgun. He removed the rifle, checked the load, and squatted on the deck using the wheelhouse as cover.

The choppers were coming toward the boat in a line. He sighted the CAR-15 on the lead helicopter.

Hawkins called out that Minnie was at the surface. The vehicle rolled in the waves around ten to fifteen feet from the boat. Miguel lowered the cable but it was impossible to snag the eye-bolt because the clasp kept whipping back and forth over the moving ROV. Hawkins kicked off his shoes, climbed onto the rail and launched himself into the water in a shallow racing dive.

He quickly covered the distance to the vehicle and grabbed on to a sled runner. Then he reached up with the other hand and hooked his fingers on the edge of the plastic housing. The captain had been watching from the pilot house. He edged the boat closer to the vehicle.

The weight of Hawkins's body tipped the vehicle and he struggled to hold on. The clasp dangled a few feet above his head, but it swung out of reach. When the cable swung back, he leaped for it, fell off the ROV, grabbed the clasp with one hand, the cable with the other and held on with every bit of strength he could muster.

Miguel was quick to react at the winch controls. Hawkins was lifted into the air, then lowered onto the ROV. He snapped the clasp onto the eye-bolt. The cable went taut and the ROV stopped rolling. Hawkins straddled the vehicle like a boy on a dolphin and held onto the cable as the ROV rose from the water. The crane swiveled and stopped when its load was over the deck.

Abby reached up and grabbed on to a runner to stabilize the ROV. Instead, she was lifted off her feet and swung back and forth like the pendulum in a grandfather clock until Miguel skillfully lowered the vehicle, and its two passengers, safely to the deck. Captain Santiago gunned the engine, and the boat slowly picked up speed.

The unmarked lead helicopter broke out of formation and flew in a wide circle around the boat. After a nerve-wracking minute or so, the chopper veered off, flew back to the wreck site and hovered with the others in a holding pattern.

Two pellets dropped from the belly of the lead helicopter and splashed into the water. The helicopter darted off and the second one moved in. Two more objects fell. The third chopper followed suit.

There were two thuds and the water above the wreck site rose in foamy mounds that exploded into twin geysers. Four more explosions followed at close intervals.

The helicopters banked off and flew back the way they had come. The clatter of rotors faded and the choppers soon disappeared from view.

Calvin stood up and lowered his rifle.

"What just happened?" he said.

Hawkins pictured the ocean bottom. Ancient timbers thrown everywhere. *Falstaff's* passenger sphere now nothing but shards. The diving bell and all the other wonderful antiquities had been transformed into scrap metal.

"They bombed the living crap out of the wreck site," he said.

"I got that. But *why*?"

"Haven't got a clue, Cal. Let's see what we got in return for all the money we've thrown into the sea."

Hawkins asked Miguel to give him a hand lifting the box out of Minnie's basket. The young man was strong, but he failed to get his fingers under the edge. As they pulled the box out, it slipped from his grasp.

Hawkins jumped out of the way. The chest barely missed smashing his toes and thudded onto the deck. The lid jounced off from the impact and something fell out.

Hawkins got down on his knees and examined the object, which was circular and around two feet across. It looked to be made of bronze, fashioned into a round metal frame that enclosed a number of smaller disks and gears. What he first thought were scratches in the metal turned out to be script and pictographs.

Abby knelt beside him and ran her fingers lightly over the engravings.

"What is it?" she said.

"Damned if I know," he said. He looked off toward the wreck site where the water still boiled and steamed from the explosions. "But I've got the feeling that it's something really, really important."

CHAPTER TWENTY

Kalliste knew it had been a mistake to accuse her superior at the cultural ministry of being destroying her country's cultural heritage. Too late. Winged words, as Homer would say, had already taken flight. Not that her outburst wasn't justified. The official, whose name was Papadokalos, had set her off with his haughty dismissal of her Spanish expedition.

"Madame Kalchis goes to find what she says is a Minoan ship. What does she have to show for her work?" he said, speaking as if she weren't even in the room.

With his pink face, razor cut black hair and mustache, and his habit of looking down his nose when he spoke, Papadokalos encapsulated the smugness of many male colleagues. He got his position thanks to the influence of his brother-in-law, a minister of Parliament who had voted to cut archaeological budgets. The cuts had spared the jobs of their own do-nothing relatives on the payroll.

She tried to moderate her temper.

Speaking in a calm voice, she said, "Perhaps Mr. Papadokalos is unaware that the expedition did not cost the Greek government a single Euro. I worked on my own time. A television network paid for the boat. The American engineer volunteered his expertise and equipment."

"But failing to find a single artifact cost us our prestige."

"*What* prestige? The Greek archaeological establishment is the laughing stock of Europe."

An angry murmur came from the half dozen ministry bureaucrats gathered in the conference room at the Greek Archaeological Museum in Athens. It was no secret that the country's debt crisis was crippling their archaeological reputation.

A threatened strike of security guards almost shut down the Acropolis. The ministry had lopped thousands of people from the payroll, closed monuments and museums and cut back hours at others. Even the country's archeological jewel, the museum they were sitting in, was operating with a third of its staff.

Kalliste's own position hung by a thread. Yet, she would never consider pandering to Papadokalos.

When he said, "As you can see, your intemperate remarks have upset your colleagues," she lost it.

"Their anger is misplaced, and should be directed at ministers who are allowing foreign investors to build hotels and roads that are destroying our heritage."

He lowered his chin into the flesh around his neck. His eyes narrowed in a tight squint.

"Are you implying that I am responsible for this desecration?"

Kalliste knew Papadokalos was stuffing his Swiss bank accounts with kickbacks earned for approving the fast-tracking of construction projects on ancient sites.

"I am implying nothing of the sort, Mr. Minister. I am *accusing* you and your government cronies of cultural vandalism that surpasses even the worst acts of that English bastard Lord Elgin, who vandalized the Parthenon. Consider this my resignation."

She stood and pushed her chair back, then marched for the door and slammed it behind her. Her heart thumped like a pile driver as she strode through the museum corridors. She emerged into the Athenian heat and noise. Hailing a taxi, she barked out the address then sat back in her seat and stared out the window, fighting to get her emotions under control.

How did I ever get into this crazy archaeology business? She fumed. Stupid question. She knew exactly how. Her grandfather. He worked the land, producing delicious olive oil from his grove on the northeast side of Crete. It was in those olive groves that he unearthed the ancient artifacts that had fascinated her as a little girl and led to her insatiable quest for knowledge of long dead civilizations.

Recalling the startled look on the minister's pink face at her accusations, she began to calm down. By the time the taxi dropped her off at her apartment complex in the fashionable neighborhood of Kolonaki, Kalliste felt like herself again. Her sixth floor apartment had a view of Lykabettus Hill. Kalliste would miss her work, but she wouldn't starve to death. Her parents, both successful professionals, had left her a sizable inheritance, and her late husband had made sure she was well taken care of in his Will.

She didn't know whether to laugh or cry, so she did both. When her tears stopped she poured herself a healthy shot of Metaxa brandy. She had drained half the glass when she got a text message on her phone from Hawkins. He was trying to Skype her.

She powered up her computer and Hawkins's face appeared on the monitor.

"Glad I found you at home," Hawkins said. "I've got some interesting news."

Kalliste was eager to tell Hawkins about her resignation, but she was curious about the serious expression on his face. "Me, too. But you go first, Matt."

"I'm calling you from a boat on its way back to Cadiz. Captain Santiago took us out to the wreck site. We were able to put an ROV in the water."

"That's more than interesting, my friend. What did you see?"

Hawkins described the holes punched in the hull of the *Sancho Panza*, and Calvin's theory of a missile strike. "We found *Falstaff* not far from the salvage boat. The sub was in pretty good shape. Then we took another look at the ship, itself. The object near the stern is definitely an antique diving bell."

"I'm stunned. That's truly amazing."

"Even more amazing are the objects we found near the bell. Dive gear that goes back centuries. Helmets and pressure suits, indicating multiple dives made on the wreck. It appears that none of the divers made it back alive."

"That would suggest that the wreck's location was passed along for hundreds of years."

"Exactly my take on it. Someone knew about the ship long before we did."

"I can't wait to see the photos and video."

"I'll send the footage along to you for analysis."

"Wonderful!" She clapped her hands. "This couldn't have come at a better time. I just quit my job. This is the material I need to persuade the television network to fund a full-fledged expedition to salvage the wreck. I'll call Lily Porter immediately."

"I wouldn't do that just yet," Hawkins said.

Hawkins told her about the attack helicopters.

Kalliste was almost numb with grief. "You're sure everything was destroyed?" she said, looking for a ray of hope.

"The barrage was pretty intense," he said. "It's not all bad news. Minnie brought us back a present. It was in a water-tight bronze chest we found on the ship."

He held the artifact up in front of the camera, and rotated it slowly to give Kalliste a full view of the other side. She gulped down the rest of the Metaxa, excused herself, and went to the bar. She poured out a double shot of brandy and carried it back to her computer table.

"Please show the object again," she said. When he went through the display, she said, "Do you have any idea what you are holding?"

"You're the expert. I was hoping you would know."

"I would have to see the actual artifact. But my first impression is that you have recovered a version of the Antikythera mechanism— the ancient astronomical computer found in a shipwreck near Crete."

"I thought of the Antikythera device, too."

"As you know, the computer had gears and dials that could compute the position of the sun, moon and stars. It would have been invaluable in navigating the seas."

"This has dials inscribed with pictographs and letters."

"This wonderful machine could have been used in navigating an entirely *different* type of sea. I'd like you to talk to someone, Matt. His name is Professor Vasilios Vedrakis. He's an expert on Minoan script who works out of the Heraklion museum. He has written extensively on the Phaistos disk."

"I'd be glad to talk to him."

"Good. Then we will make arrangements to get together as soon as possible."

Kalliste hung up and emptied her brandy glass. She thought she was going to faint from excitement. Forcing herself to rise from her chair, she walked to a wall safe located behind a stunning painting of the Acropolis. She punched out the combination, opened the door and reached inside for a metal jewelry box, which she placed on her desk.

Taking a key from her desk drawer, she opened the box, flipped the top back and removed a leather pouch. Her trembling fingers undid the drawstring and removed the vellum scroll inside, which she then unrolled on the desktop. It was about ten inches wide and when unrolled, was around three feet in length.

The vellum was covered with line after line of ancient Minoan script known as Linear A. The mysterious language had defied all attempts at decipherment, yet she had been a young girl when her grandfather showed her the script for the first time. Growing up, she had taken every opportunity to study the scroll. More than anything she could think of, it was the scroll she held in her hands that drew her to the study of archaeology. She had dreamed of the day it would be deciphered. But she never imagined that she would be the one to do it.

Papadokalos was in his office going over a doubtful resume, wondering where he was going to put all the relatives who needed government jobs. The latest application was from a cousin of a cousin. He stroked his chin between his thumb and forefinger. He suspected family members were selling jobs to friends and passing them off as family. Well, two can play that game. He would hire the so-called cousins, or uncles, or whatever they may be, but it would cost them dearly.

He was jotting down payback calculations when he got a phone call from the woman whose resignation had saved him the trouble of firing her. Kalliste's insult had gone over his head, even though he would never state that out loud. He actually had no idea who this Elgin person was, but he was happy because her exit would open up another job needed by family.

"How nice to hear from you, Dr. Kalchis. To what do I owe the pleasure?"

"As you may recall, you had some doubts as to the worth of my Minoan expedition."

"No offense meant, Dr. Kalchis. I'm a numbers man. Some of your colleagues in the archaeological ministry suggested that line of inquiry."

"In that case, would you kindly distribute the photos I've emailed you for their inspection? Tell them that they can direct their queries to Professor Vedrakis. I have designated the professor as the first one to have access to this remarkable artifact. Thank you."

She hung up. Papadokalos shrugged and turned to his computer. The email from Kalliste had an attachment that included several photos of an ugly disk-shaped object. He pondered the images, thinking about his lucrative sideline. Months before, an anonymous caller asked him to forward news of any Minoan discoveries. He had given it a try, and with each tidbit, a substantial amount of money had been deposited into his bank account.

He had no intention of doing what Kalliste suggested, but her photos meant a new injection of Euros for little or no work done. Hitting 'Forward' then 'Send,' with a great sigh, he turned back to the resumes piled on his desk.

CHAPTER TWENTY-ONE

The black Citroen limousine pulled up to the front gate of the imposing mansion set on a tree-lined street off one of the exclusive Second Empire avenues in the Chaillot quarter of Paris. Built in the 19th century for an opera singer, the mansard-roof house had been the scene of many glittering gatherings, where Paris artists mingled with the wealthiest residents of the city.

After the original owner died, the mansard was converted into a sanatorium where the well-to-do could stash family members with mental illnesses or infirmities. The wealthy called them *imbeciles*, a term that referred to any mental condition that could embarrass a prominent family.

Medical care was secondary to incarceration. The straitjacket was the main method of treatment. The sign on the cast-iron gate, *Maison de Bonheur*, was a lie. Under no circumstances could the two-story structure that housed the schizophrenic, paranoid or mentally challenged be considered a "house of happiness."

The mansion was now owned by a dummy corporation. The sign still hung from the gate, but there was only one patient in the house, surrounded by medical attendants and guarded closely by hard-faced security men. Two of them occupied a guardhouse at the gate. They were tall and wore black uniforms and berets. Machine pistols hung from their shoulders. While one guard walked over to the car to check for identification, the other kept his pistol aimed, ready to fire at the least sign of danger. The ID checked out, the gate was raised and the limo drove up a long curving driveway.

The house, surrounded by trees, was largely invisible from the street. The Citroen pulled up to the entrance where a woman wearing a nurse's uniform, loose white smock and slacks, awaited. A figure shrouded in a black hooded cloak got out of the car and approached the nurse.

"She knows I'm here?" she said.

"She's waiting for you," the nurse said. "We notified her as soon as you called from the plane."

"What's her condition?"

"Deteriorating. But still in command. She ordered us to move her from her bed to the throne room. It's not as comfortable, but being there seems to give her new strength."

"Take me to her."

The nurse led the way into the house, through a grand entryway, and into an elevator. The hooded figure got into the elevator alone and pressed a button. Seconds later the door opened and she stepped out into a windowless chamber. A blast of cold air penetrated her cloak. The recessed ceiling lights illuminated walls decorated with gryphons—creatures with the bodies of an animal and the head of a plumed bird.

The room was carpeted in red and devoid of furnishings, except for a throne-like chair that had a high, scalloped back and thick armrests.

The figure seated in the chair was small and bent over, head held low and resting on the chest. The top of the face was hidden behind a black veil. The ankle-length black ruffled skirt identified the shrunken figure as female. She was linked to an intensive care monitor; the blinking screen provided a constant picture of her faint heartbeat and low blood pressure. An intravenous feeding bag hung from a mobile stand. Plastic tubes from a portable oxygen generator led up, under the veil. Despite the ventilation, the air was heavy with the odor of decay.

As soon as the visitor stepped into the room, two huge creatures that had been sitting on their haunches next to the throne trotted forward and bared the fangs in their odd, pointed muzzles. She instinctively reached up to touch the oval medallion hanging from a gold chain around her neck. Inscribed on the metal medallion was an axe design. Inside the medallion was an electrical circuit that broadcast a silent signal, not unlike that of a dog whistle. The animals had been trained to attack anyone not wearing such a device.

Each creature weighed around two-hundred pounds. Standing on their hind legs they were taller than the average man. The breed had been developed centuries before to look like the gryphons painted on the wall. The mythical creatures were the followers of the Britomartis, the Minoan goddess of wild animals.

Instead of attacking, the animals nuzzled the visitor's legs with their cold noses. With nothing to kill, they returned to their posts and curled up like large puppies. The figure in the chair patted the creature on her right and made cooing sounds, before she spoke.

"You said you had an urgent matter to discuss, Daughter. I trust it must be important to bring you here."

"I would not trouble you otherwise, Mother. May I approach?" she asked.

A boney finger beckoned. The visitor stepped forward and handed over the photos. The woman called Mother pushed her veil back from her wrinkled face and shuffled through the pictures one-by-one.

"Where did you get these?" she said. Her voice had gained a hard edge.

"From a source within the Greek government. The American engineer working with the Greek woman brought it up from the great ship."

"How could that be? I understood that the ship was to be destroyed."

"I ordered Salazar to destroy the ship. Hawkins, the American engineer, salvaged the ship before the helicopters came in with their depth charges."

"Where is this American engineer now?"

"Hawkins is still in Spain and presumably has the device with him."

"I thought we put an end to this nonsense when we attended

to Ventris and his English friend. Now this American threatens our secrets."

The hooded figure waited in silence.

Finally, the old crone stopped her muttering, and said, "Do you know the function of this device?"

"Only that no one was to be allowed to salvage it from the great ship."

The crone tapped the stack of photos with the tip of her finger.

"An instrument like this was carried aboard *every* great ship. The machines were the keys to our empire. With these devices, the great ships communicated with people of different nations: the Egyptians, the Syrians and the Greeks. But in the wrong hands, the device would allow someone to translate the Sacred Word."

"That would be a disaster," the visitor said.

"Yes, Daughter. A disaster. We are older than Rome, older than the Greeks and Carthage and all who have followed. The Way of the Axe goes back to an age when humans were just emerging from caves. The Old Order endures because we communicate in a tongue only we know. We have conducted our affairs for centuries using the Sacred Word. If the device falls into the wrong hands, all our secrets kept through the centuries will come to light. Our plans to regain power and influence will be in jeopardy."

Her voice had been rising with each sentence. She was out of breath and wheezing. The electronic monitors began to blink in alarm.

"Should I call someone for you?" the visitor asked.

She dismissed the offer with a wave of her hand. "Listen to me. There can be only one explanation for this misfortune. *She* lives. The king's foul spawn. The daughter of Minos. She is the cause of our ills. I can feel her presence. She is near and she must die, as the prophecy instructs."

"I don't understand, Mother. The king and his daughter have been dead for four thousand years."

"No! I smell her. *She* is the reason our equilibrium has been disturbed."

The crone's head dipped to her chest, but she brought her chin up again quickly. "First, the machine must be retrieved. Hawkins and the Greek woman must be killed. I will call forth the Priors to carry out the prime directive."

The hooded figure nodded. The Priors were the remnants of a monastic order, but their numbers had dwindled through the centuries. Now, only four of the trained assassins whose main mission was to kill anyone likely to translate the sacred script, remained.

"I will immediately forward the information on Hawkins and Kalliste Kalchis to the Priors."

"Good. What do you hear from Salazar of the other business?"

"The event is on schedule. His people will be in place. He says there will be no mistakes."

"There better not be." She paused. "Tell me, Daughter, what is your opinion of Salazar?"

"I don't trust him."

"The Salazar family has been our loyal servants for centuries," the crone said.

"Maybe Salazar tires of the role. He is the last of the family and has no heir."

"This is why I chose you to succeed me, my daughter. I knew you were blessed by the Mother Goddess when I saw your skill with the sacred dagger, even as a child. But you have wisdom too. Tell me what you think we should do about Salazar."

"Nothing for now. Let him carry out the event, then convene a gathering at the Maze where we will deal with him."

"Who would take his place as head of Auroch?"

"Me."

"An interesting proposition. But you may be premature. I would have to be convinced that he is a danger to the Way before taking drastic steps. We have more important matters we must deal with for now."

"I understand, Mother."

"Good. Go now. I am getting tired."

The visitor bowed, and backed into the elevator. As the doors were about to close, the croaking voice called out from the throne room.

"Remember the prophecy, Daughter."

"Yes, Mother."
"She is near. She must die."

CHAPTER TWENTY-TWO

Tensions were high on the *Santa Maria*. The helicopters could return any minute. The fishing boat would make an easy target. But the return trip to Cadiz was uneventful. The boat pulled safely back to the dock late in the afternoon.

Hawkins thanked the captain and his son, then he got into a taxi with Abby and Calvin. Hawkins carried the artifact in a backpack. At the hotel, they made plans to meet for dinner and went to their rooms to shower and change clothes. Hawkins washed away the sea grime, changed into fresh slacks and was just buttoning his shirt when his phone signaled a text message.

Matt. Please Skype Dr. Constantine Vedrakis at this number and show him your exciting find. Thx. KK

Hawkins sent Kalliste a quick reply and connected his tablet with the number she had given him. A wide, sunburned face, framed by snowy-white hair and beard appeared on the screen. Hawkins estimated Vedrakis to be in his sixties. Eyes the hue of a New England winter sky peered through wire-rimmed glasses.

"Hello, Professor Vedrakis. My name is Matt Hawkins. Kalliste Kalchis suggested that we talk."

Speaking with a trace of an accent, the professor said, "I find it hard to believe Kalliste ever *suggested* anything in her life. She has the guile of Odysseus and the relentlessness of Artemis."

Hawkins nodded his agreement; he knew from personal

experience that Kalliste was an accomplished arm-twister. "I was being diplomatic."

"No need, Mr. Hawkins. I have the highest regard for my brilliant colleague. Otherwise I might have brushed her away when she *suggested* I talk to you. Our conversation must be short. I have my hands full herding fifty energetic young college students who are in Crete under a program with the University of Buffalo."

"Then I'll cut right to the chase. What did Kalliste tell you?"

"Only that you have made a discovery that will take my breath away. She tends to talk in superlatives. Tell me, Mr. Hawkins, was she exaggerating?"

"You'll have to be the judge of that. Hold on."

He held the artifact in front of the tablet camera lens and turned it in his hands. Like Kalliste, the professor asked that he repeat the rotation.

"Thank you, Mr. Hawkins," Vedrakis said. "Please tell me where you found this object."

"I hauled it up from a shipwreck around thirty miles off the coast of Cadiz, Spain. Kalliste believes the ship is Minoan."

The gray eyes narrowed under bushy brows. "Cadiz. Of course. That would make sense. The city was the site of a Minoan mining and trading colony."

"Then Kalliste wasn't exaggerating?"

"Not at all. Your discovery has taken my breath away. I'm amazed at the condition it is in."

"It was in a watertight bronze chest. My first impression was that this was similar to the mechanism of the Antikythera computer. Kalliste said it was a navigational device, but for a different type of sea."

"There are similarities between the two mechanisms, but this instrument may be even more important than the Antikythera machine because of its different features."

"You're talking about the script?"

"That's correct. Are you still in Spain, Mr. Hawkins?"

"I'm staying at the Hotel Cadiz."

"I would fly there immediately to examine the artifact firsthand, but I'm tied down with this blasted student program. I have a great favor to ask. Can you bring the artifact to Crete?"

"I'll see if I can be there tomorrow."

"Thank you, Mr. Hawkins. I would be forever in your debt. It's going to be difficult keeping my mind focused on these students while I await your arrival."

After they hung up, Hawkins called Abby's room and told her about the professor's request that he bring the device to Crete. She checked with her company's traffic controller and called back a few minutes later.

"We can fly to Zurich tomorrow on a freight plane and hitch a ride from there on a smaller jet to Crete. Best I can do. We'll arrive in the afternoon. Might get there faster on a commercial flight."

"Not a good idea. The device would look like an infernal machine on the X-ray screen. Airport security would throw me into a holding cell. Besides, the mechanism is pretty fragile. I don't know if it would survive being tossed around by baggage handlers."

"Both good points. We fly later but safer. See you at dinner."

Hawkins called the professor with the travel details. They agreed to meet at the archaeological museum in Heraklion. Hawkins was uneasy about leaving the artifact in the hotel room, so he wrapped it in a spare pillowcase and tucked it into the backpack which he slung over his right shoulder.

Calvin was cooling his heels at the entrance to the hotel restaurant. He had a sour expression on his face. The *maître d'* who had been studiously ignoring Calvin's request for a table for three had disappeared completely by the time Abby arrived. She had exchanged the jeans and sweater she had worn at sea for a long, silky, white dress that set off her tanned skin and auburn hair.

Her arrival brought the *maître d'* out of hiding, all smiles and heel clicks. He glanced with obvious distaste at the backpack on the tall man's shoulder, then turned to Abby. He could hardly take his eyes off the attractive woman. He practically groveled when Abby asked for a private table, escorting them to a quiet corner of the dining room away from the ordinary guests. He clapped his hands and a waiter appeared instantly to take their cocktail order.

Calvin watched the *maître d'* strut back to the entrance to defend the restaurant from riff-raff. "Glad you showed up and lured Mr. Fancy Pants out of his hidey hole, Abby."

"Can't blame the guy," Hawkins said. "Rough-looking characters like Calvin and me probably scare the regulars away."

"Nonsense," Abby said. "I couldn't ask for more dashing escorts." She gave their arms a quick squeeze, then her Annapolis and corporate persona asserted itself. "I suggest that we adjourn this meeting of the mutual admiration society and get down to business."

Hawkins filled Calvin in on the plans to fly to Crete to see Professor Vedrakis.

"That works with me," Calvin said. "Thinking of talking to a couple of arms dealers. Maybe they can put me on the track of Spike missiles."

"Coordinate with Molly. She's researching missile sales."

"Will do. I apologize for the excitement today on the boat. Never figured on an air approach."

"And I never expected to play bucking bronco with an ROV," Hawkins said.

"I don't understand why they didn't go after us," Abby said. "We witnessed their destruction of the archaeological site."

Hawkins said, "I'd guess their orders were to get in, drop their firecrackers, and get out."

"Orders from who?" Abby said.

Hawkins tapped the backpack nestled next to his leg. "Whoever wanted this gadget and every trace of the ship blown to smithereens." He looked across the dining room. "Here come our drinks."

There was little talk of business over cocktails, and the Spanish wine and dinner that followed. They were simply three old friends laughing over good times shared. After dinner, Calvin excused himself, saying he had to make some phone calls.

Abby watched Calvin leave the dining room; a smile on her face. "Do you have the feeling Calvin wants us to be alone?"

"More than a feeling, Ab. He's taken on the role of matchmaker. Or should I say *rematch*-maker."

"And—?"

"I don't know where this is going, Abby. Until we do, I suggest that we avoid anything that doesn't have to do with the business at hand. Leave emotion out of it…for now."

She nodded in agreement. "Sort of the equivalent of a sterile cockpit on a plane. I can live with that."

After dinner they took a stroll around the hotel, breathing in the sights and sounds of the old city. They stopped at a sidewalk café for a nightcap. On the walk back, they held hands like a couple of school kids out on a date. Walking Outside her room, Abby opened the door, then turned and gave him a light kiss on the lips.

"We are officially in sterile cockpit mode," she grinned. "For now."

Giving him a seductive smile, she closed the door behind her.

Hawkins stood there a moment, thinking that the usual description of their relationship—*complicated*—didn't even begin to describe the situation.

The long day, combined with alcohol, had caught up with him. He was headed for the bedroom when Professor Vedrakis called with a change of plans.

CHAPTER TWENTY-THREE

The Gulfstream G650 executive jet lifted off the tarmac, ascending over the meadows around Zurich Airport, and rapidly reached a speed of more than six hundred miles an hour on a course that would take it southeast across Europe and the Mediterranean to the island of Crete.

Hawkins and Abby were the only passengers on the eight-seat plane. Abby spent most of the flight on the phone talking with company headquarters in Virginia. Hawkins pecked away at his tablet, continuing the insurance claims process for *Falstaff* that he had started earlier in the flight.

It was going to be a formidable task. The insurance company wanted to know what happened. Hawkins explained that it had been an equipment malfunction. He omitted one detail. That the equipment failed after being hit by a sinking ship. Asked if the submersible could be lifted off the ocean floor, he wrote that it had been damaged beyond repair.

He detested paperwork and was ecstatic when the pilot announced that the plane was starting its approach. Hawkins shut down his tablet and glanced out the window. An ash-colored crescent rose from the turquoise sea. The unmistakable contours of Santorini, the volcanic island directly north of Crete.

He heaved a sigh of relief. "Escaping certain death at the bottom of the sea is a breeze compared to dealing with an insurance company."

"Will they cover the loss?" Abby said.

"Eventually, maybe. My claim must sound a bit fishy."

"Simply tell them the truth. A sinking ship hit *Falstaff* after a missile attack. The submersible was later depth-bombed by black helicopters. Probably because of a mysterious artifact people are willing to die and/or kill for."

Hawkins pinched his chin, like Sherlock Holmes pondering a puzzle. "Sounds reasonable when you put it that way. The choppers were gray and white, though."

She dismissed him with a wave of her long fingers. "Whatever. Tell me about Professor Vedrakis."

"Good sense of humor. Very serious about his work." Hawkins pointed to the knapsack buckled in the seat next to him. "When I showed him the trinket, his response was scientific. But his excitement was obvious. If he weren't so dignified, he would have done a Greek dance."

"The dancing professor. I can't wait to see that."

The pilot's voice came over the intercom advising them to buckle their seat belts. Minutes later the landing gear thumped down. The plane taxied to within a few hundred yards of the terminal at Nikos Kazantzakis airport, named after the famed author of *Zorba the Greek*. They stepped through the plane's door into the withering heat and descended the gangway. The tarmac baked under the sun, even with the lateness of the day and the cool breeze skimming off the Cretan Sea. They had changed into shorts and casual shirts and merged easily into the lines of tourists at the Customs gate. Their passports were quickly stamped.

The car rental agency was across from the terminal. They piled their two duffel bags in the trunk of the compact Renault hatchback. Offering to drive, Hawkins got behind the wheel and followed the line of traffic from the busy commercial sprawl around the airport. Traffic thinned out and soon they were heading east on E75, the highway along the island's northern coastal plain.

The road gradually rose higher. Hawkins glanced off at the turquoise sea on one side and the mountains on the other, and felt liberated after the confines of the plane's cabin. He thought back to the conversation he'd had with Professor Vedrakis when he returned to his hotel room.

"I've been thinking about the mechanism you showed me," the professor had said. "I hesitate to make a definitive assessment until I hold the artifact in my hands, but I've become convinced that what you discovered is an ancient translating computer."

"How did you come to that conclusion?"

"The mechanism is a system of interlocking gears, or wheels. There are Egyptian hieroglyphics inscribed on a large wheel. The other gears are inscribed with eastern Mediterranean pictographs and script. What has me hyperventilating is the wheel etched with the Minoan script known as Linear A. We know of two written scripts—Linear A and Linear B."

"One script was decoded, if I recall," Hawkins said.

"Correct. Michael Ventris deciphered Linear B. The other script has defied all efforts at translation. This device may be the key that unlocks the secret to understanding a language that hasn't been understood for four thousand years."

"A mechanical Rosetta Stone, in other words."

"An apt comparison. But this is far more important than the stele Napoleon's soldiers discovered in Egypt. The Rosetta Stone had the same decree written in Greek and Egyptian, which allowed for the translation of hieroglyphics. With this wonderful machine, we may translate Linear A and possibly other lost languages."

"Can't wait to get started," Hawkins said. "I'll bring the artifact to the museum as soon as we arrive in Heraklion."

"That's the reason I called. I won't be in Heraklion," Vedrakis said. "I'll be at the archaeological museum in Sitia looking over rubbings of Linear A Minoan tablets from the Robsham collection."

"Not familiar with the name," Hawkins said.

"The tablets were found in a mountain cave and acquired by an English amateur archeologist named Howard Robsham, back in the 1950s. He died in a car accident on one of our treacherous roads. The tablets were destroyed in the crash, but what's not generally known is that the museum had made paper copies of some inscriptions shortly after he acquired them."

Sitia was around two hours from Heraklion. Vedrakis proposed that they meet halfway at the ruins of *Gournia*, an ancient Minoan settlement being excavated by the students from the University of Buffalo. As project supervisor, Vedrakis would be checking on the progress of the dig after the students left for the day.

"I'll leave the gate open for you," he said. "The ruins will be a great setting for the opening chapter when we write the book on this discovery."

"You're way ahead of me, but I'll be sure to sharpen up my quill pen," Hawkins said.

CHAPTER TWENTY-FOUR

While Hawkins and Abby were still on the road, a black Suzuki Sidekick sports SUV turned off the E75 at a sign marking the Gournia ruins. The vehicle followed a dirt and gravel service road that lay between an olive grove and the ancient settlement. The Suzuki pulled up behind a vintage Land Rover parked near the entrance. A tall man got out of the SUV and walked to the gate.

The man was dressed in baggy shorts, a brightly-colored Hawaiian shirt with a hibiscus motif, and leather hiking sandals. Unruly hair the color of hay stuck out from under the brim of a wide-brimmed tan Tilley hat. The ruddy features visible below the mirrored sunglasses were on the fleshy side. A black leather camera case hung from his shoulder. He could have been a British tourist on holiday, which was exactly the look Leonidas was trying for when he'd assembled this latest identity.

He had listened to the recorded conversations between Hawkins and Vedrakis and the discussion of travel plans with Abby. Then he had gone to the lobby and asked the concierge to arrange a flight to Crete for the next day. A last-minute decision, he explained. He and his late wife had traveled to the island years before her death and he wanted to return to some of the spots they had visited.

The sympathetic concierge worked the computer. An Iberia Air flight was scheduled to leave early the next morning and connect with an Air Berlin flight traveling from Zurich to Heraklion.

Leonidas made sure he gave the concierge a big tip.

The Air Berlin flight landed a couple of hours ahead of the Gulfstream and its two passengers. Leonidas pick up his rental car and headed east. He stopped to enjoy a Greek lunch at a *taverna* in the resort town of Aghios Nickolaos before continuing on to Gournia.

A sign on the chain-link fence announced that the site was closed to the public, but the gate was unlocked, allowing Leonidas to enter. He walked for about a hundred feet and studied the narrow, stepped streets and foundations covering the slope. Movement at the top of the hill caught his eye.

Leonidas took a pair of binoculars from his camera case and focused on the bearded face of the man walking along the ridge. He recognized Vedrakis from photos he had seen while checking the Heraklion museum's website. The professor walked a short distance before he disappeared on the other side of the hill.

Leonidas checked his watch. If Hawkins were following the schedule he had discussed with Vedrakis, he would arrive soon. Heading back to the Suzuki, he drove around to the other side of the olive grove where he parked under the cover of trees.

Leaving the Suzuki, he walked back through the grove to a stone wall located around fifty feet from the service road. He sat on the wall and studied the site. He could see the road and gate from his chosen perch, and would be almost invisible in the shade. Closing his eyes, he inhaled the heady fragrance of rosemary and ripening olives and went into a calming, almost Zen-like state.

For a few minutes, the only sounds were a chorus of cicadas and the rustle of the wind in the olive leaves. Then his ears picked up the growl of a car engine. His eyelids snapped open like window shades. The sun glinted off the hood of a silver Mercedes moving along the service road. The car slowed to a crawl near the Land Rover, then sped up and kept going. A short distance from the gate, the car pulled into the olive grove where it would be hidden, much the same as Leonidas had done with his ride.

Highly suspicious behavior. Leonidas swung his legs to the other side of the wall and dropped belly-first to the ground. His hand reached into his camera bag and came out with a Sig Sauer pistol. He checked the load, then peered through a gap in the wall and saw four men dressed in black, moving single file along the road. He did a double-take. Their skulls were shaved and painted blue. They paused at the entrance, pushed the unlocked gate open and entered the site.

Waiting until they went past the ticket booth, Leonidas then stood and climbed back over the wall. Dangling the pistol at his side, he bent low in a half-crouch, dashed across the road and squatted behind a clump of oleander bushes where he'd have a good view of the slope. The group had broken up. Each figure was climbing a stairway, moving parallel to one another through the ruins. He spotted more movement at the top of the hill. Professor Vedrakis had reappeared and was silhouetted on the ridge.

He looked at his watch.

Hawkins could arrive at any time.

CHAPTER TWENTY-FIVE

Professor Vedrakis was lost in the mists of time. His body existed in the present but his mind had traveled four thousand years into the past, when Gournia was a thriving seaport. He was exercising the most important talent an archaeologist can possess—the ability to see things not as they are, but as they were. In the eye of the virtual time-traveler, a shard of plaster becomes an ancient pot. A piece of rock becomes a tool used for cutting or pounding.

He stood in the central plaza of the old city. As he swept his eyes over the network of stone foundations spread across the slopes, his imagination reconstructed houses, storage buildings and workshops. People thronged the narrow streets. Potters and bronze smiths pursued their trades.

The professor brought his gaze back to the low stone platform at the summit of the hill and imagined a multi-story palace, similar except for its smaller size to the edifice at Knossos. The sound he heard in his ears was not the soughing of the wind in the stunted trees but the voices of kilted Minoans. Hundreds were gathered in the plaza before a sacrificial altar surmounted by the stone carved horns of consecration. Dancers gyrated to the piping of flutes.

The ruins only hinted at the original size of Gournia, which would have spread across what was now the E75 highway and down a valley to the port. Years of painstaking excavation would have to be done before the full extent of the city was known. The college students who sweated under the sun were enthusiastic and energetic, undaunted by the heat, dust and boredom that make up the less glamorous side of archaeology. The students had removed rectangular sections of topsoil marked out with stakes and twine in the central plaza. On most days, teams painstakingly scraped the earth with trowels while others ran shovelfuls of the loose soil through sieves that rested on four legs. The piles of earth under the sieves were high, which meant that the students had worked hard while he was in Sitia.

Vedrakis had made copies of a dozen Linear A tablet rubbings at the Sitia museum. He'd stuffed the rubbings into his briefcase along with a volume of commonly used Egyptian hieroglyphics. It was only a short while later that he was driving along the winding highway to Gournia.

He'd parked at the entrance, left the briefcase in the Land Rover and locked the car. The only thing he carried was a replica of the Phaistos disk he had acquired from the Heraklion museum gift shop. He hiked to the top of the hill. *Good*, he thought. The mournful wind blowing in from the sea would add drama to the first chapter of the book he had already started writing in his head.

He had worked out the Prologue on the drive from Sitia.

Alone amid four-thousand-year-old ruins, my only companions the ghosts haunting the remnants of this once-magnificent city, I anxiously awaited the discovery that would allow me to strip the veil off one of the most mysterious civilizations of all time.

Hawkins would arrive with the machine that would allow the translation of Linear A. Of course, he would give Hawkins credit for finding the device, but Vedrakis would quickly write him out of the narrative. He imagined himself holding the Phaistos disk high above his head to catch the rays of the setting sun.

Snap.

The noise of a breaking twig ended his literary reverie. He lowered his arms and turned around. He was no longer alone. A tall, slender figure dressed in black had emerged from behind an outcropping of rock.

The sun was setting behind the figure so the face was in shadow, but the professor could see that the man had a narrow waist and

144

barrel chest.

"Hawkins?" Vedrakis asked.

No reply. Vedrakis frowned. This wasn't the friendly man he'd talked to on the telephone.

Someone must have strayed through the gate he'd left open.

"This site is closed," he said, making no attempt to disguise his annoyance. "You'll have to leave. Come back tomorrow when you can buy a ticket."

"When will Hawkins be here?" the man said in a deep, accented voice.

The tone was menacing. This was no tourist. Vedrakis pondered his response. Maybe he could say he didn't know who Hawkins was, but he sensed the man would know he'd be lying. He went for a half-truth.

"I'm meeting Hawkins later at the museum in Heraklion," Vedrakis said. "If you give me your name I'll pass it on when I see him."

The man ignored the offer. He moved closer.

"Give that to me," he said.

The disk had only cost a few Euros, but Vedrakis clutched it to his chest. The man took a couple of steps forward until he was close enough for Vedrakis to see that his head was shaved and painted blue. Three other figures dressed in black emerged in the dusky light and closed in from behind and both sides. Astonishment overcame his fear.

They, too, had bald blue scalps. They wore identical jumpsuits snug to bodies that were narrow at the waist and wide at the shoulders. All four men had similar almond-shaped yellow eyes.

He realized he had seen them before, but not in real life. Surrounding him were men who seemed to have jumped off the walls of a Minoan fresco.

But these were not painted images. They were flesh and blood. And they were coming for him.

Leonidas crossed the service road and ducked behind the unoccupied ticket booth. He studied the diagram of Gournia on the fence, then took a circuitous route that led to the top of the hill.

Using bushes and rocks for cover, he made his way along the ridge until he came to the edge of the central plaza. He crossed the deserted open space and came to a boulder that stood at least ten feet high. He edged around the corner, only to pull back quickly.

Leonidas had almost stumbled into the midst of the four weird-looking guys who were holding the arms and legs of a body. He recognized the shock of white hair and beard. Vedrakis. They tossed the body off a cliff as if it were a rag doll.

Leonidas saw one of the men point at a car that had slowed at the entrance to the site and turned off the highway onto the access road.

It had to be Hawkins. Rather than trying to make a run for it, the men spread apart. They were setting up an ambush. They would allow Hawkins to enter, then close in, cutting off any escape. He didn't know who these weirdos were, but he'd have to babysit Hawkins if he hoped to use him to get to Salazar.

Leonidas could be subtle but it wasn't in his nature. He raised his pistol and squeezed the trigger. There was a soft *thut* and a puff of dust exploded from a waist-high rock next to one of the men who called out a warning and reached under his shirt.

He pulled out a handgun; the other men followed his lead. They stood back to back, looking in four different directions for the source of the fire.

Leonidas had moved a short distance from his original shooting position. He climbed some rocks to a position that was above the group and fired off two more rounds, aiming near the feet of his targets.

The strangers realized that they were dangerously exposed. At a word from one, who must have been the leader, they ran across the plaza. Leonidas sent a couple more rounds whizzing over their heads. He didn't want to kill them. He was trying to herd them off the site. He emptied his pistol and slid a fresh magazine in, then followed the trail of the killers to the brow of the hill. Four figures could be seen from this viewpoint running single file along the service road. He hoped they wouldn't double-back or reconsider their escape.

Shifting his attention to the base of the hill, Leonidas watched the Renault pull up directly behind the Land Rover.

CHAPTER TWENTY-SIX

The shadows were creeping across the mountain peaks when Hawkins and Abby arrived at Gournia. Parking behind a Land Rover near the entrance, they got out of the car. Hawkins noticed a parking sticker for the Heraklion museum on the windshield. Looking through the window of the locked vehicle, he spotted a briefcase on the passenger seat.

"This is the professor's car," he said to Abby.

They pushed the gate open and entered the site. They then walked past the ticket booth and turned onto a trail that ran along the base of the hill. After a short distance, they started up an ancient stairway leading to the ridge.

About halfway to the top they heard shouts from a man standing at the base of the hill. He was waving both arms like a landing officer directing a plane on an aircraft carrier.

In a booming voice, he shouted again, "Halloo. Wait up for a minute."

He lumbered up the stairway and was puffing like a steam locomotive when he got to where they stood.

"Good afternoon. Thanks for waiting, folks," he said. "Whoosh. Not used to all this exertion. Out of shape."

Abby and Hawkins exchanged glances at the statement of the obvious. "It's a pretty steep climb," she said.

"Maybe not for a mountain goat." He spoke in brief shouts, as if he were talking to someone who was hard of hearing. "Got delayed on my way out here. Almost missed the road. Saw the sign. Closed. Noticed the gate was open. Saw you up on the hill. Thought I'd see what's going on. Is the site open or not?"

"It's closed to the public today," Hawkins said.

"Damn. I can't come out from Rhethymon tomorrow. Reginald Pouty's the name." He extended a sweaty hand and showed them his top and bottom teeth in a horsey smile. "Would it be all right if I wandered around the place? I can leave a few Euros at the ticket booth. Wouldn't want to be a freeloader."

Even as he shook hands with Pouty, Hawkins thought it was odd for the Englishman to show up out of nowhere. The attacks of the last few days had put him on alert. He would feel better if Pouty weren't around and went to tell him to come back another time, but the Englishman was a looking off at a silver Mercedes traveling along the service road.

He turned back and said, "I may do this another time. Winded. This site is a disappointing, if you ask me. Not as grand as the Palace at Knossos."

"Nice to meet you, Mr. Pouty," Hawkins said. He was glad to see him go.

"Mutual." The full mouth smile re-appeared. "Toodle pip."

Moving with more athleticism than he'd shown on the climb, he quickly descended the stairway and strode toward the gate.

"Toodle pip," Hawkins repeated in a stage British accent.

Abby shook her head. "Mad dogs and Englishmen."

"Go out in the midday sun," he said, finishing the Noel Coward lyric. "Since it's not midday, we'd better get moving."

He continued across the plaza past the excavation pits. There was no sign of Vedrakis. They took turns calling his name.

Abby stooped to examine some pieces of pottery left in a pit. Hawkins walked over to the brow of the hill. As he was about to climb onto a knob of rock for a better view, he looked down to make sure of his footing and saw the sun glinting off glass. He picked up a pair of broken eyeglass frames identical to the ones he had seen on the professor. Next to them was a fragment of pottery. He tucked both objects into his shirt pocket, then climbed onto the rock.

On the other side of the outcropping was a gully, and at the bottom of the shallow ravine was the body of a man with white hair. He lay on his back, arms and legs bent in impossible angles. Vedrakis. Hawkins climbed down into the ravine, knelt by the body and placed his fingers on the professor's neck. The skin was warm, but there was no pulse. The eyes were wide open in a death stare.

Hawkins looked up at the outcropping silhouetted against the sky. Vedrakis could have slipped and fallen, but there was no sensible reason why he would have climbed onto the rock. The body was too far into the ravine to have fallen. He would have had to make a running leap to land in his present position.

Abby was calling his name. He gave the professor a last glance, then climbed back up. Abby had walked over to where she had last seen Hawkins and was surprised when he suddenly appeared out of nowhere.

"Had me worried for a sec," she said. "Where were you?"

Putting his hand on her shoulder, he spoke in a soft voice, "Abby, I want you to listen to me. I found the professor. He's dead. His body is at the bottom of the ravine behind me. I think he's been murdered."

"Who—?"

"Don't know. I'm wondering if that English tourist might have something to do with it. We can talk after we get away from here."

Abby nodded. "I saw a path that will take us directly down to the gate."

The trail led down, past some Minoan tombs, then around to the front of the ticket booth. Hawkins handed his backpack to Abby and asked her to start the Renault's engine. He found a rock the size of a cabbage and smashed a hole in the passenger window of the Land Rover. Reaching in, he quickly unlocked the door and grabbed the briefcase.

Sliding into the passenger seat beside Abby, Hawkins buckled up and placed the briefcase on his lap.

"Maybe there's something in here that explains why the professor is dead. I'll check it out while you drive."

Abby dropped the transmission into low and accelerated, then spun the car around in a cloud of dust and headed back to the highway.

"Nice move," Hawkins said in admiration.

"I learned the reverse spin-out on the first day of my evasive driving course." They were coming up on the highway.

"Where to?" she said.

Hawkins had driven the coastal road on his last visit to Crete and knew that the mountainous countryside to the east had more goats than people.

"Go back to Heraklion. We need to tell the police about the professor."

Abby kicked the Renault up to seventy miles per hour. Traffic was light; they would be back in the city in less than an hour. Hawkins pushed the latch on the unlocked briefcase, reached inside and came out with the rubbings. He held a sheet of paper up for Abby to see.

"The professor said he was bringing along some Minoan inscriptions."

Abby glanced at the rows of script, then back to the rearview mirror.

"I think we're being followed," she said in a neutral voice. "Dark silver Mercedes. Like the one that went by when we were standing at the top of the hill. Been behind us for five miles."

"Can you see the driver?"

"Uh-uh. Tinted windows. Every time I pass, change lanes or speed up, it does the same. They've stayed back just far enough to keep me in sight."

"Slow down and see what happens."

She took her foot off the gas and glanced in the mirror. "They've slowed down too."

She pulled over to the side of the road. The Mercedes did the same. "Any idea who they are and what they want?"

"Worst case scenario is they had something to do with the professor's death."

"What's the best case scenario?"

"There is none." He gave her a tight smile. "Sorry. SEAL graveyard humor."

"Pardon me if I don't double over in laughter. What should we do?"

"We could keep on going to Heraklion and snag the first cop we see, but the E75 has isolated stretches. They could do a drive-by or run us off the road. We're coming up on a big resort town. We might be able to lose ourselves in the crowds."

Abby pulled back onto the highway and the Mercedes followed. Several miles further, she turned off. They attempted to lose their pursuers in Aghios Nikolaos, but the driver of the Mercedes stuck with them like glue.

"This isn't working," Hawkins said. "I've got an idea. Might be risky, and it depends on luck, timing and improvisation."

"A typical SEAL op, in other words."

"In a way. Remember when we were having our marital issues, how we talked about getting away on a cruise so we could talk things through?"

A sad smile came to her lips. "I also remember that things were too far gone by then. One of us would have jumped or thrown the other overboard. Why do you ask?"

"I think it's time to take that cruise."

CHAPTER TWENTY-SEVEN

The island of Spinalonga rises from the emerald waters of the Gulf of Mirabello off the bustling town of Elounda like the shell of a giant stone turtle. Venice fortified the island in the 1500s to guard the entrance to a wide harbor. The next occupants were the Ottoman Turks. When they left, the island became a leper colony, making it the perfect place to hide a clandestine radio during the German occupation. After World War II, Aristotle Onassis wanted to build a casino on the island, but he was stymied by the formidable ranks of the Greek bureaucracy.

On his last visit to Crete Hawkins had wandered the narrow streets and alleyways, climbed the looming battlements and wondered how life must have been for the soldiers, the lepers and caregivers who made the forbidding pile of rock their home.

After leaving the highway, he had directed Abby along a high road that offered sweeping views of the bay and mountains before descending into Elounda. Hawkins asked Abby to pull the Renault into a public lot next to the marina and the harbor side tavernas. Instead of following them, the Mercedes circled like a prowling tiger, then disappeared around a corner.

They left the Renault in the parking lot. Hawkins hid the professor's briefcase under the seat but he carried the backpack that held the device. They bought tickets to Spinalonga, boarded a high-prow wooden boat with a couple of dozen other passengers and sat on benches along the starboard side.

The boat eased out of its slip, and Hawkins got up and went to the stern. His eyes scanned the marina; two figures caught his attention because unlike other tourists strolling along the dock, they were running. They dashed up to the empty slip and stared at the departing boat. They were tall and thin, dressed in black running suits. Denim floppy-brimmed hats were pulled down low over their foreheads.

Training, combat experience and instinct combined to set off a loud alarm inside his head. Hawkins knew without a doubt that he was looking at the professor's killers.

He ambled back to his seat and leaned close to Abby's ear. "I saw two guys on the dock. My guess is that they're the ones in the silver Mercedes."

"Did they see you?"

"Unfortunately, yes."

She looked toward the purple mountains across the bay and let out a deep sigh. "Beautiful, isn't it, Matt? Someday we'll have to do this when we don't have murderers dogging our footsteps."

"It's a date," Hawkins said. "Sorry, Abby. First things first."

"Yes, I know. Sterile cockpit. What next?"

"They'll find another boat to take them to the island. We'll have time before they get there. We'll try to hire a private boat to take us back to the mainland. There were a few fishermen hanging around last time I was here. We'll leave those guys high and dry on the big rock."

"And if we don't find transportation?"

"We take this boat back. They follow. We get to the mainland first and lose them with your fancy driving."

"Pretty thin, Hawkins, but it will have to do."

Minutes later they stepped off the landing dock and merged with the crowd of sightseers milling around below the bastion. The huge curved fortifications had gun emplacements for the cannons that once guarded one end of the island. A couple of private power boats were anchored near the dock. Hawkins started walking towards them, but another tour boat was about to land. The vessel had an upper deck. Leaning on the rail looking down on him were the two men he had seen at the marina.

Hawkins grabbed Abby by the arm and guided her behind a souvenir kiosk.

"Change in plans," he said. "Check out the two guys in black on the top deck of that boat. Don't be too obvious."

She peered around the corner of the kiosk. "I see them."

"Good. Stand near those tour groups until the men in black are out of sight. Then head over to those anchored boats, wave a wad of Euros, and line up a ride to the mainland."

"What about you?"

"I'll lose our pals in the fortress and circle back."

She stared at the approaching boat. "Do you think that will work?"

"If that's a nice way of asking whether my gimp leg will slow me down, don't worry."

"I never meant it that way. I was talking about the backpack slowing you down. Why do you have to be so damn sensitive?"

"Sorry. To answer your question, I can handle it. We can have a sensitivity session later over glasses of ouzo."

She gave him a quick kiss on the cheek. "Go! And for God sakes, be careful."

Hawkins strode toward the entrance to the fortress where he paused to look back. The boat was almost at the dock. The two men had moved to the bow of the lower deck where they'd be the first to disembark. Hawkins stood in full view until one of the men pointed in his direction. Satisfied they had sighted him, he followed an alleyway through a tunnel to the old town—several small buildings the Ottoman Turks had constructed for residences and markets. Following a path that ran along the perimeter of the island he passed a French tour group and walked by an old mosque that had been used as an infirmary. Staying on the path would gain him nothing. His pursuers would catch up, jam a gun in his back and point him to a quiet place where he could be disposed of with a knife to the ribs.

Near the old city gate, he left the path and climbed a set of steep steps that ran between two high walls. The backpack seemed heavier with each step. He would never admit it to Abby, but the stiffness of his bum right leg did slow him down.

He doubled back toward the ferry landing but that plan was soon dashed. Someone in black was climbing the hill ahead in an effort to cut him off. They must have anticipated his move.

Hawkins climbed another level. His haste, combined with the burden of the backpack and his bad leg, threw his balance off. He tripped and his knee came down hard on a stone step. Struggling to his feet, he tried to ignore the pain stabbing in his bruised kneecap.

He realized he was losing the race to the top. Taking a right between two walls, he loped along, catching glimpses of black-suited men in the network of alleyways. They would move in when there were no tourists around, Hawkins knew. They would want to avoid any inconvenient witnesses wandering the hill. He decided to take the offensive. He stopped at the open door to a small chapel. Stepping inside, he removed the artifact from the backpack and tucked it into a corner of the vaulted room.

Then he filled his pack with chunks of masonry. Hoisting the pack on one shoulder, Hawkins exited the chapel and kept moving. The sun's warmth was blistering and at an intersection he stopped to catch his breath. He looked down and saw one of his pursuers standing below on the path that ran parallel to his. The large aquiline nose under the brim of his hat was out of proportion, as if it had been pasted onto his narrow face. The chin was pointed and the mouth was shaped in an upside down V.

The man parted his feral lips in a smile and began to climb, taking each step as if he had all the time in the world.

Hawkins tried to divert him. "Did you kill Professor Vedrakis?"

The man stopped and said something in a strange language.

"I'll take that as a yes," Hawkins said.

The man climbed another step and reached under his shirt. Hawkins hefted the backpack, trying to make it seem lighter than it was. "Do you want this?"

There was no gun in his hand when the man removed it from under the shirt. He climbed another step and reached forward. He was no more than six feet away when Hawkins lifted the backpack.

"Okay, pal. You want it, I'll give it to you."

He tossed the backpack like a basketball player making a two-handed foul shot.

The rock-filled bag soared in a tight arc and hit the man squarely in the chest. He instinctively grabbed onto the backpack, which threw him off balance, throwing him backwards so that his head smashed into a step.

Hawkins hustled down the stairway. The man's body was limp. Saliva dripped from the corner of his oddly-shaped mouth. Hawkins removed the hat, which is when he discovered the man's shaved blue scalp.

Hawkins went through the pockets of the black jumpsuit. He found a billfold containing some Euros and tucked it in his shirt pocket, then went to lift his pack only to freeze at the sound of a voice.

"Nice work, bloke. Is he dead?"

Pouty was standing at the top of the stairs. His English accent was gone and in his hand he held a Sig Sauer with a sound suppressor extending from the barrel.

"He might be, Mr. Pouty," Hawkins said. "Is that your real name?"

"Doesn't matter. What does matter is I'm someone who's got your interests at heart. I was close by when I heard a shout and thought you were hurt."

"Well it wasn't me who was hurt, Mr. Pouty."

"I can see that. How about giving me that bag. Please don't throw it."

Hawkins started up the stairs and put the bag down on the top step. Pouty told him to dump out the contents. Hawkins unzipped the pack then turned it upside down so the rocks tumbled out. A puzzled expression came to Pouty's ruddy features and then, he began to laugh.

"Quite the beanbag. No wonder your playmate crashed and burned."

"He isn't alone on the island. He's got a friend out there," Hawkins said.

"I know that. I'll take care of him." He paused.

"Who are these guys? And what's with the blue head?"

"Damned if I know. Too bad we can't ask him."

"Sorry, but he didn't introduce himself."

Pouty chuckled, and said, "We're not all that different, you know. You and me."

"I don't understand what you're talking about."

"You will." He tucked the pistol into his belt. "Better get moving."

Pouty slipped into an alley on his right. Hawkins hurried to the chapel and replaced the mechanism into the backpack. He descended to the main path and hurried past groups of camera-toting visitors to the landing. Abby was nowhere near the souvenir booth. He cursed himself. He should never have left her.

"Matt!"

Abby waved at him from a white wooden launch hovering a few yards off shore. The young Greek fisherman at the tiller moved the boat closer. Hawkins hurried toward the dock, handed the backpack to the Greek and climbed into the boat. The fisherman powered up the outboard and the boat headed to the mainland.

"Damn it, Hawkins. I was worried," Abby said. "Are you all right?"

"Knee got banged up in a fall, but I'm okay otherwise."

Abby gave him a hug and a kiss. "Hell with the sterile cockpit," she said.

Within minutes, the boat approached the harbor port, leaving the mysteries of Spinalonga, old and new, in its foamy wake.

CHAPTER TWENTY-EIGHT

Amsterdam, The Netherlands

The jetliner Calvin had boarded at Cadiz taxied toward the sprawling terminal at Airport Schiphol. Making it quickly through customs, Calvin was now on the train to the city. As it trundled through the suburbs, he saw a new message from Molly on his electronic tablet. She had dug up more dirt on the man he was about to see. He read her latest tidbit, studied the photos and a smile crossed his broad face.

Calvin caught a cab outside the main entrance of Central Station. Dressed in a dark blue suit he'd bought from a fashionable clothing store in Cadiz, and carrying a leather portfolio case, Calvin fit right in with the working crowd. The taxi dropped him off on a quiet, tree-lined residential street bordering a canal. Calvin stepped across a bicycle lane and walked to a narrow four-story house constructed of dark brick with a white trim. He read the name written in Dutch and English on the small brass plaque next to the front door.

Security Technologies Ltd.

Calvin flew to Amsterdam after talking to a couple of contacts in the arms trade. If he wanted exotic weaponry, they advised he go see Broz at Security Tech.

He rang the doorbell and seconds later a female voice came

over the speaker. "How may I help you?"

"My name is Calvin Hayes. From Secure Ocean Services."

"We've been expecting you, Mr. Hayes. Come right in."

The latch unlocked with a soft click. Calvin opened the door and stepped into a small lobby. A tall, middle-aged woman conservatively dressed in a gray jacket and skirt emerged seconds later from an elevator. She extended her hand in a strong grip.

"I'm Gertrude Doost, Mr. Broz's assistant. Thank you for coming to see us, Mr. Hayes."

"Thank you for seeing me on such short notice."

Her expression didn't waver. "We operate 24/7. Our clients must often deal with the unexpected."

Calvin guessed that the "unexpected" had to do with the strategy that went back to the Stone Age: Never have a smaller club than the other guy. They went into the elevator and she pressed the button for the top floor. He followed her through a reception area into an office of moderate size, tastefully furnished with a shiny wood desk and comfortable-looking leather chairs. Paintings of Dutch village life, canals and windmills adorned the papered walls.

The man at the desk with his back to the street-side windows rose from his chair and came around to shake hands.

Speaking with a slight accent, he said, "Welcome, Mr. Hayes. I trust you had a good trip from Spain."

"Yes, thank you, Mr. Broz. It was an easy flight."

Hayes surveyed Broz as they exchanged pleasantries. The arms dealers Calvin had met up till now were either tanned, clean-shaven, fit and fashionably dressed; or paunchy, scruffy and badly in need of a shave. Both types had "sleaze" written all over their uncaring faces.

Yosef Broz was cut from a different mold. He wore a pinstriped navy suit with a pinched waist that emphasized his shoulders. His black hair was cut so short to his scalp it looked gray. He could have been a banker for Goldman Sachs or a high-end real estate agent with Sotheby's.

He appraised Calvin with light blue eyes, invited him to have a seat and returned to his desk.

"What sort of weapons system are you interested in procuring, Mr. Hayes?"

"As you know from the references I supplied, my company provides marine security for commercial ocean-going vessels susceptible to piracy."

"I called up your website. Very impressive. You've had a high rate of success using your armored safe rooms and professional hit squads."

"I prefer to call them maritime security details. They are basically sniper teams that knock out boarding pirates while the hidden crew removes the vessel from the attack zone. It's been an effective formula but still leaves a hole in security."

Broz leaned back and tented his fingers. "Those left in the attack boats could launch one or more hand-held missiles, sinking the ship and its crew."

Calvin was glad that he didn't have to lead Broz to the conclusion he wanted him to make.

"Correct. I'm looking for something that can pick off a swarm of attacking boats."

"I have just the item. It's called a Spike. Portable, powerful and designed to deal with swarming tactics. It can pick multiple attackers off before they get in close enough to use their rocket launchers."

"That's exactly what I'm looking for."

Broz pecked at his computer keyboard, then swiveled the monitor around for Calvin to see the screen.

"This is a video of the Spike being tested. Ten drone boats were sent in to attack a target. All were destroyed before they got closer than two miles. Fast-loading capacity allowed the whole operation to take less than two minutes. Only one defender was involved."

Calvin watched the screen for a moment, then said, "Wonderful! What will these babies cost my company?"

Broz's fingers played over the keyboard and a price list appeared on the screen. "The unit price is reduced according to the number ordered. Bulk discounts, in other words. Tell me how many you need and I'll start the ordering process. It will take a few days for delivery."

"You must sell a lot of these things."

Broz paused. A mental tic. He was being asked about his

business.

"I've only recently acquired a reliable supplier."

It was a non-sequitur answer to a non-question.

"Pardon me. I don't mean to pry. I was wondering if I could draw on the experience of someone who may have used the product in a combat situation."

"Of course." Broz seemed to relax slightly but the blue eyes were still wary. "I'm only the supplier. I don't do follow-through. Many of my clients are regulars. I would hear from them if there were any complaints."

"And has that happened with the Spike buyers?"

Broz must have decided that Calvin was becoming too inquisitive. His voice hardening, he said, "Perhaps you would do better taking your inquiries to another supplier."

"Is that a refusal to do business with me?"

"It's merely a statement of fact. I'm a cautious man."

"Perhaps you haven't been cautious enough." Calvin unzipped the portfolio case and pulled out his electronic tablet which he powered up and placed on the desk.

Broz read the list of names on the screen. "How did you get this information?"

"Nothing is private in today's world."

Broz sat back in his chair. "I don't see your point. This is nothing more than my client list."

"Which includes known terrorist organizations. Selling weapons to them could land you in jail."

"Come now. Today's terrorist is tomorrow's statesman. Even George Washington was considered a terrorist by the British Crown. I have many friends in high places who value and depend on the services my company provides them."

"So I've heard. Which is why I thought you would be interested in this."

Calvin clicked on another file and pushed the tablet back across the desk. The photo album showed Broz stretched out on the deck of a yacht. Lying next to him was a leggy blonde woman wearing the lower half of a bikini. Broz stared at the picture.

"You're treading in dangerous waters," he growled.

"Not half as dangerous as the waters you and the young lady were testing off the coast of Croatia while your wife was back here in Amsterdam. There are more pictures in the album. I assume the young lady is not your daughter."

"You, sir, are no gentleman."

"And neither are you, based on these photos. "

Broz pushed the tablet away. "What do you want?"

"A little information. I want to know who bought Spike missiles from you over the past six months. If you are honest and upfront with me, these embarrassing photos will never see the light of day."

"How can I know you won't come back again and again with more demands?"

"Your marital status doesn't mean a damn to me, Mr. Broz. What I want is an answer to the question I asked."

Broz sighed. "When someone new approaches my company I ask for a reference. Sometimes more. I did it in your case. Evidently there is much more to you than what I knew."

"I'm a nice guy when you get to know me. Back to the Spikes. Who bought them?"

"I've had three buyers. Two governments wanted the missiles for harbor patrol boats. The third buyer was an independent contractor. The security company he gave as his reference said he had been in special operations in Iraq where he was wounded and got an early discharge."

Broz checked his computer, jotted down the name of the security company, and shoved it across the desk. Calvin glanced at the paper before folding it and placing it into his pocket.

"You said he was independent, which means he no longer worked for the company."

"That's right. He had gone private. He told me he needed the missiles to protect his wealthy employer who lived on his yacht."

"Did he say who that employer was?"

"Only that he could be a prime target for kidnapping. I left it at that."

"How many missiles did he buy?"

"A set of four, plus the launcher of course."

"He must have given you the name he used when he worked

for the security contractor."

"It's Chad Williams. I don't know what name he uses now."

"How did he pay you?"

"The usual. Through a Swiss bank account."

"Did he give you his address?"

"You're not serious."

"A shot in the dark. How did he take delivery?"

"All sales go through a distribution point in Croatia. My home country. From there the missiles were trucked over land to Cadiz, Spain. They were delivered to a warehouse to be picked up."

"When was the last time you heard from him?"

"When he sat in that very chair and placed his order several weeks ago. Are we through here?"

"One last question." Calvin looked around. "Where are the security cameras?"

Broz smiled. "You're the security person. What do you think?"

"At the front door. In the lobby and elevator. In the reception area."

"Not bad. You forgot the one behind the windmill painting."

He went to his computer again and a moment later the printer on his desk spit out a photograph which he handed to Calvin.

"Good looking guy," Calvin said. "This should do it."

"Good. Then I expect our business is concluded."

Calvin raised his palm. "Not quite."

Broz listened to the last request and a smile crossed his face.

"I'm sure we can accommodate you, Mr. Hayes."

Broz called in his receptionist and she escorted Calvin to the front door.

"Come again," she said, sounding more like a retail clerk than part of a slightly sordid arms dealing operation.

Stepping out of the building he walked across the street, narrowly missing a collision with a bike. Calvin hailed a cab. He had a couple of hours before his flight back to Cadiz, and although Calvin was not above dealing with the shadowy world of arms dealing, he needed a strong dose of sunlight.

"Please take me to the Van Gogh Museum," he said.

CHAPTER TWENTY-NINE

Athens, Greece

Kalliste sealed the last cardboard box and placed it on the stack of cartons. Movers would come in later to transport personal possessions from her office to her apartment. She glanced around the small space with sadness in her eyes. Earlier, she had said goodbye to her colleagues at the Hellenic Ministry of Culture. A few co-workers had whispered that they might soon be following her out the door.

She left the office key at the reception desk and stepped out of the ministry building. As Kalliste made her way along the busy sidewalk, her glum mood began to fade. She had a new sense of freedom in her step. She practically raced up the stairway and strode between the tall Ionic columns leading to the entrance of the Athens National Archaeological Museum.

The artifact Matt had salvaged before the Minoan ship was destroyed offered endless possibilities. Life and career, she knew, were about to become exciting indeed.

She made her way to a gallery that'd been set aside to exhibit the cargo of the ship that had sunk in a storm after striking a rock wall off the island of Antikythera. Sponge divers had found the wreck of an ancient Greek freighter around the turn of the century. The ship had carried bronze, marbles and jewelry. But the most amazing object found was a clock-like machine whose purpose had baffled scientists for years.

She stopped at a display case and gazed through the glass at the Antikythera device— a piece that'd been at the museum since 1901. At first, it was thought to be an astrolabe, a navigational instrument that allowed mariners to chart latitude position using the sun and stars. Not until technical advances such as X-ray and imaging did scientists piece together the fragments. They concluded that the corroded assembly of gears within a circular bronze framework was an analog computer that could track the cycles of the solar system. Dated to the second century B.C., it had been fashioned hundreds of years after the Minoan mechanism.

Kalliste wondered how Hawkins had made out with Professor Vedrakis. She left the Antikythera gallery and walked through the museum to the garden in the classical exhibition section. She found a bench in a quiet corner and called Hawkins on her cell phone.

He answered right away. "Hello, Kalliste. Sorry I haven't called you. I had a few issues to deal with."

"That's all right, Matt. I've spent most of my day moving out of my office at the ministry. I assume you've been busy talking to Professor Vedrakis."

There was a pause at the other end of the line, before Hawkins said, "Where are you now, Kalliste?"

"I'm in the garden at the Athens archaeological museum. Why do you ask?"

"I wanted to make sure that you were in a private setting. I've got bad news."

"Don't tell me. The professor told you that the device was nothing like we thought it was."

"The professor didn't have the chance to tell me anything, Kalliste. He's dead. He died at Gournia, where we were supposed to meet."

Kalliste's smile vanished. "Dear God. I always told him he'd have a heart attack digging in the hot sun."

"I wish it were that simple. The professor was murdered."

Struggling to keep her composure, Kalliste glanced around the garden to make sure no one was near enough to pick up the conversation. Tears brimmed in her eyes. Speaking with a catch in her voice, she said, "I want to know what happened."

Hawkins told her how he had found the professor's body at the bottom of a ravine.

"What makes you think he was murdered? He could have fallen."

"That was my first guess," Hawkins said. "But there's more to the story."

Hawkins described how a car had followed them from the Minoan ruins to Spinalonga, saying only that they had managed to elude their pursuers at the old leper colony.

"The professor was a wonderful scholar and a gentleman," she said. "There was no reason to kill him."

"Someone apparently thought there was, Kalliste. It's no coincidence that he was murdered just before he was going to meet with Abby and me. Any idea how word of our meeting got out so fast?"

"I can't—oh…Matt."

"What's wrong?"

"It was me. I told someone at the ministry. I wanted to rub it in the faces of those bastards. Now, because of me, the professor is dead."

"Don't go there, Kalliste. You didn't kill the professor. The creeps who tried to nail me are the guilty ones. Tell me who you talked to."

"A fat pig named Papadokalos. He's a bureaucrat in the ministry. Totally dishonest and unscrupulous. He'll do anything for money."

"Even act as a paid informant?"

"Yes. I have no doubt of that. I'm going to rip his heart out and step on it when I see him."

"I'll look forward to the stomping party but it will have to wait until we deal with more important matters."

"You're right of course, Matt. I have an ancient scroll written in Linear A. It could be important. Is the machine functional?"

"It will be when Calvin gets through with it. He'll have this thing purring like a Swiss watch. We'll need a quiet location to work without interruption."

"I know just the place. Remember my house on Santorini?"

On the last night of the Kolumbo expedition she and Matt had celebrated at a taverna with a bottle of ouzo and wound up at the little marshmallow-shaped house perched on a cliff overlooking the volcanic caldera. He'd spent the night and nature had taken its course.

"The house will be perfect. I'll ask Cal know to meet us there," Hawkins said. "Leave Athens as quickly as possible. Don't tell anyone where you're going, and make sure that you're not followed."

"I'll gather up a few things and take an island ferry. See you later today." She sighed heavily. "I can't get over Dr. Vedrakis, but I'm so glad that you are all right. Before I hang up, could you tell more about the men who murdered the professor?"

"They were dressed in black and they had wide shoulders and narrow waists. One of them was bald and his scalp had been painted blue. Don't know about the others because they were wearing hats. Ring a bell?"

She sat there in stunned silence, then said, "I'm afraid it does, but it's too fantastic."

"Nothing about this day would surprise me. We'll talk about it when I see you. Be careful, Kalliste."

"You too, Matt."

Hanging up, she went back into the museum, climbing to the Thera exhibition gallery located on the second floor. The room held artifacts excavated from the ancient city of Akrotiri on Santorini. She walked past the cases of vases and urns, the graceful paintings of swallows and ships, until she came to a fresco that depicted two boxers dressed in loincloths.

Kalliste stared at the painting as if in a trance. They had narrow waists and barrel chests; the scalps had been shaved and painted blue.

CHAPTER THIRTY

Hawkins swept his gaze around the waterfront and adjacent streets after the fisherman had dropped them off at the quay. He spotted the silver Mercedes almost immediately. They went over to inspect the car.

"This is it. I remember the license plate," Abby said. "We'd better get going. That thing can catch the Renault before we're halfway back to the airport."

"Let's make sure that doesn't happen."

Hawkins took Abby by the arm and guided her across the street. "Where are we going?" she said.

"To that mini-market's wine section."

"Are you crazy, Hawkins? Those guys could be here any minute, and you want to get a bottle of wine?"

"I never said anything about buying wine," he said.

Inside the market Hawkins picked a corkscrew from a rack and made a twisting motion with his hand. Abby gave him a 'now-I-get-it' grin.

Back at the parking lot she leaned against the car, using her body to shield Hawkins, who knelt on his good knee and went to work on the Mercedes' tires with the corkscrew. When they walked away, the shiny ride had four flats in the making.

Abby got behind the wheel of the Renault. They were headed for the highway when Hawkins answered the call from Kalliste. After they talked, he filled Abby in on the full conversation.

"I'll text Cal and tell him to join us on Santorini," he said. "We'll try to get the device working there."

"I'll call my company pilot and say we'll be at the airport in about five minutes."

"You'd better allow an hour's leeway. I want to swing by the archaeological museum." He reached into his shirt pocket and held up the clay fragment from Gournia. "I'm hoping to find the jigsaw puzzle this fits into."

Abby drove past the airport into Heraklion. They found a parking spot near the museum. Matt reluctantly checked his knapsack at the security desk and they made their way to the Minoan collection.

Hanging on the walls were the famous frescoes from Knossos. The colorful paintings were like a slide show of the past. Playful blue dolphins. The three fashionable Minoan ladies in the portrait known as, *La Parisienne*. Acrobats somersaulting over the back of a huge bull. A graceful female dancer.

"It was a beautiful civilization, wasn't it?" Abby said, gazing at the painting of the regal kilted figure known as the Lilly Prince.

"It's fascinating to contemplate what the world would be like now if they hadn't vanished from the face of the earth." Hawkins stopped in front of a display case and pointed at a small figurine. "But they had their sinister side, too."

Inside the case was the small ceramic figure of a woman wearing a tall conical hat, long flounced skirt, an embroidered apron and a tight open bodice that exposed her breasts. In each hand she gripped a writhing snake. Her eyes were round and staring as if she were under a spell.

Abby said, "The Snake Goddess would have been a fearsome figure in real life."

"I'd be more worried about her pets," Hawkins said.

"Things aren't all that they seem," a voice said. "The snake was a symbol of fertility and renewal in ancient times." The speaker of these words was a pleasant-faced, middle-aged woman dressed in a museum staff uniform. The badge on her blouse identified her as Maria Constatinos, a museum conservator.

"Thank you. That's very interesting," Abby said.

"Didn't mean to eavesdrop, but I heard your American accents. I studied at Boston University many years ago. I had a wonderful time, so I always go out of my way to speak to visitors from the U.S. Is there anything else I can show you?"

"We were hoping to see the Phaistos Disk," Hawkins said.

"Of course. Everyone does."

She led the way to a glass case that contained a round object covered with signs spiraling clockwise toward the center. Abby said, "It's smaller than I thought it would be."

"Many people say that. It's just under six inches in diameter, made of fired clay. It dates back to the late Minoan Bronze Age, which would put it at the second millennium B.C., and was discovered in the palace at *Phaistos* in 1908. The size is deceiving. You're looking at one of the world's most intriguing archaeological mysteries."

"Are those Linear A symbols?" Hawkins asked.

"Some people think they are, at least in part. But I'll say this; whoever translates those little symbols will be the most famous person in the field of archaeology. I wish Dr. Vedrakis were here to talk to you. He's our resident expert on the Phaistos Disk, but he's off on a dig at a Minoan site. Perhaps another time."

Hawkins and Abby exchanged glances. He was thinking that the only way they would see the professor is if they took a cruise on the Styx, the legendary river of the dead. "Thank you," he said. "That would be nice."

She said, "You may want to read the book that Professor Vedrakis wrote. It's called *The Minoan Enigma* and is available in the gift shop."

"Thank you. We'll pick up a copy on the way out."

Constatinos excused herself and went off to tend to her other duties. "That was damned eerie," Abby said. "She's going to feel awful when she learns about the professor. I wish we could tell someone."

Hawkins remembered the body sprawled at the bottom of the cliff and felt a sense of guilt, but things were moving too fast. "I don't like it any better than you do, Abby. But an interrogation room in the Heraklion police station is the last place we want to be."

"I know," she said with an angry shake of her head. "Well, at least you can tell me why we came here."

Hawkins reached into his pocket for the clay shard he'd found next to the professor's broken glasses and held it close to the glass. Several figures on the shard matched an area on the disk. A fish, a head, and a bare-breasted woman similar to the ceramic figuring holding the snakes.

"It's a piece from the disk," Abby said with wonderment in her voice.

He put the fragment back in his pocket. "I recognized the figures from the last time I was here. Since we're looking at the real thing, and it's not damaged in any way, the piece I found must have come from a replica."

"Why would the professor bring a fake disk out to the site? Did he think we'd be able to decode that script with the device?"

"He was pretty excited. My guess is that he thought it might be worth a try. Mostly, he wanted to take a close look at the device before he confirmed that it was a translating machine. Too bad those jerks got to him before he could do that."

"But he *did* confirm that's exactly what it was, Matt. He had already concluded that the mechanism was a translator or he wouldn't have brought the disk replica with him."

Matt gave his skull a light knuckle rap and kissed Abby on the cheek.

"You are the smartest woman I know."

She looked at her watch. "I'm smart enough to know we shouldn't press our luck. Let's get to the airport."

Hawkins didn't argue. They headed for the exit, stopping at the gift shop to buy a copy of the professor's book and a replica of the disk. Hawkins retrieved the knapsack that contained the mechanism.

As they walked back to the car, Abby said, "I've been thinking about Kalliste's scroll, wondering if it will help us unravel the mystery."

"Which mystery?" Hawkins said with a shake of his head. "There seem to be an infinite number of them."

The pensive smile vanished from Abby's lips. "The one that keeps getting people killed."

CHAPTER THIRTY-ONE

Molly rolled the raw hamburger into little balls that she put in a saucepan. She carried the pan outside to the shed behind her house. She flipped the latch, went inside and closed the door behind her.

A mesh cage sat on a wooden table, visible in the sunlight streaming in from the windows. The cage door was wide open. A large bird with dark brown feathers hopped out of its home onto the table, opened its beak and fluffed its wings. Molly placed the pot with the raw meatballs on the table.

"Suppertime," Molly said.

Several weeks earlier, Molly had been shooting photos in the forest near Mount Bachelor and discovered the injured bird lying on the ground, blood clotting on its wing. She had learned at the museum about *Cainism*, named after the Biblical brother Cain who'd killed his sibling. The oldest Golden eagle hatchling attacks its younger siblings, killing them or driving them from the nest.

Sutherland had picked up the weakened fledgling and put it in her camera bag. Back home, she lined a wicker basket with a towel to provide a nest. The bird looked to be at death's door but, like Lazarus, it'd recovered and started to eat the scraps of raw meat she fed it. Before long, it could stand, spread its wings, and clack its beak.

The bird was too young to be released. If she brought it to the museum, it would be put in a cage. It would be well fed and cared for. Visitors would gawk and take pictures. But she couldn't bring herself to do it. Like the eagle, she had been attacked and thrown out of her army nest.

Molly knew she couldn't keep the bird forever. This was no canary. The Golden eagle was one of the deadliest birds of prey in the world. Falconers used teams of the raptor to hunt down antelopes and wolves.

The eagle now measured more than two feet from the top of its head to its tail and could easily grow to more than a yard. When it stretched its wings the span was nearly six feet. The four talons on each yellow foot were like curved daggers and the hooked beak was more than two inches long. Gold-colored feathers grew around the back of the crown and the nape. The white plumage of a juvenile bird were quickly being replaced by feathers of rusty brown.

She had named the eagle Wheeling after the capital of her home state of West Virginia. The name fit the way the eagles flew—in wide, lazy circles. Since she didn't know whether the bird was male or female, the uni-sex name would work for now. The bird was used to her, but if she got too close, it would spread its wings and shift from claw to claw. She didn't know if Wheeling would attack when provoked, but this wasn't a creature to be toyed with.

Since moving to mellow Oregon, the emotional numbness of her post-Army days had ebbed. She was making connections at the museum, but nothing strong or permanent. She had done better at making friends with a fierce raptor. Pathetic. She would be sad to see it go, but she knew that it was time to release the bird.

"Fixin to let you go by an by," Molly said. "Better enjoy the room service while you can."

She left the shed and returned to the kitchen to toast a bagel. Tromping around in the woods with a load of camera equipment was good exercise, but she knew that if she didn't modify her own diet she'd blow up like a tick having dinner. She didn't want to be like her triple-chinned Auntie Flo who used to wash French fries down with Diet Coke. So, instead of slathering the bagel with an inch of cream cheese, butter and jelly, she only used a dab, skimming the mixture lightly over the crust. It made her feel good, but she knew it was only a gesture.

After breakfast she went into her office and powered up the computer. Dozens of photos needed editing and filing. She read the email Calvin sent after his visit to Amsterdam and put the photo project aside. Finding someone who had been in the armed services would take little effort. Some people saw hacking into a database as a sneaky intrusion. She pictured it more like parting curtains and stepping into the room. The trick was to make yourself invisible to those already in the room.

She clicked on the Department of Defense site and parted the curtains wide enough to peek inside for her first sighting of Chad Williams.

Within fifteen minutes a photo popped up on her screen. Even with his buzz haircut Chad Williams was good-looking enough to be a movie star. Digging around, she learned he had been injured in Iraq and spent several months in Walter Reed hospital. She got into the hospital files and saw that he had extensive plastic surgery. He was honorably discharged. There was no forwarding address, so she tracked down family listed in the DOD files. Unmarried. Only child. Father and mother deceased. Molly forwarded the information to Calvin and Hawkins and went back into the kitchen for another bagel. This time she left out the jelly.

Seven thousand miles away from Oregon, Hawkins sat in the Gulfstream, reading the professor's book. The cover art was a reproduction of the bull and acrobats fresco from the museum. Hawkins opened to the index section and looked under the *R*'s. He found *Robsham, Howard*, turned to the page and read the professor's words.

"Howard Robsham was a self-educated Englishman whose family fortune allowed him to pursue his obsession with the ancient world. Professional scholars worked from their offices and conducted research in libraries and archives. They never went into the field, and looked down with disdain at those who scratched the dirt from an ancient ruin with a trowel. They castigated self-schooled archaeologists, like Heinrich Schliemann and Arthur Evans, for the sometimes destructive methods of investigation they used. To the dismay of these desk-bound academics, amateur

Indiana Jones's had made the big discoveries.

"Evans uncovered the ancient capital of Knossos and the palace that had been at the center of a lost civilization. He called it 'Minoan' after its leader, King Minos, and named the two writing scripts Linear A and Linear B. Michael Ventris was an architect by training, but he deciphered Linear B. It was a close-knit community. Howard Robsham had been a friend of Ventris.

"In the last year of his life, Robsham had come to Athens to read a paper at a conference of philologists, people who study historic languages. After the conference, he sailed to Crete looking for examples of the Minoan script known as Linear A. He heard about some inscribed tablets and tracked down the shepherd who had found them in what was apparently a cave shrine. Robsham negotiated the sale of more than two dozen tablets. A short time later, Robsham drove his car off a mountain road and died in the crash.

"It was a double blow to Minoan investigation. In a strange coincidence, the same year, only months earlier, Ventris died in a car accident in London. What has come to be called the Robsham Collection was never found; it was presumed the tablets had been destroyed in the accident."

Hawkins put the book down and stared out the window at the shimmering turquoise sea. The accidental deaths of two major Minoan scholars was a strange coincidence. But what did it mean? Did it mean anything? He looked over at Abby, who had dozed off. He let his eyes rove over her perfect nose and lush lips. Many things had changed since their divorce, but he still thought she was the loveliest woman he had ever met.

"Beautiful," he whispered.

He had forgotten that Abby had the hearing of a cat. She woke up, saw Hawkins looking at her, and said, "What did you say?"

Hawkins pointed out the window at the black cliffs and crescent shape that distinguished Santorini from other Aegean islands. A moment later the pilot asked them to make sure their seat belts were fastened.

CHAPTER THIRTY-TWO

Paris, France

The man splashed through the Paris sewers with a look of sheer terror on his handsome face. He would have run faster, but he was carrying an unconscious young woman over his shoulder and the dead weight slowed him down. In the other hand was a sputtering torch. He kept glancing over his shoulder, but the danger lay ahead. The creature that stepped out of an alcove and crouched in his path wore a ragged shirt and pants, and was standing on two legs like a human. But its face, hands and paw-like bare feet were covered with thick fur. The teeth that it bared as it uttered a low growl were those of a canine. With no other weapon to protect him, the running man thrust the torch into the creature's face. It reeled and let out a loud howl, then turned and disappeared into the darkness.

Someone yelled, "Cut!" and the tunnel was flooded with light.

The woman slung over the man's shoulder lifted her head, "Let me down, you brute."

He set her on her feet and squinted against the glare of floodlights.

"Where's Wolfie?"

The creature walked into the light, and said, "Where do you think I'd be after you tried to set my whiskers on fire?"

The woman laughed, "Poor doggy. You wouldn't get such rough

treatment if you didn't jump out and scare people." She went over and kissed the furry cheek. "Ugh. Smells like burnt plastic."

The young man grinned, "Sorry Wolfie. Didn't mean to singe you. We'll buy you some dog biscuits after the shoot."

The creature lifted the mask off his face to reveal another handsome actor. "I'll settle for a Pernod, unless I have to do another take."

Lily Porter stepped out from behind the lights. "If this was Masterpiece Theatre that's exactly what I'd do. The Hidden History channel is a cheapskate and we can't afford to wreck another mask. But I think there's room in the budget to celebrate the end of the shoot. Let's put *Werewolves of Paris* in the can with style."

The three actors cheered, joined by the electricians and cameraman. No one liked working in the damp, smelly, rat-infested sewer system. The technical crew started to take down the lights and pack up the camera. Chatting happily, Lily and the actors headed for the ladder that would take them to the street. Yellow tape had been stretched on pylons around the manhole opening.

Lily said she would meet them in a nearby brasserie after they had a chance to shower and change their clothes. She waited for the technical crew to emerge from below the street and filled the team in on the plans, then headed to the hotel to clean up.

She showered for a long time, dried her reddish-blonde hair, and changed from her coveralls into a short leather black dress, high boots, horizontally-striped leggings and a waist-length black leather jacket. Lily was tall and slender and would have looked good in a burlap bag. She left the hotel and was walking to the brasserie when she heard her phone chirp. She put the phone to her ear and looked up the street.

"I see you," she said.

The black Citroen sedan pulled up to the curb seconds later. A rugged-looking driver got out and opened the back door. She slid in beside Salazar who ordered the chauffeur to take them for a drive.

"You should have told me you were coming," Lily said. "I don't like surprises."

"My apologies. I thought it best to meet in person and was on my way to your hotel. I heard from Crete. The news is not good."

"Don't waste my time with unnecessary drama, Salazar."

"Then I'll get right to the point. Hawkins has escaped."

"And the device escaped with him, I assume."

"As far as we know, it is still with him. It gets worse. Two of the Priors who went after him are dead."

Lily's jaw hardened.

"Tell me what happened. From the beginning. Omit no detail."

"Our informant told us that Hawkins was going to Crete to see Professor Vedrakis at Gournia. As you asked, I passed the information on to the team of Priors, who went there, killed the professor, making it look like an accident, and waited to ambush Hawkins, only to flee when someone started shooting at them."

"Did they see the shooter?"

"No. He or she was hiding behind some rocks."

"Is Gournia where the Priors died?"

"That came later. They followed Hawkins to the island of Spinalonga. A short time later, the Priors were found dead. The police believe that they fell down some stone stairways."

"What of the others in their team?"

"The Priors, called North and South, stayed on the mainland to cut off escape. When they lost contact with the other men, they followed them to Spinalonga. The bodies of East and West had been found by then. Hawkins. He had escaped."

The temperature in the car seemed to drop twenty degrees. Salazar squirmed under the unrelenting stare. When Lily spoke again, her voice was harsh.

"Priors are trained assassins, Salazar. They don't fall down stairways. Was Hawkins alone?"

"No. He was with a woman."

"Find out who she is. Where are the surviving Priors?"

"Still on Crete, waiting for orders."

She thought for a moment about the crone's comment back at the Paris sanatorium. How the descendant of King Minos was disturbing the equilibrium of the Way of the Axe. It had all started with Kalliste's intention to identify the ancient shipwreck. It was Kalliste who brought Hawkins in, Kalliste who connected Hawkins to Vedrakis. It had been right in front of her eyes all this time.

"Tell them I want them to go to Athens immediately," she snapped. "Kalliste Kalchis has an apartment there." She rattled off the address of the apartment building. "Make her tell them where Hawkins is."

"Should she be disposed of once she does that?"

"No. Keep her alive. Now tell me about the status of the event in the United States."

"Good news there. The demolition team has the explosive charges in place. All is ready when you give the word. Nothing can go wrong."

"Things have been going wrong since the discovery of the ship. This is too much to be coincidence. There are unseen forces at work here, Salazar."

"I don't understand."

"The Mother Goddess is angry. She is warning us that she is thirsty for blood. The sacrifice must be of the highest order. No prostitutes dragged off the street as in the past."

The car had gone in a circle and was back where it had originally picked Lily up. She got out and watched it disappear into the Paris traffic. She stood there as if in a bubble that insulated her from the noise of the city. In that unnatural silence, the voice of the crone called from afar.

The prophecy must be fulfilled. She is near. She must die.

She was starting to understand what the old priestess had told her. It had all started when the girl escaped thousands of years ago, never to be found. Through his daughter, the king still lived. Someone alive now carried the king's seed, and until that person was killed—as the prophecy said must happen—one thing was very certain: The Mother Goddess would continue to hunger for blood.

CHAPTER THIRTY-THREE

The key to Kalliste's house on Santorini was kept at a taverna owned by her cousin, who insisted that Hawkins and Abby have a glass of raki and a plate of local snacks called mezes. He peppered them with questions about how they knew Kalliste, the famous archaeologist, then said that his mother would open the house for them. They could hardly keep up with the skinny lady in the black dress and stockings as she scuttled through a network of narrow alleys to a small, tree-lined square and down a narrow set of stairs to the two-story house that looked like one marshmallow stacked on top of another.

They had flown into the busy tourist town of Thera and caught a cab to Oia, a quiet village at the westerly tip of the island. It had been a couple of years since Hawkins had been to the house to celebrate the end of the research expedition, and he was glad to have a guide, especially after the raki.

The old woman unlocked the turquoise-painted door and pushed it open.

"*Kali mera*," she said, flashing a gold-toothed grin. "Sleep good."

"*Kali mera efaristo*," Hawkins replied. Good evening and thank you.

The old lady cackled like a happy hen, handed him the key and scuttled off.

"She's a joyful old soul," Abby said.

"I think she was waiting for me to carry you across the threshold."

"You didn't even do that on our honeymoon, Matt. You were too much in a rush to consummate the marriage."

"Then I owe you one." He picked her up, stepped inside and set her back on her feet.

Abby burst into laughter. "I never knew you Neanderthal types could be so gentle."

They were standing in a large combination living room and kitchen. The white-washed walls were decorated with colorful Greek textiles and photos of Santorini's famous cliff towns.

He led the way to the rear of the house, outside to a paved terrace. Below a wrought-iron fence, cube-shaped houses and domed churches were built into the dark gray cliffs that wrapped partially around the flooded caldera. Hawkins pointed to an island almost directly opposite the house.

"That's Therasia. Off to the left is Nea Kamini where you can still see volcanic fumes that seep to the surface."

"It's breathtaking," Abby said. "Is there any danger of another eruption?"

"It's never really stopped erupting or shaking things up with earthquakes. A monitoring system should give plenty of warning for the next one. Let's see if we can find a good spot for the sunset."

They locked up the house. Hawkins shouldered the knapsack that had become part of him and they strolled through the warren of alleyways to the foundation of an old castle that was jammed with visitors gathered to watch the spectacular sunset. The fiery sun painted the sky red as it plunged into the Bay of Ammoudi. After the show, the selfie-snapping tourists boarded the buses for Thera. Hawkins and Abby stopped for coffee and made small talk, then headed back to the house.

Kalliste had arrived. Through the open window she could be seen bustling around in the kitchen. The pungent fragrance of garlic and oregano wafted on the breeze. Kalliste greeted them with a warm smile and hugs. She had picked up groceries on the way in from the airport and was cooking fish with tomatoes and onions.

A taxi dropped Calvin off around a half hour later. After a dinner washed down with a dry white Santorini wine, they gathered at the table.

Hawkins glanced around at his friends and he smiled. "I'm reminded of the scene in *Dracula* where Dr. Van Helsing pulls the troops together and spells out what they're up against. Kalliste's house is a lot more comfortable than a rat-infested old chapel, but the forces we're dealing with are just as murderous as the old bloodsucker."

"Damn it, Hawk," Calvin drawled. "After all that garlic we had for dinner, no self-respecting vampire would come closer than a hundred miles."

Laughter rippled around the table.

"Wish it were that simple, Cal. First of all, a question for Kalliste...or Calvin. Did you notice anyone on your travels that aroused your suspicions?"

"Got anything specific in mind, Hawk?"

"Yep. Tall, skinny guys dressed in black. They shave their heads and paint their scalps blue."

"You serious, Hawk?" Calvin said.

"Deadly serious, Cal."

"No blue heads in black," Calvin said. "Just run-of-the-mill tourists on my flight."

"The same with me," Kalliste said. "Please tell us, Matt, exactly who and what are those forces that we're dealing with?"

"First, let's go over what we do know. A Minoan ship is discovered off the coast of Spain. Kalliste pulls together a survey expedition to check it out. Someone sinks the survey boat with missiles. A second survey indicates failed attempts to dive down to the boat going back centuries. Finally, helicopters come in and blast the crap out of the wreck site. Right so far?"

Abby nodded. "The helicopter part isn't exactly eloquent, but it's an accurate description."

Hawkins asked Calvin to close the window shutters. Then he unzipped the knapsack, lifted out the treasure and set it on the table.

"Kalliste and I think this is similar in design to the Antikythera computer, but instead of computing the position of the stars, it is a language translator. Abby and I went to Crete to show this device to an expert. Before we could talk to him he was murdered by the blue-headed characters who chased us down."

Calvin slowly spun the device around. "Looks like a prototype can opener."

"You may be right, Cal, but this little can opener is worth killing over."

"It's not what it is, but what it can do," Kalliste said. "I believe it can translate the Minoan script known as Linear A."

"Why is that so important?" Abby said. "Who cares, outside of historians and linguists, whether the script can be translated or not?"

Speaking in a quiet voice, Hawkins said, "Someone does. Can we get this thing to work, Calvin?"

"I'll give it a try."

He got a plastic case out of his duffel bag and opened it on the table. The case contained an assortment of tools. Calvin took out a small but powerful flashlight and a magnifying glass attached to an extending handle. He examined the mechanism like Sherlock Holmes studying a spot of blood, then switched off the light and looked around the table.

"There is corrosion, but the gears are workable if we're careful. Haven't figured out the power driver yet. Probably had a crank arrangement. Gears are going to need a squirt or two of lubricant."

"How long will it take to get it working?" Kalliste said.

"Can't say. This gadget didn't come with an operating manual." Sensing her impatience, he added, "Maybe you can study the lettering, zero in on the linguistics capabilities while I figure out the mechanics of the device. Then we'll compare notes."

Hawkins and Abby volunteered to act as research assistants, jotting down the observations of the experts.

The front door of the house opened and the old woman stepped out into the square. She was bent over, talking to a hungry stray cat that was meowing loudly. Her eyesight was poor, but even with 20/20 vision she might never have seen the shadowy figure that emerged from the stairway leading down to Kalliste's house.

Leonidas waited until she went back inside before dashing across the square to the door of his rental property.

He had hovered near a window that gave him a view of Hawkins and his friends clustered around a strange object. He couldn't hear their voices clearly after the window was shuttered, but from the excited expression he'd seen on their faces, he could tell that the thing was very, very important.

CHAPTER THIRTY-FOUR

Fueled by generous amounts of wine, the party was going full tilt. The actor who'd played the werewolf role got drunk, put his mask back on and growled at a woman sitting at a nearby table. With typical Parisian imperturbability, she asked if he was an American. When he said yes, she accepted his invitation to join the celebration.

Lily whooped it up with the rest of the Hidden History crew, but her thoughts were light years away. She had her hand resting on her purse and felt the vibration signaling a call. Pulling the phone out, she held it under the edge of the table. On the screen was the image of the Prior known as North. Each one of the Priors was named after the cardinal directions on a compass. The one named North was their leader.

She excused herself and walked outside to the relative quiet of the sidewalk. The smile left her lips and when she spoke her voice had a hard edge to it.

"Well. Do you have her?" she said.

"We're in the apartment now. We came here immediately after your call but she was gone when we arrived."

"Then you must wait until she returns."

"I don't think she will be coming back soon. Clothes are missing from the closet and drawers. We found no luggage."

"Show me."

The face disappeared and the screen showed a sofa and chairs in a living room. The camera spun slowly around, then the view moved into the kitchen and bedroom. The hangers were empty in the bedroom closet and spaces in the drawers showed where items had been removed. There was no sign of a toothbrush or hairbrush in the bathroom.

The camera phone moved into a small office. On the neat desktop were photos of Kalliste with her colleagues on a research vessel, and a picture of white, cube-shaped houses hugging black cliffs. The drawers were pulled open, but contained only office supplies. Of course, Kalliste would keep her files electronically and would have taken her computer with her. The face reappeared in the screen.

"Enough," Lily said. "Go back into the bedroom and examine the pillows on her bed. Look for hair. Do the same in the shower drain."

Less than a minute later, the voice came on again, "I found two long hairs."

"Now go into the kitchen and place the hairs in a plastic bag. Bring the bag and its contents to me at the Cadiz Airport. I want you to carry it personally." Lily clicked off and made a call to Salazar. "Send a plane to pick me up. I'll need a helicopter in Cadiz, as well."

"I'll order an Auroch jet to Le Bourget right away," Salazar said. "The helicopter will be at the Auroch corporate hangar. Anything further I can assist you with?"

"I'll let you know."

Lily went back to the party and stayed only long enough to excuse herself. She said the office called and assigned her to scope out a new assignment. She thanked the crew for its work, posed for photos with the French woman, who had donned the werewolf mask, and said she would see them back in New York. She took a cab to the hotel and asked the front desk to arrange for a limo to the airport while she packed.

Le Bourget Airport is used primarily for business aviation. The executive jet that landed minutes after her arrival was distinguished from the other corporate aircraft only by the stylized bull horns insignia of Auroch Industries on the fuselage. The jet taxied up to the limo where she was waiting. The jet kept its engines going while she boarded and an hour later it touched down in Cadiz. A tall thin figure dressed in black was standing near the Auroch hangar. He handed her the plastic bag as she walked to the helicopter.

The helicopter lifted into the air, headed east at two hundred miles per hour and soon approached its destination. Lily felt the tension slip away as she glimpsed the crenelated towers of the old castle looming like dragon's teeth against the blue-black sky. The helicopter touched down inside the castle walls. Lily got out and strode across the courtyard under a translucent roof that had been built over a structure consisting of three towers, the tallest resting between the others.

Lily entered the door of the middle tower, walked through a dimly lit antechamber, then descended a wide set of stairs.

She placed the axe medallion hanging around her neck against the metal pad next to the doors to identify herself. When the doors opened, she stepped through into a passageway lit by electrical wall torches to a second set of steel doors and opened them with another press of her medallion on an ID plate. As she stepped into this new room and the doors silently closed behind her, she was enveloped by a sickly sweet odor of ancient decay. Anyone else would have retched, but Lily inhaled the miasma deep into her lungs. With each breath, she underwent a transformation.

The soft features of her face became rock hard. The corners of the lush mouth turned downward. The brow dipped into a shallow V. The warmth drained from her eyes. She elevated her chin at a haughty, uncaring angle and her long fingers curled into claws. The friendly, outgoing woman who had caroused with the film crew in Paris just a short time ago disappeared. In its place was a cruel caricature of herself.

She was in a huge chamber lined on four sides by red and black columns. The panels that decorated the walls between the columns included none of the finer aspects of Minoan art, such as flying fish or graceful swallows. These were pictures of death and destruction: An erupting volcano; bloody battle scenes on land and at sea; a bull being sacrificed.

She made her way between two lines of marble platforms. Lying on the biers were the mummified remains of high priestesses going back four thousand years. She walked further through the centuries with every step until she stopped at an altar surmounted by two up-swept stone horns. On a dais behind the altar was the first of the high priestesses.

Unlike the other mummies, she sat upright on a granite throne flanked on each side by a metal stand holding a double-edged axe. The round eyes that stared out through the horns at the lines of mummies were made of ivory. She wore the traditional dress of the priestess; the open bodice and long ruffled skirt. On her skull was a flat cap with a wide brim. Her desiccated skin was the color of old leather.

Lily gazed at the figure as if in a drug-induced haze. Although the silent thing on the throne was nothing but a pile of dry skin and bones, the High Priestess still exerted a power that was only somewhat diminished since that ancient time when she spoke with the voice of the Mother Goddess.

Lily had been aware that she was considered special even as a girl, when she was removed from an orphanage in California and placed under the guardianship of a foundation that had moved her to the Paris mansion where she was educated by the priestesses who lived there. Later she learned that she had been chosen because her blood contained what some psychologists canned "the murder gene," an inherited characteristic that blots out normal human traits, such as empathy and sympathy. Her cold-blooded persona had been refined by bloody rituals that stretched back to the dawn of time, grooming her for the role she would play. Now…that time had come. Only the faint heartbeat of the crone lying in a room of the Paris sanitarium separated her from joining the line of high priestesses that stretched back forty centuries.

Set in the folds of the mummy's apron, clutched in boney fingers, was a skull. The long ragged hole in the crown of the skull suggested that the owner had died a swift and violent death. Lily reached into a bronze chest at the feet of the mummy and came out with a dagger that would have been used for sacrifices. With the skill of a surgeon, she scraped a shaving of bone from the skull's forehead into the plastic bag and put it in her pocket.

Lily turned to face the altar. Lifting the dagger in both hands, holding it high above her head with the deadly blade pointed downward, her voice rang out, echoing off the walls of the huge tomb.

"She is near. And she *will* die."

CHAPTER THIRTY-FIVE

Calvin leaned back in his chair. "I've figured out how this contraption works."

Sitting at the table with Calvin were Hawkins, Abby and Kalliste, who brushed a strand of hair away from her forehead, saying, "And I think I understand the linguistic program the ancients loaded onto this amazing mechanism."

"Kudos to both of you," Hawkins said. "Let's start with the hardware. Then Kalliste can tell us about the software."

Calvin said, "The engineering is similar to the Antikythera computer. Sizes are also comparable. Roughly sixteen inches high, half that wide and around three inches thick."

"Are those dimensional similarities more than a simple coincidence?" Abby asked.

"I'm just a dumb mechanic. What do you think, Kalliste?"

"Some experts think Archimedes designed the Greek computer. He lived in Sicily when it was a Greek colony. The Minoans had established settlements on the island years before."

"That establishes a link," Abby said.

Kalliste nodded. "The provenance is comparable as well. Not the exact location, but the fact that both computers were found on cargo ships and both were designed for navigation. Using the Greek computer a ship could navigate the sea. With the other, Minoan traders could find their way through the cultural seas of different languages."

"Might have a military application too," Hawkins observed. "It would come in handy if you intercepted the enemy's battle plans."

Calvin tapped the top of the device with a ballpoint pen. "Both computers were housed in wooden boxes, although the wood has disintegrated. They both used bronze gears. Thirty wheels in the Greek device; less than a dozen in the older gadget. The biggest gear meshed with smaller ones in both computers. When you spun the large disk in the Greek gadget it gave you the position of the moon, sun, eclipses, phases, even the years for the Olympic games."

"How was the big gear powered?" Hawkins said.

Calvin stuck the pen into an opening on the side of the mechanism. "Both devices had a crank. Give it a turn and your computer starts computing."

"How accurate was it?" Abby asked.

"Not very. Engineering was impressive, but the hand-made gears didn't allow for precision. I'll turn it over to the software expert."

Kalliste borrowed the pen and pointed to the largest gear on the Minoan mechanism. "The gears contain letters or language symbols rather than celestial information. The big disk moves the smaller ones into position so that the corresponding letters are aligned."

"What languages does it translate?" Hawkins asked.

"The alphabets used by Minoan trading partners: Egypt, Mesopotamia and Greece. The script doesn't match symbol for symbol. That was an issue in the Rosetta Stone. But you have enough matches to make a rudimentary translation. We have computers now that could fill in the blanks, but it is going to be a slow process at first."

"How soon can we start translating the scroll?" Hawkins said.

"I'll rig a crank and give the gears a lube job," Calvin said. "We'll have to run tests on the movement to make sure it doesn't fall apart, since we can't send it back to the manufacturer to repair."

Hawkins said, "In that event, let's turn in, get a good night's sleep and attack the problem first thing in the morning."

Calvin yawned. "Good idea. Where's my rack?"

"Take the bedroom on the first floor. I'll stretch out on the sofa.

The master bedroom is upstairs, if you ladies don't mind sharing. There should be plenty of room for two."

Hawkins noticed Abby's raised eyebrow. He realized too late that he had stepped off a cliff, and flapping his arms wouldn't help. He could have thanked the gods of Olympus when his phone chirped, signaling a text message. He excused himself and went outside to sit at the table on the terrace overlooking the caldera. The text was from Sutherland.

Bingo. Found a Howard Robsham in London.

Molly had added an email address and links to a number of articles about Robsham, who was a successful international financier. Hawkins scanned the stories, then wrote a quick email to Robsham.

"Dear Mr. Robsham. My name is Matt Hawkins. I'm a robotics engineer with the Woods Hole Oceanographic Institution. I'm working on an archaeological project where your grand-uncle's name has been mentioned a few times. Wondered if we might talk?"

A reply with a phone number came back almost immediately.
Call me. HR

Hawkins punched in the number. A man with a crisp patrician accent answered. "Thank you for getting back to me, Mr. Hawkins. I'm well acquainted with the Woods Hole Oceanographic Institution. You say you're in robotics?"

"That's correct. I design underwater vehicles for the military and scientific community."

"I'm not unfamiliar with the ocean technology field through my investment companies. Fascinating stuff. What can I tell you about my grand-uncle Howard?"

"As I wrote you, I've been helping an archaeologist survey involving a shipwreck that may have originated in Crete. A researcher at the Heraklion museum said that Howard Robsham specialized in Minoan studies."

"Uncle Howard was an imposing figure. Looked like those *Punch Magazine* cartoons of John Bull. I live in his house, which he left to my father who passed it down to me. As a boy I loved to come over here. Place was full of exotic artifacts. I'd read *King Solomon's Mines,* and Uncle Howard was Allan Quatermain in my young imagination."

"What can you tell me about the Robsham collection?"

"Apparently the collection was destroyed in the car crash that killed Howard. Bloody shame. He was far and above many professionals. Good friend of Ventris and Evans and the other amateurs who brought passion and knowledge to their work."

"What happened to the artifacts you saw as a boy?"

"My father turned them over to the British Museum and the museum in Heraklion you mentioned. You can see them there."

"Thanks, Mr. Robsham. You've been a great help."

"Wish I could do more. Hold on. There was one document that the museums weren't interested in because it was written in Spanish. Luckily, Uncle Howard had left it with a colleague in Athens, so it wasn't destroyed in the car crash. I had a Spanish translator look at it. Said it's a real estate transaction going back to the 1400s. Sandwiched in between a couple of pages was a document written in another language as well. Odd script. Pictures, symbols and so forth."

The comment about 'script' caught Hawkins attention.

"I'd love to see a copy. You never know."

"I have a photo on my computer. I'll send it to you via email."

"That would be very kind of you." He thanked Robsham for his trouble.

"Not at all. And thank you for reminding me what a wonderful character Howard was. Proud to be named after him."

Hawkins said goodbye. As he hung up, he heard the house door open and shut. Abby walked across the terrace and sat down next to him. She stared off at the vast darkness of the caldera. "It's just as beautiful even when you can't see it. Did you sit out here with Kalliste?"

"A few times. Why do you ask?"

"You seemed to know your way around Kalliste's house, especially the master bedroom."

Hawkins chuckled. "I guess that's pretty obvious, Abby."

"More than obvious."

"We were both in mourning. She had lost her husband. I'd turned into a gimp and had been tossed out on my butt by the Navy."

"Did it help? Being here, I mean?"

"Yes. At the time."

Abby was silent for a few seconds, then said, "You made a good choice. Kalliste is special. That's more than obvious, too. Goodnight."

She leaned across the table, kissed him on the cheek, then rose from her chair and went back into the house. Hawkins pondered the brief exchange. Abby always had a way of making his head spin. This time it was whirling like a top. He'd admitted to his ex-wife that he'd slept with another woman and she'd shown her approval with a kiss.

He went back into the house. Everyone else had turned in. Before stretching out on the sofa, he checked his electronic tablet. The email from Robsham had come through. He called up the attachment, skipped past the Spanish text and studied the lines of symbols. He immediately recognized the script as Minoan. He forwarded the attachment to Captain Santiago, asking him to take a look at the Spanish text and get back to him.

As he stretched out on the sofa, he thought about Abby again. What had he told Calvin? That their relationship was complicated. String theory is complicated. A Bach concerto is complicated. World peace is complicated. His relationship with Abby was just plain crazy.

CHAPTER THIRTY-SIX

From the balcony of the house set into the cliff above Kalliste's place, Leonidas had watched Hawkins and Abby sitting on the terrace and wondered what they had talked about. He missed having a real conversation with a beautiful woman. Isabel had filled a niche in his life, but she was more like the nubile females in bikinis who flocked around him back in his lazy drug-filled days as a surf bum. Damn. He wished he had a joint.

Putting the thought out of his mind, he concentrated on Hawkins. The guy had everything. Good looks, brains and babes. He was resourceful too. Leonidas had watched with amazement as Hawkins had coolly taken out that creep on the fortress island with nothing more than a sack full of rocks.

The technique worked so well Leonidas used a modified version on the second man in black. Leonidas was able to get above him. He pried loose a boulder the size of a football out of a wall and waited. The man came to the intersection below and started to climb. Leonidas popped up from behind the wall like a jack-in-the-box and dropped the rock on the man's head. Quick, effective, practically silent except for the wet melon sound.

Leonidas had hurried back to the dock and lost himself in the crowd waiting for an incoming boat. Two men who looked like clones of the dead guys disembarked, brushed right by him and headed for the fortress.

On the way back to the mainland the ferry passed a police boat screaming out to the island with lights flashing. One or both bodies must have been found. He figured the local gendarmes would write it off as an accident. Back on land, Leonidas checked the parking lot. No other men in black, and Hawkins's car was gone.

No big deal. He'd planted a location device on the car at the Minoan ruins. His phone app picked up the signal. He drove to the main highway, expecting Hawkins to turn off at the airport. Instead, the blinking blue dot representing the Renault continued into the city. He found the car parked near the museum.

He decided not to go in, seeing as that he was in his 'Pouty' outfit and Hawkins would spot him in a second. He quickly removed the positioning device from the bumper. It only took a few seconds to break into the car to retrieve the recorder he'd planted under the front seat. He locked the car, went back to the Suzuki and listened to the recording of the conversation.

He heard Hawkins say he planned to go to Santorini and jotted down the address Hawkins had given to Calvin over the phone. A short time later, Hawkins and Abby came out of the museum and got in their car. Leonidas was right behind them. Watching them drop their own car off and head for the airport, he then returned his own rental.

Now that he knew where their destination was, he took his time. He caught a taxi to the port and boarded the next ferry to Santorini. While most passengers were out on deck, he went into a restroom. When he emerged, Pouty had disappeared. Leonidas had on shorts, sandals, a T-shirt, and a Yankees baseball cap. In addition, he had sprouted a beard. He'd flipped from British tourist to American tourist. He was getting to like the garrulous Englishman, but he needed to blend in.

A few hours later the ferry landed at Thera and he took a bus to Oia. His first stop was the tourist office. The young woman at the desk marked the address of Kalliste's house on a map. He strolled through the narrow alleyways until he came to a small square. He walked down the stairs from the square, past the house which overlooked the caldera. It would be hard to keep it under surveillance without being seen. He went back up the stairway and saw the rental sign on a house built into the cliff above Kalliste's place. The landlord showed him a studio apartment that he immediately took, paying paid the man a week's rent in cash.

Leonidas walked through the neighborhood, memorizing the streets and alleyways. As he strolled along, his nostrils picked up a familiar scent. He followed the smell to the Kastro and found a gathering of young Americans getting high on pot. He accepted their invitation to join the party. When they had smoked all their marijuana, he offered to buy a round of drinks at a taverna.

One round turned into others and they ended up closing the place down. As he stumbled home in the darkness he thought that it was a good thing he'd memorized the neighborhood. He took a few wrong turns, but made it safely back to his apartment and passed out.

Hawkins tossed and turned on a sofa that was too short to accommodate his long body. He gave up finally and checked his watch: Five o'clock. Throwing off the blanket, he rose from the sofa and pulled his clothes on. His friends were still in bed. He made coffee, sat at the table with his tablet and read the message from Captain Santiago. Apparently the captain couldn't sleep either because the message had been sent only minutes earlier.

Dear Matt: Please get back to me immediately. I have done a partial translation. The document speaks of evil deeds.

He typed a reply.

What sort of evil deeds, Captain Santiago?

The very worst kind. This document is very dangerous. We should meet in person. Can you come to Cadiz?

Hawkins wrote that he'd come to Spain as soon as he could. He pondered the captain's message. Even after his boat sank under him the captain had displayed a calm that was almost uncanny. Yet the centuries-old parchment had spooked him. Hawkins climbed to the upstairs bedroom and knocked softly. Abby came to the door fully dressed. She and Kalliste had smelled the brewing coffee and were about to come down.

Calvin was up as well. When the group was together again, Hawkins showed them the message.

"Damn," Abby said. "Wish I had held onto the Gulfstream." She checked commercial flights on her phone. "If we leave within the next ten minutes we can catch a flight to Frankfurt. Forty-five minute layover and we can hop a plane to Cadiz. We'll be there in time for lunch."

Kalliste called a taxi. They threw their toothbrushes and a change of clothes into their bags. Within minutes, they headed out the door on the way to the main square where the cab would pick them up.

A few hundred feet away, Leonidas heard someone speaking English in the quiet of the morning.

He parted the curtains of his hangover fog, got out of bed—still wearing his rumpled clothes—and staggered to the front window just in time to see Hawkins and Abby disappear around the corner. They were carrying bags, which told him that they weren't simply going for a walk around town. He pictured himself chasing after them but decided against it. His wig had fallen off, revealing his scarred scalp. Then the waves of nausea churning in his stomach sent him running for the bathroom sink.

CHAPTER THIRTY-SEVEN

Cadiz, Spain

Lily met the DNA expert from Madrid at the courtyard restaurant of the Melia Santi Petri hotel. He had called the night before to say he had the test results. When she told him that she wanted to meet with him as soon as possible, he said he would catch a flight to Cadiz in the morning.

The slightly-built, well-groomed man in the dark blue suit and gray tie emerged from the hotel, glanced around the courtyard and saw Lily waving him over to her table. They shook hands.

"You must be Ms. Porter," he said.

"And you would be Luis Flores from the genetic profiling lab. Please have a seat."

Flores sat at the table and placed a leather briefcase on his lap.

"I'm sorry I couldn't get the test results to you earlier," he said. "Genetic testing has come a long way, but the process still involves several steps. The sample goes through a machine that isolates it from the other material, then it must be heated to magnify the DNA and frozen before it can be analyzed."

"Don't worry, Senor Flores. This was an unusual request to toss at you on such short notice. I appreciate your company's decision to give it Priority as I asked."

Flores beamed. "I was glad to do it, Ms. Porter. I'm a great fan of Hidden History. I particularly enjoyed that segment you did in Madagascar about the zombie batmen."

"Thank you. I'm sure you will also enjoy the program we just finished filming, called *Werewolves of the Paris Sewers.*"

The eyes behind the circular wire-rimmed glasses widened. "Werewolves! You certainly cover the spectrum of the supernatural." He grinned. "Anyway, on to the subject at hand. The analysis we just completed was somewhat unusual. Is it something related to a future program?"

"Hidden History is constantly researching possible projects. There are only so many zombie or vampire stories you can run."

"I can hardly wait," he said. He unsnapped the briefcase and reached in for a file folder, placing it on the table directly in front of him. He asked Lily if she knew much about genetic profiling.

"I was a reporter before I became a producer," she said. "I know a great deal about many things but not very much about one thing in particular."

"Picture the human cell as a bubble, and within that is a smaller bubble called the nucleus. Within that nucleus, both men and women have twenty-three pairs of chromosomes. When men and women conceive a child, one chromosome in each pair comes from the mother and the other from the father. The 'Y' chromosome is passed down from the father, whereas women pass along their DNA from the mitochondria that float in the space between the nucleus and the outer layer of the cell."

"All very informative, Senor Flores." She glanced at her watch. "I don't mean to rush you, but I'm on a tight schedule."

"Sorry. I felt I had to lay a foundation so you would appreciate the special problems we had to deal with in analyzing these samples."

"What kind of problems?"

"None with the hair sample. Using the polymerase chain reaction, we easily developed a genetic profile of the subject."

"Was the bone sample too old to analyze?"

"Not at all. With the latest techniques, ancient DNA can be traced back tens of thousands of years. All the way to the African 'Eve' who is supposedly the mother of all mankind. The bone sample you provided was dated between three thousand and four thousand years old. A comparatively recent period when we look back in human history."

"I'm afraid you're losing me, Mr. Flores."

"Had this been a sample from the tissues of a mummy, we could have dated the sample using the PCR process. The problem with dating ancient specimens is that skeletal remains, bones and teeth, are fragile and highly degradable. No cells are preserved, which means we can't use the PCR lab procedure I described a moment ago. It is *mitochondrial*, not the nuclear DNA, that survives."

"You said you could date a specimen back to Eve."

"Yes, Eve, but not Adam. Mitochondrial markers are passed down from the maternal line, not the paternal one. The bone sample came from a male, so it was impossible to make the genetic connection between the two samples."

"That's disappointing, Senor Flores. I had hoped you could do better," Lily said in a flat tone of voice.

"I had hoped so as well," he said with a sigh. "This is a fascinating assignment, and I would have loved to establish a connection between the two samples. But not all is lost. It's possible that circumstantial evidence may establish a link."

He opened the file folder, extracted two sheets of paper and slid them across the table. Printed on each sheet was a pie-chart and a map of the world's continents with areas that were color coded. He tapped the pie-chart labeled "Subject A" with the tip of his finger. "This is the genetic profile from the bone sample. What do you see?"

"It is almost entirely in red except for a small sliver in green."

"Correct. The island of Crete on the map is also in red, indicating that the individual we're interested in is almost entirely of Cretan origin. The green sliver corresponds to the area around the eastern Mediterranean where the subject had ancestral antecedents."

Lily stared at the other pie-chart. "Tell me more about the diagram."

"As you can see, most of the chart is red, indicating that the subject is around ninety percent Cretan. Subject B is around fifty per cent pure Cretan, with the balance mostly Spanish and other western European areas."

"What's this?" she said, pointing to an irregular black section of Crete that was the same in both maps.

"You have a quick eye. That's the circumstantial evidence I mentioned. This is the Lassithi Plateau. Some scholars refer to it as the *Machu Picchu* of the ancient Minoan civilization. As Crete was overrun by various invaders, the last of the Minoans retreated to the plateau and the adjoining mountain slopes."

"Are you saying that both subjects go back to Lassithi?"

"Their genes do. In fact, they go back to the Neolithic people who first settled the island more than seven thousand years ago. These were small settlements. Families intermarried, so it's entirely possible the subjects were related. I can't confirm that. You'll have to go back along the maternal line. We'll try to refine the search and see if we can come up with anything that we didn't pick up with the initial analysis."

"Thank you, Senor Flores. May I keep these charts?"

"I printed them out for you to keep. I'll be looking forward to the Paris werewolves. Please let me know when the program airs."

"I'll do that," Lily said, forcing a smile.

After a quick handshake Flores headed back into the hotel and Lily sat down again and studied the pie charts and maps. The skull sample produced no surprises. Minos could trace his Cretan ancestors back for centuries. But the chart based on the hair sample from Kalliste Kalchis really intrigued her.

The Cretan section indicated that Kalliste and Minos *both* descended from inhabitants of Crete who had arrived on the island in Neolithic times. The king's daughter had moved from Crete which accounted for Spanish and European DNA in the genetic profile of her descendant.

One pie slice caught her eye. It was much thinner than the others and constituted only a small percentage of the chart for Kalliste. The sliver showed that she had a distant ancestor from the Caucasus. Lily tapped out Caucasus in the Google space of her phone. The northern part of the region on the coast of the Black Sea in ancient times was known as *Colchis*.

She Googled *Colchis*. As she read further, her pulse began to race. *Colchis* was the home of Medea, daughter of the king who lost the Golden Fleece to Jason and the Argonauts. Medea had a niece named, Persiphae. Lily looked up Persiphae and confirmed what she already knew; Persiphae was the wife of King Minos. How could she have missed it?

Names often change over time. Even her own, Lily, came from Lil-ee, the sacred flower of the Minoan goddess Britomartis, who went back to the Neolithic era. But Lily's ancient name was not Porter, but Portina, Minoan Mistress of the Animals.

Colchis. *Kalchis.*

It was no coincidence. Kalliste was descended from the daughter of King Minos.

She had to bring Kalliste to her long overdue fate in the Maze. The decree from the High Priestess whose mummy sat on a throne in the Maze had been passed down through the centuries. The spawn of Minos must be given to the Mother Goddess if the Way of the Axe were to prosper.

Lily silently mouthed the old chants, murmurings that had their roots in the primitive rituals when men lived in caves. The past seemed like a river rushing through her brain, but the sound it made was not water but a chorus of voices. An image flashed before her eyes. The photograph on the wall of Kalliste's apartment. White cubical houses set against black ashen cliffs. The Mother Goddess was leading the way.

"Would you like more coffee, Madame?"

The waiter standing at her table had come over to see if Lily needed anything. She snapped out of her trance, gave him her playful TV producer smile, then scooped up the graphs and stuffed them into her pocketbook. She rose from her chair.

"I'm fine, thank you. I'm very fine indeed."

CHAPTER THIRTY-EIGHT

Miguel picked up Hawkins and Abby at Malaga Airport and drove them to the Santiago apartment in an upscale part of Cadiz. Captain Santiago greeted the visitors with effusive bear hugs and introduced his wife, Louisa, a pretty woman with the broad smile that had been passed down to her son.

The sturdy dining room table groaned under the weight of the Spanish appetizers known as *tapas*. The dishes included meatballs in spicy tomato sauce, garlic prawns and olives of every size and color. All washed down with an oak-aged *Rioja* wine.

After lunch, Captain Santiago led his guests to his dark-paneled study. He pointed out the painting of Cervantes hanging over the fireplace. Photos of the salvage boats that had given the captain and his family a comfortable living hung on the walls.

Hawkins recognized a photo of the *Sancho Panza*. Santiago noticed his pained expression. "It's all right, Matt. The sea giveth and the sea taketh away. So make sure you have insurance."

"Words of wisdom from Cervantes?"

"No." The captain jabbed his chest with a forefinger. "From Santiago."

He unlocked a desk drawer and pulled out a large mailing envelope. Inviting his guests to take a seat, he settled into a stuffed leather chair. He opened the envelope and extracted a print-out of the document Hawkins had sent him.

"I must ask you a question," he said to Matt. "Where did you get this?"

"From an Englishman named Robsham. It was among papers he inherited that once belonged to his great-uncle. Do you know what it is?"

Santiago nodded. "A deed of penance. Basically a real estate transfer that dates back to the 16th century, regarding the transfer of property in the *Castilla La Mancha*."

Hawkins glanced at the portrait of Cervantes. "As in 'Man of La Mancha'?"

"The very same countryside where the Knight of the Sorrowful Countenance roamed. It's a region in the central part of Spain. Very flat and desolate. Known for its windmills, like the one Don Quixote battled, while imagining they were giants. I've traveled there a number of times. I've seen the property described in the document. It's a medieval castle, surrounded by abandoned vineyards and farmlands. No inhabited villages or towns lay nearby."

"You would think that the vineyards would generate local commerce," Abby said.

"Perhaps at one time; long ago," Santiago said. "According to the legends I've heard, the area has long been plagued by strange happenings that drove people away."

"What sort of happenings?"

"People disappeared. Mostly young and mostly female. The villagers suspected the disappearances had something to do with the castle, which was home to a secretive order of monks. Many of the locals moved away. After some people were killed by some huge creatures who attacked them in church, the remaining inhabitants decided that even the Almighty couldn't help, so they deserted their village."

"What sort of creatures?" Abby said.

"They were said to be demonic dogs. The story goes back to the mid-1500s. It was on a Sunday and the people were at worship when two massive dogs burst down the doors and ran among the kneeling congregation, maiming and killing. They ripped the throats out of six people. Churches could be targets for brigands, so the villagers always carried weapons under their cloaks. Some attacked the animals with their knives and swords. Witnesses heard a whistle and saw one dog go to a man standing outside the church. He appeared to be a monk from the castle. He left without a word with the dog at his side. The other animal ran off, leaving a trail of blood."

"Tell us more about these dogs," Hawkins said.

"The animals were as tall as a man and had eyes that were flaming red; or bright yellow, depending on the storyteller. Their heads were skull-like, with a thick ruff around the neck, and they had long, narrow snouts."

"Good thing it's only a legend," Hawkins said.

Santiago hiked up his thick eyebrows. "Maybe not. A few years ago researchers digging near the foundation of the old church found the bones of a gigantic dog lying in a shallow grave. The dog would have stood more than seven feet on its hind legs and weighed more than two hundred pounds. Its skull shape matched the descriptions and led the researchers to believe that it was a hybrid of some sort."

"Fascinating, but maybe we should get back to the document Matt sent you," Abby said. "You described it as a 'deed of penance.'"

"The deed was an invention of the Inquisition. Loss of your property was part of the penalty paid by the accused. The document was basically fiction to make the theft of property legal. No money was mentioned in the papers. The Salazar family listed as beneficiaries took ownership for what was termed a 'consideration.' In other words, it was never paid for," Santiago said.

"Lucky buyer."

"The Salazar family has always made its own luck."

"Who are the Salazars?" Hawkins asked.

"They are a prominent family that go back a long time. They are very rich and own many businesses. Their biggest one is Auroch Industries. It started as a mining company and now has holdings around the world."

"Impressive."

"That's the *who*. More important is *what* the Salazars are. The family has a bad reputation. There are stories of their rivals mysteriously disappearing in the old days. It's very strange, but the Salazar family was never prosecuted. Most of the family has died out in recent years so you rarely hear anything about them."

"Your message mentioned 'evil deeds,'" Abby said. "Were you talking about the family's criminal activities?"

"What I mentioned is the sort of thing you would expect of any criminal organization. The document suggests that the Salazars have a past that is much more evil than I knew of."

"More evil than murdering rivals?" Abby said.

"Sadly, yes. I'm a simple mariner. If you're ready, I'll introduce you to an expert on evil."

CHAPTER THIRTY-NINE

Minutes later, they were in the captain's car heading out of the city. After about a half-hour's drive, Miguel parked in front of a chapel at the end of a quiet street. A man was kneeling at the edge of a flowerbed in front of the building.

With the others following him, Santiago got out of the car and went over to the gardener. "*Buenos Dias*, Father Francisco. Good to see you on your knees doing honest work."

The man turned and a broad grin came to a face that closely resembled the captain's, except for the pale complexion and the shorter haircut.

"*Buenos Dias*, Brother. Have you come to my church to confess your sins?"

"You would need a bigger church to hold all my sins."

"Then we had better start now."

Both men burst into laughter. The gardener stuck the trowel into the flowerbed and extended his hand to the captain who helped him to his feet. He brushed the dirt off his sweatshirt and the knees of his baggy pants, then the two men gave each other a big hug. The priest offered the same greeting to the captain's son.

Santiago then introduced Hawkins and Abby. "These are the friends I told you about. This is my twin brother, Francisco, who chose to follow the church instead of the sea."

"We are not so different. My brother salvages ships and I salvage souls. Excuse my un-priestly appearance. The diocese considers my church too small to employ the services of a gardener, so I tend the grounds myself. Come, I'll show you around."

Father Francisco led the way through the front door into the chapel. The interior was of simple design, long and narrow, with rows of oak pews squeezed between whitewashed walls. The air was heavy with the smell of incense. An ornately carved gilded altarpiece was flanked by statues of saints and angels.

Abby glanced around the chapel, and said, "It's beautiful."

"Thank you, senora. The 16th century, when the Capilla de St. Vincent was built, was a time when the visual arts flourished. Unfortunately, it was a time when the Church succumbed to the basest of human instincts."

"I told my friends that you were better qualified than I to speak of evil deeds," the captain said.

"That description doesn't even approach what happened during the more than three hundred years of the Spanish Inquisition. The torture and killing have been well-documented, but one of the most pernicious aspects was the right the Inquisition gave itself to confiscate the property of the accused. They were held prisoner, sometimes for years before their trial. Those who were part of the inner circle of the Inquisition became very wealthy at the expense of the poor souls who suffered."

"Which meant that they had little incentive to judge someone as innocent," Abby said.

"The senora is astute. Stolen property fueled the Inquisition and made it an unstoppable force. At first confiscated wealth went to the king and queen. Later, the loot went to the Holy Office and made its way down the line to the central council, tribunals, and the various officials who processed the victims like animals on a slaughterhouse conveyor belt."

"Where does the document figure in?" Hawkins asked.

"The Inquisition kept detailed records of its financial dealings to aid in its persecutions, to justify their criminality and, like any big business, to keep track of cash flow. The document my brother showed me is a letter regarding the transfer of property from a victim to a new owner."

"Captain Santiago said the property was a castle in Castilla La Mancha."

"This is true. It was originally owned by a lesser nobleman named Hernandez. Someone wanted the property. That was that. He was imprisoned, tortured, tried and put to death."

"What crime was he accused of?" Abby said.

"Heresy, which was broadly defined. People were arrested for offenses as trivial as wearing clean linen or not eating pork."

"Even Cervantes came to the attention of the Inquisition," the captain said. "He had to censor his writing to avoid prosecution."

"Cervantes was lucky," Father Francisco said. "Hernandez was doomed to the stake for being a *negativo*, which meant he denied the charges and refused to confess. Of course had he admitted his heresy, he would have been convicted as well."

"Captain Santiago said that the castle went to the Salazar family."

"Correct. Eduardo Salazar was a mining tycoon who must have enjoyed favor with the Inquisition to have been the recipient of such largesse. It's a mystery why he was chosen, seeing as that most of the people who benefited from the confiscations were part of the Inquisition bureaucracy."

"Maybe it was for services rendered," Hawkins said.

"What kind of services would get him such a big pay-off?" Abby said.

"There is mention in the document of Salazar providing labor to do some work on the castle."

"Maybe it was a run-down property that needed work. What American real estate agents call a fixer-upper," Abby said. "Salazar ran mining operations. He could have provided people from his labor pool to do the work."

"Perhaps," the priest said. "Whatever the reason, he apparently enjoyed great favor of the *Promotor Fiscal*, the public prosecutor for that council. His name was Henrique del Norte."

"Norte, meaning North?" Abby said.

"Yes. I can show you his portrait. It's in the church library."

"If it's not too much trouble," Hawkins said.

They went through a door into a room lined with ornately-bound books and smelling of old paper. Father Santiago slid one volume off a shelf and placed the book on a table. He slipped on a pair of white cloth gloves and carefully turned the pages. He stopped at a back-and-white portrait that took up a full page.

"May I introduce you to Senor del Norte."

The man dressed in a dark robe and floppy hat had piercing, almond-shaped eyes set in a cruel face. His dark hair hung in bangs over his forehead. The chin was pointed and the nose far too large for the narrow face. Even more interesting, except for having hair, he was a clone of the blue-headed man Hawkins had killed on the fortress island of Spinalonga. Hawkins had to do everything he could to keep from bursting out in the colorful language he had picked up as a Navy SEAL.

Instead, he said, "Thank you for your time, Father Santiago."

"No trouble at all. I needed a rest from my gardening. And it's always good to see my brother. Please let me know if I can be of further help."

On the drive back into Cadiz, Hawkins asked the captain to drop them off near the harbor. Their plane back to Santorini didn't leave for a few hours. Captain Santiago said to call him for a ride to the airport.

As the car pulled away, Abby said, "Okay, what gives? I saw the way your jaw dropped when you looked at the portrait of Senor del Norte. I know from experience that it takes a lot to make that happen."

"This *was* a lot. Except for the hair, Del Norte was a dead ringer for the guys who chased us all over Crete."

It was Abby's chin that now dropped. "How could that be?"

"Dunno." He jerked his thumb at a nearby waterfront café. "Let's talk about it over a cup of coffee."

They sat at a table and ordered a couple of espressos. When the waiter went off to retrieve their order, Abby said, "I noticed that you didn't give the captain the section of document written in Linear A."

"I wanted him to focus," Hawkins said. "It would have been confusing."

She hiked an eyebrow. "How much more confusing can it get?"

Hawkins smiled. "What do you make of all this, Ab?"

Abby's keen mind had propelled her to the top of her class at

Annapolis and her analytical skills had built the foundation of a successful worldwide corporation, so she was definitely the person to ask.

She gazed off at the harbor.

"It all goes back to Crete," she began. "Crete is the hub of a big wheel. Spokes reach from the center. The sunken ship came from Crete. So did the device. Robsham visited Crete, where he found his collection of Linear A tablets and died. Professor Vedrakis was murdered there."

"The wheel is good analogy as far as it goes. We've found more spokes. Now we've got the Inquisition, Auroch Industries, castles in Spain, the Salazar family past and present, and del Norte." Hawkins said. "All apparently unconnected to Crete."

"Maybe we don't see the connection because the spokes are a blur as long as the wheel is moving. Let's try a linear approach. Start with the Salazars and work our way backwards to Eduardo Salazar who leads to del Norte, who leads to someone or something else. Maybe Molly could work up a time line."

"Good suggestion, Abby. I'll get her on it right away."

He texted a message on his cell to Molly asking her to dig up what she could on the Salazars and Auroch. He said he would give her a complete update after he returned to Santorini. After contacting Sutherland, he texted Calvin, asking how things were going.

Calvin replied almost immediately. Hawkins read the message to Abby.

"Device working. Slow going. But have deciphered the name of the scroll's author."

"Don't keep me in suspense," she said. "Who was the author?"

Hawkins relayed the question.

Calvin's text came back in a flash. When Hawkins read the word, the right side of his mouth turned up in a smirk.

"You remember asking, how much more confusing it could get?"

"I remember saying something like that."

He handed the phone over so Abby could see the reply displayed on the screen.

"This is the name of the guy who wrote the scroll. *That's* how confusing it can get."

CHAPTER FORTY

Calvin had fashioned a hand crank for the device after rummaging in a kitchen drawer. Using a paring knife, he carved the narrower end of an old-fashioned potato masher to fit the square opening. Then he screwed the handle of a meat-grinder into the wider end. He inserted the makeshift crank into the socket and cautiously turned the handle. A wide grin came to his face.

"How old did you say this gadget is?" he asked Kalliste.

"Four thousand years or so."

He chuckled softly. "Folks who designed this gadget would have a good laugh if they saw the primitive operating system I've rigged."

Kalliste had been watching with doubt in her eyes, but she applauded when the olive oil lubricated gears began to turn.

"It's working! You're amazing, Calvin."

"Matt and I had to improvise a few times back in Afghanistan."

"Matt told me about his Navy experiences. I'm glad to see that he is not as bitter as he was when we first met."

"Me, too. I'm surprised Matt opened up to you. He kept things close to his chest for a long time."

"We had both suffered personal loss, so we had lot in common. I was pleased to meet Abby. Matt talked about her a lot. They are obviously good friends. Too bad they can't be closer."

Calvin made a zipping motion across his lips. "Matt's told me in so many words to butt out of his personal life."

She mimicked the gesture. "Then I will, too. For now." She glanced down at the scroll and thought back to the hours she had spent as a girl gazing at the symbols until they seemed to dance before her eyes. "I will choose a pictogram. You will line it up to the corresponding Egyptian hieroglyph. Then we'll go from there."

"Sounds good," Calvin said. "Ready when you are."

She unrolled the scroll further. "There is a word at the end of the text, where we would place a signature. Maybe if I start there we can learn the name of the scroll's author."

She copied a symbol onto a pad of paper. Calvin cranked the handle until the pictograph matched a hieroglyph on an adjoining disk. At the same time, another part of the gear was placed in line with the disk Kalliste had identified as archaic Greek. She copied the Egyptian pictograph and the Greek letter, as well.

They went to the next letter, going through the same labor-intensive procedure, until Kalliste had listed eight symbols. She told Calvin to take a break while she tried to figure out the Greek script. This entailed going through a couple of thick textbooks to translate the archaic language into ancient Greek, then into modern-day language.

Minutes stretched into hours. While Kalliste poured through her volumes Calvin made coffee, then whipped together a Greek salad which she ate as she worked. At one point she speared a black olive but, instead of eating it, placed the fork down on her plate.

"Calvin," she whispered. "I think I have figured out who wrote the scroll. It doesn't make sense, though."

"You're not going to tell me those pictures spell out 'Kilroy Was Here.' "

"Mr. Kilroy was definitely *not* here," she said. She spun the notepad around so he could read the English translation:

M-I-N-O-T-A-U-R

"Joke's on us, Kalliste. Guy used a pen name."

"I'm not sure why he would pick the name of such an ugly creature. The Minotaur was the half-man, half-bull monster buried in the core of the Cretan Labyrinth where he guarded the treasure of Knossos. Athenian youth were sacrificed to the Minotaur. An intended victim was Theseus, who killed the Minotaur with the help of Ariadne, the daughter of Minos."

"This Minotaur sounds like a busy guy. In between chewing on Athenians and getting killed, it's amazing he had any time to do any writing at all."

She tapped the device with her pen.

"At the rate we're going, it might take another four thousand years to decipher the entire script."

Calvin looked at his watch and saw that it was afternoon. "What say we take a break? I'll go into town to fetch some grub for when Matt and Abby return. When I get back, we'll dig into it again. Maybe we can polish off the first thousand years before midnight."

"That's a good suggestion, Calvin. I'll go over my notes. Maybe ghosts of the past will rise from the caldera and whisper secrets in my ear."

"Whatever works, Kalliste. See ya in a bit."

Leonidas was returning from a stroll when he saw Calvin emerge from the house without Kalliste.

With nothing else to occupy him, Leonidas followed Calvin down an alley and into the commercial section of the village. He lingered outside an all-purpose market until Calvin came out with some bags of groceries and headed back towards the house. Leonidas thought about following him, but Calvin might suspect something if he saw the same American tourist everywhere he went.

He strolled to the main village square and was sitting at a taverna having a beer when a taxi pulled up at the curb and three men got out. His hand automatically slid under his shirt and rested on the holster at his belt. The first two men exiting the cab looked like the thugs he had chased away from Gournia and later encountered on Spinalonga.

Leonidas couldn't believe his eyes when he saw who the third man was. Salazar. He was dressed casually and the brim of his Borsalino straw hat was pulled down over his dark sunglasses. Leonidas recognized the wide jutting chin and the muscular shoulders bulging under the blue linen jacket. The Spaniard paid the taxi driver, then he and the other men headed into the village. Leonidas was right behind them.

Kalliste sat on the terrace behind her house and gazed out at the caldera. She pondered her situation. She had been blessed as an archaeologist to start unraveling not one, but a number of the mysteries that had defied historical scholars for centuries. The gods of Olympus must be laughing at their joke; the tantalizing gifts they had bestowed upon future humanity were still out of reach.

She possessed the key to Linear A, but using the mechanism to decipher a lost language that consisted of hundreds of pictograms was a fool's errand. She needed the help of expert linguists, philologists and computer capacity. And all that would cost money.

She had cut her ties to the government, but Greece wouldn't have the funds to sponsor her project even if they wanted to. She knew of only one potential source of financing. She went back into her house, picked up her phone and punched in a number.

Lily Porter answered, "Kalliste! How wonderful to hear your voice."

"Yours, too, Lily. I have a great favor to ask."

"Yes, of course, Kalliste. I want to know all about it."

CHAPTER FORTY-ONE

Molly pointed her D3X Nikon camera at the olive and yellow bird sitting on the top branch of a rabbit bush. She sat on a folding stool, hidden in the wheat grass in the high desert region known as the Badlands Wilderness, around fifteen miles east of Bend. The camera rested on a carbon fiber tripod, the 600mm lens pointed at the fat, little short-tailed bird. She pressed the shutter release and banged off a dozen or so photos of the MacGillivray's warbler before it flew away.

Her camera had captured images of dusky fly-catchers, yellow-rumped warblers and a Golden eagle to add to her photo files. She had taken pictures of these birds on previous field trips, but like any photographer, she was always looking for *the* photograph. The click of the shutter when action, light and color conditions were perfect.

Time to wrap things up. Her knees creaked from sitting and she was getting hungry. In line with her vow to keep to a healthy diet, Molly had dined on oatmeal and fresh blueberries before she'd left the house, and ate a protein bar out in the field. Packing up her camera and stool in a carry-all bag, she slung the tripod over her shoulder and hiked back to the dirt road where she had parked her motorcycle.

After returning to her house, she went out to the shed to see how the eagle was doing. He seemed content, but that didn't lessen her guilt. She would set him free tomorrow. Having made her decision, she headed for the kitchen. She made herself a toasted ham and Havarti sandwich on multi-grain bread, opened a bag of sweet potato chips and popped a can of Diet Coke. Carrying her lunch to her office, she clicked on the computer. The message from Hawkins popped up on the screen.

Hi, Molly. Hope you're well. Need you to dig into Auroch Industries and CEO Viktor Salazar. Thanks. MH.

The email was around two hours old. She munched on her sandwich as she reread the request. Molly was glad to help. So far, it was easy stuff, like tracking down the arms dealer in The Netherlands, but she didn't want Matt or anyone else to take her for granted.

Relax girl, you can't spend the rest of your life talking only to birds.

She finished her Coke, thought about heading back into the kitchen for dessert, but pushed the temptation aside.

Eventually, she'd weaken, but Molly was energized by her temporary resolve. Auroch Industries. *Funny name*, she thought to herself.

Looking up Auroch on the internet, images of a weird-looking cow popped up on the screen. She'd come from a farming community, but had never seen anything closely resembling this animal. Probably because the Auroch was an extinct species of cattle. The last one died in 17th century Poland. The breed had a pretty good run until then, and was probably domesticated in Neolithic times.

Dang thing was big. Stood six feet high at the shoulders and could weigh more than a ton. The critter had crazy-looking horns that went up, forward, then turned in. Its body shape looked like pictures she'd seen of Spanish fighting bulls. Like those animals, it could move fast and was sometimes aggressive toward humans. Nothing like the friendly dairy cows that grazed the scraggly fields behind her family's shack in West Virginia. She wondered why anyone would name a corporation after a big cow.

The company name was familiar…as well as odd.

She Googled Auroch Industries and pulled up a pile of news articles. Molly may be reclusive, but she was not uninformed. She read a number of on-line publications, which is how she had first come across the article on sexual abuse in the military. One of the stories was a report in the *New York Times* that she had read a few months ago. The headline caught her eye because it had to do with the latest in a series of mining accidents occurring at or near Auroch sites. Auroch was the target of some environmental groups. Good luck pitching a hissie fit, she remembered thinking. West Virginia mining companies got away with murder.

She proceeded to the company's website.

The logo was a stylized bull's horns like those on the flesh and blood animal. Auroch was one of the worlds' ten largest mining, metals and petroleum companies with headquarters in Cadiz, Spain. The corporate history said that Auroch was an old company, its origins stretching back to the 17th century. It came into existence with the consolidation of a number of mining companies in Spain and had expanded into more than thirty countries around the globe.

Flowing from that wellspring was a river of iron ore, coal, diamonds, manganese, gold, petroleum, aluminum, copper, natural gas, nickel, uranium and silver. The statistics were stunning. Auroch earned more than fifty billion dollars a year and had more than forty-thousand people working for the mining operation and a dozen subsidiaries. It owned smelters and refining companies and was a major producer of fossil fuels.

Molly puffed out her cheeks. This was no fly-by-night operation Hawkins was asking her to stick her nose into. Its security wall would be tough to breach. A company as big as Auroch could hardly be invisible. She would comb the information available on unsecured sources first. She clicked off the website and skimmed the dozens of files.

After twenty minutes or so, she had built a mental image of the company in her mind. They stayed under the radar for the first few hundred years. Then Auroch got into steel manufacturing in 1915, on the eve of World War I, putting it in a position to profit from massive arms production.

She started digging into the company's more recent history. Auroch was one of the world's major polluters, joining a group of ninety responsible for two-thirds of the globe's greenhouse gas emissions. Auroch operations had been responsible for hundreds of deaths, from landslides, explosions, poisonous emissions—even an earthquake triggered by its fracking techniques. All lethal. All summed up as 'accidents.'

A news clip caught her attention. It was an account of a mine accident in Africa that killed more than a hundred miners. An explosion had occurred in a poorly ventilated gold mine. Auroch claimed that the mine was owned by the subsidiary of a subsidiary, thus it bore no responsibility. The corrupt government investigators agreed.

Molly got a lump in her throat. A similar mine explosion had killed her favorite uncle back in West Virginia. Uncle Gowdy had left a wife and six kids behind. His mine was cited with hundreds of safety violations but the owners pulled strings and spread bribes. Like the case in Africa, no one was called into account. Her family tried to help her aunt and cousins. They would bake fried chicken, make cold potato salad and toss a few coins their way when they had any, but they couldn't erase the grief and misery.

Her curiosity now stirred, she looked up the company her uncle had worked for at the time of his death. It had gone out of business decades ago, its assets acquired by other companies which in turn went bankrupt or sold out. There was still coal in the ground, attracting the attention of a large corporation that started huge strip copper mining operations, devastating the once-beautiful countryside and polluting the air and water. The mines no longer worked, but the scars they inflicted remained.

Molly was on a roll. Her fingers flew over the keyboard. Images flashed onto the screen. Government records. Company reports. News clips. Legal filings. She hacked into data banks when necessary, her photographic memory categorizing the details. She had a funny habit of blinking when she sunk her teeth into something that excited her. By the time she reached the end of her search, her eyes were fluttering so hard behind the circular eyeglass frames that she could hardly see. What made her stop was a footnote in a government investigation of Uncle Gowdy's accident.

The real owners of the mine had been hidden under layers of corporate insulation. But in the small print of the national mine safety board she found what she was looking for. The corporate owner of the mine was Auroch Industries. She set her jaw. This had just become personal.

She went back to the Auroch website and looked up the company officers. The corporation was privately held. The CEO and President was Viktor Salazar, the man Hawkins had asked her to investigate. She gazed at the photograph of the olive-skinned man with the bullet head and beetling brow. She'd been asked to dig up dirt on Salazar, but she wasn't going to stop there. She was going to wipe the phony smile off his ugly face.

Molly kept digging. Minutes after she began, she read a news story out of Cadiz, saying that Auroch Industries had donated money toward the establishment of a foundation to explore alternatives to fossil fuel. The news seemed at odds with what she had learned about the company and its leader. She read more and discovered she wasn't the only one who had expressed disbelief. Several environmentalists were quoted, including one who referred to Auroch as a 'wolf in sheep's clothing.' She looked up the name of the environmental organization and discovered their headquarters was in Portland, Oregon. She called the telephone number listed. The recorded message said that the phone was no longer in use and forwarded her to the number for a law firm. Molly always had a direct manner, so when the phone was answered, she told the receptionist that she wanted to talk to the environmentalist about Viktor Salazar.

A woman came on the phone, said the organization was defunct, and asked why she had called.

"I'm from West Virginia," she said. "My name is Molly Sutherland. My favorite uncle was killed in a mine accident that shouldn't have happened. Auroch Industries was the owner of the mine. I want to get to Viktor Salazar."

"Do you want to sue him?"

"No," Molly said. She had darker reasons in mind. "I just want to find out more about him. I saw that the organization is in Portland. I live in Bend."

"Hold on, Ms. Sutherland. I'll see what I can do."

A few minutes later the lawyer came back on the phone.

"I can set up a meeting with someone who is knowledgeable

about Mr. Salazar. Can you come to Portland?"

Molly had a flashback of her Uncle Gowdy strumming his guitar and singing on the front porch of his house.

She didn't hesitate. "How about tomorrow morning?"

CHAPTER FORTY-TWO

Salazar didn't know who had put two Priors out of commission on Crete but he could have jumped for joy when he heard the news. The assassins who did the bidding of the Way would have to be eliminated if he were to carry out his plan, and that could have been a problem. One never knew where they were. They didn't even have real names, except for the four cardinal directions.

With only two Priors remaining of the monastic order that had once protected the Maze, Lily found it necessary to call on Salazar to back up their mission to Santorini, where they would retrieve the translating device, kidnap Kalliste and kill Hawkins. He had said he would get right on it, speaking in the same subservient tone that the Salazar family had used with its masters since they had established their unholy alliance centuries before, but he could barely keep himself from gloating.

Salazar was determined to end that arrangement and, to do so, had secretly been building his power base. He had to be extremely careful, especially around Lily who had the ear of the High Priestess. Any hint that he was forming a private army to counter the Priors and the mercenaries who protected the priestess would have brought quick retribution from the Maze. He'd characterized the group of bodyguards he'd gathered around him as his personal security staff, the type needed to protect the CEO of a major corporation.

Lily reluctantly allowed Salazar to bring his men into the plan after he pointed out that a kidnapping in a crowded neighborhood would be tricky. Hawkins was a former Navy SEAL and had already eluded two attempts to kill him. Just using the Priors would put them at risk. Sunglasses covered their strange eyes, and the Greek fishermen's caps hid their brightly-colored scalps, but not their wolfish features. The collarless Greek shirts they had bought in Thera added color to their otherwise funereal outfits. The result was slightly grotesque, and there was still something repellant and menacing about their appearance that would be imprinted in the memory of anyone who encountered them.

Salazar's team had arrived separately. Some sharp-eyed taverna waiter or shop owner would remember the hard-faced men, with physiques like gorillas, wandering suspiciously around the narrow streets and alleys. Their polo shirts and shorts only emphasized their muscular arms and legs. But he had recruited the most elite of his mercenaries for this mission. They would be in and out before anyone put things together.

As he walked along under the hot Greek sun he reveled at the opportunity to unleash his more violent instincts. His career had come full circle. Here he was again managing a team of killers. Salazar had worked his way up the family criminal organization ladder as an enforcer and enjoyed the killing and maiming that went with the job.

He had ordered his men to spread out around the village until he located the house. Even with the address, Kalliste's place was hard to find. He walked along a walled path above the jumble of houses that sprawled along the terraces of the caldera until he came to a small square with a fountain in the center. An elderly woman in a black dress was crossing the square. He asked where he could find the address.

She gave him a 14-karat smile and pointed to stairs that led down off the square. He thanked her and descended a stone-paved stairway to a house built into the cliff. He raised his camera and took pictures of the cliffs, but his mind was busy planning the assault.

Salazar approached the kidnapping of the Greek woman as he would a mining operation. Locate. Extract. Transport. Process. His men would knock on the door, burst in like a SWAT team, kill Hawkins and the Greek woman and procure the device. He had asked the Priors to cover the square to intercept anyone who escaped the assault.

He would summon the Priors down to take charge of Kalliste. His men would kill them and set fire to the house. Lily would be told that the device was destroyed in the fire. With no Priors to intimidate them, the Auroch corporate officers he'd been cultivating would come over to his side. He'd persuade them that Auroch no longer needed the Minoans and their mumbo-jumbo. With the High Priestess on her death bed, the time was ripe for a coup.

He was under no illusions. His ambitious plan was like an inverted pyramid. Success or failure depended on what happened in the next few hours.

Leonidas was having a hard time finding a coil of rope. Oia had no shortage of tavernas, jewelry and souvenir shops that sold refrigerator magnets of the Parthenon. But he was unable to find a good, old-fashioned hardware store. He would have given his right arm for a Home Depot. Coming to the mule path at the edge of the town, he looked out at the fishing boats tied up at the quay.

Suddenly inspired, he made his way down the switchbacks and headed to the nearest boat. The captain was too polite to ask why this crazy tourist wanted rope, and he dug out a fifty-foot coil of manila rope encrusted with dry seaweed, handed it over and gladly accepted the wad of bills. Leonidas asked if he had more. The fisherman dug out another coil. Leonidas hung the coils over his shoulder and caught a mule ride to the top of the path.

Back in his apartment, he attached one line to the balcony railing. It was about a thirty-foot drop to the cliff below. He tied knots in the rope at intervals. Not exactly a department store escalator, but it would have to do. Next he needed an escape route. Taking the second coil of rope with him, he left the apartment and followed a path along the rim of the caldera. The sun was setting, transforming the violet waters into a shimmering lake of silver, when he found what he was looking for.

Half an hour later he was back on the roof of his apartment. He stoked up the doobie he had scored from the German kids on the old kastro. After a few tokes of the high-powered cannabis a foolish grin came to his face. He took another drag, snuffed the joint and went back into the house. He pulled a chair up to a mirror and dug into his disguise kit.

As he peeled the tourist face off and begin to apply his new features over the scarred flesh, he was already praising himself that this would be one of the best make-up jobs he'd ever done.

Hell, maybe it would even earn him an Oscar.

CHAPTER FORTY-THREE

Kalliste peered through a magnifying glass at the inked symbols on the vellum. To the left of the scroll was a thick lexicon of archaic Greek. On the other side was a yellow, legal-sized notepad filled with symbols and pictograms. Calvin sat patiently at the table waiting to give the handle another crank.

When she finally raised her head from her work, Kalliste had a weary, but triumphant smile on her face.

"Eureka," she said. Her voice came out as a croak. "I've got it. Correction. I've got *part* of it, but I don't know what I've got."

She turned the pad around so Calvin could see what she had written below the word Minotaur. The first sentence of the scroll read:

"O my King as thou hast (commanded) thy humble protector of thy treasure(s) has (written) the story of thy greatness and wisdom."

Calvin had listened to Kalliste's sighs of frustration for the last hour. He tapped the notebook with his fingertip. "Looks like you're getting somewhere."

"After the first flush of victory with the Minotaur I thought I would quickly make progress, but this is the best I can do after hours of painstaking work. It reinforces my decision to seek outside money from the Hidden History channel for linguistics expertise. Maybe I should put this off until I know if that's a possibility."

Calvin tried to back her up. "That might not be a bad idea," he said. "Why don't we decide what we want to do after we go over the latest stuff?"

"A good idea. My brain is frazzled. Tell me what you think this means. The words in parenthesis are educated guesses."

He read the sentence again. "Easy call. Our pal Minotaur worked for the king who ordered him to write his boss's biography. Like anyone in that position, he's gonna butter up the guy who signs his paycheck."

"Very good, Calvin. As to the author?"

"He's been given an important and sensitive job. That means he's pretty close to the king. Maybe even a confidant." He paused. "He describes himself as a protector, which may mean he's military." Calvin read the notebook again. "You've got *treasures*, plural. Is that a mistake?"

"It could be, but I'm pretty sure I got it right. There was more than one treasure. Based on the link to the Minotaur, I'm assuming this was the treasure of King Minos. He was one of the richest rulers in the world."

Calvin shook his head. "Treasure could mean diamonds and gold. Land holdings and ships. The list could go on forever."

"There's something else you should see. Minotaur left another mystery."

She turned vellum over. On the other side of the scroll was a diagram drawn with the same ink used for the text. "Do you know what this is, Calvin?"

"Looks like a maze."

"Yes. Maybe *the* maze. When I was young I used to imagine myself in the Labyrinth I think I could navigate the network of passages with my eyes shut. This diagram must have been drawn by the person who calls himself the Minotaur. Looks like our work is just beginning," she said.

"I heard from Matt while you had your nose in the scroll. The captain and his wife asked them to stay overnight. He and Abby will fly back tomorrow morning."

"Maybe we'll have something exciting to tell them. I relax best when I'm cooking. Why don't we have dinner on the rooftop? The view will calm my inner turmoil."

"Fine with me. I picked up some shrimp at the market."

"Wonderful. I'll whip up a shrimp and feta casserole."

Kalliste rummaged through the refrigerator and discovered she was out of tomatoes.

"I'll borrow some from the old yiayia who lives on the square," Kalliste says. "She stays up late and watches reruns of *Dallas* on the television. I'll be back in ten minutes."

Calvin volunteered to peel the shrimp and pop the wine.

Kalliste took a ceramic bowl from the cupboard, left the house and climbed the stairs to her neighbor's. As she had predicted, the elderly woman was watching a Greek-speaking Larry Hagman on the small television set. She filled a bowl with tomatoes and went back to her program to watch J.R. Ewing plot against his brother Bobby.

As Kalliste hurried across the square to the stairway two figures in black darted from the shadows and came up behind her. One put his over her mouth. The other placed a shiny object on her neck. The bowl fell from her hands and shattered on the pavement. Seconds later her body went limp and she was dragged back into the shadows.

Leonidas was watching from the rooftop, and had seen Kalliste walk from the stairway to a house on the square. When she emerged minutes later carrying the bowl, he assumed that she had borrowed something. He was taken off-guard by the swiftness of the kidnapping. An alarm clanged inside his skull. All hell was about to break loose. His experience and training kicked in. With calm deliberation, he slipped the bag containing his arsenal onto his right shoulder, slung a leg over the low wall and dropped off the roof into the darkness.

Salazar waited with his men who'd taken up positions close to Kalliste's house. When he gave the order, one man would go up to the door and knock. As soon as the door opened, the point man would blast his way in. The others would follow and take care of business.

The phone in his shirt pocket vibrated. He brought the phone to his ear. The Prior leader, North, spoke, "We've got the Greek woman."

Salazar tempered his rage. "Good work. I can't talk now. The operation is about to commence. We'll see you at the plane with the device."

North clicked off. Salazar cursed under his breath. Those ferret-faced fools had spoiled his plans. No matter. He would still deal with Hawkins. And he would soon have the device. He pursed his lips in a soft whistle. The point man waved to show he heard the signal, then brought his machine pistol to his hip and advanced toward the door.

Calvin had cleaned the last of the shrimp and rinsed them in a plastic colander. As he worked, he hummed a variation on the old New Orleans standby.

"Oh when the shrimp go marching in, oh when those shrimp go marching in..."

Hearing the knock at the door, he stopped singing. Maybe Kalliste was back and needed help. He rinsed the shrimp juice off and dried his hands on a dishtowel. The few seconds it took for that task saved his life.

As he started toward the door, a man's voice called from behind.

"I wouldn't open that. A bunch of guys are on the other side waiting to gun you down."

Calvin turned and a grin came to his face. "Hey, Hawk. What are you doin' here, man? Thought you were still in Spain. How'd you do that voice?"

Leonidas had copied every detail he could of Hawkins's face. He'd started with the usual blank mask, dyed it an oaken complexion, and trimmed the dark wig.

"Been working on it."

Doubt crossed Calvin's face. The stranger's shoulders were not as broad as those of his friend and he was shorter than Hawkins.

"You're not Matt."

Leonidas smirked. "Yeah, that's right. I'm not your pal. You gotta admit it's pretty close, though."

"Who the hell are you?"

"I'm the guy who saved your buddy's ass on Crete and I'm trying to do the same for you."

Calvin glanced at the pistol hanging by Leonidas's thigh.

"If you're thinking of grabbing for my gun I'll save you the trouble." Leonidas hooked his finger through the trigger guard and handed the weapon to Calvin, who hesitated, thinking the offer was a trick.

There was another knock at the door. Louder.

Calvin shouted over his shoulder, "That you, Kalliste?"

No reply.

Leonidas knew that they had seconds to act. "They got your lady friend and they're going to get us if we don't get outta here."

Calvin weighed the warning. Kalliste would have answered his voice. He snatched the pistol and tucked it into his belt. Then he stuffed the device, the scroll, and the notebook into the knapsack and slipped his arms through the straps.

"You got in. Maybe you can get us out," he said.

Leonidas had produced another pistol from a holster in the small of his back. He gestured with the barrel at the stairway leading to the second floor. Then he dashed for the patio door, with Calvin right behind. There was a thud from the front entryway followed by the sound of wood splintering. By then the two men were on the patio.

As Leonidas led Calvin to the iron fence, he said, "I had you made as military. What branch were you in?"

"Navy SEALs. Why you askin'?"

"I don't want to carry you around piggy-back. See if you can keep up with an Army Special Ops."

Leonidas climbed over the fence and disappeared. Calvin didn't have to be coaxed. He followed Leonidas over the fence, grabbed onto the rope and began his hand-over-hand descent down the face of the cliff.

Salazar entered Kalliste's house on the heels of his men, who had cleared the first floor and streamed up the stairs to the second level. His fierce eyes glanced around the living room. He expected to see the bodies of Hawkins and whoever was unlucky enough to be in his company. But there was no one. Salazar was at his most dangerous when his blood lust went unsatisfied. No sign of the mechanism either. His frown deepened. He picked up a *demitasse* cup from the table. The coffee was still warm.

His lead man called from the patio.

"Something you should see here, Mr. Salazar."

He went out to see his man pointing his electric torch at the end of the rope knotted to the fence. Salazar borrowed the torch and leaned over the railing. The rope dangled down to the narrow shelf of rock at the base of the house's foundation. Salazar handed the torch back.

"Give me your pistol," he said.

He held the gun so he could see the screen of the night vision sight and surveyed the cliffs. Two ghostly blurs were moving off to the left.

"There," he said, pointing. "They're trying to escape along the cliffs. We could lose them if they make it to the stairs that run from the village to the harbor. Split your men into teams of three. One team will follow them. The other will cut them off at the stairway. Get moving."

"What do you want us to do when we spot them?"

He handed the gun back.

"My orders haven't changed. *Kill* them."

CHAPTER FORTY-FOUR

Calvin stumbled blindly along the rim of the ancient volcanic caldera behind the pseudo version of Hawkins. The black lava cliffs sloped down to a ragged edge a few feet off to his right. Below the cliffs a striated wall dropped more than two hundred feet as if it'd been sheared off by a giant cleaver. Calvin's feet kept slipping on the loose pieces of pumice that covered the ground. A single misstep and he'd slide over the cliff to his death.

"Hey," he called out. "You know where you're going?"

"Yeah. Away from the posse on our ass," Leonidas replied without slowing his pace. "The guy back there was carrying a Cobray M11 with sound suppressor and night vision scope."

"I know all about Cobrays," Calvin said. "You can empty the magazine in the time it takes to sneeze. You still haven't told me where we're headed."

"I'm following a goat path along the ridge. Scouted it out in the daylight. Not exactly the LA Freeway, but we've only got a short way to go."

"Hope so. They're moving faster and can see in the dark. Bound to catch us at this pace."

"Not if we disappear."

"You got a Harry Potter invisibility cloak on you?"

"Better. Whoops!"

Leonidas caught his toe on a black lava knob. He pitched

forward, twisting his body to avoid a face plant and a deathly slide down the slope. Calvin's arm shot out and his thick fingers closed on a wrist, but Leonidas kept sliding. Calvin jammed his downhill foot into a crease in the lava to keep from slipping, leaned into the hill and braced himself. His arm felt as if it were being pulled from its socket. Leonidas came to a jerking stop; one leg dangled over the cliff. His weight pulled Calvin closer to the edge.

"Climb or you'll take us both down!" Calvin yelled.

Leonidas dropped the pistol. The weapon clattered down the slope and disappeared over the edge. He reached out and clawed at the pumice until his groping fingers found a crease in the rock. Calvin got both hands around the wrist and pulled him to a standing position.

They backed away from the edge and paused to catch their breath. "Thanks, man," Leonidas said. "Almost lost it."

"You must have something damned important in that bag of yours. It almost pulled us over the edge."

"You should talk, dude. Kept a tight hand on that knapsack."

"You got a name, *dude*?"

Leonidas hesitated. He switched identity so often he'd forgotten he had a real name.

"It's Chad Williams," he said. "What's yours?"

Chad Williams was the name of the man who'd bought the Spike missiles from the arms dealer in the Netherlands.

"Calvin Hayes." In a level voice, he said, "You know a guy in Amsterdam by the name of Broz?"

"Never heard of him."

"Funny, 'cause he knows you." He pulled the gun out of his belt. "I'll bet that if I rip that Halloween mask off your face I'll see the same mug the security camera caught when you bought the Spikes."

Chad's reaction wasn't what Calvin expected from a man staring into the muzzle of a gun. He laughed and looked over Calvin's shoulder.

"Glad to take that bet, but we've gotta move before they get into shooting range."

Every instinct warned Calvin not to take the word of a stranger who could switch colors like a chameleon. He changed his mind when the pumice exploded in small clouds of dust just inches from where Chad had fallen seconds before. The next shot would find its mark. Calvin raised the pistol and fired a spread of six shots, hoping to slow down their pursuers, knowing that the muzzle flashes would reveal their position. There was a pause, followed by the sound of someone yelling or crying out. Then an intense fusillade began.

"Nice going. Now they're really pissed off," Chad shouted over the rattle of gunfire.

"Time to make us disappear," Calvin said.

"Follow me. Gets tricky, so watch your footing."

Chad plunged into the gloom with Calvin close behind. Another round ricocheted off the lava a dozen feet to their left. Bullets zipped through the air like angry bees. The rounds would have ripped into their targets, but the path descended at a steep angle and the bullets passed overhead. The rocks at Calvin's left elbow began to encroach, transforming the path into a ledge that narrowed to about a yard in width. On his right side lay darkness and potential death; on the left, was a ridged wall of rock.

The curve in the wall offered protection from the probing gunfire, but the ledge narrowed by a foot. Calvin pressed his body belly-first against the rock, arms spread like an eagle's wings, fingers looking for hand-holds. If the ledge narrowed more, or simply disappeared, they could go neither forward nor backward. The wall bulged again. He inched his way around the curving rock.

When he got to the other side of the bulge he saw that Chad had disappeared. A hand reached out of a dark cleft in the wall and grabbed his arm.

"Keep on coming," an echoing voice said. "Ground's flat. You'll be okay."

A cell phone screen light flashed on, showing a smooth floor and timber supports in the wall and ceiling.

"We in a mine?" Calvin said.

"The island is a honey-comb of shafts and tunnels. Follow me. Floor slopes down. When I say stop, make sure you *stop*."

After walking another thirty seconds, Chad said, "Stop!" The bobbing light showed a rectangular opening in the floor. "We go down this shaft. Me first."

He handed the phone over, then grabbed onto a rope tied to a timber and lowered himself into the shaft. Calvin tucked the phone away and rappelled down the rope until his feet touched solid ground. Chad was in the mine entrance, silhouetted against a square of blue. Behind him were shimmering waters.

They exited through the opening and descended a ramp to a rotting pier. A winding path ran from the dock along the base of the cliffs until it opened up into the parking lot of a busy taverna. The fragrance of oregano and garlic wafted on the sea air and wailing music blasted from speakers on the patio. Calvin went inside and asked the owner to call a taxi. He and Chad waited out on the patio and ordered a couple of beers.

Calvin silently pondered his options. First order of Priority was to get the hell off Oia.

"I'm leaving the island," Calvin said. "I'd suggest you do the same."

"I want to talk to Hawkins. And he needs to talk to me."

"Talk to him about what?"

"About everything. You guys don't have a clue what kind of crap you're dealing with. Tell him I'm the guy who saved his ass twice on Crete."

Calvin gave Chad a suspicious look. "Okay. I'll call Hawkins and see what he says."

He got up and walked away from the restaurant until he could hear above the music. He reached Hawkins in his hotel room and told him Kalliste had been kidnapped.

"Tell me what happened," Hawkins said.

"Salazar's men got her when she went to the neighbor's house. They came for me, but I got out the back door. I managed to save the device and the scroll."

"That's good news. Are you okay?"

"Yeah. Few bumps and scrapes after running along the rim of the caldera."

"You were lucky to get away."

"Not all luck. I had help. Same guy who came to your rescue on Crete."

"You can't be talking about a British tourist named Pouty."

239

"That's the phony name he was using then, but he's actually American as apple pie. His real name is Chad Williams."

"Sounds familiar."

"It should. He's the guy who bought the Spike missiles."

"You're kidding."

"Nope. Crazy, huh?"

"It's insane. Why would he help me and give you a hand?"

"You can ask him yourself. He says he knows what's going on with Salazar and wants to talk to you."

"Where is he now?"

"Sitting at a table having a beer."

"Tell him I'll talk to him. He could be the only lead we have to Kalliste. I'll send a plane to bring you back to Spain. Call me from the airport after you land."

"He could be angling to take another shot at you. Like they say in the bayou, you don't invite a water moccasin into your house."

"I'll have to take that risk. Kalliste's life may depend on what this snake has to say, Calvin. But don't take any chances. Make sure he's defanged."

Calvin clicked off and went back to the table. "Hawkins says he'll talk to you. You're going to have to do something about the way you look, though. I think Hawk will be spooked to see a copy of himself."

Chad drained his glass and removed the make-up kit from his bag. "Don't worry. I'll put on my best face."

CHAPTER FORTY-FIVE

Abby had just begun to doze off when she heard the soft knock. She got out of bed, and after a quick look through the peephole, opened her hotel room door and greeted Hawkins with a warm smile.

"What a nice surprise! I thought I had wasted my time with all the eye flutters and knee bumps at dinner. Come to bed while the sheets are still warm."

"The sheets may have to get cold for now, Abby. Calvin called a few minutes ago with bad news. Kalliste's been kidnapped."

The smile faded. "Come in."

Hawkins stepped into the room and closed the door behind him. "Salazar and his men grabbed her outside of her house. They tried for Calvin, but he got away with the translating device and the scroll."

"Thank God Calvin's not hurt. I feel awful about Kalliste. I know how much she means to you. I'll do everything I can to get her back safely. How can I help?"

"I need Calvin back here as soon as possible. I told him I'd send a plane to pick him up. The person who helped him escape from Salazar will be coming in with him."

"That's not a problem. Who's the other passenger?"

"His name is Chad Williams. We met him before when he was calling himself Pouty."

"The mysterious British tourist we met in Crete?"

"Mr. Pouty gets around. He's the guy who sank Captain Santiago's boat and sent *Falstaff* to the bottom."

Abby searched his face for any sign that he was joking. Seeing none, she said, "Are you crazy? That man is a killer."

"I had the same reaction. But he's got another agenda that evidently involves coming to my rescue. I want to find out what it is. He says he can help us find Kalliste."

"I can see your reasoning, Matt, but it could be a trick."

"Yes it could, Ab. But I have to go with what I've got."

"In that case, you should talk to him. I'll get a plane to Santorini."

"There's something else. I'd like to check out the Salazar castle. Which means I'll need a helicopter."

Picking up her phone, she made a number of calls. Minutes later she hung up. "I found a company plane in Frankfurt. I've talked to the pilot and he's on his way to the airport. Plane will be gassed up and ready to go pick up Calvin and company in Santorini. We'll have them back here by morning. My people are still working on the helicopter."

"Incredible as usual, Abby."

"I'm not doing all the work. You'll have to come up with a safe meeting place. Having a chat with the man who tried to kill you doesn't seem like something you would do at a café over lunch."

"I was thinking of a more private setting where we'd be in control. The *Santa Maria* is docked at the harbor and we're still paying for her lease."

"Sounds perfect. Do you want me there?"

"Might be simpler if it's just Calvin and me."

"Okay. Now tell me why you want to look at the castle."

"From what we know about the deed Father Francisco translated, the Salazar castle seems to be the key to this mess. I want to see it in the flesh. Just a feeling."

"I understand. I've had a feeling that there might be something we missed when we talked to the captain's brother. I think I should see him again."

"Good idea, Abby. Thanks for all you're doing."

"No problem. Well, then, I guess we're done for the night," Abby said.

There was an awkward moment when no words were spoken. Abby was standing close and he could feel the heat from her body. Hawkins had the mental discipline that was a holdover from his days as a Navy SEAL. But his mind belonged to a healthy male in the presence of a beautiful woman whose nightie failed to hide the curves he knew so well. He glanced over at the bed.

"Maybe not," Hawkins said. "We've got some time before Calvin arrives. I've been thinking what a shame it would be to waste those warm sheets."

Abby raised an eyebrow. "I totally agree."

CHAPTER FORTY-SIX

The next morning after a breakfast of gluten free raisin bread, Molly got into her leathers and straddled her Harley. Leaving Bend, she followed the road through the forests around Mount Hood. She rolled into Portland late in the morning and pulled up in front of the Dragonfly coffee shop on Thurman Street.

A few blonde wood tables were occupied. A man and woman sat at one to the rear of the shop. When she stepped inside they waved her over. She walked past a man in a Red Sox baseball hat who was bent over his laptop.

"I'm Molly Sutherland," she said. "I think you're waiting for me."

With his long, graying, brown hair tied in a pigtail, and a neatly trimmed beard, the man at the table looked like an aging hippie. He maintained a grim expression on his gaunt face, told her to take a seat and introduced himself as Jared Spaulding. The woman in the business suit identified herself as Attorney Alberta Mullins. Her manner was crisp rather than cold, Molly thought, but her attempt at a warm smile wouldn't have melted an icicle.

"Thank you for coming all this way, Ms. Sutherland. After your call, I ran your name and telephone number through a private investigator. He said you were retired Army. Is that correct?"

"Yes, ma'am. That's correct."

"What do you do now?" she said.

"I'm on an Army pension but I work as a bird photographer

and trainer at the High Desert Museum in Bend. You can call them if you want."

"Thanks. I'll do that." She jotted down the information in a small notebook. "Would you tell us again why you're interested in Auroch Industries and Viktor Salazar?"

Molly was ready for the question. "Like I said, my Uncle Gowdy died in a coal mine explosion. While I was working on a family history project, I found out that the mine was owned by Auroch. I started poking around and learned that they were never called into account for safety violations. Mr. Salazar is the boss, so I thought maybe he might do the right thing and apologize, even though it was years ago."

Spaulding let out a barking laugh. "Good luck with that."

"I see what you're saying," Molly said. "Big company like that wouldn't pay any attention to me."

"Uh-uh," he said. "They would pay a *lot* of attention, and that's the problem."

Molly furrowed her brow. "Not sure I understand."

Attorney Mullins reached into the briefcase by her side, pulled out a folder and opened it on the table. She extracted half a dozen photographs and spread them out. Taken from different angles, at ground level and from the air, the photos showed a village, or what was left of it. Most of the corrugated metal shacks had disappeared into a sinkhole.

His voice cracking with emotion, Spaulding said, "I've got photos of the same scene repeated over and over again in different places. Only the body count varies. In this incident, twenty-three people—men, women and children—died when an Auroch mining operation weakened the ground under their village."

"Mr. Spaulding was the chairman of an environmental and humanitarian organization when these disasters occurred," Ms. Mullins chimed in. "After a series of highly-publicized disasters near Auroch mines, Jared pulled together an international consortium to confront the company. He can tell you what happened next."

"We had lots of momentum," Spaulding said. "Their public relations department folded under the world-wide criticism. They put me directly in touch with Salazar. To my surprise, he took full responsibility, said he would provide restitution to those impacted, and would be open to suggestions on how Auroch could make amends and prevent further disasters. He said Auroch was heavily involved in alternative energy."

Molly nodded. "I saw that Auroch belongs to an energy council working on stuff that could put him out of business. Seem funny to you?"

"Yeah. Go figure. Maybe that's one reason we believed him when he said he'd tend to our demands personally and have his staff carry out his wishes."

"Salazar was a man of his word," Attorney Mullins interrupted. "Auroch had an army of lawyers, investigators and accountants in-waiting. They must have been prepped for weeks because we were served with subpoenas within hours of the telephone call. Offices and cars were vandalized. Our computers were hacked. Worse, the police came in with false charges that were brought against the organization; our donors were warned against giving any funds to help us. People followed our staff everywhere."

"That's an awful lot of trouble."

"We planned to hang in, but we had some amazing bad luck. Our treasurer was killed in a car accident. Hit and run. That put us over the edge. In a matter of days, our organization was dead as well."

"Sorry to hear that. Sounds like you tried to do some good."

"We did lots of good," Spaulding said. "And if you know what's good for *you*, stay away from Auroch and Salazar. They're poison."

"Thanks," Molly said.

Spaulding must have noticed the firm set of her jaw. "You're not going to take our advice, are you?"

"Uncle Gowdy's wife was my favorite aunt and their kids are my best cousins."

The attorney shook her head. "Weren't the Hatfields and McCoys from West Virginia?"

"Hatfields were. McCoys came from Kentucky. I'm probably related to both of them. That's the way it is where I come from. We're all kin."

Spaulding sighed. "If you persist in going ahead, promise me a couple of things. One, come to us if you need help. Two, be careful."

"My Maw and Paw didn't raise any dumb kids," Molly said sarcastically. "I'll keep looking over my shoulder."

If Molly heeded her own advice, she would have paid more attention to the man in the Red Sox cap who was positioned so he could glance up from his laptop without seeming too obvious. He had purchased the cap in Boston, where he had been the day before when the call came in telling him to fly to Portland. He had arrived that morning on the red-eye and taken a cab directly from the airport to the café. He wore a hearing aid that could shut out extraneous sound. He had been listening to the conversation, typing out notes on who said what. He had already taken down the license plate number of the Harley. When the conversation ended, he typed out the time, then sent the notes as an attachment to the email.

Within milliseconds, the words spoken at Molly's table winged their way across the continental United States and the Atlantic Ocean to the security department of Auroch Industries. The recipient glanced at the source, printed out the message and then placed it in a folder that was delivered by hand to the big office with the strip-mining murals on the walls.

As Molly was throwing a leg over the seat of her motorcycle, her words were being studied by the subject of her discussion. Salazar was back in his office after a quick flight from Santorini. He read the notes again. It was a small annoyance, but he was a man who abhorred loose ends, and after the Santorini debacle, he wanted someone to pay. He reached for his phone, punched a button, and said:

"Tell our man on the scene to deal with this Sutherland person. *Immediately.*"

CHAPTER FORTY-SEVEN

The castle perched on a hill overlooking the wind-swept plains of the sparsely-populated central region of the Iberian Peninsula was known as, *Castillo de Cuernos*, or Castle of the Horns. The guidebooks said that the name was derived from the cattle farms that once surrounded the castle. Most of the grazing land had been turned over to olive and grape cultivation, but the farmland hadn't been tilled for decades; all that was left in the sere soil were blackened vines and twisted tree trunks.

A river ran past the castle, and in the heyday of agricultural production, boats transported goods from the fields and vineyards to market along the winding waterway. Workers lived in a bustling village built on the bank of the river, but the settlement had long ago been abandoned.

The figure in black stood on the east tower of *Castillo de Cuernos*, eyes fixed on a star-like pinpoint of light that rapidly grew in brightness. The pulsating sound of air being thrashed echoed across the plains and the star materialized into a helicopter that came in low over the parapets. The rotor air-wash blew back the hood to reveal the marble white features of Lily Porter. Circling the castle once, the helicopter hovered, then dropped into the courtyard. By then, Lily was in an elevator on her way to the base of the tower. She stepped out into the courtyard and strode through the cloud of dust that the rotors had kicked up. The fuselage door opened, a ladder flipped out and two Priors maneuvered a stretcher through the opening.

Kalliste lay on the stretcher, her body covered with a blanket and tied down with nylon straps. The restraints were necessary because she was starting to come out of the deep sleep induced by the powerful drugs injected into her bloodstream. Lily gazed down at Kalliste, awe-struck at her beauty. She had truly earned her name: the fair one. But Lily's appraisal was the cold assessment of a farmer admiring the perfect features on an animal before sending it off to slaughter.

Locked within that still body was the dangerous DNA going back to King Minos.

The sacrifice that had been delayed for thousands of years would at last be accomplished. Kalliste would be the end of the Minos line. The Mother Goddess would have more blood than she could drink, and as a reward would bestow unimaginable blessings on the Way of the Axe.

She leaned close to Kalliste's ear. "Don't be afraid," she whispered. "It's me, your friend Lily."

Kalliste's eyes remained closed, but her lips parted slightly.

"Your friend Hawkins wants to come to you. Tell me where he is."

Kalliste scrunched her eyelids tight but made no reply. Lily leaned over and placed her hand on Kalliste's shoulder.

"Tell me, Kalliste. Tell me where Hawkins is."

The lips remained silent.

Lily shook Kalliste's shoulder, but to no avail. She felt her phone vibrating in her robe pocket. She recognized the number on the caller ID. It belonged to the nurse at the Paris sanitarium where the High Priestess was being treated. She ordered the stretcher-bearers to go on.

"This had better be important," she said into the phone.

She heard a sob, followed by the whispered words, "She's gone."

Lily needed no more detail to know what happened. The Head Priestess had died. Lily knew after her last visit that this day would come, but the announcement was still a shock.

"When?"

"Minutes ago. In her sleep. The monitors flat-lined. It was too late to bring her back. What should I do?"

"Have you talked to anyone else?"

"Only you."

With icy calm, Lily said, "Prepare the body immediately for transport. Alert the security detail to be ready. I'll be in Paris tonight to escort the High Priestess home."

As she clicked off, grief washed over Lily, but not for long. With the death of the crone, Lily would become the new High Priestess. *Her* word would be law. She looked down at Kalliste and said to the Prior holding the front of the stretcher, "How much longer will she sleep?"

"Several hours. Longer, if we inject more drugs, but that could be dangerous."

"Take her to the Maze. Keep her unconscious until I get back, but she must not come to any harm."

She watched the Priors carry the stretcher toward the shrine entrance and considered the moves she would make after she had been made High Priestess. She had quietly watched Salazar gather together his private army. She knew of his conversations with the corporate managers. He had been subtle, hinting that change was needed, but she wasn't fooled. Salazar wanted to take over the Auroch corporate empire.

When the first High Priestess had arrived on Spanish shores, she had needed the help of the local inhabitants to consolidate her hold. The Salazars had lent their services as thugs for hire, and the relationship had worked for centuries. The Salazar family became the public face of the mining company that evolved into Auroch. But behind the curtains, the Maze pulled the strings.

Lily would deal with Salazar at the Gathering, when her spirit would merge with all those who came before her, going back to the first High Priestess. But the loss of the translation device worried her. As long as the machine was out of her control, the possibility existed that someone would figure out how to use it to translate Linear A.

This must never happen. That rule had been drilled into her head since she was a girl, then later as a promising young priestess.

For thousands of years those who followed the Way of the Axe had communicated in the ancient script, secure in the knowledge that its secrets were safe from prying eyes. The script bound them together, shielding from public view the horrifying theology of blood that had allowed them to expand their wealth and influence. Anyone who came close to decoding the script was dealt with in the same way—sudden death, made to look accidental. The practice had worked. Until now. Until Kalliste and her friend Hawkins interfered.

She needed to find Hawkins and the device. She had sensed that he and Kalliste were close when she met him in the Cadiz hotel. Kalliste would be the perfect bait to lure him to the Maze. Lily would have to be careful, though. Hawkins had shown that he was no fool.

She gazed at the Tripartite Shrine for a moment, absorbing the power of the Mother Goddess that seemed to flow from the three-towered building that housed the entrance to the Maze. Then she climbed into the helicopter, barked an order to the pilot, and started off on the first leg of her trip to bring the body of the High Priestess back home to rest with the others.

CHAPTER FORTY-EIGHT

Abby awakened to discover Hawkins gone. A note on his pillow said he would call her later. Hawkins was right when he warned of the danger of bringing emotions on a mission. Abby hadn't reached the high levels of the Navy by being a worrywart. The best way to take her mind off Hawkins was to throw herself at a problem.

She called Captain Santiago and said she wanted to see his brother again. He called her back a few minutes later. Francisco would love to talk to her. Miguel was on his way to the hotel to give her a ride to the chapel. She quickly got dressed and was ready when Miguel knocked on her door. When they arrived at the chapel, Miguel stayed with the car. Abby went in to see Father Francisco and found him sweeping the main aisle.

He gave her a broad smile. "Blessed are those who clean up after others," he said. "As you can see, I serve St. Vincent as his janitor as well as his gardener." He put the broom aside, brushed his hands, and said, "My brother told me you wanted to talk more about the deed of penance."

"Yes. I'm wondering if I missed something hidden in the bureaucratic language."

"That's possible. The deed deliberately disguises what essentially was a vast killing machine, and was intended to divert people from the monstrous evil of the enterprise."

"One clause stood out. Something about the property being

cleansed of demons before it could be transferred."

"I agree. It is a curious phrase. Let's take another look at it."

He led the way into the musty-smelling library, unlocked a desk drawer and pulled out the Spanish copy of the deed. Placing the document on a reading table, he ran his index finger down the text. "Here it is. Actually, several references describe the property as being 'unclean' or 'unholy.'"

"What exactly does it mean?"

"When I translated this section, I thought it referred to the fact that the property had been owned by a heretic, who the church could claim was unholy."

"That seems like a logical supposition," Abby said.

"But now that I have given it further thought, I have my doubts. As you recall, the owner, Fernandez, was tossed into prison and later burned at the stake. Fire was seen as the ultimate cure for heresy. The lucky sinner was cleansed of all their sins. 'Relaxed,' as they said. So there would be no need for additional cleansing, as suggested in the deed. Then there's the section about the work crews."

"The ones who built the castle?"

"Correct. This line that says a priest was delegated to accompany the work crews. The Inquisition had spies everywhere. I took it to mean they were sending along someone to keep an eye out for heretics. What it actually said is that the priest would 'go before' the crews to cleanse. It was, in fact, an exorcism of the property."

"Exorcism has to do with demons, doesn't it?"

"Yes. Certain priests could sweep out demons the same way I swept dirt from the chapel floor. When I first read this, I translated it as old demons. Now that I look at it, I see that it could mean, 'Old Gods.' Pagan gods, in other words."

"I don't get it," Abby said. "Does that mean that the owner of the land was a pagan?"

"Highly unlikely. Under the Inquisition you could be accused of heresy for simply taking a bath or cooking the wrong type of food. Someone who worshiped pagan gods might just as well hand the executioners a box of matches."

"So if it wasn't the owner who was pagan; it was the property itself?"

"That's what I'm thinking. The plains of *La Mancha* have been inhabited by humans since long before the country of Spain ever existed. Roman ruins abound. It's not uncommon for newer settlements to be built over old ones. The castle may have been built on pagan ruins."

Abby pointed to the page of pictographs that had been found with the deed. "This is old Minoan script. Is it possible that the ruins were Minoan?"

"The Minoans were very active in Spain for trading and mining. It wouldn't be out of the question."

"That could explain the castle's name, *Castillo de Cuernos.*"

"Castle of the Horns? How so? I thought that had to do with cattle."

"That may be true, but the bull was sacred in Minoan religion. The altar used for Minoan religious ceremonies was called the Horns of Consecration. Is it possible that the castle was built over a Minoan temple?"

"Yes, of course! That would explain it. The Inquisitors were happy to take property and convey it to favored individuals. The Salazars, in this case. But the purity of the Inquisition could be challenged if the property were pagan, thus heretical and unclean."

"It would be like a real estate agent in our country getting in trouble for selling a contaminated house lot."

"Your American agent could merely lose his license. During the Inquisition a mistake like that could cost someone their life."

Questions whirled in Abby's mind. Did the Salazars acquire the land in spite of the pagan contamination or because of it? Why would the Salazars be interested in a lost civilization? Especially at a time when the world had forgotten the civilization that had once flourished on Crete.

She couldn't wait to tell Matt what she had discovered. But Abby was not one to jump to conclusions. She had built her successful career as a logistics expert on her ability to analyze complex situations and use her findings to carry out complicated tasks. She sat down at the table and motioned for Father Francisco to do the same.

"If you don't mind," she said. "Let's go over this again."

CHAPTER FORTY-NINE

Hawkins paced the deck of the *Santa Maria*, his mind churning. Every minute that passed put Kalliste further out of reach and deeper in danger.

He was about to start back toward the bow when a taxi drove along the dock and stopped near the boat slip. Calvin got out of the cab and gave him a wave. Another passenger emerged and followed Calvin up the gangway. The man looked to be in his thirties. He had a movie-star handsome face and a rugged build. He was dressed beach casual in shorts, leather sandals and a blue polo shirt. An LA baseball cap was clamped down over a thatch of long, platinum-colored hair.

As Calvin came up the gangway he noticed the stony gaze in his friend's eyes. "It's okay, Hawk. He's clean. Carrying his hardware in my backpack. This is Chad. I guess his name was Pouty when you met before."

Hawkins was in no mood for games. He had expected to see the red-faced Englishman, not an aging beach bum. "We've got a problem, Calvin. This isn't the guy I met on Crete."

Lapsing into a British accent, Chad said, "You've got a short memory, guv'nor. How could you forget the delightful chinwag we had atop a hill in Gournia and our lovely chat on Spinalonga?"

Hawkins stared at Chad in disbelief. The voice was definitely that of the loquacious Englishman.

"That was *you*?"

"One and the same, old chap." Chad switched back to an American accent, "I was trying to get your attention. Hope it worked."

"It worked, whatever your name is. Time to talk."

Hawkins led the way into the pilot house. He slid into the captain's chair and told Chad to take a seat. "Tell me who you are."

"It's a long, sad story," he said.

"I'm sure I've heard longer and sadder ones."

Chad took off his ball cap and brushed the hair out of his eyes. "To begin with, I was born in California."

Chad laid out his progression from California beach bum to Special Ops and the encounter with the IED that ended his acting career and his engagement. He described how he'd parleyed his actor training into being a master of disguise, which led to a mercenary career using the name Leonidas, up until Salazar fired him. That's when he became Hawkins's shadow and protector.

Hawkins could have kicked himself. "I must have been asleep at the switch not to pick you up trailing us in Crete and Santorini."

"Don't beat yourself up. I ditched Pouty and changed my persona to the American tourist you see before you. I'm good at what I do."

"Evidently." Hawkins narrowed his eyes. "My question is *why* you do it? One minute you've got me and my friends in your sights. The next, you're risking your ass to save mine. What gives?"

Chad shrugged. "Salazar wanted you dead. I took the contract, but he reneged after I screwed up. Figured if I kept you alive I could use you as leverage so he'll pay up."

"I don't buy it, Corporal. You could have turned me over to Salazar any time you wanted. Instead, you kept me out of trouble. Not once, but twice. Then you did the same with Calvin. Why?"

"Maybe I'm just a nice guy."

"You're not a nice guy, Chad. You're a cold-blooded killer for hire."

"And you were a SEAL. Part of your job was killing people."

Chad was closer to danger than he knew. Under the calm exterior, Hawkins was like a sleeping volcano.

In a quiet voice, he said, "I wouldn't go there if I were you. You cost me a million dollar submersible and you sank my friend's boat." He made a pinching gesture with his thumb and forefinger. "I'm this far from taking you thirty miles out to sea and letting you swim back to Spain, the path you planned for me."

Chad glanced at Calvin, who nodded in agreement.

He swallowed hard and the smug expression vanished from his face. "I was out of line. Maybe I came over to your side because we'd both got busted up. You in Afghanistan. Me in Iraq."

Without shifting his hard gaze from Chad's strangely perfect features, Hawkins said, "You've been listening to our guest, Calvin. Think Chad's being straight with us?"

Calvin folded his arms across his chest. A lazy smile came to his lips. "I could hear the violins playing when he got into that band-of-brothers, us against the rest of the world stuff, Hawk. We've gotta remember Chad's an actor."

Hawkins said, "Why didn't you find another gig, Chad? Salazar is rich and powerful. Why do you want to go up against him? The cost-benefit ratio doesn't add up."

"I wanted to score big so I could get out of the business."

"I don't think so," Hawkins said. "Guys like you are the maggots of this world. And there's plenty of decaying flesh to keep you busy. I don't trust you, I don't like you, and I don't believe you. Calvin, please escort Mr. Chad off this boat before I change my mind about the long swim home."

Chad raised his palms. "Wait." No change came to the perfect face, but his voice was emotional, "I met a girl in Cadiz. Young kid. Pretty thing. Name was Isabel. She was a prostitute, but I got to be more than a customer. She accepted me for what I am."

"What are you, Chad?"

"I'm a monster." Slowly, he peeled the mask off his face to reveal the massive scarring. The lip-less mouth opened wide. "Boo," he said.

During his recovery in Walter Reed hospital, Hawkins had seen lots of men with burn injuries, but these were the worst he'd ever encountered.

"What happened to you?"

"Convoy outside of Mosul. Road was supposedly cleared, but

the bad guys snuck an IED in before we got there. Humvee was one of the early ones with no bottom armor. My crew was killed. Vehicle became a bonfire. I was the marshmallow."

"Sorry, Corporal." His voice had lost its edge. "Where does your Cadiz girlfriend fit in?"

"After I messed up the job on your boat, Salazar said he was still going to pay me. He said he was sending someone to my hotel with the money. Salazar doesn't play nicey-nice, so that should have raised a red flag with me, but I was high on grass. Couple of his thugs showed up. Isabel answered the door. They killed her. I was getting out of the shower. I nailed one, then the other." He paused. "Now do you know why I want to get to Salazar?"

"Revenge is the most plausible reason you've given us. How'd you screw up the missile attack?"

"I was stoned there, too. I wasted a Spike on the guy on deck."

"Rodriguez, the government observer."

"Don't know his name. He had it coming. Salazar had used his connections to get a spy on board. Rodriguez called in when you were over the shipwreck and Salazar gave me the order to launch."

"Why did Salazar want me killed?"

"He wanted to torpedo the expedition. He'd got the government to refuse a permit for the project, but the Spaniards changed their mind when you joined the project. He needed to stop things fast. I'd done some at-sea stuff for him before, and had been on call to stop the expedition."

"Which is exactly what he did after you screwed up."

"What are you talking about?"

Hawkins told Chad about the helicopter attack on the wreck site. "Could Salazar order up an operation like that?"

"In a heartbeat."

"From the sounds of it, Salazar has a lot of clout," Calvin said.

"No doubt about that, but I always had the feeling that he was working for someone else," Chad said. "He seemed afraid of making a quick decision. He'd tell me to wait. Almost as if he were checking with a higher up."

"Any idea who it was?"

"Only that it was someone who wanted to stop you from diving."

"What do you want from us, Chad?"

"You want to help your friend. I want to get to Salazar. Maybe we can work together."

Hawkins turned to Calvin. "What do you think?"

"Dunno," Calvin said, "A stoned-out pothead with a score to settle isn't the kind of guy I want watching my back."

"Don't blame you. But I know I can't take Salazar on alone," Chad said. "You would still call the shots. I haven't forgotten how to follow orders."

"I don't trust you either, but we've got to get to Kalliste." He glanced at Calvin who gave him a nod.

"Okay, Chad. You're in, but one screw up and you're dead meat."

"The only dead meat I want is Salazar."

"In time. You can deal with Salazar after we rescue our friend."

"Okay. Where do we start?"

"At Salazar's castle. Let's go for a ride in the country."

CHAPTER FIFTY

The three black Mercedes GL class SUVs carrying Salazar and his lieutenants emerged in a line from the garage under the Auroch Industries tower. The caravan wound its way through the Cadiz traffic to the highway that led out of the city.

After traveling around twenty miles, the SUVs took a ramp off the highway, drove to a secondary road, then turned onto a little-used country lane that ran past a heavily wooded section enclosed by a fence festooned with 'No Trespassing' signs.

The SUVs pulled onto a driveway marked by a 'Private' sign. The lead driver remotely activated the gate. The vehicles followed a gravel driveway hemmed in by thick growth. The tract of land was under the control of a realty trust anonymously owned by Auroch. After traveling a few miles, the vehicles parked in a cul-de-sac. Salazar's driver got out and went around to the back of the SUV. He opened the hatch door and lifted out a wooden box. Then he followed Salazar, trailed by the other lieutenants, all heavily armed, onto a path leading into the woods.

They walked past a shooting range, stopping to pick up pairs of ear protectors, then continued on to a cleared rectangular area a couple of hundred feet across. In the center of the open square was a metal platform resting on a waist-high steel framework.

Salazar was still fuming over the Santorini debacle. He had left the island empty-handed, and one of his men had been killed during the exchange of gunfire on the cliffs. He was already down the two fools who had fatally botched their mission to kill Leonidas. Then, on the way into the city from the airport, Lily Porter called to say the High Priestess had died. She had called for a Gathering and expected him to be at the Maze.

"I will look forward to bearing witness to your ascension," Salazar said.

Lily made no attempt to acknowledge the compliment. "Tell me what happened."

"My men broke into the Greek woman's house. Hawkins must have had warning. He and another escaped along the caldera cliffs. One of my men was killed in the chase."

"No sign of the device?"

"We searched the house and found nothing."

"It's fortunate the Priors were able to carry out the will of the Mother Goddess."

It was a subtle rebuke. Lily showed no sympathy for the loss of his man. More telling, she had said nothing about his previous failures. The failed attempt to stop the ship expedition, to deal with Hawkins and the loss of the translating device. She was keeping her anger in check, but he knew that he would soon be finished. The situation was deteriorating even without the troublesome security breach in Oregon.

Salazar had to move fast on all fronts. As the next in line, Lily would be anointed the new High Priestess, giving her vast powers of life and death and total control of Auroch Industries. Before the death of the crone, Lily lacked the power to go head-to-head with him. The authoritative tone to her voice now, signaled that she was already enjoying a taste of the authority that would come with her rise to the High Priestess throne.

Salazar saw this not as a challenge but as an opportunity. With a single blow he could destroy the new High Priestess and her assistants and eliminate the last two Priors. With the core of the Believers gone, he would take total control of Auroch. Once the mission in the United States was carried out, he would be sitting at the top of a multi-national corporation that controlled most, if not all, of the world's mining, petroleum and gas extraction operations.

With the money and power that came with an energy monopoly, political influence would follow. He would be able to do what he wanted, where he wanted. His first step would be to eliminate, or bend to his will, the members of the Way who held key positions in the company. And that would be easy once they saw there was nothing to fear from the priestesses or the Priors.

In a supreme irony, the bull that the Believers held sacred would be the key to carrying out his goals.

Salazar's driver placed the box on the ground, lifted out an object and set it on the platform. The bull's head was around twelve inches high, fashioned from a greenish-black material. Sharp, curving horns gleamed in the sunlight. Red eyes blazed from the broad face.

Salazar ran his fingers over the bull's crown and down the blunt muzzle to the white line defining its snout.

"Gentlemen, this is a Minoan vessel called a *rhyton*, and was designed to hold liquid which can be poured out through the nostrils. The original was found in the ancient city of Knossos and was made of Serpentinite with inlays of shell, crystal and jasper. The horns were born of gilded wood."

He turned to his explosives expert. "Bruno, could you tell us how this *rhyton* differs from the original?"

"Glad to, Mr. Salazar. The head here is made mostly of PETN, the same explosive being used for the show we'll be putting on in the U.S. The horns enclose chemical detonators."

"And this is the triggering remote," Salazar reached into his right ear with his fingertip and dislodged a contoured piece of pink plastic. He held it in the palm of his hand. "This is capable of sending a signal more than a hundred feet. Shall we give it a test?"

He led the way behind an earthen bunker. Small viewing ports enclosed in tinted blast-proof glass allowed a view of the platform. Salazar and his men donned ear protectors, then he took the ear plug in his fingers, turned a knob on it and pressed three times. The bull's head vanished. In its place was a miniature sun of yellow and red fire. Even with the protectors, the explosion hurt their ears.

As the blast echoed through the forest, Salazar walked through the smoke and inspected the splintered trees around the edge of the clearing. The head had disintegrated. There was no shrapnel damage, but the shock wave from the explosion would have been fatal to anyone in the open.

He complimented his explosives expert on the extensive kill zone.

"Thanks," Bruno said. "The second bomb I had built will work just as well, killing anyone within a radius of thirty feet."

"That will be more than adequate. The targets will all be clustered in a small area of the sanctuary of the snake goddess. The procession of the priestesses will move toward the Horns of Consecration, flanked by the Priors and by musicians chanting and playing the pipes. The new High Priestess will dispatch the victim. I will present the *rhyton* to catch the blood of the sacrifice. The attention of everyone in the room will be on the altar. I will slip out of the sanctuary and trigger the bomb."

"Okay. The bomb goes off. What next?"

"The Auroch security guards will be waiting in the courtyard for the announcement that the ceremony is over, waiting for the new High Priestess to emerge. They will rush into the sanctuary after the explosion. Finding only the dead, they will come out of the shrine. They will be confused. We will quickly dispatch them. Once that is done, I will broadcast a message to the Faithful worldwide saying that everyone in the old order was killed and that I am taking charge."

"What about the big dogs?" another man asked.

"The Daemons will be in the ceremonial room with the Priors."

"What's the time table, sir?" the man asked.

Salazar looked at his watch. "The ceremony is set for tomorrow night. I'll deliver the second bull's head personally. You will accompany me. Your loyalty will soon be rewarded. As soon as I'm in power, I'll make you rich beyond your wildest dreams." He glanced toward the empty bomb test platform and in an uncharacteristic display of humor, added, "And that's no bull."

CHAPTER FIFTY-ONE

Uncle Gowdy was talking to Molly from the grave.

She pictured him in a rocking chair on the sagging porch, with his children and their cousin Molly at his feet, telling what it was like to mine coal. From time to time the narrative would be interrupted by a coughing fit brought on by the coal dust irritating his lungs.

"Diggin' coal is easier'n making pie," he said in his soft West Virginia accent. "You ride down a shaft a coupla hundred feet, careful you don't go too deep 'cause you'd come out in China. Then you blast the seam out with dynamite, bust the big hunks to bitty pieces." He wrapped his coal-stained fingers around the hammer of an invisible pick handle. "Pickety-pick, pickety-pick. Then you go on to the next seam."

Molly sat in front of her computer, thinking how digging coal wasn't much different from mining the internet. She'd blasted out the Auroch Industries seam and had picked her way through the hunks of data. The company's deplorable behavior as an international corporate citizen. Its disdain for public opinion. The damage caused by its mining and drilling operations. The lawsuits filed against anyone or anything in its way. And most troubling, the strange deaths associated with its mergers and acquisitions.

Yet, Salazar, the CEO who presumably orchestrated all this bad behavior, came out smelling as sweet as yam pie. He served on charitable boards and contributed heavily to the arts. Most puzzling, was not only his support, but his leadership of a consortium focused on alternative energy research. He had even funded a foundation that was backing an important conference to be held in Cambridge, Massachusetts, within a few days.

Molly's life experiences had taught her that people like Salazar could back all the concerts and lectures money could buy, but the halos over their heads still wouldn't take a polish. She asked herself why Salazar would invest in research that might put him out of business. Maybe he actually wanted to do something to help the planet, but she doubted it. She read the *Wall Street Journal* headline again:

Experts to Unveil Important Energy News at MIT Conference

The article described the excitement over a revolutionary energy source to be demonstrated at the conference organized by the Salazar Foundation. The presenters were the world's best-known experts in the fields of physics and energy distribution. It was a stellar scientific line-up and the first time all the leaders in new technologies would be in the same place at the same time. *The Journal* speculated on turmoil in the markets. Energy stocks would plummet.

Guys like Salazar stood to lose a bundle, but here he was, saying Auroch was well-positioned to embrace cleaner technologies that would reduce the carbon footprint. She shook her head. Salazar was a skunk. Plain and simple. You could clean him up but he'd still stink to high heaven. There was no way he would back something that was bound to put him out of business. Yet here he was giving people the shovel that would bury him. *Why?*

Thinking made her hungry. She put the computer in sleep mode and went into the kitchen. Her shelves and refrigerator were filled with gluten-free products. She didn't have celiac disease, with its intolerance to grain, but eating gluten-free food sounded healthy. She cooked up a gluten-free pizza and ate half of it, washed down with a couple of cans of diet soda. Time to feed Wheeling. She got some calves liver pieces out of the fridge and put them in a dish.

The big bird clucked his beak in anticipation when she entered the shed. She watched him chow down, knowing it was wrong to pamper this magnificent wild creature. Being accustomed to gourmet meals would hamper him when he had to hunt for his own food. Heck. Maybe that's why she was doing it, trying to come up with a reason to postpone Freedom Day.

The chirp of her cell phone was a welcome diversion from her guilty wallowing. She checked the screen. The alert had been transmitted by a motion-activated camera at the front of the house.

Molly had decided not to install a fence, a safe room and full-fledged camera and alarm system like the one she had in Arizona. After all, her house burned down in spite of all her precautions. But she had placed four cameras around the property, each capable of transmitting photos to her cell phone. Mostly, the cameras snapped photos of bats and owls, but the image on her phone now was that of a man who'd triggered the automated flood light.

He was walking toward her house, slightly crouched over. Cradled in his arms was a short-barreled automatic weapon. He wore a baseball cap with a B on it, like the one on the man who'd been bent over his laptop in the Portland coffee shop.

Another camera picked up the man walking along the side of the house. He may have found the front door locked and was making his way around to the back. She turned out the shed light, went to the door and pushed it almost shut, leaving it open just a crack to allow her a glimpse of the man as he turned the corner. He glanced at the shed, then headed for the kitchen door, which she'd left unlocked, and went inside.

She could see him through the windows. He paused to examine the partially-eaten pizza on the table, then went from room to room on the first floor. The second floor lights clicked on. She felt a rush of anger at having the privacy of her bedroom violated by this stranger. She thought of trying to break out of the shed, but Sutherland was in no shape to run for it, even without the pizza sitting like gluten-free lead in her stomach.

The best she could do would be to keep watch and hope that he'd give up and leave. She waited. Moments later she glimpsed him again through the kitchen window. Then he stepped out the back door, stared thoughtfully at the shed, and walked slowly toward it. She moved away from the door, loosened the overhead light bulb and crawled under the shelf in front of Wheeling's perch to the back wall of the shed.

The unexpected intrusion into his space made the eagle nervous. He spread his wings slightly, shifted from claw to claw and made a soft 'wonk' sound.

The crunch of footsteps stopped outside. A man's voice said, "You in there, sweetheart? Come out, come out, or I'll huff and puff and blow the place down. Okay. Guess you're shy. Maybe I'll just burn the place down."

A chill went down her spine. She would be trapped. She stayed silent.

"No answer? Hey, girl, maybe I won't burn you. They said you were in the Army. So you know what a machine pistol can do. I can just riddle that little hen coop full of holes with you in it. So why don't you come out and we'll talk?"

The voice was closer. Molly figured the stranger was moving in as he talked, and that he'd kick the door in when he got close enough. The eagle was even more nervous after hearing the stranger's voice. She placed her hands on the bird's wings and felt it shudder.

Then she yelled, "Changed my mind about coming out, you stupid man. I called 911. Cops are on their way. You'd better get your sorry ass out of here."

That did it. He kicked the door open. He was holding a flashlight against the machine pistol, which was raised to his shoulder. He stepped inside.

Molly stood up suddenly and launched Wheeling at the intruder. The bird flapped its wings. The man stood in the way of the only avenue of escape. The eagle landed on his head, sinking its sharp talons into his scalp through the thin fabric of the baseball cap. He tried to knock the bird off with the short barrel of the machine pistol. This only frightened Wheeling more, and it dug in deeper, wings beating furiously.

The stranger dropped the weapon and staggered out of the shed, the eagle still clutching his head. The noise was awful. The stranger was screaming in pain. The eagle screeched in fright and then spread its wings and flew off into the night. The man wiped away the blood streaming down his face and turned to go back for his weapon. Molly was standing in the shed doorway, machine pistol in hand. He spun around and drunkenly staggered off away from the shed and around the corner of the house.

Cautiously, she followed in his tracks. The stranger might have gone to his car for another gun. She was relieved when she heard a car engine start. Headlights snapped on from the woods off to one side of her driveway where the stranger had parked his car in the trees. The car accelerated, its tires kicking up gravel, and pulled out onto the road, but instead of navigating the curve, it went straight. There was a horrendous *crump* sound. Then silence. She trotted down a couple of hundred feet to where the car had hit a tree.

The headlights were still on. The windshield was cracked from the impact of the stranger's head. He was slumped over the steering wheel. She pushed him back into the seat and felt for a pulse in his neck. He was dead. His eye sockets were filled with pools of blood from his head wounds. He must have been blinded and not seen the bad curve in time. She went through his pockets and pulled out a wallet and cell phone. She used a corner of his jacket to wipe the blood away, turned his head to face her, and took a photograph with her phone. She hid the machine pistol in the shed. Then she called 911 to report the accident.

Molly was waiting next to the wreck when the police and rescue squad arrived. She said she heard the noise of the crash and went out to see what it was. After giving her account, she went back to her house and sat at her computer table. She took out the wallet and spread its contents on the table. The man's name was William Thomas and his home address was in Nebraska.

She remembered the words the man spoke when she was hiding in the shed.

"They said you were in the Army."

Who were *they*? And why was this man sent to kill her?

She woke up her computer and started piecing together a biography of the late Mr. Thomas. She didn't find much until she got into the FBI file. The facial recognition program identified the dead man as Tommy Lee Crimmins from Fort Collins, Colorado. Going back from the present, she saw that he had been released from prison where he'd served a term for assault and battery. Before that, he'd worked for a couple of security companies. And his training for those jobs came in Afghanistan where he worked in demolition with the Marines.

Using his credit card number, she hacked into his account. Crimmins, or Thomas, had only arrived in Oregon early that morning, when she had seen him at the café. *Pickety-pick.* She worked back and saw that he had flown in from Boston. He'd stayed at an expensive Boston hotel, which suggested someone else must be paying the bill. And he had several dinners that ran more than five hundred dollars, which indicated he was not dining alone. Boston is across the Charles River from Cambridge, home to MIT.

Molly stared at a list of credit card charges on the screen.

Something was to going to happen. And it involved explosives, and the energy conference.

CHAPTER FIFTY-TWO

Kalliste opened her eyes and gazed at a painting of a half dozen flying fish dancing in the air over an azure sea. She thought, *what a beautiful dream.* As she became fully conscious, the painful throb in her forehead told her this was no dream.

She pushed herself onto her elbow, then sat up and swung her legs over the edge of a platform bed. She looked down and saw that she was wearing an ankle-length layered skirt of pale blue and a white, long-sleeved blouse.

The room was around twenty feet square. The other three walls were also covered with frescoes heavy on an ocean theme: Octopi. Dolphins. Graceful, square-sailed sailboats. The artistic style was unmistakably Minoan.

The only other furniture in the windowless room consisted of a chair made of lattice wood and leather and a small table next to the bed. On the table was a ceramic drinking vessel, a pitcher and a bowl of fruit and nuts. The pieces of pottery were decorated with pictures of mollusks. She had an awful taste in her mouth, as if she'd been eating ashes. Ugh. Worse than an ouzo hangover. With an unsteady hand she poured water from the pitcher into the glass and took a deep swallow. She was starving as well as thirsty, and hungrily devoured several dates, some figs and a bunch of deep red grapes.

As she chewed on a juicy grape, she saw the bug-eyed octopi

begin to move. Then a sliding door opened in the wall. She gasped with surprise. Lily Porter stepped into the room and shut the door behind her. The trademark short leather skirt and matching vest were gone. She was dressed in an outfit similar to Kalliste's, except for the blue-black color of the flounced skirt.

Lily's skirts rustled as she settled into the chair. "Hello, Kalliste. Surprised to see me?"

"Of course I'm surprised. What is this place?"

"We are in the royal apartments of the Maze, or Labyrinth if you prefer the more poetic name."

"The only Labyrinth I know of is at Knossos."

"We're in Spain. A very special part of Spain."

Kalliste was more confused than ever. The last memory she had was of walking across the square near her Santorini house, deep in thought about her translating work. She didn't notice the figures in black dart from the pool of darkness under a spreading tree until it was too late. Rough hands grabbed her around the shoulders, pinning her arms. She felt a sharp sting in her neck. And a curtain of darkness descended.

"How did I get to Spain? Wait. I get it now. Hidden History is doing a piece on the Knossos maze." She glanced around. "This is a set."

"No, Kalliste. This is not a set for a television program."

Her voice was low and almost monotone. Her unsmiling face was as hard as marble. She was no longer the scatter-brained producer of zany TV shows. Kalliste was still slightly confused from the drugs, but she was alert enough to know that something was dangerously wrong about this bizarre encounter.

Suppressing the fear that threatened to choke her words, she said, "In that case, I would appreciate it if you could tell me what is going on."

Lily cracked her lips in a slight smile. "What I am about to tell you is true, although you may find it hard to believe."

Kalliste glanced around the room. "These days there is nothing I find hard to believe."

Lily ignored the comment and stared off into the distance.

"The story begins nearly four thousand years ago on the island where you were born, and whose name you bear. The volcano on Kalliste erupts, causing earthquakes and triggering a tsunami that wipes out Knossos and the other seaports along the northern coast of Crete. The Minoan empire is weakened. An invasion from the mainland threatens."

"So far you have told me nothing new," Kalliste said.

Lily dismissed the comment with a flick of her long fingers.

"You know only what you read in the history books. What I'm about to tell you few people know."

"Go ahead then. I'm listening." Trying to preserve the illusion of calm, Kalliste plucked a grape from the bowl and popped it in her mouth.

"Civil war ensues. One side is loyal to King Minos. The other supports the High Priestess of the Snake Goddess sanctuary. The king is about to be overthrown, and places his young daughter in the hands of the commander of the palace guard who leaves Knossos with the Minoan treasure. They sail aboard a cargo ship to the west, with the High Priestess and her brother in pursuit. There is a fierce sea battle off the coast of Spain. Both ships are heavily damaged by fire. The king's daughter escapes in a sailboat. The priestess and her party make it to land, but their ship has been damaged beyond repair. They are stranded."

Kalliste remembered the dark stains on the wreck of the sunken ship.

"The timbers of the Minoan vessel off Cadiz were charred from fire. That's quite the coincidence."

"No coincidence at all. You dove on the king's ship."

"We saw no sign of treasure."

"That's because there is none. Numerous dives were made on the ship over the centuries before it was determined that the commander disposed of the treasure before the battle."

Kalliste remembered the diving bell and the other antique underwater equipment that littered the shipwreck.

"The divers all died looking for a treasure that wasn't there," she said.

Lily nodded. "At that point the wreck was abandoned and its location was lost over time until the fisherman caught his net."

"What happened after the battle?" Kalliste asked.

"The priestess, her brother and a handful of followers made their way to a Minoan mining colony. They took control and prospered. The king's people vanished. They hid their tracks well. Search parties went out from the mining colony, but with no success. There were no DNA footprints to follow in those days."

"What's DNA got to do with it?"

"In this case, everything. I borrowed some hairs from your pillow and had them analyzed."

"You broke into my apartment to find some hairs?"

"Not me, but those under my command."

The intrusion on her private property seemed trivial after having been kidnapped, but Kalliste was furious.

"I liked you much better when you were a TV producer. Too bad you went through all this breaking and entering and stealing for nothing."

"No trouble at all, considering what I learned from the DNA tests. That your genetic line goes back to King Minos."

"Oh, stop it, Lily. That's ridiculous."

"The DNA doesn't lie. You are a direct descendent of King Minos's daughter."

"Fascinating. I always wanted to be a princess. You still haven't told me what we're doing in this place, and why we're dressed in these foolish costumes."

"I understand why you're angry, but you will feel better after I put things in perspective."

"I doubt it, but go ahead." Kalliste's curiosity overshadowed her anger.

"I told you how the priestess and her people entrenched themselves in the mining colony. The priestess remained pure so she could conduct the old rituals, but her brother and the other men intermarried with local women. As their line grew, they expanded their wealth and power throughout Spain and into other parts of Europe. They went into the highest levels of government and business. No matter where they were, they kept to the old traditions and rituals."

"They practiced the Minoan religion?"

"It was modified to adapt to changing circumstances, but it endured in its basic form through the centuries."

"You're saying there are people alive in the world today who belong to a cult that worships the Snake Goddess?"

"The Way of the Axe is much more than a cult. It took an organization with power and wealth to build this replica of the original maze where they could practice their religion and be reminded of their ancient roots."

"Does that religion include the bull dancers?"

"The farms around here bred the Auroch bulls for centuries and young men and women were trained in the ritual. It became more difficult to maintain the breed and train the dancers while keeping our existence a secret. We had to make other arrangements."

"It's hard for me to believe an 'organization' like the one you describe could operate in secret for so long without being discovered."

"Oh, their secret was uncovered from time to time, but those revelations were quickly reburied. Important communications were transmitted using the ancient script, Linear A. I believe you're familiar with it."

"Of course. Linear A is one of the world's great mysteries."

"Apparently, it is a mystery no more. The translating device you and Hawkins brought up from the ship is similar to those used to keep the old language alive. We use computer programs now, not unlike the one you hoped the Hidden History channel would finance. Within minutes, we can decipher the scroll that gave you so much trouble. Simply figuring out the author's name was an amazing accomplishment on your part, though."

I have a big, fat Greek mouth, Kalliste thought. She had told Lily everything about the device and the scroll when she called from Santorini to ask Hidden History to fund a computer-aided translation.

Attempting to divert Lily, she said, "Thank you, but all I learned was that the author's name was Minotaur."

"Don't sell yourself short. The Minotaur was the nickname of King Minos's second-in-command. He was the guardian of your ancestor, the king's daughter."

"Now I understand. You were behind the attack on my expedition and the destruction of the ancient ship," Kalliste said.

"We couldn't let the translator get into the wrong hands. Our prime directive is that Linear A be kept a secret. Once the script is deciphered, all our secrets, going back centuries, would become public."

"As you can see, I don't have it. So, maybe you can arrange transportation from this lovely place."

"You can leave any time you want to," Lily said. "Just press on the octopus image on the fresco to the right of the door."

Kalliste was suspicious. *This* was too easy. She got up and went to the door. When she placed her palm on the octopus, the door slid open. She glanced back at Lily, who was still in her chair, and stepped out into a long passageway lit by electric wall sconces.

She set her jaw and began to follow the passageway toward another door. She had made it almost to the end when the door slid open on its own. Beyond the portal was darkness, except for two pairs of blazing red orbs at eye level. She thought they were some sort of lights until they moved in her direction. She turned and ran. The patter of paws was right behind her.

Lily was waiting in the doorway to the apartment. She stepped aside, then followed Kalliste into the room and closed the door.

"Are you done playing with our pets?" she said.

"What are those awful things?" She could barely speak.

"They're called the Daemons. They're a hybrid of dog and wolf, developed through the years to resemble the griffins on the wall drawings. You were never in any danger. The medallion around your neck protected you."

Kalliste's trembling hand reached to her throat and her fingers felt the metal pendant shaped like a double-headed axe.

"I don't understand," she said.

"The medallion emits a signal that tells the Daemons that you're not prey."

She reached out and hit the wall switch that slid the door back. Sitting on their haunches, tongues hanging out over their formidable teeth, were the supposed hounds that had chased her. They made no move to come into the room but, in fact, got to their feet and moved aside to make way for Lily.

"Come," she said. "I'll show you the Maze."

Keeping a wary eye on the dogs, Kalliste closely followed on Lily's heels, trying to ignore the patter of paws behind her once again.

CHAPTER FIFTY-THREE

Hawkins drove his rental car to a private aircraft hangar at the Cadiz Airport and pulled up next to a helicopter emblazoned with yellow suns. The word HelioTours was printed in large letters on the red fuselage. He checked the instructions Abby had given him, and said, "This is it."

"You gotta be kidding," Chad said.

"This was the only chopper available on short notice," Hawkins said. "Belonged to a tour company that went bankrupt. It's been maintained pending sale. Let's take a look."

They got out of the car and walked around the helicopter.

"It's an Astar model," Calvin said. "Good machine. They fly these babies in the U.S. tourist trade."

Chad had a doubtful expression on his face. "Guess the SEALs did things different. Special Ops choppers were painted in camouflage. Maybe you guys can explain what's smart about using a flying billboard for a recon mission."

"Calvin, please explain SEAL tactics to our Army friend," Hawkins said.

"Glad to, Hawk." Turning to Chad, he said, "This *is* camouflage. We're doing a daytime recon. No way to sneak in without someone spotting you. With this paint job anyone who sees us peeking in their windows will think we're tourists."

Chad thought about it. "Might work." His lips tightened in a smirk. "Then again, it might not."

"That's a fifty-fifty chance of success," Hawkins said. "Better odds than pumping the slots at Vegas, right Cal?"

"Tell you after I check this baby out."

Calvin squatted to inspect the underside and pronounced the fuselage in good shape. Then he climbed into the pilot's seat and fiddled around with the instrument panel. Satisfied, he gave the others a thumb's up.

Hawkins got in beside his friend. Chad climbed in the back and set his duffel bag on the bench seat. They tested their headsets. Cal started the engine, the whirling rotors picked up speed and the helicopter lifted off the tarmac. Quickly clearing Cadiz, they headed inland at a speed of one-hundred-thirty-five-miles per hour. The sprawling suburbs thinned out and were replaced by farmland.

"Here's the mission plan," Hawkins said, speaking over the cabin communication system. "Calvin keeps us in the air. I'll act as primary spotter. Chad will shoot photos of stuff I point out or anything that looks significant. We'll keep our survey short, stay at a distance and avoid engagement."

Flying at an altitude of around a thousand feet, the helicopter cruised over cultivated fields. The farms and villages grew fewer in number and further apart. The countryside became a wild-looking expanse of dark, tangled woods and stretches of uninhabited flatland. The overcast sky intensified the gloominess of the landscape. Hawkins could understand why Don Quixote thought he encountered monsters roaming the desolate plains of *La Mancha*.

Hawkins scanned the horizon through binoculars and saw the spikes of the castle's towers jutting from a low hill into the slag-gray sky. He handed the binoculars to Calvin.

"Looks like we made a wrong turn and ended up in Transylvania."

Calvin peered through the lenses.

"Either that, or it's Disney channeling Dracula's castle."

Passing the binoculars back to Chad, he peered at the high walls of dark stone and the looming towers and let out a low whistle. "Getting into that pile of rocks is going to be a challenge."

"Every defensive position has its weak spots. Get your camera ready," Hawkins said. "Calvin, move us about a quarter of a mile closer, then put the chopper in a wide clockwise circle."

They passed over a river and Calvin brought the helicopter down to around five hundred feet. He cut speed by half, steered left of the castle and banked to the right, drifting the helicopter into a wide circle that gave Hawkins a clear view out his side window. As the helicopter passed the corner of the crenelated wall, Hawkins saw a number of masts sprouting from the tower.

"Get some shots of those communication antennae, Chad. Might help us figure out their electronic defense perimeter."

The chopper rounded the castle and came back to where it started. Calvin put it into a hover with the nose pointing toward the castle.

Hawkins wasn't sure how long the tourist helicopter disguise would hold, and he didn't want to press his luck. The castle was a magnificent example of architecture, and it wouldn't be unusual for it to be the focus of attention. But there was a fine line between curiosity and nosiness.

The recon had yielded little information of value. Yes, there was a big building on a hill, but Hawk wanted to know what was on the other side of the high walls.

"We'll have to fly directly over the castle," he said.

"Risky move," Calvin warned. "They could hit us with a rock thrown from the top of the walls."

"If we only make one quick pass we might catch them off-guard. What do you think, Chad?"

"I'm game. We'd better make a move soon, though. We look suspicious just sitting out here."

Hawkins said, "Set your camera on video so we won't miss anything. Any time, Cal."

Calvin tilted the helicopter's nose down and accelerated, flying directly toward the main gate. The helicopter passed a hundred feet above the top of the wall, then over a second line of lower fortifications that hadn't been visible before. Hawkins only saw a blur before the chopper swept over the outer walls, did a quick turn-around and flew back over the castle.

"Anyone see what was beyond that secondary wall?" Hawkins said as the helicopter came to a hover.

"We were going too fast," Calvin said. "Feel like risking a slower pass?"

"Why not?" Hawkins said. "Looks like nobody's home."

Chad said, "I think I got some good video, but it doesn't hurt to have an insurance shot."

Hawkins gave Calvin the thumb's-up. The helicopter started toward the castle again, gaining speed. It was within seconds of passing over the wall when an object that looked like a large black bug rose from the other side and stopped to hover directly in the way.

"Drone!" Calvin warned. "Hold on."

He steered the helicopter sharply off to the right to go around the remotely piloted aircraft, which mirrored Calvin's tactic. He brought the helicopter to a sliding hover, and moved to the left. The drone mimicked the move. Both aircraft stopped and hovered nose-to-nose, a hundred feet apart, in an aerial Mexican standoff.

The blunt-nosed aircraft of gleaming black metal was roughly six feet long. It had a tail propeller for forward motion and twin rotors for vertical movement. The configuration gave the aircraft high maneuverability. Hawkins stared at the undersides of the tubby, square-tip wings jutting out from each side and a chill ran down his spine.

Speaking in a level tone, Hawkins said, "Calvin. Don't make a move."

Calvin had his eyes fixed on the drone. "Yeah, I get you. What do you want me to do?"

"Wait."

"Wait for what?" he said.

"Wait until we figure things out."

Calvin maintained the helicopter in its face-off hover. As they hung in the air as if suspended by an invisible cable, Hawkins heard the sound of the duffel bag being unzipped in the back seat. He turned around and saw Chad extract a machine rifle from the bag, snap the folding stock into place and slide the window open.

"I've *already* got things figured out," he said. "Swing this chopper around and I'll fill the little birdy full of buck shot."

Hawkins grabbed the barrel of the gun before Chad could stick it out the open window.

"What the hell are you doing?" Chad said.

"That pop gun is going to get us killed," Hawkins yelled. "Take a look under those wings."

He moved his body to one side to allow an unimpeded view of the missiles under each wing of the drone. Chad swallowed hard, lowered the gun, and carefully folded the machine rifle back into its bag.

"Your call." He sounded as if he had swallowed a mouthful of sand.

Keeping his eye fixed on the hovering drone, Hawkins stretched his lips so wide it hurt. "The camera's probably picking up our faces, Cal. Give it big smile. You too, Chad boy. Look like a toothpaste commercial."

Calvin and Chad forced toothy grins.

"That's more fiendish than friendly," Hawkins said.

"That's the best I've got, Hawk. What next?"

Speaking through half-clenched teeth, Hawkins raised his hand. "Give our little friend a wave. Pray that our HelioTours cover does what it is supposed to do. Count to thirty, and if we haven't been blown out of the sky, slowly start to back up."

Hawkins mentally kept count. Calvin moved the chopper with the caution of a new driver backing a car out of a garage. The drone made no move to follow. When they had a couple of hundred yards of air between them, he instructed Calvin to keep on going.

They were still fair game. The drone could pick them off at any second. Which is why he almost shouted for joy when the drone did a pivot and headed back to the castle like a dog who had successfully chased away a trespasser. Hawkins let out the breath he'd been holding and told Calvin to take them back to Cadiz.

He called Abby to let her know they were safe. She sounded relieved and said she would meet them at the airport. The helicopter touched down less than an hour later. Abby was waiting by the hangar. She gave Hawkins and Calvin big hugs. Chad, who'd been standing off at a distance watching their reunion, came over and said, "I've been thinking maybe I don't want this gig."

"You pulling out?" Calvin said.

Chad nodded. "I know when I'm outmatched. Salazar's too big to take on."

"I thought you wanted a shot at Salazar because of your girlfriend," Hawkins said.

"I don't want to die trying. Besides, she was only a prostitute."

"What are you going to do?"

"Dunno. I'll figure it out later. In the meantime, I'd appreciate it if you'd drop me off at a taxi stand."

Hawkins decided there was no use arguing. He was of two minds. Chad offered additional needed firepower, but Hawkins didn't trust him in a pinch. Chad had been too eager to shoot at the drone without sizing up its overwhelming fire power. They gave him a ride to the main airport terminal where he got out, handed Hawkins the camera, and said it was a pleasure meeting them. Then he walked off to hail a taxi.

Abby watched him go and said, "He's lying. He's still in love with that girl Salazar killed. He's up to something."

"I've got a feeling that not a minute goes by when Chad *isn't* up to something," Hawkins said.

CHAPTER FIFTY-FOUR

The explosion that had melted Chad's handsome features into a mass of scars had cauterized the emotional center of his brain. But he had been touched by Hawkins' reaction to his disfigurement. Hawkins hadn't been revolted, nor did he show pity. He had been scarred as well; the only difference being that his wounds weren't visible.

Hawkins had said little on the flight back to Cadiz. Chad figured he was analyzing the recon. The news wasn't good. The unseen castle defenders were alert and ready to deal with any intrusion. Even if infiltrators made it past the double defensive walls, they would be operating blindly. If Salazar had Kalliste prisoner there, she was dead meat.

Back in his hotel room, he liberated a bottle of single-malt whiskey from the courtesy refrigerator, poured a glass straight up and settled into a chair. He took a few sips of whiskey, enjoying the smooth burn of the liquid trickling down his throat, then punched a number on his phone. The call was patched through a series of connections to the top floor of the Auroch Industries building. An unmistakable voice came on the line.

"Salazar."

"Hello, Mr. Salazar. This is Leonidas. Hope I didn't catch you at a bad time."

Silence. Then, "I told you not to call me."

"I just wanted to say I'm sorry I was nasty to the two guys you sent over to see me."

"You're not really sorry, Leonidas, but I'm curious how you managed to kill two professionals?"

"They got sloppy."

"In that case they deserved to die."

"They were sloppy about delivering my money, too. Wondered if we could try again without the fireworks."

"Count yourself lucky that I'm too busy to follow up, Leonidas. Consider your life as payment enough. Don't call me again. Ever."

Slam.

Chad stared at the phone in his hand. "I guess that was a no."

He drained his glass, went to his bedroom and opened his make-up kit. Peeling off his handsome California surf bum face, he replaced it with a new layer of fake skin that was several shades darker. He tucked foam under the skin and darkened the eye pouches with touch-up. Then he added fleshy cheeks and jowls. He hid his hair under a fake bald scalp and touched up the edges with make-up so they would blend into the skin. Next came the beetling eyebrows. He smiled at himself in the full-length mirror and practiced Salazar's silky voice. After several tries he got it within range.

He phoned a men's clothing store he had seen in the hotel lobby, said he needed a suit immediately and was willing to pay for it. He gave the clerk his measurements and said he wanted black, with a light blue shirt and yellow tie. Black dress shoes, too.

"Can you find me a briefcase?"

"No problem. There's a leather shop in the lobby."

"Make it alligator skin. Remember. One hour."

Thirty-five minutes later the clerk arrived carrying a cardboard box and an alligator briefcase. Chad took the box from the clerk and gave him a fat tip.

He stripped off his jeans and sweater and slipped into the suit. Salazar was heavier in the shoulders. He cut up strips of towel and used them as shoulder pads. A little lumpy but they'd have to do. Then he went back in front of the mirror, lowered his head and practiced Salazar's menacing glower. Satisfied, he imitated Salazar's purposeful walk on the way to the elevator and across the lobby to the entrance where he gave the door attendant a substantial tip and asked him to hail a limo.

Ten minutes later the limo dropped him off in front of the Auroch Industries tower. He had been there once before when Salazar had hired him. He remembered Salazar presiding in a long room decorated with photos of mining operations.

On the other side of the revolving door was a vast lobby, circular in shape, with highly polished marble walls and floors. At the center of the lobby, balanced on a platform of dark granite, was a perforated greenish-black hunk of copper ore as big as a car. According to a bronze plaque, the nugget was unearthed at an Auroch mine in Bolivia.

On his last visit to the building, a limo brought him to an underground garage. A private elevator whisked him to Salazar's office. He guessed that Salazar rarely came in the front door. He hoped the novelty of seeing Auroch's CEO in the flesh would bring down a veil of confusion he could exploit.

The uniformed security man standing next to the reception desk was the first to recognize him. His jaw dropped. As Chad strode directly toward the guard, he pulled out his cell phone and stuck it to his ear. Playing the role of the distracted executive, he gestured toward the bank of elevators.

In his best Salazar imitation, he said, "If you don't mind, I'm in a hurry."

The guard acted as if he'd been stuck with an electrical prod. "Of course, Mr. Salazar."

He led the way to the last elevator in the row and used a key to unlock the doors. Chad stepped into the elevator and glanced at the name on the man's badge.

"Thank you, Manuel."

The guard grinned, most likely savoring the prospect of a pay raise and promotion, then reached in and pressed a button that closed the doors. The elevator was silent, but Chad could feel the G-force pressing against the soles of his shoes. The doors opened again and Chad stepped out into Salazar's office suite. He walked briskly toward the door he remembered from his last visit, opened it, and went into the combination office and boardroom.

He stood there without speaking. Salazar sat at his desk, his massive head bent over paperwork. After a moment he looked up and furrowed his brow. Chad had to admire the man's steely self-discipline. Salazar's scowl got impossibly deeper, but he didn't miss a beat.

"Is this some sort of joke?" he said.

"Only if you think it is, Mr. Salazar."

Hearing a close approximation of his voice caught his attention. He stood up, came around the table and approached Chad, who tensed, expecting Salazar to get physical. But instead, he stuck his face into Chad's, and said, "Leonidas?"

"Good call, Mr. Salazar," he said in his natural voice.

Salazar turned and went back to his desk. He told Chad to take a seat. "I could have you killed, you know. One touch of my finger on a button will summon men who will take you away."

"I understand that."

"So why did you come here? Did you think I'd be amused by your antics?"

"No," Chad said. "I came here because I needed work. And I wanted to remind you in the best way that I could, why you hired me in the first place. I'm good at getting into places where I haven't been invited." He glanced around at the mining mural. "Places like this."

Salazar sat back in his chair and tented his fingers. Narrowing his eyes, he said, "You caused me a great deal of trouble with your incompetence."

"I'll admit it. I screwed up. I underestimated Hawkins. Nobody warned me about him. Next time he won't be so lucky."

"I have bigger fish to fry than Hawkins." He paused in thought, then he smiled. "I may be able to use you for an operation where your shape-shifting talent will come in handy. "

"I'm up for anything, Mr. Salazar. When do I start?"

"About twenty-four hours from now. I'll let you know the details as soon as I work them out. You have work to do before then. You're going to have to do something about the eyes. They're the wrong color, but contacts can fix that. And you'll have to work on the voice. You've got the tone and the inflections, but not the delivery. A keen ear would notice the difference. That suit looks like it came off the rack at a flea market. I'll have my tailor come up with something that fits."

"Are you saying what I think you're saying?"

"I've never been accused of being vague or imprecise, Leonidas. And I don't like repeating myself. But I'll make an exception in this once instance. Yes, I am saying what you think I'm saying. I want you to be Viktor Salazar."

CHAPTER FIFTY-FIVE

On the ride into the city Abby peppered Hawkins and Calvin with questions about the recon mission. She absorbed every detail, from the description of the castle walls to the shape and size of the drone. By the time they reached the boat that would be their unofficial command center, she had analyzed the possibility of success and balanced it against the probable rewards.

"I don't mean to be pessimistic, Matt," she said, "but the cost-benefit ratio doesn't look good for Kalliste."

"You must have read my mind. Maybe our basic assumption is wrong and Kalliste isn't behind those walls. Or, worst case, she might be dead, and that's something I can't accept."

"Then it's something I can't accept, either." She glanced at Hawkins' stony profile. "Kalliste's special to you, isn't she?"

"Very special, but not in the way you might think. You know better than anyone how mean and crazy I got after the Navy cut me loose. I thought I'd flushed all the bile out of my system after I changed careers and landed in Woods Hole. But I was fooling myself. Every time my bum leg twinged where the doctors patched it together, the rage would come to the surface. It still does, sometimes. Kalliste understood that."

"Unlike your loving wife."

Hawkins could have kicked himself. Abby was still guilty about ditching him after she could no longer take his bitter outbursts.

"Hell, Abby, I was the one who let *you* down."

Sitting in the back seat of the car, Calvin cleared his throat more loudly than necessary.

"What say we work on the assumption that Kalliste *is* in the castle," he said. "We know she's been kidnapped, and that Salazar had a hand in it. Smartest thing is to figure out what to do."

"Sorry for subjecting you to our apology competition," Abby said. "As usual, you're a fount of common sense."

Calvin let out a whooping laugh. "If I had any common sense, I'd be back in New Orleans, strolling down Bourbon Street, instead of trying to figure out where to find a copy of Siege Warfare for Dummies."

"I've got a better idea," Hawkins said. "Let's do some foraging in the galley."

They climbed down into the cabin. Hawkins rummaged around the galley and found a bottle of drinkable wine in a cupboard and spicy sausage in the refrigerator. Calvin came up with rice, canned tomatoes and kidney beans. In short order, they were sitting down to a hearty meal. They talked about the Navy, mostly, three old friends and comrades sharing their fonder memories.

After they cleaned up the galley, Hawkins set his electronic tablet on the table and played the video Chad had shot on the castle flyover. The video showed that behind the castle walls was an open courtyard surfaced with large, irregular paving stones.

"I don't get it," Hawkins said. "The walls are protecting empty space, like a Hollywood movie set. There's nothing there."

"Maybe it's there but we can't see it," Abby said. "I met with Captain Santiago's brother again to talk about the Inquisition deed that transferred the castle property to Salazar's ancestor. I was curious about the references to the property being unclean or unholy. Francisco said the castle may have been built over pre-Christian ruins and that old pagan gods were thought of as demons. The deed was also written in the ancient Linear A script, which suggests a Minoan palace or temple."

"Are you saying that the castle is there to protect buried Minoan ruins?"

"*Castillo de Cuernos* means Castle of the Horns. The bull was sacred in Minoan mythology. Can we take a closer look at the plaza in the center of the enclosure?"

Hawkins zoomed in on the screen image. The enlarged photograph showed something that hadn't been apparent on the more expansive view. Some paving stones were shinier than others. The stones with the sheen were not placed randomly, but were laid out in parallel rows that ran from one side of the enclosure to the other.

"I didn't know the Minoans had solar panels."

"Ground level is a funny place to put solar panels," Abby said.

"Maybe we're not looking at ground level," Hawkins said. "The last time I visited Santorini, Kalliste took me to see the archaeological excavation of the ancient Minoan town that had been buried in the Theran eruption. Let me show you what I'm thinking."

He Googled the town's name, *Akrotiri*, and pulled up photos of tourists wandering through the network of streets lined by one and two-story buildings. Columnar steel supports had been placed throughout the ruins to support a corrugated roof. Translucent fiberglass panels built into the roof allowed light to filter through, casting the ruins in a soft ocher glow.

"I get it," Abby said. "We're not looking at a courtyard. This could be a roof made to *look* like a courtyard."

"Figures," Calvin said. "The castle walls kept the ruins hidden, but once planes and satellites were invented they had to cover it up somehow. Only way to confirm is to take a close look."

Hawkins tented his fingertips, and said, "Any idea how we're going to do that?"

Seeing blank looks all around, he said, "That's what I figured. Time to get to work."

CHAPTER FIFTY-SIX

Kalliste was living the dream of every archaeologist who'd scraped dirt off a piece of ancient pottery. She had stepped through a time warp, traveled thousands of years into the past and was seeing the Labyrinth not as a pile of reassembled stones that only hinted at its grandeur, but as it actually *was*.

She would feel better if the dream had not turned into a nightmare. As Lily led her through the network of passageways and rooms, the Daemons padded behind them. She tried to pretend that the living griffins were simply very large canines. But the massive heads and cruel jaws, the skull-like faces and powerful haunches, were not likely to bring them "Best in Show" at Westminster.

She touched the medallion hanging from her neck.

Lily noticed the gesture. "You have nothing to worry about as long as you're wearing the pendant."

"Your pets still make me nervous. Do they need to follow so closely?"

Lily said something in a strange language. The hell hounds bounded off like spaniels chasing a rabbit and disappeared through a darkened doorway.

"What language were you speaking?" Kalliste said.

"A form of ancient Minoan. I told the puppies to resume their patrol duties. Well, what do you think of the Labyrinth?"

"I'm stunned at its sophistication. Who built it?"

"The first High Priestess and her followers. They wanted something greater than Knossos to please the Mother Goddess and to serve as the administrative center of a growing empire."

"It sounds like an old English Priory, where religious and secular interests merged."

"That's exactly what Knossos was until the king went against the High Priestess, who conveyed the word of the Mother Goddess, and had to be disposed of."

Detecting a tightness in Lily's voice, Kalliste changed the subject. "Why is it here in Spain, so far from Crete?"

"The volcanic disaster had ruined the island. There were famines and civil wars. The High Priestess wanted to preserve the old ways. And for centuries, the dancers risked their lives on the bull court."

"You no longer do the bull dancing ritual?"

"It became difficult to maintain a herd of bulls as in the old days. We chose certain rituals to continue and the People of the Axe prospered."

"The People. Is that what you call yourself?"

"We who follow the Mother Goddess have called ourselves many things over the ten thousand years of our existence."

"I thought that worship of the Mother Goddess had vanished, except for a cult or sect here and there."

"You've seen too many episodes of Hidden History, Kalliste. We're not a bunch of crazies beating drums and chanting meaningless mumblings. Our rituals are based in the natural world. We will continue to reap bounty from the earth as long as we make the Mother Goddess happy."

"You make it sound as if she is no longer happy."

"We have seen the signs of her anger. Mortals who ignore the demands of the Mother Goddess do so at their own peril."

"Mortals like Professor Vedrakis?"

"The professor would have deciphered our sacred script. Our prime protocol is that Linear A cannot ever be translated by an outsider. The penalty is death. This has been going on a long time with others who got too near, like Ventris."

"He died in an accident."

"Did he? Well, we did our job well with that one. Robsham,

too, going off that cliff. Bad drivers, these scholars. Don't look so horrified, Kalliste. You bear responsibility for Vedrakis. His death could have been avoided if you and Hawkins had not pursued diving on the ship and recovered the translating device."

The chirp of a telephone was like a gunshot in the quiet precincts of the dead. Lily reached into the folds of her skirt and pulled out a phone. She glanced at the screen and a smile came to her saturnine face.

"It seems we had visitors."

She showed Kalliste the photo of the man sitting in the cockpit of a helicopter. He had a smile on his face and was waving.

"It's Matt!"

"Your friend must miss you. It would be rude not to invite him to visit the Maze and meet its guardian."

"Guardian? What are you talking about?"

Lily responded with a lilting laugh. "I'm surprised that you wouldn't know. The Minotaur lives here. Now, I have a request to make of you."

Kalliste was convinced more than ever that Lily was insane, but if she wanted to survive she would have to play along.

"Of course. Tell me what you want me to do."

"I want to take a photograph to send to Mr. Hawkins."

"Why would you do that?"

"Hawkins has our property—the translator—and I want him to return it."

Kalliste's face flushed in anger. Lily was using her as bait. But she sensed an opportunity. She glanced around at her surroundings and moved a few steps so she was directly in front of the doorway to the apartment under the double axe-head lintel. She crossed her arms.

Lily gave a sharp whistle. The two hell hounds shot out of the shadows. She spoke to them again in the strange language. The command must have overridden the signal from the medallion, because they growled and moved toward Kalliste from both sides.

Lily used her phone to take a picture of Kalliste being menaced by the giant animals, then she called them off with another command.

Kalliste was still trembling when she said, "Are you through?"

"For now." She called off the hounds and showed Kalliste the photo on her cell phone. "This should get your friend's attention."

CHAPTER FIFTY-SEVEN

Salazar called Chad, "Be outside your hotel in thirty minutes."

Chad had been waiting for the call, and was already dressed in a black sweatshirt, sweatpants and running shoes. Loose and nondescript. Standard hit man gear. Good for hiding weapons and confusing eye witnesses.

He tucked a short-barreled pistol into a sock holster. He was standing on the curb when the black Mercedes SUV pulled up in front of him. Salazar rolled down the window and beckoned from the front passenger seat for him to get in.

The two bulky men in the back seat slid over to make room. His seatmates and the driver had stuffed themselves into black running outfits that looked like they'd come off the rack at Assassins "R" Us. Baseball caps were pulled down over aviator sunglasses. Their heads seemed to sit on their shoulders without benefit of a neck. Salazar was dressed the same way.

Salazar introduced Chad as the replacement member of the team. There were grunted responses and a couple of hard stares.

The SUV pulled away from the curb, headed out of the city and after a short drive, left the highway and traveled on back roads. The Mercedes turned onto a driveway marked Private and plunged into thick woods. The vehicle stopped in front of a log house at the end of the road. Chad and the other men got out of the SUV and followed Salazar into the cabin to a room that had a TV monitor filling an entire wall.

Salazar went over to a table that held an object covered with a sheet. He told everyone to take a seat and clicked the remote control of a Power Point projector. Chad almost fell out of his chair with surprise. He was looking at a photo of the castle he had seen from the helicopter.

Salazar said, "This castle is called *Castillo de Cuernos*. It was built by my family, but for five hundred years it has been under the control of a small group. Our goal is to take it back. Bruno will fill you in on the operational plan."

Salazar sat down and Bruno got up and flicked on a laser pointer. He placed the red dot on an entrance to the castle.

"The castle is defended by two sets of walls and has only one land entrance. All Middle Ages stuff. It's also protected by sensors, inside and out, that detect intruders and respond accordingly. Signs and recorded messages warn trespassers that they will be met with lethal force. Guns mounted on top of the walls are programmed to fire on anyone in the kill zone. Any air incursion will be met by a drone armed with missiles."

That explained the warm reception when the tourist helicopter got too close.

"Okay. I'm impressed. How do we get past the air defenses?"

"The defenses can be temporarily disabled allowing visitors to land on a helipad within the castle walls. About a dozen guys will be in the courtyard. All top guns for hire. But we go in with Mr. Salazar, who is there by my invitation. He's allowed four bodyguards. Once we are admitted past the first line of walls we will make the switch."

"I don't get you. What switch is that?"

"I've told Bruno and his men about your unique shape-shifting talents," Salazar said.

"Don't know if I'd call it shape-shifting, Mr. Salazar. I'm pretty good with make-up."

"Don't be modest. You were more than good when you borrowed my face and walked past security into my office. I want you to impersonate me again after we pass through the second wall enclosure."

Bruno clicked the remote control. The castle photo vanished to be replaced by a picture of an odd-looking structure that had two towers flanking a taller one.

Chad shook his head. "Looks like something on the Strip in Vegas."

Salazar said, "We'll make the switch in this building. We'll all be wearing face masks, so the transition should be simple. There's another level below this one, and that's where the ceremony will be."

"What sort of ceremony, Mr. Salazar?"

"It's a religious ceremony. It will be attended by a dozen or so priestesses and two bodyguards. Your role is a minor one." He removed the cloth covering the object on the table, revealing the bull's head; rhyton. "You will carry this to an altar in the ceremonial sanctuary."

"That's it?"

"Not quite. You'll be given a small remote device. You will place the rhyton on the altar. Then you will step back; when the ceremony begins you will press the remote button which will send a signal to us. While all attention is on the ceremony we will disarm the bodyguards and take control of the sanctuary."

"Getting past your office security guard was one thing. Do you really think we can pull off an identity swap?"

"I don't just think it. I *know* it. The light inside the sanctuary will be dim. You will be wearing a costume that will disguise you. You won't have to worry about opposition. Only women and chosen male attendants are allowed in the sanctuary for the ceremony."

Stretching his lips in a slop-sided grin, Chad said, "How'd you get so lucky?"

"My special status allows me to participate in the ceremony," Salazar said. "That's all you have to know."

"Okay. When does this go down?"

Salazar said, "I can't give you an exact time, but expect to get a call within the next twenty-four hours. You must be ready to move in disguise on a moment's notice."

The ride back to the hotel was uneventful. Chad got out of the SUV and watched until the taillights disappeared around a corner. He went back to his room and poured a tall glass of whiskey. He sat in a chair and sipped from his glass.

Salazar had seemed irritated when asked for details. There was also an edge to that silky smooth voice when Chad asked how he had access to the women-only party in the sanctuary.

The question popped back into his mind. Why would Salazar be allowed entrance into a female ceremony? The answer was so far-fetched he pushed it aside, but the thought kept nudging him like a hungry puppy. All the signs were there. The feminine flesh around the cheeks and mouth. The lack of any facial hair; not even a whisker. The heavy physique of someone who worked hard to keep the pounds off.

He clicked on his cell phone and after a short Google search found some photographs whose subjects could have been Salazar's brothers. Eunuchs. Young men had once been castrated to give them the amazing singing voices that echoed off the walls of great cathedrals. Salazar had been modified early in his life not to change his voice, but to allow him to take part in a ceremony that excluded males. He poured himself another half glass and slugged it down. For a second, he entertained a fleeting sympathy for Salazar at the barbaric operation that had turned him into a freak. It quickly passed, to be replaced by a cold appraisal. It didn't make any difference in his hatred, but at least he knew now why Salazar was so damned bad-tempered.

CHAPTER FIFTY-EIGHT

Calvin snapped his fingers. "Got it. We build a *trebuchet* siege engine, buckle on a couple of parachutes, then catapult over the wall and float down like feathers."

"Poetic, but not practical," Abby said. "If it worked, the castle defenders would have been toast a long time ago."

"That's because parachutes hadn't been invented yet," Calvin said.

Abby rolled her eyes and turned to Hawkins. "Calvin didn't quite get the concept when you said we would need to be creative."

"Thanks for the suggestion, Cal, but Abby's right. Back to the drawing board."

Calvin took his pen and crossed an X over the imaginative diagram he'd sketched out to demonstrate his plan. "Guess it was kinda dumb, but I was getting desperate."

They were sitting around the table in the galley. The tablet was in the center of the table. Scattered on the tabletop were sheets of paper with diagrams and notes scrawled on them. The gloom in the cabin was so thick it could have been cut with a butter knife.

"Let's go back to the beginning," Hawkins said. "We know from our recon that the walls may enclose a camouflage roof. We think that the roof hides a replica of the Maze."

Abby said, "That's the problem, Matt. We're trying to act on supposition rather than knowledge, and that's dangerous. We may

299

have to admit that there is no viable way to get in and out."

"Damn it, Abby. There's *always* a way." He quickly squelched his flash of anger. "Sorry, Ab, that outburst was uncalled for."

"I stepped into it, Matt. We've known each other a long time. Defeatism isn't in your vocabulary."

"Yeah, but realism should be. Let's go through our choices. Option one is standard SEAL insertion strategy. Come in over a target, rappel down from a chopper, find the target and get out before anyone knows we dropped in."

"The late Mr. Bin Laden would testify that isn't a bad strategy," she said.

"Main difference is that the SEAL team's intel had a pretty good idea of what they were getting into," Calvin added.

Hawkins nodded in agreement. "So let's go over SEAL Option Two. We come in by sea, we get dropped off by a fast boat or sneak close to shore in a mini-sub."

"Not applicable here," Abby said. "It's a long way from the ocean."

"No ocean, but there is water. A river."

Abby picked up the salt and pepper shakers and moved them a foot apart. "Okay, the castle is pepper and the river is salt. How do we get from one to the other?"

He brought up the satellite photo of the castle and its environs on the screen. "Tell me what we're looking at."

"The castle sits on a low hill rising above grassy plains, where it overlooks a winding river. The structure seems to be built on layers of rock, the strata immediately below the castle is grayish-brown in color. How am I doing, Sherlock?"

"Excellent, Abby. Go on with your analysis, but think about the natural environment for a SEAL op; water."

"Aside from the river, the only water in the castle environment is in the form of a moat." She drew her finger along a faint line on the photo connecting the river and the moat. "What's this?"

"I asked myself the same question. I also wondered about the water source for the moat. It was the river, obviously, which feeds the moat with fresh water to counter evaporation."

"We could be looking at a sluiceway," Calvin said.

300

"Maybe. Maybe more than that."

Hawkins flattened out the scroll next to the computer. Calvin studied the diagram of the maze that had been drawn on the vellum and placed the tip of his forefinger on two parallel lines drawn at right angles to one wall.

"This projection matches the sluiceway," he said.

"Maybe," Hawkins said. "There's no moat shown in the original construction. The sluiceway goes directly from the river into the maze. I think this connector was for water supply or drainage for the maze. The castle builders found it and incorporated it into the design as a way to fill the moat with water. And what's at home in water? SEALs."

Abby pursed her lips. "This assumes that the maze shown in the diagram and what's under the castle are the same. Do you want to base a dangerous mission on that assumption?"

There was silence in the galley as three pair of eyes examined the network of lines in the diagram. Then Hawkins said, "We'll need to pull together some SCUBA gear."

"Guess that's a go," Abby said. "I'll take what intel we have and lay out a mission plan. If Kalliste is in there, you'll have to get her out. What's the extraction strategy?"

"We'll bring along a backup air tank. Kalliste is an experienced diver and will know what to do. I'm still wondering about the insertion. Can we make a helicopter drop close to the castle without being detected, Cal?"

"We'll be flying low enough to mow the lawn. I'll land us up-river and we can make our approach from there."

"Let's do a quick inventory of the gear we'll need."

They grabbed pen and paper and were ten minutes into their work when Hawkins' cell chirped. It was Lily Porter, the producer for Hidden History.

"Matt, thank God I got you," Lily said in a breathless voice. "I've been trying to reach Kalliste. Have you heard from her?"

"Not recently. Is there a problem?"

"A very big problem. I can't explain over the phone. I have to talk to you in person. Immediately."

Hawkins remembered the effusive young woman who'd babbled

about her goofy TV series when he'd met her in the hotel lobby.

"I'm sorry," he said. "I'm up to my eyeballs."

"Please, Matt. You don't understand. I'm going to send you a picture I just received. Please call me back."

A second later a photo appeared on the screen of Hawkins' cell phone. The picture showed Kalliste standing in a dimly lit place. The last time he saw her, in Santorini, she was wearing a T-shirt and shorts, her normal work-a-day uniform. The woman in the picture was dressed as if for a costume ball in a waist-length white shift, and a flounced skirt that went down to her ankles.

Kalliste was staring directly at the picture taker. She had her arms crossed and determination burned in her dark eyes, but fear lurked there as well. And with good reason. Flanking Kalliste were a pair of monstrous creatures. They resembled gigantic dogs, but they were like no canines Hawkins had ever seen. Their tapering, satanic skulls were vaguely human. The massive jaws hung open in fiendish grins, long sharp fangs only inches from her throat. Either one of the creatures looked capable of snapping Kalliste's head off in a single bite.

There was a message under the photo which read:

Wish you were here, Matt.

Hawkins called Lily back.

"Tell me where we can meet," he said.

CHAPTER FIFTY-NINE

Kalliste sat on her bed, legs crossed in a yoga lotus position, her eyes tightly shut, her thoughts focused like a laser. Lily had removed the pendant from Kalliste's neck after escorting her back to the apartment. She left the door unlocked. The giant guardians prowling the Maze were enough to keep Kalliste in her room.

She wasn't fooled by Lily's assurances that she would be a "guest" at the ceremony. She knew exactly what her role would be—a sacrifice to the Mother Goddess. She channeled all her energy and intellect on a single goal. Escape.

She heard the door slide across, opened her eyes and saw the tall priestess who'd been her keeper. The woman was dressed in a long flounced dress with a half-open bodice. She wore a flat, rolled cap on her head. An axe medallion dangled between her breasts. The priestess silently advanced and set a tray on the table, then left Kalliste alone. She stared at the dishes on the tray. Fruit, yogurt, bread, honey and water. Should she eat it or not?

She knew that bulls about to be sacrificed in Minoan days were fed grain laced with drugs to dull their senses. Kalliste was no thousand-pound animal whose resistance could pose a danger, but it was common sense that when the time came, her captors would revert to old habits. Her last meal would be sumptuous. After being half-starved, she would devour every drugged morsel.

The serving of a sumptuous *prix fixe* would be her signal to act.

She stared at the tray, hoping she was right. She hadn't had food for hours and was famished. She had to eat if she were to have the strength to cope with what lay on the other side of her door. She picked up a slice of bread, slathered it with honey, and popped it in her mouth. The outline of a plan was forming in her mind.

CHAPTER SIXTY

Calvin wished Hawkins luck and dropped him off at the *Plaza de las Flores* near the Central Market, the meeting place Lily had suggested. Using the cell phone GPS, he followed a route through block after block of deteriorating neighborhoods.

He parked in front of a nondescript warehouse on a street strewn with broken glass. The windows were boarded over with plywood. A chain link fence topped by razor wire enclosed the warehouse, but the wide open main gate was falling off its hinges. The walls were covered with fading paint. Even the graffiti artists avoided the place.

The warehouse was one of a dozen or so similar structures in what must have been a bustling commercial center. There was no number on the building. He'd been advised on the phone that the green light bulb glowing in a wire cage next to the door would tell him he had the right place. He got out of the car, walked through the gate to the warehouse and pushed the doorbell.

A voice came from a square grate a few inches below the light. "State your business."

"I'm the friend of the gentleman in Amsterdam."

The man who opened the door was slight of build. He wore a white shirt, loosely knotted tie and dark slacks. His gray hair was disheveled and he had pouches under his eyes. Calvin thought he looked like an overworked accountant chasing a deadline for filing tax returns.

He stepped aside. "Come right in. My name is Higgins."

It wasn't a hard accent for Calvin to pick up. "Aussie?"

"Good call. Melbourne. And you're from southern U.S.?"

"New Orleans."

"Great town. C'mon. Let's get you fitted out."

Their footsteps echoed across the concrete floor. Higgins pushed open a sliding door and led Calvin into a cramped space that functioned as a combined office and living quarters. Higgins told Calvin to take a seat in a folding chair, then plunked himself behind a metal desk and pecked away at the computer keyboard.

Calvin thought back to the plush surroundings where Broz conducted business.

"After Amsterdam, I expected an operation this size to be more elaborate."

Higgins looked up from his work. "More here than meets the eye. Security cameras are everywhere. Even the street you drove in on is under surveillance. You were checked out before I opened the door. Facial recognition. Voice ID when you called. We've got personnel on hand 24/7, but they stay out of sight unless there's trouble. Some of our guys are pretty scary and we don't like to frighten legitimate customers."

Calvin glanced at the cot in a corner, the refrigerator and the folding table. "Looks like you spend a lot of time here."

"Twenty-four seven. Changing shifts is a big deal security-wise. Okay, here's your order." He printed a sheet of paper and handed it to Calvin to read.

Calvin read the list. "Looks okay. Got all the main stuff and the special order."

Higgins got up from his chair, and with Calvin following, went out onto the warehouse floor and walked to a stack of corner shelves that was almost lost in the cavernous space. He explained that goods were stored in a central distribution center, and orders were shipped to the warehouse as needed. The warehouse was like a post office and he was Postmaster.

Higgins asked Calvin to help pull three wooden boxes off the shelf and set them on the floor. He pried the tops off so Calvin could check the contents against the order.

The first box contained two lines of SEAL underwater gear and paraphernalia. A second carton had the weaponry he had ordered. Calvin lifted a Spike missile out of the third box and hefted it in his hands.

"Cute," he said.

"Potent, too," Higgins said. "We pride ourselves on the latest technology. Launcher is under the other stuff."

He replaced the cover, then he and Calvin loaded the boxes onto a dolly which they pushed to an overhanging door. Higgins opened the door and told Calvin to drive around back to the loading platform for a pick-up. They loaded the boxes in the trunk.

Higgins said the order would be billed to the numbered Swiss bank account Calvin had set up. All products had a thirty-day guarantee. The surveillance system would watch him leave and if anyone tailed him, personnel would take care of it. Once out of the three-kilometer safety zone he'd be on his own. Calvin didn't know why he had ordered the Spike missile kit. He didn't see any use for the weapon in the operation he and Hawkins contemplated, but he'd learned to expect the unexpected.

Heck, maybe he simply liked to make things go 'boom.'

CHAPTER SIXTY-ONE

Lily had been waiting for Hawkins at a sidewalk cafe near the Central Market. She saw him dodging the traffic as he crossed the street, popped up from her chair and waved her arms like a semaphore signalman. She was wearing a short purple leather skirt and matching jacket. When he walked over to her table, she wrapped her arms around him in a desperate hug.

"Thank you so much for coming," she said. "I don't know what I would have done if I hadn't reached you. I'm practically falling apart with worry."

Hawkins disentangled himself from her embrace and sat down. He put his cell phone on the table.

"Before you fall apart, can you tell me where you got this photo of Kalliste?"

Lily was taken aback by his abrupt tone and relentless gaze. Her face crumpled. She started to blather in an unbroken stream of words. Hawkins reached across the table and gave her hand a gentle squeeze.

Speaking in a soft tone, and with more deliberation, he said, "Sorry for snarling at you, Lily. Please tell me the whole story from the beginning. Take your time. Try to remember every detail."

Lily smiled through her tears. "My specialty is fake television, Matt. I don't do well with reality."

The creatures menacing Kalliste were unlike any reality Hawkins could recall, but he kept his thoughts to himself. He signaled the waiter and ordered two coffees. Lily took a sip from her cup. Her eyes still brimmed with tears, but she had regained her composure.

"Kalliste called me from Santorini," she said. "She was trying to translate an ancient scroll, using the device you brought up from the Minoan ship. She was very frustrated. The work was going slowly and she needed help."

"Why call you rather than an expert in her field of study?" Hawkins said.

"I asked her the same question. Kalliste said the translation work was labor intensive. She could hurry things along if she had access to computer technology and wondered if Hidden History would foot the bill for technical services. I told her I'd ask my boss. He said no, because the project was too speculative."

"More speculative than werewolves in Paris?"

"Paris was a proven formula. Dig out an old legend, throw in some movie clips, make it relevant with a hook that pulls the story into the present, and trot out pseudo-experts who drag up obscure historical tidbits to make the case. Paris had a series of unsolved mutilation murders. Probably the work of a sicko, but it fit the formula. *Voila.* The murders were the work of werewolves stalking the Left Bank."

"Interesting," Hawkins said. "But what does it have to do with Kalliste's disappearance?"

Heaving a sigh, Lily said, "It goes back to research my team was doing on modern-day Druids."

"The nuts who dress up in robes and prance around Stonehenge on the solstice?"

She nodded. "My researchers talked to an Oxford professor who had written books about secret societies. During the interview, he mentioned hearing about a cult much older than the Druids that went back to ancient Sumer. The cultists migrated to Crete and built the Minoan palace at Knossos." She leaned forward on her elbows and lowered her voice. "Here's what caught our attention, Matt. These folks are still around."

"Around? As in, still alive and kicking?"

"Very much so."

"How did the professor know about this society if it's so secret?"

"The Oxford guy knew about it from a colleague in the anthropology department at the University of Cadiz. When I heard about the Minoan connection I thought about the shipwreck off the coast of Spain." With excitement growing in her voice, she said, "If I could put this bunch of crazies together with Kalliste's project, my tightwad boss would leap at the chance for an exclusive."

"Is that what happened?"

"He was practically drooling when I gave him the pitch. I sent my team to see the professor in Cadiz. Big disappointment. He said the society was a harmless bunch of back-to-nature types. They got dressed up in funny costumes, made offerings to the earth goddess and had a big feast. My researchers were packing it up when the professor mentioned yet another group that made animal sacrifices to the earth goddess. And maybe more."

"What did he mean by *more?*"

"He clammed up, even when we waved money under his nose. Said he had talked too much already. I wasn't about to let the story go, so after Kalliste called from Santorini I went back to the professor and told him about her Linear A scroll and the translating device. I said I would give him exclusive access to the story. He'd be a star."

"That's a tempting offer to an academic."

"He couldn't resist it. He said he'd gone to witness a ceremony of the harmless nature lovers. A woman he met there got into the sacrificial wine and let loose about a friend, even told him her name, who'd joined the animal sacrifice cult but pulled out after going to a ceremony. Too bloody, she said. When the woman sobered up, she told the professor she had made it up. The shadow society didn't exist."

"Did the professor believe her?"

"No. He even tried to track down the former member, but she had died in a car accident."

Hawkins pondered the reply. Yet another accident. "What else did the professor's source tell him?"

"She said the cult went back thousands of years; said they believed in continuous sacrifices to ensure good fortune. Anything less would anger the earth goddess. She was constantly thirsty for human blood, apparently."

"Which this gang provided."

"That's what we were told."

"Did this cult have a name?"

"It was called the Way of the Axe. They're spread around the world. All the pieces were starting to fit. A Minoan cult. A Minoan ship. Human sacrifice. I saw stars, especially after I heard about Kalliste's scroll in a lost language and the translation device you salvaged from the ship. I envisioned a mini-series that would give Hidden History the kind of respectability it never had."

"People who practice human sacrifice would do everything they could to stop that from happening."

Lily bit her lower lip. "I know that now. I got worried and called Kalliste to let her know what was going on. She didn't answer her phone. Today I got the photo of her with those two…things. What in God's name are they?"

"Nothing I want breathing down Kalliste's neck."

"I know it sounds crazy. That's why I called you instead of the police. Was that the right decision?"

"The Spanish cops still don't believe someone blew our dive boat out of the water." He stared off into space, working his jaw muscles, then said, "Let's assume your theory has legs. The kidnappers could have killed Kalliste at any time, but they sent the photo instead. My guess is that they want the scroll and translation device."

"That seems like a reasonable assumption, but where does it leave us?"

"With leverage. We'll say that we'll give them what they want in exchange for Kalliste."

"You have the scroll and the translator?"

"I can put my hands on them. Setting up a deal will keep Kalliste alive and give us time to figure things out."

"She could already be dead. They could have killed her after they took that picture."

"I'm aware of that possibility. I'd like you type out the following message:

Miss you too. Let's get together. Stay well. Matt."

She finished typing and hit Reply. "Now what?"

"We wait. And we try to learn whatever we can about the Way of the Axe."

"Maybe we should talk to the professor again."

"Good suggestion. Maybe we can pry something out of him that will give us an edge."

"I'll try to arrange a meeting."

She said she would call Hawkins as soon as she heard from the professor. She gave him another hug and waved down a cab to take her back to the hotel. She sat back in her seat with a smile of satisfaction on her lips. The eyes that had been moist with tears were desert dry. The quivering lips were compressed into a tight smile. There was not a shred of resemblance to the helpless female who'd fallen on Hawkins' broad shoulders.

Hawkins had made her work even easier. He was a modern-day swashbuckler, a man of immense courage and resources. The same qualities that could make him a formidable foe would be his downfall. His friend was in trouble and he would do anything he could to rescue her. His fierce determination would blind him to the real dangers that threatened.

She had lured him in with the mix of fact and fiction. The Way of the Axe was real. The Oxford professor was fiction. The University of Cadiz scholar was real but she had never talked to him.

After she got back to her hotel room, she would call the Maze and instruct the priestesses to prepare Kalliste for her meeting with the Mother Goddess. Then she would contact Hawkins, and say the professor wanted to meet him. Before the night was over, she would have the scroll and translator in her hands, Hawkins would be dead, and Kalliste offered up to the Mother Goddess.

She stared out the taxi window at the busy Cadiz street scene, but her mind's eye saw the sanctuary of the Snake Goddess. As she pictured herself walking toward the altar and the Horns of Consecration, her long slender fingers closed around the jeweled hilt of an invisible bronze dagger.

CHAPTER SIXTY-TWO

Molly stood in the yard behind her house, eyes fixed on the cloudless blue sky. Her ears were cocked for the plaintive whistle of a Golden eagle, but the only sound she heard was the breeze soughing in the aspen trees.

On the ride back from Portland she had passed the accident site. A wrecker had towed the car away. She examined the raw scars on the tree and wondered what the medical examiner would make of the claw marks on the stranger's head, but decided she didn't really care.

When she got home, she garaged the motorcycle and went around behind the house to stand near the shed. Maybe Wheeling would drop by for a snack, but probably not. After its traumatic escape, the bird was probably so danged scared it would never come back.

Molly lowered her chin and rubbed the back of her neck. She took a final glance at the empty sky and headed into the house, stopping in the kitchen to rummage through the cupboards. She filled a bowl with tortilla chips and opened a jar of cheese dip. To take the edge off her guilt she liberated a can of diet soda from the refrigerator and carried her snack into her office.

She sat down in front of her computer, munched some chips and stared vacantly at the screen. Her mind methodically checked off a mental checklist. She ran a test of her computer. The firewalls and protections were in place. Some hackers throw every possible password at a wall to see what sticks. The technique was known as brute force. Amateur move. Time-consuming. Unlikely to reach higher levels of authentication. Guaranteed to alert the target.

Molly decided against a direct approach, such as running a scan to see how high the Auroch protective walls were. This was her first foray into Auroch. Poking around the edges of a target as big as Salazar's company would likely trigger alarms and a counter attack.

Molly finished her chips and salsa. Then she flexed her fingers like a piano virtuoso preparing to dig into a Chopin etude, tapped the keyboard and called up the Auroch company logo with its stylized bull's horns. She glanced with contempt at the photo of Salazar, thinking that he looked like a big old smiling lizard. Then she dissected the website.

She zeroed in on the Auroch subsidiaries. There were dozens, nearly all in the fossil fuel industry, mining or related businesses, such as, equipment manufacture or transport. With the patience of a Swiss watchmaker, she studied each company one-by-one, but made no attempt to get into their files.

After finishing the first pass, she gazed at the monitor, imagining herself on the other side of the screen. She put herself in the place of the computer experts who would have built defensive walls around Auroch. In their position, she would have made a few entry points accessible. Nothing too easy, just enough to pose a reasonable challenge to a competent hacker. She'd use sloppy programming, as if by mistake. The hacker who went down that pathway would eventually encounter a no-nonsense barrier. But by then the trap would have been sprung. The hacker would have no idea he'd been traced until he heard someone pounding on his door.

After a few minutes of contemplation, Molly came to a reluctant conclusion. There was no safe way she could get directly into Auroch or its subsidiaries. The barriers were too formidable. But every wall has a finite height and width. The Chinese had learned that with the Great Wall. So had the builders of the Maginot Line. If she couldn't go through the cyber wall she could go over or around it.

The lavender eyes blinking behind the round lenses were the

only outward sign of her inner excitement. She scrolled down the website. Her cursor came to rest on the section entitled 'Corporate Responsibility.' She reread the puff piece that had caught her eye on the first pass. Probably written by a committee of company public relations hacks, it was a surprising candid admission that Auroch could have been less than a good corporate citizen.

Without going into detail the piece described the damage some Auroch operations had caused. To demonstrate that the company had changed its ways, the article contained a list of two dozen environmental and green energy organizations that Auroch now sponsored. The benevolent attitude was at odds with the company's history. The same corporation that destroyed the Oregon environmental non-profit in a few days' time, was like a born-again sinner preaching Salvation.

She followed the links and read everything available about each non-profit. It was grinding, time-consuming work. She had to replenish her snacks a couple of times. Her computer-like memory stored every pertinent fact about each organization. One name blazed in her mind like a neon sign. She went back to the link for Fusion Technologies Research. FUTR for short.

Molly had noticed on the first run-through that FUTR had its headquarters at the Massachusetts Institute of Technology. She was about to pop a tortilla chip into her mouth but she stopped short. MIT was in Cambridge. The dude who'd attacked her and scared off Wheeling had been in Cambridge only a week before. Funny coincidence.

She dug into the FUTR website. The group had been created by some of the world's leading scientists in the field of fusion power, in which atoms are joined together to produce heat that drives a turbine to produce energy. FUTR's goal was to lay the groundwork for a clean energy source that would be cheap and plentiful. The organization coordinated a number of research labs experimenting with ways to harness the atomic reaction that powers the sun and the stars.

An MIT plasma physicist named Dr. Moncrieff Gardner was the chairman of FUTR. The photo of Dr. Gardner showed a middle-aged man with short pepper-and-salt hair, a friendly smile and intense blue eyes that looked as if they could see through solid objects. Molly got dizzy from reading his scientific accomplishments.

Under the photo was a message from Dr. Gardner reminding readers of FUTR's annual conference at MIT. The conference was in a few days. The entire FUTR scientific board would attend. An announcement of global importance would be made at the conference, whose subject was: The FUTR of Energy. Dr. Gardner referred back to his first column, made at FUTR's founding two years ago.

Molly clicked on the Archives. Summaries appeared of all Gardner's past messages. His first outlined the non-profit's goals, and said there hadn't been such a concentration of intellectual power since the Manhattan Project scientific team developed the atomic bomb in a mere twenty-seven months. Gardner hoped this group accomplished its far more peaceful goal in twenty-four months.

She went back to a recent column under the title:

Auroch CEO: An Inspiration

Her frown deepened as she read the message that described in glowing terms how Viktor Salazar was sponsoring FUTR even though fossil fuel alternatives would damage his company. Gardner had enclosed the copy of a 'thank you' letter he wrote after a telephone conversation with Salazar. The letter said in part that, "the selfless example of Auroch would encourage other companies to come forward for the good of mankind."

Molly looked up Gardner's email and phone number on the website. With that information, it was a simple matter for her to hack into Gardner's business and personal files and follow them to Salazar. The cyber watchdogs who defended Auroch would not expect an indirect assault. Just in case, she built a firewall to prevent her probe from being traced back to her.

Within minutes she had Salazar's list of calls made from a mobile phone. There were hundreds. It would take days to analyze all the numbers. Instead, she used his phone to connect to his computer. File after file popped onto her screen. She clapped her hands like an excited child.

She skipped over the files identified by numbers and concentrated on a few labeled with corporate names. None had appeared on the Auroch website. She guessed that Salazar didn't want it known that Auroch had links to these off-the-books outfits. She hesitated, wondering if these files had the same level of protection guarding the corporate portals. Salazar was careful, but from what she knew of the man, he was arrogant as well. He'd never dream that anyone could get this close to him.

She hoped.

She decided to take the chance. She rubbed her palms together in anticipation only to pull back. First, she'd reward herself in advance with a snack.

CHAPTER SIXTY-THREE

Abby had no illusions about the challenge involved in rescuing Kalliste. The operation was somewhere between foolhardy and insane. If anyone could pull off a mission this dangerous, it would be Hawkins and Calvin. But they would need all the help she could provide.

While they were off on their separate errands, Abby had been alone in the galley of the boat. She sat hunched over a table that was covered with the notes and diagrams she had sketched out suggesting ways to penetrate the castle's ramparts. She had blocked out the creaks and burbles the boat made as water nibbled at its hull, and was so intent on her work she didn't hear the footfalls on deck.0

Sensing she was no longer alone, she turned and saw Hawkins standing at the bottom of the companionway.

"How long have you been there?" she said.

"Less than a minute. I didn't want to startle you."

"Sorry. I was totally engrossed."

"So I see." Hawkins pointed at the 3-D diagram of the castle slowly spinning on the computer screen. "That looks like *Castillo de Huernos.*"

"It's a close rendition. I pulled the schematic together using the video you shot on your recon and combined it with material from the internet."

He sat next to her and gazed at the diagram. "If attacking armies had this program back in the Middle Ages, not a castle in the land would be left standing."

"Having a detailed picture of potential weak points would definitely have given the assaulting army an edge. They'd still have been stuck with the traditional siege tools. Fire, battering rams, catapults and starving to submission."

"After you left, I did some research on Minoan construction. Their engineers were far ahead of their time when it came to urban hydraulics."

"Moving water in and out of cities?"

"I'm talking about cities, palaces and villages. Thousands of years ago their plumbing was more advanced than what you'd find in Europe in the late 19th century. They had indoor bathrooms and bathtubs. Their water systems had aqueducts, cisterns, filtering systems, ways to collect rainwater, and terracotta pipes. They knew about gravity, flow and pipe pressure. They brought water in from rivers and springs, built distribution and disposal systems that worked quite well."

Abby placed the scroll diagram of the maze in front of Hawkins.

Hawkins studied the diagram. "What do you see that I don't?"

"Look at this opening in one wall of the maze. It's in an odd place for an entrance. Now look at this satellite photo of the castle. See the faint double line running in from the river to the moat?"

"A conduit of some kind to bring water into the maze from the river?"

She drew her fingernail from the tip of the conduit, across the moat to the wall of the castle where the opening was indicated in the diagram. "Or it could have been a sluiceway that brought effluent from the maze to the river. Either possibility might provide a way to get close to or into the castle."

"If you're right, we could land up-river and drift down to the sluiceway. Would the conduit be big enough for a man to pass through it?"

"I can't say for sure. Minoan water systems all have the same characteristics; a water main, cisterns or wells, internal distribution lines and refuse disposal. When the castle was built over the maze, a section of the conduit may have been removed to make way for the moat. The builders might have been satisfied with a plumbing system that was not as sophisticated as the Minoan design, but they would still need part of the sluiceway to bring water from the river to the moat. But if I'm wrong, even if you get from the moat into a pipe, you might find that it leads nowhere. All I can give you is my educated guess."

"Good enough for me," Hawkins said. "Beats flying out of Calvin's catapult."

She gave him a hug. "I can't wait to fill Calvin in."

"He's on his way. He texted me a while ago and said all went okay with his errand."

"I'll start pulling things together."

"Good. I want to push ahead with the castle plan, but my talk with Lily Porter put a new spin on the situation."

Hawkins gave her a shortened version of his meeting.

Abby shook her head. "I've seen Hidden History. It's all crap. She prances around in a mini-skirt looking for vampires and ghosts. Maybe she's trying out a new script."

He took the cell phone out of his pocket. "Someone sent Lily this picture."

"Dear God!" Abby said. "What are those awful-looking things with Kalliste?"

"Dunno, Ab, but they're not waiting for her to throw a stick. Check out the expression on Kalliste's face. She's hanging tough, but she's scared."

"We've got to get her out of there damned fast."

He pointed at the 3-D castle image on the computer screen. "Can't wait to tell Calvin that the way we're going to get into that pile of rock is almost as crazy as his catapult theory."

They heard footsteps on deck, then Calvin's voice saying, "Anybody home?"

"Looks like you'll have your chance sooner than later," Abby said.

Hawkins shrugged and called out, "We're down here, Cal."

CHAPTER SIXTY-FOUR

Kalliste felt as if she were crawling out of a coal pit. Although her eyes had blinked open, darkness encroached at the periphery of her vision. She pushed the shadows aside by sheer will power, slowly sat up and swung her legs over the side of her bed. Her lips were dry, she had a coppery taste in her mouth and her head pounded.

She couldn't understand why she had a super hangover. She hadn't had a drop of wine. After downing a slice of bread, she had nibbled on fresh fruit. She glanced at the bowl and the partially-eaten orange. *Of course*. They had drugged the fruit *and* the wine. She swept her arm around in anger. The bowl and its contents crashed to the tiled floor. She was about to consign the wine jug to the same fate, but a gurgling below her breastbone warned that she had a more urgent Priority.

Staggering to her feet, she rushed to the washroom and made it to the sink barely in time to disgorge the tainted fruit. She stuck her head under the tap and washed away the sour taste. Then she splashed cold water on her face and brushed her hair back with her fingers. Kalliste was glad there was no mirror. Her face must be a fright.

Her captors wanted her out cold. If she had sampled the wine as well as the food she would have been in la-la land when they came to take her away.

Kalliste went back to her bedside and used her fork to tear the blue fringe away from the tablecloth. She twisted the tassels and wrapped them around the fork handle to create a crude brush. She dipped the makeshift brush into the wine and drew an outline on the tablecloth of the Maze from memory that went back to her childhood days. She was ninety percent sure she'd got it right, even down to the bull's head in the center of the diagram.

Seconds after she hung the tablecloth in the shower to dry, she heard someone at the door. She emptied out the rest of the wine, dashed for the bed and pulled the sheets over her body. Lying on her left side, she held the jug by its handle behind the crook of her bent knees. Through the slits of her slightly open eyes she saw the priestess enter and shut the door behind her.

Unlike earlier visits, when she carried a tray of food and wine, the priestess was empty-handed. As Kalliste concluded, the last food delivery must have been planned as the final meal. That's why it packed a drug punch. She clamped her eyelids tight. There were the soft footfalls of sandals on tiles, then she felt the brush of warm air against her cheeks and heard soft breathing. The priestess was leaning close to make sure Kalliste was unconscious.

The warm air stopped. Next, Kalliste heard a scraping sound. She opened an eye. The priestess was down on one knee, sweeping pieces of broken pottery with one hand into another. She went to put the shards on the table, but stopped short and stared at the tabletop. Kalliste's heart sank. The priestess must have noticed the tablecloth and the wine jug and figured something was amiss. Kalliste could imagine what was going through the woman's mind. If the fruit and wine had knocked Kalliste out, when did she have time to dispose of the tablecloth and the jug?

She looked straight into Kalliste's face. Kalliste flipped the sheet back and swung the jug around in a short arc. The vessel shattered in pieces against the woman's skull. Her hands went limp. The shards fell from her hands onto the floor. Her eyes rolled in her head and she keeled over like a felled tree.

Kalliste vaulted out of bed. She picked up the table and held it high over the limp body, but the priestess was out cold. Kalliste slipped the axe medallion over the woman's head and looped the chain around her own neck.

She shimmied out of the flounced skirt and tossed it aside. The ankle-length garment would slow her down. She pulled the light outer skirt off the priestess and wrapped it around her waist. She couldn't help noticing the ropey muscles and the thick calves. The woman was an Amazon who would have squashed her like a bug if Kalliste hadn't put her out of commission.

She thought of tying the priestess up with the discarded skirt, but she didn't have time to figure it out. She gambled that the priestess would never venture out into the Maze without the protection of her medallion. Kalliste took several long deep breaths to slow the beating of her heart, then slid the door open.

Waiting in the passageway like a couple of puppies eager to go for a walk were the two dog creatures. Even sitting on their haunches, the heads of the animals were at her eye level. Kalliste took a deep breath and started forward, only to stop. *Damn.* She had forgotten her map. She went back inside to retrieve the tablecloth. It took superhuman effort to march past the unconscious priestess, then out into the passageway again. The dog creatures pattered behind her.

Kalliste tried to ignore her companions and concentrate on finding her way out. She made steady progress toward the center of the maze. She had to back out a couple of blind alleys. The foul-ups were more due to the slap-dash nature of the tablecloth map than her cartographic skills.

Despite her fear and anxiety, Kalliste couldn't help but appreciate the ingenuity and labor that had gone into the construction of the Maze. Knossos was like child's play compared to this network of tunnels. The passageways were at least twenty feet across and she estimated the ceilings that dripped with moisture were around ten feet high. Lily said that the Maze builders could trace their origins back to Neolithic times.

The Maze must have had its inspiration in the caves their ancestors called home tens of thousands of years ago. As perverted as Lily and her followers were, they had been the jealous guardians of rituals and language born at the dawn of civilization. Kalliste couldn't wait to write a scientific paper. She almost laughed at her presumptuousness. Here she was, trying to make her way through a gigantic puzzle deep in the earth, followed by a couple of toothy monsters, and she had herself practically accepting a Nobel prize in science.

According to her map, she was practically halfway through the Maze, approaching the large rectangle where the bull's head had been drawn on the scroll. Because of the size and location of the space, Kalliste assumed that it might be the bull court Lily said was no longer used. She would make quick time across the open space, and pick up a passageway on the other side.

The lighted tunnel jogged to the right and the left, then ended abruptly. There was nothing ahead but pitch-black darkness. Not a pinpoint of light. She brushed aside fears of falling into yawning pits. She would let her eyes get used to the darkness, allow her senses to take over and try to move ahead in a straight line. Keeping her hands extended until she encountered the wall indicated on the map, she would then grope her way along the surface until she found the opening for the passageway.

She turned to check on her companions. They had disappeared. They must have fallen silently back as she approached the bull court. They were hideous creatures, but it wasn't their fault. They had been bred as killers by humans who were the real monsters.

She took a tentative step into the darkness, then another and another. She moved with more confidence with each step, thinking that this was what a blind person experienced every day of his or her life. The lack of sight heightened her other senses. Her nostrils picked up a musty, damp smell. From somewhere came the sickly-sweet scent of rotting meat. Her heartbeat ratcheted up at the prospect of stepping on a dead animal that may have wandered into the court, but she continued resolutely on, arms waving in front of her like the antennae on an insect.

After a few minutes passed, Kalliste guessed that she might be halfway across the court, which is when she heard the scuffling noise from directly in front of her. She stopped and listened. A different sound echoed in the darkness.

Clop-clop.

The noise sounded like hooves on stone.

Then came a snuffle and a snort. She was not alone. An animal was moving around the unlit court. She froze. Her mind was whirling. She didn't know whether to make a dash for the opposite wall or turn back to the portal she had entered. The decision was made for her. The clopping moved around behind her, and when she turned, two blazing red eyes blinked on in the darkness.

She began to run.

CHAPTER SIXTY-FIVE

Chad stared at his ruined face in the mirror. He had come to think of the pale mass of scar tissue as a fleshy version of the blank canvas a portrait artist would put up on an easel. But this was different. The identity he was about to assume belonged to Salazar, the man he most hated in the world.

He began to mold Salazar's face over his own, improving on the hastily-assembled features that had got him past Auroch security. Tinted contact lenses took care of the eye color. Make-up hid the edge of the skullcap covering his hair. He evened out the flesh he'd added to his cheeks and chin. When he finished the transformation, he tried to replicate the distinctive voice.

Salazar said Chad had the tone and the inflections, but his impersonation lacked depth. Chad was soft-spoken, a holdover from his Army days. Special Ops were trained to speak quietly on a mission. Chad still spoke in his drowsy, half-stoned surfer's voice, but his acting school voice lessons had come in handy. He had a wide range and he could fit the tone to the disguise of the moment.

He went through a series of vocal exercises that raised his speaking voice to a mellow tenor. His dry enunciation was impeccable. Although his impression lacked the brilliance that was part of Salazar's natural speech patterns, he came close. He could elevate his voice a few octaves without sounding too feminine. His speech was penetrating but not loud.

"Is this some sort of joke?" he asked himself, painting his question with amused scorn.

Not bad. It was as far as he could go without putting himself through the same surgical procedure that had turned Salazar into a freak. He could never replicate the large bones of the rib cage that gave Salazar the added lung capacity to squeeze his powerful voice through vocal cords the size of a child's. Nor would he want it.

Chad would make his move at the rendezvous with Salazar. When the Mercedes pulled up at the log house, he would get out of the SUV and draw his pistol from its sock holster. He would shoot Salazar first, then tend to his men. Chad had practiced the attack in his hotel room. Four quick pulls of the trigger. Bang-bang-bang-bang.

Salazar's men were pros. They wouldn't stand there with Shoot Me signs around their necks. They would fight back. He might die. He didn't care. Maybe it was the loss of his girlfriend. Or maybe he had come to terms with the destructive uselessness of his life. A peaceful feeling had come over his mind since his decision to kill Salazar. He would do so no matter the cost.

Chad's phone chirped. Speak of the devil.

"The time has come," Salazar said. "We'll pick you up at your hotel in thirty minutes."

Chad took a deep breath and expelled the words through his constricted larynx. "I'll be ready, Mr. Salazar."

There was silence at the other end of the line, then Salazar said, "You've been working at it, I see."

"You told me I had the tone and inflections. Now do I have the depth?"

"That would never be possible, but it's close enough for our purposes. Thirty minutes."

Chad hung up. Being in Salazar's skin was creepy enough. Speaking in his voice was even worse. He got into his black running suit and tucked his pistol into the sock holster. He pulled the baseball cap low over his face and laced up his sneakers. He used the stairs to get to the ground floor and crossed the busy lobby with his head down. Anyone giving him a second look would see only a man dressed as if he'd been using the hotel's fitness center.

The Mercedes SUV picked him up at the curb exactly on time. Salazar wasn't in the vehicle. The rear door opened, a man emerged and motioned for Chad to get inside next to another of Salazar's thugs. The first man got in after Chad, sandwiching him between two sets of wide shoulders and hard thighs.

The driver was the man called Bruno. No one spoke on the ride out of the city and into the countryside along the same route they had taken on the earlier trip. When the SUV stopped in front of the log cabin, his seat companions muscled him out between them. As soon as Chad's feet hit the ground, one man enveloped him from behind in a bear hug. His companion bent over and plucked the pistol from its holster.

He jabbed Chad between the shoulder blades with the gun.

"Get moving," he growled.

Salazar's gorillas dragged him up the stairs and into the log cabin. Salazar was waiting in the living room. His man handed him the pistol. Salazar glanced at the gun, then tossed it into the cold fireplace.

"You won't need your little toy for this mission," Salazar said. There was derision rather than anger in his manner.

Chad decided to bluff it out. "No one said I couldn't bring along some insurance."

"True, but it would simply complicate matters."

"You're the boss, Mr. Salazar." He turned to Bruno and gave him a lop-sided grin. "Must be getting careless. How'd you make me?"

"No-brainer. Your piece got picked up by a metal detector built into the framework of the front door. It's got a link to my cell phone."

Chad remembered the call Bruno had taken on the first visit to the cabin.

Forcing a chuckle, he said, "Guess things have changed a lot since my Special Ops days."

"Guess they have," Bruno said with a sneer lacing his voice.

Salazar raised his hand to signal an end to the discussion, then moved closer to Chad, examining him from a foot away like an entomologist studying a rare insect.

"Not bad at all," he murmured. "The hairline is barely discernible. The eye color is almost right. What do you think, Bruno?"

"Dead ringer," Bruno said.

Salazar stretched his lips in a wide smile. "Give me another demonstration of your vocal talents."

Chad barked, "Why did you come here? Did you think I'd be amused by your antics?"

Salazar wrapped his arm around the shoulders of his body double and guided him to the door. "Now let's put your skills to a real test."

CHAPTER SIXTY-SIX

Calvin was twelve minutes overdue at the airport and to Abby that was an eternity. She went to shoot him a text but hesitated. Headlights were approaching at a high rate of speed. As the lights neared, she saw that they belonged to a truck. Someone was waving madly out of the driver's window. The truck screeched to a stop and the door flew open. Calvin leaped out, a bright smile on his face, strode across the tarmac and gave Abby a hug that squeezed every ounce of anger from her body.

"Sorry I'm late," he said. "Had to swing by Captain Santiago's to borrow the truck. Where's Matt?"

"He got the call from Lily Porter and drove into Cadiz to meet her and the professor. He doesn't expect it to amount to much."

"Mission's still on as far as I'm concerned. When I told the captain we were headed to *La Mancha* he quoted a bon voyage from Cervantes. It's been whirling around in my skull all the way to the airport."

"I'd love to hear it," Abby said.

"I'll give it a try," Calvin said. " 'May you come back sound, wind and limb out of this dreadful hole which you are running into, once more to see the warm sun which you art now leaving.' "

Abby laughed. "I'll be glad when we *all* see the warm sun again."

Calvin gave her a thumb's up. He went over to the back of the truck, unloaded some boxes and laid out the contents on the tarmac.

Abby brought out her iPad and went down the list with Calvin. Black dry suits. Draeger rebreather units. Night vision goggles. Six M67 "baseball" grenades. Two tear gas canisters. A pair of Heckler and Koch machine guns with sound suppressors. Ammunition magazines. Two limpet mines. Dive knives. A compact raft that could be inflated in seconds. And miscellaneous equipment, such as radios, medical kits and wire cutters.

She stopped next to a long bag. "Planning to get in a round of golf?"

"That's gator repellant," Calvin said with a straight face.

Abby was responsible for making sure Calvin and Hawkins weren't encumbered by even an ounce of excess gear.

"Is it necessary for the success of the mission?"

Calvin smirked. "Might be. If we run into any gators."

Abby sighed and shook her head.

This was going to be a long night.

While the equipment was being checked out at the airport, Hawkins was driving across the city to meet with Lily and her professor friend. He hoped the professor had information that would help, but no matter what he said, Hawkins was certain he and Calvin would have to penetrate the castle defenses.

A SEAL mission goes through a standard protocol that starts with a problem to be solved. The platoon comes up with one or more solutions, operations and intel are brought in to massage the plan, and it goes to the commander. Upon his okay, the platoon comes up with an action schedule and collects the resources needed to carry the mission out.

Hawkins was commander and team leader. Calvin was operations and Abby was intel. This simplified things. They could move faster without the usual back-and-forth and negotiations that went with a full-blown SEAL mission. As far as combat forces go, the team was pretty pitiful.

To be successful, a SEAL operation must follow a simple rule. *Haul ass.* Get in, accomplish the mission and get out. Combat should be avoided at all costs.

The objective was to rescue Kalliste. He had figured out the *when*. Damned soon. But not the *where*. Kalliste could be anywhere in the Maze. He pictured the Maze drawing on the scroll. His brain fluttered. A thought flew around inside his skull like a bird in a cage.

He glanced at his watch. Traffic was heavy because of an accident. He was running late for his appointment with Lily at the University of Cadiz campus, and this delayed him even further. All he could do was sit behind the steering wheel and fume.

The Cadiz campus was in the old city, clustered in a warren of narrow streets, squares and plazas bordered on the waterside by Caleta Beach and Genovese Park. In the daytime, it was a shady oasis of palms, topiary cut trees sculpted in the shape of giant corkscrews, duck pools and bubbling fountains. At night, much of the park was in darkness.

Lily waited in the shadows of an unlit area under some tall palms.

She had instructed Hawkins to leave his car in the lot next to the seawall, and make his way to the park. She would be watching for him. She would call his name and tell him that the professor was waiting with her. Then she would lead him to the place she had chosen as the killing ground. As they strolled under the trees, she would stop and whisper something pitiful like, "Oh Matt. I'm so glad you came."

Then she would embrace him as she had at the café, draw the bronze dagger from her sleeve and drive the point up under his ribs. Hawkins was a big man, but she had dispatched thousand-pound sacrificial bulls with cold-blooded efficiency. She gripped the hilt of the dagger. At times of sacrifice, the dagger seemed to quiver with life. She was merely the instrument of the Mother Goddess who directed her hand.

The sea shimmered in the moonlight. It was a beautiful night. Soon she would add the sickly-sweet smell of blood to the fragrance of orange trees carried on the soft, warm breeze. When she had eliminated Hawkins, she would head back to the Maze where a new High Priestess would be born. Lily Porter, the vapid chattering woman whose role she had played for so long, would disappear forever.

CHAPTER SIXTY-SEVEN

Six thousand miles to the west of Cadiz, Molly Sutherland sat in front of the glowing computer screen surrounded by empty diet soda cans, half a cold pizza and various empty snack bags.

She had spent hours going through Salazar's off-the-books list of corporations. Her head was spinning. Her butt was numb from sitting. Her stomach was queasy from junk food. She felt like a lone lumberjack trying to hack his way through a forest of redwood trees. The extent of the Auroch holdings was mind-boggling.

Most of the businesses had to do with energy, mining and related industries, which is the reason she raised an eyebrow when she came across the media subsidiary known as the Hidden History channel listed under Auroch ownership.

She Googled Hidden History and concluded that the show was the broadcasting equivalent of the junk food that was making her sick. A number of files referred to Lily Porter. She called up a photo. Porter was pretty in a dippy kind of way. Had she seen the name before? Oh yeah. Hawkins had been sending her short updates on where he was and what he was doing. She went back and read where he had met Lily Porter in a hotel. She was Kalliste's producer. Molly's mind must have been as bloated as her stomach. She didn't catch the significance of the recollection at first. When she did, it was like being hit with a hammer. Lily Porter worked for Hidden History, which was owned by Auroch, which was run by Salazar.

It only took minutes to do a quick people search using a biography program that could reach back to the gleam in a father's eye. Porter's biography was brief. She had been born in Stockton, California, went to U-Cal and the Columbia School of Journalism. After graduation, she went to work for Hidden History and in a short time as a reporter, became its producer. Molly ran a check of the Stockton birth records. No mention of Lily Porter. Lily just seemed to have appeared out of nowhere.

Her long eyelashes went into full blink mode. She typed a quick text.

Matt. Call me now.

When Matt didn't reply she called him directly.

No answer. She tried again and left a message on his voicemail saying she had urgent news.

Damn, Matt. Where are you?

Molly started to hyperventilate in her panic. With a trembling finger she punched in a number on her contact list. As she listened to the unanswered ring, she was filled with a sense of foreboding.

Abby heard the phone chirping but she finished helping Calvin stow the raft in the helicopter before she answered the call.

"Abby, do you know where Matt is? I can't reach him. Tried texting and calling."

Molly's excited voice was high-pitched, but Abby recognized the West Virginia drawl.

"He's on his way to a meeting with a TV producer named Lily Porter."

"Darn. Matt could be in danger," Molly said. "Lily Porter works for Auroch."

Abby was stunned by the revelation, but her Navy training took control. "Thanks, Molly. I'll stop him. Talk later. Bye."

She hung up and called Matt's number. She got his voice mail and left a quick message, "Matt, it's Abby. Don't meet with Lily Porter."

Calvin walked over, brushing his palms to signify a job well done. "Why shouldn't Matt meet with Lily?" he said.

"That was Molly. She found a connection between Salazar and

Lily. I *knew* there was something slimy about that over-made-up dame."

Calvin swore. "Whole thing was a set-up. You get through to Matt?"

"Just his voice mail. Texting is out, too. His phone is off."

Calvin reached into his pocket and pulled out his own phone.

"Damn it, Calvin, I just called. You're wasting valuable time."

"Maybe not," Calvin said with a maddening calmness.

He showed her the phone screen which displayed a map of Cadiz. A pulsating blue dot was moving slowly through the city.

"You've got a locator?" Abby said.

"Matt and I installed the program on our phones. Seemed like a good idea if we got separated."

Abby's elation faded as quickly as it had appeared. Matt was getting closer to danger. Even if they drove out of the airport now, they could never arrive in time. She stared at the screen. She had never felt so helpless.

CHAPTER SIXTY-EIGHT

As Hawkins pulled into the parking lot he finally figured out what was nagging him. He sat in his car and called up the photo Lily had relayed to his phone. When he'd first seen the picture, his eye had been drawn to Kalliste's face and the creatures at her sides. This time he saw something he hadn't noticed before.

Kalliste had her arms crossed in what he had taken to be a defensive posture. The thumb of her right hand was extended vertically in an unnatural position. The invisible line from her thumb tip pointed toward the archway above her head. Painted on the lintel was a double-headed axe that matched the one in the maze diagram. Kalliste had used the photo to show where she was being held.

There were two calls on his phone as well. Molly and Abby. He was already twenty minutes late for his meeting with Lily. He tucked the phone in his pocket, got out of the car and headed toward the opening in the wall bordering the park. A hard-packed sand path led to a boulevard that ran between the rows of benches and odd-shaped trees.

No sign of Lily. He wondered if she had left because he was late. He started to walk down the boulevard. Ahead of him, a figure in black stepped out from the trees into the yellow puddle of light cast by one of the tall lamps that lined the boulevard. The figure waved. It could only be Lily. By the time he got to the lamp, she had stepped back into the woods.

He stood under the light and called her name.

Her answer came from the shadows. "I didn't want anyone to see us together. Follow my voice. You'll come upon a path. The professor is with me."

The last thing Hawkins wanted was to play hide-and-seek with the spacey TV producer. He stepped between two topiary trees and came upon a narrow path into the woods. After walking for a hundred feet he stopped where another path intercepted the first; he was uncertain which way to go.

Lily called from the darkness to his left, "Over here, Matt."

He followed her voice through some bushes and broke out into a clearing. Lily was standing in the open area, barely visible in the moonlight. As he started walking toward her, she spread her arms. Hawkins steeled himself for the inevitable embrace. That's when all hell broke loose. From overhead there came an ear-shattering thrashing racket. The palms whipped as if in a hurricane. The downdraft kicked up a blinding cloud of sand and dust. He was caught in the staccato glare of blinking lights from a hovering helicopter.

Calvin's voice thundered down from the heavens, "Matt, get out of there!"

Hawkins covered his face with one arm and waved with the other.

"Do it now, Matt," the voice said. "Head for the sea."

Hawkins made his way through the palm grove to the path leading to the seawall. As he emerged from the park, he saw the red fuselage and yellow suns on the side of the hovering HelioTours helicopter, which was starting its descent.

The downdraft had nearly blown Lily off her feet. She buried her head in her arms until the helicopter flew off, then she brushed away the sand that covered her black dress. As the dust settled, she looked around. Hawkins was gone.

CHAPTER SIXTY-NINE

When the red orbs had blinked on in the darkness Kalliste froze like a rabbit being stalked by a fox. The clop-clop sound and the snorts grew louder. She was too terrified to run. Her feet seemed to be glued to the floor.

Then came the bellow. Part human moan. Part the bawl of a huge animal. The unearthly sound echoed off the walls of the dark chamber and triggered her flight response. She turned and fled.

The thing gave chase. The reddish glow cast from behind by the burning eyes helped show the way, but it also indicated that the thing was about to catch her.

She drew on every ounce of strength in her body, and seemed to be outdistancing her pursuer when the sole of her right sandal came down hard on a round object that moved underfoot. It was like stepping on a bowling ball. Her ankle twisted and she pitched off to one side. Her arms wind-milled in the empty air. The tumble was ripe with the potential for broken bones, but Kalliste crashed into what felt like a pile of dry kindling that snapped under her weight and cushioned her fall.

She rolled off to one side and the *thing* barreled past Kalliste instead of over her. Then came a metallic crash that sounded like an SUV in a collision test. Kalliste pushed herself up on her knees and watched, spellbound, as the beams from the twin red orbs pointed up, then off to one side, then at the stone wall. The thing finally seemed to regain its balance. It spun slowly around. The probing eyes found Kalliste and moved in her direction.

In the quick glimpse of pale light she saw that she had fallen onto a heap of bones. Dried flesh still clung to some of them, including the grinning skull that'd tripped her up. If she didn't move she'd end up like the thing's previous victims. Kalliste was up and running. She almost fell again on the scattered bones, but managed to stay on her feet. Again, she was surrounded by a rosy halo as the thing gained on her.

A stone wall loomed up at the forward edge of the sweep of light. She saw a dark rectangle in the wall. A doorway. She plunged through the opening and her extended hands slammed into a second wall. She groped her way along the rough stone surface until she found another doorway. Kalliste stepped through the portal and followed the wall right, then left, until she emerged into a tunnel lit by flickering sconces.

The thing was too big to follow her through the narrow passageway. She could hear it snorting and clomping around in its lair. She stood there catching her breath, her mind whirling. Had she nearly been killed by the Minotaur—the legendary half-man, half-bull that guarded the heart of the Labyrinth? The bones she'd tripped over and the odor of rotting flesh indicated that others had been less fortunate. She had leaned back against a wall to rest, and that's when her legs turned to rubber and she slid down to a sitting position.

Curling up on the hard surface, Kalliste waited for the mad hammering of her heart to slow down. She pulled the tablecloth tighter around her shoulders. The thin fabric provided a degree of insulation from the cold. She still shivered but her teeth stopped clacking. She got to her feet and ran her fingers over her arms and legs. Both elbows and one knee were bruised, but if she hadn't fallen she might not be alive.

She unwrapped the tablecloth and held it under a sconce. Her heart fell as she saw that the diagram she'd hastily drawn was smeared from contact with the moist floor. But it was then that she realized a map of the Maze was constantly with her—carried around inside her head. She let her mind drift back through the years. She was a little girl again, sitting at a desk in her bedroom, studying the script and lines written on her grandfather's scroll. She pictured the Maze and saw that the passageway she was standing in led to a stairway. Could this be the way out of the Labyrinth? Seemed logical.

She pushed on and passed a number of portals. According to the map in her head, the doorways led to dead ends or would take her back the way she came. A few minutes of walking brought her to a set of steel doors. The Maze diagram indicated a big room on the other side of the doors. There was no handle or lock, but to the right of the doors, where the up-down button of an elevator would be located, was a green, glowing double-edged axe around six inches from top to bottom. Kalliste pressed her palm against it. Nothing happened. She stared at the axe, thinking it was identical to the medallion hanging around her neck. Of course! She leaned close and pressed the medallion against the weapon carved in stone. The doors silently slid open.

Kalliste stepped through the portal and the doors shut behind her. The atmosphere was cool and dry. She detected the same type of cloying odor she'd smelled in newly-opened tombs that contained centuries-old air and desiccated bodies.

The vast chamber was lined on all four sides by red and black columns that bowed out slightly in the middle, as was common to Minoan architecture. Panels decorated the wall spaces between the columns. She had seen similar scenes on the frescoes from Thera and Knossos depicting warships, battles and sacrificial processions.

The smell of decay became even stronger. She kept going, drawn by her curiosity, and discovered the source of the odor, the mummified remains that rested on two parallel rows of stone platforms.

She walked between the silent biers and saw that the corpses were adorned with jewelry made of gold and precious stones. Carved into the front of each platform was a sacred horn design. Since Minoan religion was matriarchal, Kalliste guessed that the mummies were probably high-ranking priestesses. She counted forty mummies in all, twenty on each side. At the end of the walkway that passed between the mummies was a stone altar surmounted by two swept-up horns.

To either side of the altar was a cylindrical metal stand that held a double-edged axe. Kalliste gazed at the granite throne that sat on a raised dais behind the altar. A mummy sat upright in the throne. The skeleton and skull were held in place with thin metal straps. The teeth revealed by the fleshless lips set the mouth in a permanent grin. Ivory eyes stared out of the dead sockets. The mummy wore the traditional ruffled skirt of a Minoan priestess, but the breasts that would have been revealed by the open bodice were lost in the leathery folds that enveloped the protruding ribs.

The mummy's bony hands rested on the cranium of the skull that lay in her lap. The ragged hole in the crown suggested the skull's owner had died a violent death. Kalliste wondered who the skull belonged to and why it had been given such an important placement. It was almost like a trophy. The thought hit her like a thunderbolt. Lily had said that an ancient priestess had vanquished King Minos before sailing to exile in Spain. Could she be looking at all that was left of her long-ago royal ancestor?

Reality intruded. She was still in extreme danger. Once the alarm was raised, she'd be cornered in the Maze and dragged back to this evil place for the sacrifice. She was tantalizingly close to the exit stairway. No time to waste. Turning, she ran back between the silent rows of the ancient dead.

CHAPTER SEVENTY

A couple of seconds after Hawkins dove into the helicopter, it had lifted off the parking lot and flown over the harbor, leaving behind angry lovers whose romantic strolls along the seawall had been spoiled by the noisy intrusion.

Calvin's voice crackled over the headset Hawkins had slipped on after his dive into the helicopter.

"Sorry about that messy extraction, Hawk. We were in a hurry. You okay?"

Hawkins wiped the dust from his lips. "I'm fine. What's going on?"

Abby's voice came through his earphones. "That ditzy blonde bombshell Lily Porter, or whatever her name is, works for Auroch Industries. She was setting you up."

"Hold on! How'd you know that?"

"Molly discovered that Auroch owns the Hidden History media company. Lily has been playing a game the whole time."

"It all fits," Hawkins said. "She was the one who contacted Kalliste with the offer to finance the dive. She knew the position of the shipwreck. She worked with Salazar to scuttle the project. Kalliste was kidnapped after she called Lily from Santorini."

"I don't want to think about the plans she had for you," Abby said.

"Neither do I. Thanks for yanking me out of her clutches."

"Thank Molly. She tried to warn you. When you didn't answer she called us."

"The phone was on airplane mode. How did you find me?"

"The positioning app we put on our phones," Calvin said. "We used it to track you down."

Hawkins shook his head in disgust. "Can't believe I bought Lily's phony story about the professor."

"The professor is real enough, but he's nowhere near Cadiz," Abby said. "Molly found out that he's on an archeological dig in the Middle East."

"Ouch. I should have done the same thing. Lily used the photo of Kalliste like a bullfighter waving a red cape. That's all I could think about, especially after she embellished it with the info on the gang of crazies holding Kalliste."

"She told you about her gang of crazies because it didn't matter what you knew."

"Right again, Abby. Dead men tell no tales," Hawkins said. "Especially gullible dead men. Lily's been keeping Kalliste alive to lure me in with the scroll and translator. But with me out of reach, she's got no reason to keep Kalliste alive. We've got to get to her."

"Way ahead of you, Hawk. I've set a course for the castle. Chopper's loaded with all our gear. I'll kick it up a notch and maybe we can shave off a few minutes."

"Put the pedal through the floor if you have to. With Lily on the warpath, there's no margin for error."

"We've got to go over the mission schedule to reduce the possibility of error to zero," Abby said, switching on the iPad that seemed to be an extension of her body. "I'll start with the landing procedure."

The helicopter flew beyond the city, which curved along the harbor like a sparkling diamond tiara, and passed over the suburbs, then over open farmland, following the track of the earlier reconnaissance visit. As the helicopter reached the wind-swept plain *Castilla La Mancha* the lights of villages and houses became more scattered with each passing mile until they disappeared almost completely.

Abby ticked off the mission's time markers. When she finished the briefing, she said, "That's the best I can do with limited intel. How does it sound?"

The plan sounded good on paper, but Hawkins knew that even the best-planned SEAL operations ran into trouble. "Not bad. It might even work except for the exit plan."

"You haven't filled me in on an exit plan," Abby said.

"That's because we don't have one. The best course will be to use an extraction route that's different from the insertion. Everything depends on what we find once we get inside."

Hawkins knew that Abby didn't like uncertainty, which was why they were not still married, so he wasn't surprised when she said, "I know SEALs are adept at improvisation, but the lack of an escape plan worries me."

"We'll be fine, Abby. Isn't that right, Calvin?"

"Hawk's cool, Abby. This is nothing compared to Afghanland. Hoo-yah!" he said, giving the SEAL war cry.

Abby shook her head and switched her iPad onto its GPS function. After a glance at the screen, she said, "Coming up on the river, Calvin."

Calvin cut speed and brought the helicopter down in a long shallow angle toward a river that looked like a silver ribbon lying on black velvet. He leveled off about ten yards above the water and followed the winding path of the river. It was a wild and exhilarating experience, like a ride in a futuristic amusement park.

Three miles from the castle, Calvin warned his passengers to prepare for a landing.

"We'll be on the ground in five minutes. I'll try for a soft landing but it could get bumpy, so hold tight."

He brought the helicopter to a hover and made an angled descent to one side of the river. Hawkins leaned out a window. The landing lights illuminated what looked like a green carpet.

"All clear for landing, Cal."

The helicopter settled onto the ground. Hawkins was out the door. He did a quick perimeter patrol through the waving grass then swept the river bank with the beam from a powerful electric torch. The chopper was solidly in place around twenty feet back from the river. He walked around in front of the helicopter and slashed his hand across his throat in a signal to cut power.

The engine died and the rotors slowly spun to a halt. Abby and Calvin stepped out onto the knee-high grass. The helicopter had silenced the normal insect chorus and there was only the chuckle of river water. The air was heavy with the scent of muck.

Hawkins led the way to the river bank. Calvin pulled up a handful of grass, tied it into a knot and tossed it into the water. Within seconds, the clump was swept beyond the range of the flashlight.

"Strong current," Calvin said. "That's good news. Should push us right along going down. Not so good coming back against the current."

Abby had slung a CAR-15 over her shoulder and walked a short distance from the helicopter to peer through a pair of binoculars in the general direction of the castle. There was no sign that their landing had been detected.

While Abby kept watch, Calvin and Hawkins unloaded the helicopter and placed the cases in a row. They used a foot pump to inflate the three-person polyurethane raft. Weighing thirty-three pounds, the nine-foot long Wing IBXS was similar to the model they had used in the SEALs. The raft had a payload of more than five hundred pounds and easily accommodated the weapons and other gear.

They stripped down to their underwear and slipped on camouflage uniforms streaked with a pattern of black and dark green. Calvin tied a bandanna known as a "drive-on rag" around his bald scalp. Hawkins favored a floppy hat with a wide brim pinned up in front. Abby came over and said there was no sign of activity from the castle. She went over the inventory on her iPad and matched it with the gear.

When she got to Calvin's golf bag, she said, "Gator repellant."

"What did you say?" Hawkins said.

"That's what Calvin called it."

Calvin tapped his nose. "I've been smelling gators ever since I signed onto this gig. Figured they'd need special treatment."

Hawkins simply shrugged. His friend's preparedness for unknown threats had saved their butts more than one time. If

Calvin smelled gators, sure as hell there were gators. They loaded the gear into the inflatable. Hawkins glanced around at their remote surroundings and turned to Abby.

"Ready to go. I don't like leaving you alone out here."

"I'll be fine," Abby said. "Don't forget, I volunteered for this mission."

"You never bargained for something as crazy as this, Abby."

"I never bargained for a *lot* of crazy things that have happened since I met you, Hawkins. Concentrate on getting Kalliste out safely. I know your schedule, so I'll have a rough idea of your progress. One hour to the castle. One hour insertion. One hour extraction."

"If you don't hear from us within an hour of our estimated exit time I want you to leave," Hawkins said. "Call the number I gave you and talk to my Navy friend. He's my old commanding officer. He'll know what to do. When's the last time you flew a chopper?"

"Been a while. I'm rusty, but I can keep it in the air. Now get lost."

Abby gave Hawkins a hug and did the same with Calvin. They dragged the loaded inflatable and its cargo down to the water and got in. Hawkins pushed off with a paddle until the current grabbed the inflatable. Calvin started the electric outboard motor and the little raft picked up speed.

"See you in three hours," Hawkins called out.

As he and Calvin got into the raft and pushed off, Abby said, "Forgot to tell you something."

"What's that, Ab?"

The current had caught the raft and was pulling into the stream when Abby cupped her hands to her mouth and called out.

"Hoo-yah!"

CHAPTER SEVENTY-ONE

Lily had staggered out of Genovese Park onto the street and called the limousine waiting around the corner. She was coughing from the dust in her lungs when the Mercedes pulled up to the curb within thirty seconds, but she still managed to bark out an order.

"Take me to the Auroch building. *Quickly.*"

The chauffeur mashed the gas pedal. Lily raged as the big car sped across the city, running stop signs and cutting off other vehicles.

This was not supposed to be this way, Hawkins should be lying in the park with the life's blood flowing from his dying body.

The scroll and translator device should be in her hands. It was obvious the helicopter's arrival above her head was no coincidence, but she couldn't understand it. How had anyone known where she and Hawkins would be?

Lily was the classic psychopath. Charming and manipulative. But behind her brilliant smile was a cold-blooded being who was incapable of empathy. Adding to her murderous genetic heritage, the tutelage under the High Priestess, the drug-induced hallucinations at dozens of bloody rituals, her fealty to the Mother Goddess, and her immersion in the perverted religion that underpinned the Way of the Axe had drained every last human emotion from her body.

Amid all this, she had retained her outward appearance of sanity. Until now. Forces beyond her control seemed to be battling for command of her mind and body. Voices clamored in her head. She was confused at first until it dawned on her what the cacophony was about. All the priestesses who'd ever lived were calling out from across the eons, the chorus of the dead telling her that soon she, too, would be one with the Mother Goddess. When Hawkins slipped from her grasp her fevered mind concluded that his impossible escape could only have been the will of the Mother Goddess. She was telling Lily that Hawkins was a worthless diversion. The only one the goddess truly wanted was Kalliste, descendant of King Minos.

The Mercedes plunged into the garage under the Auroch tower. The elevator sped Lily to the roof. She got into the waiting helicopter, which lifted off and flew across the city to the airport. A company jet sat on the tarmac warming its engines. As soon as she was in her seat, the jet sped down the runway, quickly reached its cruising altitude and headed for *La Mancha* at more than six hundred miles an hour.

Hawkins and Calvin were still floating down the river at around five knots when Lily's plane landed on the airstrip near the castle. A waiting SUV driven by one of the crone's guards transported her along the old road and through the main gate of the castle to the torch-lit courtyard. She stepped out of the SUV and walked across toward the Tripartite Shrine. She noticed a commotion in front of the entrance where her assistant priestesses were gathered around the Prior known as North.

She stepped up to the senior priestess. "Why aren't you preparing the Greek woman for the ceremony?" she demanded.

The priestess reacted with a horrified expression.

"We can't," she sobbed. "She's dead."

A thunder cloud passed over Lily's brow. She reached out and her long fingernails dug like talons into the young woman's throat. The priestess tried to speak, but her face turned purple. She could barely breathe and would have died if not for the Prior.

"She told me that the Daemons killed someone in the Maze," he said. "I was about to investigate."

Lily released her grip. "Show me," she said.

Clutching her bleeding throat, the priestess led the way through the shrine entrance and down the stairway into the Maze, with Lily and the Prior close behind. They followed a convoluted route that took them to a tunnel near the king's apartment where Kalliste had been held.

The body of a woman lay on its side, face turned against a wall. The torso was a mass of shredded cloth and flesh. Having eaten their fill, the Daemons were curled up asleep near the body. In the dim light the woman's hair looked a deep brown, the same shade as Kalliste's. Lily knelt by the body and saw that the hair had been darkened by the blood pooling on the floor.

"Turn her over," Lily said.

The Prior rolled the body onto its back. Lily stared at a face frozen in a mask of terror. "This is not the Greek. It is her attendant."

"I don't understand," the Prior said. "The hounds would not attack someone wearing the medallion."

"Look closer, Prior. Do you see the axe medallion?"

The Prior got down on one knee. The woman's throat was a mass of bloody flesh, but it was obvious the medallion was missing. He glanced at the Daemons. "Maybe it was torn off and swallowed."

"Very creative, Prior. But as you said, they would not attack, which means she was not wearing the protective pendant. The medallion was taken from her and she foolishly decided to leave the apartment without it. The Greek is still in the Maze. I want all exits guarded. Go through the tunnels one by one."

The Prior pulled a hand radio from his belt and barked a series of orders.

"The Shrine portal is under guard," he said. "A crew will move from one side of the Maze to the other. We're checking security cameras as well. We'll catch her."

Lily turned to the priestess. "Tell my lovely flowers to be ready in the sanctuary in one hour. Go!"

Still mute from her damaged vocal cords, the priestess nodded, then she and the Prior disappeared down a tunnel leaving Lily alone. She was already enjoying the power that would soon be in her hands. The voices she'd been hearing had quieted except for the harsh cackle of the crone.

Remember the prophecy.

She is near. She must die.

CHAPTER SEVENTY-TWO

Kalliste was close to the exit portal under the Tripartite Shrine at the foot of a broad marble stairway. She sprinted up the stairs in her eagerness to escape from the foul place with its four-legged demons and red-eyed monster. Her exuberance almost proved her undoing.

As she reached the top of the stairway and entered the dimly-lit interior of the Tripartite Shrine, she heard shouting. She ducked into the shadow of an alcove. Within seconds, a group of men in uniform burst through the doorway, dashed across the floor and disappeared down the stairs into the Maze. Kalliste crouched in a corner.

Her escape must have been discovered. She forced herself to count to sixty, then she rose from her hiding place, folded the tablecloth that had been her comfort blanket and tucked it into the alcove. She cautiously approached the entrance.

The wooden doors were wide open. She peered around the jamb and saw a pair of uniformed guards a dozen or so feet from the doorway. She yanked her head back inside. Time was short. When it was discovered she was not in the Labyrinth the search would be expanded to the castle grounds.

She didn't know what to do. If she made a run for it, she'd be cut down in an instant, but it would be better than the torture of waiting to be caught and killed. She was psyching herself up to make a quick dash when she heard the unmistakable sound of an approaching helicopter.

She ventured a peek around the corner. The two guards had turned away from the door to watch the helicopter drop onto the landing pad. One guard started walking toward the helipad. Now or never.

Kalliste stepped through the doorway of the Tripartite Shrine and began to run.

CHAPTER SEVENTY-THREE

As Salazar's helicopter skimmed the castle's crenelated ramparts and hovered in preparation for its landing, Chad peered down through a window and saw that the space enclosed within the castle walls was as empty as when he'd glimpsed it from the air with Hawkins. But when the helicopter landed and he stepped out the door with Salazar and his guards, he blinked his eyes in astonishment.

Directly in front of him, barely fifty yards from where he stood, was a strange-looking building. The façade consisted of three towers, with the tallest in the center. Downward tapering columns supported raised plinths surmounted by horn-shaped sculptures. Standing on steel legs over the building was a huge tent-like structure made of pale green material.

Salazar stepped up beside Chad. "What do you think of our little illusion?"

"Amazing, but what is it?"

"An example of octopus technology. It's the latest in camouflage techniques. The roof is actually a system that includes light and temperature sensors. Color-switching controls adapt to changing light conditions the way an octopus switches color. The walls hid the castle's interior for centuries, but we live in the age of Google Earth and prying satellite eyes. Walls are obsolete, no matter how tall they are."

"Very cool," Chad said. "What's with the funky building?"

"Don't let the priestesses hear you say that. They'll cut your tongue out for denigrating the entrance to their most sacred site. This facade is called the Tripartite Shrine. It was built centuries ago to replicate the Knossos shrine that served as the entrance to the sanctuary of the Snake Goddess. The red on the back walls represents the Underworld, yellow is earth and blue is the heavens. The horns are the symbol of Poteidan, the Bull God. But enough of theology; we have work to do."

"Sure thing, Mr. Salazar."

As he waited for an order, Chad took in his surroundings with the eye of a Special Ops team member. High walls. Portals in the base of the four towers. Tall steel doors. A couple of big SUVs. The drone sitting on its launcher. Points of possible threat. Points of possible escape.

He was puzzled by the number of sentries. Only two. One was walking toward the helicopter while the other stayed near the door. Where the hell were the rest of the security guys Salazar had mentioned? The walking guard stopped suddenly and yelled. A woman had popped out of the entrance next to the shrine façade and was racing toward a castle tower.

The guard nearest Chad peeled away and did a fish hook run that cut her off. She saw the maneuver and changed course. The guards adjusted their pursuit so that both were closing in on the woman. Salazar's men joined the chase.

The woman's features were distorted with exertion, but Chad recognized Kalliste, Hawkins' friend, who'd been kidnapped by the goons on Santorini. She'd been focused on her pursuers and didn't see Chad directly in her path until she was around twenty feet away. That's when Salazar yelled:

"Don't just stand there, you fool! Grab her."

Kalliste saw Chad standing in her way. She tried to veer off to one side, but momentum carried her into his waiting arms where she fought against his tight embrace.

"Let me go!" she snarled.

He put his mouth close to her ear. "Can't do that, darlin'. They'll shoot us both."

She continued her struggle. "I don't care. Let me go, you bastard." She was breathing hard and barely able to get the words out.

He held her tighter. "I'm a friend of Matt and Calvin. Don't give them an excuse to kill us."

She stopped fighting and their eyes locked for a moment before the guards pulled her from his grasp and dragged her to the shrine entrance. Chad experienced the same feeling of rage he had when Salazar's men had killed his girlfriend. Hate for Salazar flowed through his veins like a mega-shot of adrenaline. He would not let the same thing happen to this woman.

His skin crawled when Salazar came over, put his hand on his shoulder, and said,

"Good work, Leonidas. If she'd gotten away, the ceremony would have been canceled."

"Who was that?" Chad asked, because it was a natural question Salazar would have expected.

"Her identity is of no consequence. She's an unimportant grain of sand whose escape could have brought our enterprise to a grinding halt."

"Where are those guys taking her?"

"To a place men have seen only in their fevered dreams. Come with me, Leonidas. It's time to introduce you to the Labyrinth."

CHAPTER SEVENTY-FOUR

The inflatable boat carrying the two men was about a half mile from the castle when the beat of rotors shattered the night and the helicopter swooped over the castle walls. The five-horsepower motor was at full throttle. The swift current had given the inflatable an extra boost.

Hawkins lay on his belly in the bow, his sharp eyes scanning the river ahead. The inflatable rounded a curve and in the light of the moon he saw the sluice gate cut into the side of the river bank.

The landing had to go off without a hitch. There was no room for screw-ups. He pointed. "Pull in, Cal."

Calvin cut speed, pushed the tiller over and pointed the inflatable inland. Hawkins was on his knees, bow line in hand. He had to act fast. The current was drawing the raft sideways back into the river.

Calvin goosed the throttle. Still not enough power to counter the pull of the current. They were sliding past the sluice gate. Hawkins stretched dangerously out over the prow. If he miscalculated and went into the river precious moments would be lost getting back into the raft. Setting up for another pass might even be impossible.

With a practiced hand, he looped the line around the metal framework that supported the gate. The inflatable fish-tailed to a jerking stop. He hauled on the line hand-over-hand. The inflatable bumped up against the gate. Hawkins secured the tie line with a clove hitch. Calvin tied off the stern line. The raft was snugged tightly against a rusty steel plate that could be moved up and down to control water flow. It was stuck in a half-open position, allowing water from the river into the sluiceway.

Hawkins removed his night vision goggles and peered over the top of the sluice gate. The castle was a couple of hundred yards away. Floodlights pointed down from the top of the wall and illuminated the electrical fencing around the perimeter.

He rolled out of the raft, crawled like a salamander up the muddy slope next to the sluice gate and lay belly-down on the grass, his eyes glued to the castle. If they'd been detected by cameras or sensors, all hell would soon break loose. When nothing happened, Hawkins whistled to Calvin, who passed up the waterproof bags and crawled up alongside him.

They dragged their gear through the grass to the edge of the sluiceway on the other side of the gate. The channel was around five feet across, bordered on both sides by stone walls. They got into their dry suits, pulled two compact Draeger dive rigs from a bag and clipped them onto their harnesses. Unlike SCUBA, the closed-circuit rig didn't emit bubbles and noise that could broadcast their location. The unit's oxygen cylinder would allow them to stay down for hours.

They used the oxygen flow to inflate the buoys attached to each bag, donned their masks, hoods, weight belts and flippers, then rolled over the top of the wall into the sluiceway. Hawkins almost gagged on the rotten odor rising from the stagnant water.

"Whew! Smells like a swamp."

Calvin chuckled softly. "Hell, this is like a swimming pool compared to the bayou. You'll get used to it."

Hawkins was unconvinced. He held his breath and pulled a gear bag into the water. The bag sank slightly but remained partly afloat. He released air in the lifts until the bag had neutral buoyancy and would neither float nor sink on its own. They adjusted the buoyancy in the other bags, clenched their regulators between their teeth and slipped below the water.

Using powerful kicks of their fins, they swam to the bottom of the sluiceway. Hawkins glanced at his depth gauge. Five feet. He tapped Calvin on the shoulder and began to swim toward the castle. Light from the castle walls filtered down from the surface providing enough visibility for them to see their way. At the same time, the glittering reflection would screen them from probing eyes.

The bags hindered their progress, but both men were strong swimmers. On land, Hawkins walked with a slight limp. Underwater, he was as agile as a dolphin. They followed the sluiceway, which ended in the moat, as Abby had suggested. They swam across the moat to the foundation to look for the opening that would have carried water from the sluiceway into the castle. The wall was blank. Hawkins swam to his right for several feet, then doubled back in the opposite direction. Still no opening.

Had they got it wrong? He drew a question mark inside a square on the white wrist board. Cal nodded, then drew an arrow pointing up on his board. They were too low. Hawkins gave a few fin kicks.

His fingertips grazed the slimy stones until he felt a hard edge and followed it around four sides with his hand. The rectangular opening was around four feet wide and three feet high. He flicked on the flashlight attached to his other wrist.

The pencil thin beam picked out stone walls, a floor and a ceiling before fading into the murk. Hawkins had worried that the water pipe would be too small to navigate. He gave Calvin a thumb's up signal and swam into the tunnel. If Abby had figured it correctly, the tunnel should lead to a cistern. He tried not to think that their entry strategy relied for the most part on guesswork, and the interpretation of lines drawn on an ancient document. If they hit a dead end and had to turn back, the consequences might be disastrous for Kalliste.

The clang of the Draeger against the tunnel ceiling brought him back into the moment. He swam with slight fluttering kicks, trying not to stir up the silt, his hands extended in front of him like Superman in flight. Hawkins didn't normally suffer from claustrophobia, but he was aware that the tons of stone pressing down directly over his head were held in place by walls erected centuries before.

Turning his thoughts to Kalliste, he swam even faster.

CHAPTER SEVENTY-FIVE

"It's time to put your thespian skills to work," Salazar said to Chad.

The men were standing in the cool, torch-lit interior of the three-towered building Salazar had called the Tripartite Shrine. They had entered the cathedral-like precincts after Kalliste was whisked through the doors. She was nowhere to be seen. There was only Chad, Salazar and his four bodyguards. Salazar snapped his fingers. One of his men handed Chad a folded white cloth.

"Put this on. It should be the right size," Salazar said.

Chad shook out the cotton robe. The hem and the round collar were embroidered with blue axe designs. He pulled it over his head and down past his knees. The robe fit snugly over his clothes and the shoulder padding he'd used to imitate Salazar's physique.

"Remove your mask," Salazar ordered.

Chad tossed the balaclava to the man who'd given him the robe.

"The illusion must fool all the senses." Salazar handed him a small bottle.

Chad took the top off the bottle and almost gagged. It was the same sickly-sweet cologne Salazar favored. He thought how satisfying it would be to smash the bottle into Salazar's nose and drive splinters of bone into the man's skull. His joy would be short-lived. The guards would cut him down before Salazar's body hit the floor. He had learned the value of patience in Special Ops and later as a contract killer. He could wait.

He opened the bottle, patted cologne on his neck, and in his best imitation of Salazar's silky voice, said, "Well, what do you think?"

Salazar stepped back, folded his arms and gazed at his double.

"Remarkable," he said. "You will easily pass as me, especially in the dim light of the priestess sanctuary." He handed Chad the ear plug that he had shown him back at the log cabin. "Slide this into your ear. You remember your instructions?"

"Sure. Twist the button and press it three times when the ceremony ends."

"You forgot something." Salazar barked an order to a man who stepped forward with the box that contained the bull's head bomb. He reached inside the box for the rhyton and handled it to Chad. "You will place this on the altar and step aside. No one will pay any attention to you. All eyes will be watching the victim's blood being drained into the rhyton."

Chad made a face. "Do they really do that?"

Salazar's liverish lips twisted into his reptilian smile. "The priestesses are what are known as Maenads, which means 'raving ones' in Greek. In their ecstatic frenzy they tear their victim to pieces and the life's blood is passed around in communion. Don't tell me you're squeamish. You've seen people die before. As I recall, you helped a few into the afterlife."

"Yeah, but I never drank anyone's blood. If you're going to bust up the party, why not do it *before* they do the sacrifice and have their snack?"

"These are dangerous people. I want to strike when the priestess and her followers are at the peak of their frenzy and will be most vulnerable. The victim is only a means to an end, and of no consequence in the greater scheme. She's no different than any of the targets you've eliminated at my order."

There's a big difference, Chad thought. His kills were always quick and clean. The death of Kalliste Kalchis was vital to Salazar for some reason, and that alone would make her worth saving.

"Okay, Mr. Salazar. I see where you're going."

"One more thing," Salazar said. He removed an axe-shaped pendant from around his neck and looped the chain over Chad's head.

"Keep this with you at all times in the Maze. If you remove it, the Daemons will see that you enjoy an even more unpleasant death than the sacrificial victim."

Chad went to ask about the Daemons, but Salazar shushed him and cocked his head to listen. A faint piping sound floated up the stairway into the towered shrine.

"The procession has begun. Go down those stairs and into the antechamber to wait for the priestesses. Do as you're instructed and you'll be fine."

He turned and strode from the shrine with his men. Chad listened to the eerie sound coming from the Maze. No going back now. He descended the stairway, moving slowly so he wouldn't trip on the hem of his robe with a bomb in his hands. At the bottom of the stairs he paused and took a deep breath. Inhaling reminded him of how much he could use a joint. He squared his shoulders and went through the open entryway into a room around a hundred feet square. Scenes of bulls and acrobats and aquatic creatures decorated the turquoise-colored walls. He was facing a closed door. The flute music issued from two portals, one on his left; the other to his right. It was an atonal sound, off-key and without melody, and almost hurt his ears to listen to it.

The sound of flutes grew louder. Chad expected the musicians to enter the antechamber at any second, but the two creatures that emerged simultaneously through the doorways looked as if they were stepping out of a nightmare. The muscular, vaguely dog-like animals were identical in appearance. They had narrow muzzles and boney faces that were almost at Chad's eye-level.

Each animal was at the end of a leather leash attached to a jeweled collar. The men holding the leashes had aquiline noses, their scalps were painted blue. They looked like clones of the men he and Hawkins had killed on the Cretan island of Spinalonga.

The leashes must have been for decorative purposes because the long, sharp teeth lining the open mouths of the animals looked as if they could snap tethers of chain. The men let the creatures approach Chad on both sides. He tensed, but the dogs merely poked the hem of his robe with their long snouts, then sat back on their haunches and grinned at him. He had passed the sight and sniff test.

Others were coming into the chamber. Behind the dog walkers were processions of four women, eight in all, walking in pairs. The women all had on long layered skirts made of overlapping material in blue, black and green. The short-sleeved tops they wore had necklines cut to the navel, exposing cleavage. The wide cloth belts wrapped around their waists emphasized the hips. Their hair was tucked up under flat, round caps.

These had to be the priestesses. They were in their twenties or thirties, Chad guessed, but their faces lacked the fresh allure that young women normally had at that age. Their hard features looked as if they had been chipped out of marble. Lush mouths were compressed into tight expressions that revealed no emotion. Heavy liner made the arc of their brows longer and more exaggerated so that their eyes looked larger than they were. The cheeks were rouged with make-up. Chad had spent enough time in drug-induced la-la land to know from their glazed, fixed expressions that the women were stoned out of their minds.

The leader of the procession was holding a clay vessel. Behind her marched a pair of priestesses who were playing flutes. The next pair of marchers held leafy boughs on their shoulders. They formed two lines and the music stopped. The priestess with the vessel stepped forward and offered it to Chad. Just follow instructions, Salazar said. He took the vessel and raised it to his lips. His first sip was tentative. Not bad. A little medicinal. Earthy, though, and slightly sweet. He took a second swallow and handed the vessel back.

Wham.

Chad had tried a lot of addictive substances, but nothing had ever acted with such *speed*. Not even speed. It felt as if someone had poured a glass of LSD directly into his brain. First came a flush of heat. He imagined his cheeks glowing red-hot. The hot flush passed and he felt a tingling from head to toe. He stared off at the wall. The colors glowed and pulsated. The painted figures seemed to move. The acrobats were vaulting between the horns of the bulls. The octopi and fish were dancing with each other.

His sense of hearing had become more acute. He could hear the swish of skirts and the soft padding of bare feet on the hard floor as the priestesses began to dance around him. He smiled as they morphed from humans into beautiful, whirling flowers.

The musicians started to play again. But the music that had been so awful when he first heard it was now beautiful. They chanted the same words again and again.

She is near. She must die.

The lead priestess was the most animated. She whirled around, her arms extended above her head. The circle of dancers moved faster and faster, the chanting louder. Chad was losing it. The chanting and music, the moving circle of glowing colors, the weird effects of the drugs—all were getting to him. He clutched the bull's head closer so he wouldn't drop it.

Then the lead priestess stopped dancing. The hands that had been flailing above her head dropped to waist level, palms down. She was facing the door. It was obviously the signal for the music and the dancing to stop. The priestesses had broken out of their circle. Their cheeks were still flushed from the orgiastic dance. At the head of each line was a blue-headed man holding a leash with a pit bull on steroids.

They formed lines on both sides again. With Chad in the middle carrying the bull's head as if it were radioactive, they filed into the sanctuary of the high priestess.

CHAPTER SEVENTY-SIX

Abby's technical evaluation had been right on the mark when she said the water main would end in a cistern. Hawkins played the beam of his wrist light on the stone walls of the circular chamber, then he swam up until his head broke the surface. Calvin bobbed up beside him.

The cistern was around six feet across. He pulled himself up onto the low wall, then reached down to help Calvin with the bags. Once all their gear was out of the cistern, Calvin joined him at the edge of the pool.

Hawkins removed his mouthpiece and took a tentative sniff. "Air is musty and damp, but breathable," he pronounced. He stood and walked around the cistern. "Getting Kalliste out this way could be a problem."

"I'm thinking the same thing," Calvin said. "We don't know what shape Kalliste is in, but even if she's okay, trying to muscle her back through that drainage pipe is not going to work."

"Which means we stick with standard SEAL protocol. Get in one way and go out another."

The cistern was at the center of a room around fifteen feet square that had only one doorway. They slipped the Draegers off their backs, leaving them with the spare unit they had brought for Kalliste, then peeled off their dry suits down to their camouflage uniforms. Calvin tied the drive-on rag around his head and Hawkins tucked his hair under his floppy hat. They picked up their gear bags and went through the doorway into a long, narrow room. There was a stone shelf along one wall with circular holes cut into it.

"Reminds me of the outhouse our family had, except ours was a one-holer," Calvin said. "Guess the Minoans didn't put a lot a value on privy-cy."

"Looks that way, but I wasn't *privy* to their thoughts."

"Damn, Hawk, that was worse than mine."

"Remember this moment the next time you feel the need to unleash your puns on a captive audience."

A door connecting to a passageway is where they felt a slight breeze blowing. The corridor led to a tunnel big enough to drive a car through. Hawkins surveyed the walls and ceiling that dripped with moisture. The tunnel was a remarkable example of ancient engineering. He estimated the dimensions at around twenty feet across and ten feet high. Hawkins noticed that the lichen-splotched surfaces were honey-combed with cracks.

Hawkins had taken a photo of the Minotaur's maze diagram with his tablet. Using the map as a guide, they soon found their way to the doorway pictured in the photo of Kalliste and the dog creature. Hawkins gazed up at the axe head lintel and pictured Kalliste standing in the doorway. Then, with Calvin standing watch, he checked the apartment, taking in the unmade bed, and the remnants of food on the table. There were pieces of the broken ceramic vessel on the floor. Something had happened here, and that worried him even more.

Hawkins stepped back into the passageway and shook his head. They set off along the tunnel at a fast trot and came to a junction where the passageway ended in a 'T.' The map showed that the right hand turn went to a blank wall. They turned left and picked up the pace, moving so fast that when a strange sound brought Hawkins to a sudden halt, Calvin almost bowled him over.

"What was that god-awful noise?" Calvin said.

The bawling sound that had brought them to a stop repeated itself. The noise sounded as if it were being made by an animal, but it had a mournful human quality to it as well.

"Whatever it is doesn't sound happy. Maybe we should try to

go around it."

"No argument there," Calvin said. When they checked the map they saw that they could only move forward and back. All the other outlets were dead ends.

Calvin slipped the CAR-15 off his shoulder. Hawkins took the Sig Sauer from its holster leaving one hand free to hold the map. As they continued down the passageway the bellowing grew louder. It seemed to echo from every part of the maze so that it was almost impossible to pinpoint its source at first. But as they made their way through the tunnel, it became apparent that whatever was making the noise was directly ahead.

The bawling combined with a new sound, a steady *clop-clop*, as if two coconut shells were being clapped together, like a scene from "Monty Python." Hawkins brought the pistol up in both hands. Calvin lifted the CAR-15 to waist level.

They took a right turn and discovered they were no longer alone. Framed in the tunnel, silhouetted against a bluish back light, was what looked like a gigantic bull. It stepped forward, and wall sconces that must have been motion sensitive flicked on.

The animal was a bull, but only from the waist down. The lower body was white with splotches of brown. From the navel up, the torso was that of a muscular man who had abdominal muscles that looked as if they had been sculpted with a chisel. Ropey arms dangled by its sides. The face was a combination of man and animal. Protruding from each side of the wide forehead, sharp horns curved down and forward. Each one was at least a yard long. The nose was human, but the flaring nostrils were not. Thick lips defined the wide mouth.

"Man, that is one ugly cow," Calvin whispered.

"I wish it *were* a cow," Hawkins said. "It's the Minotaur, the guardian of the Maze."

"There's no such thing as the Minotaur," Calvin said.

"*You* tell that thing it doesn't exist, Cal. I'm going to slowly make a retreat and recommend you do the same. Walk backwards around the corner. Duck into the doorway we passed on our right." They stepped back. The maneuver triggered more snorts, but the creature stayed where it was. Emboldened, they kept moving, and gained a few yards before there was a change in the Minotaur's bearing. The head had been held high in a position of watchful alertness. Now it dropped low. The elbows tucked into its sides.

With no longer any need to speak in a whisper, Calvin yelled, "He's going for it, Hawk!"

The thunder of hooves filled the passageway.

Hawkins and Calvin ducked around the corner, ran about twenty feet and slipped into a side tunnel. The animal clattered past, the sharp points of its horns were extended like twin spears. Then it spun around, clopped back and stood in the entryway looking for the two men, who stood further in the tunnel with their backs flat against the wall.

The Minotaur's head lifted and moved back and forth like a radar disk homing in on a target.

There was a jerkiness to its movements that wasn't quite natural, although agility was top-notch. The quickness of its attack was amazing. He recalled what Molly had learned about the French company whose name he had seen on the diving bell. It was owned by Auroch, and made giant robotic mining equipment. The same technique could have been used to build the monster he was looking at.

"You were right," Hawkins murmured. "That isn't the Minotaur. We're looking at a well-designed robot."

"That makes me feel a lot better, Hawk. Now tell me how we pull the plug on that bag of bolts."

"Not a chance. It must operate on batteries. Probably uses recharging stations scattered around this place. The legs must be on wheels, which means that the *clop-clop* was recorded. Damned amazing piece of engineering. I'd love to get a closer look at it."

"You may get your wish."

The bull's head had stopped its back and forth motion and was lowering, the signal for a charge. Hawkins was impressed with the robot's learning ability when he saw it advance cautiously into the tunnel rather than rush after them as it did before. He wondered if the machine knew that they were in a dead end.

"We may have a problem, Calvin. That thing could have been programmed with the maze's layout and given some sensing apparatus to keep track of its own movements."

"Which means it's biding its time because it knows we're trapped."

"You got it."

"How long before it rushes us again?"

"Its circuits are probably telling it we can't go anywhere. It will keep up that pace and make its rush when it's almost to us." He clicked the safety off his pistol. "Aim for the eyes. If we put the camera lenses out of commission we might still have a chance to make a run for it."

"Got a better idea," Calvin said. "Gator repellent."

He unzipped the golf bag, pulled out a Spike missile and snapped it into the launcher, which he raised to his shoulder. Hawkins watched his friend squint through the launcher's viewfinder.

"Oh hell, Calvin," he said.

"What's the problem, Hawk?"

"You're going to blow that thing off the map. It's an incredible piece of engineering. I'd love to get a look at its insides."

"Unfortunately, it probably wants to get a look our insides, too. Uh-oh."

The creature was starting to pick up speed, but still moving at a fast walk.

"This isn't exactly like putting Old Paint out of its misery. It's nothing but a machine."

"Yeah, I know, but—" Hawkins had noticed a slightly different motion. Rather than keeping its arms by its sides, the creature had extended them and formed the hands into giant claws. Having missed on its first charge, it was preparing to grab its targets if they tried to slip by.

"But *what*, man?"

"It's about to attack. Wait until it's closer to get a clean shot."

"Okay. Tell me when and hit the dirt."

The robot was less than thirty feet away and was picking up speed. The head had stopped twitching and was starting to lower. The attack had begun.

"Now!" Hawkins shouted.

The Minotaur accelerated and quickly halved the distance.

There was a loud whoosh as the missile left the launcher. In a normal shoot, Calvin would have watched the missile and directed it to its target, but after he fired he threw the launcher down and slammed belly-first next to Hawkins onto the hard floor. They covered their ears but the shock of the explosion in the confined space pummeled their eardrums. They felt the shock wave flow over their bodies. Pieces of hot plastic and metal rained down on their backs.

Smoke filled the tunnel. Calvin handed Hawkins one of the gas protection units he'd packed. Goggles protected the eyes and the units had small, compressed air tubes with regulators attached. He and Hawkins bit down on the plastic mouthpieces and crawled along the floor where the smoke was the thinnest and their wrist lights were somewhat effective. They had to avoid chunks of glowing debris scattered on the floor. Once past ground zero, they stood in a half-crouch and made their way to the end of the passageway. As they turned back into the main tunnel, there was a rumble and the horrendous crash of what sounded like an avalanche.

"Sounds like the roof just caved in," Calvin said.

Hawkins remembered the cracks he had seen in the tunnel walls.

"I think that's exactly what it was." He glanced up at the tunnel ceiling and saw that it was covered with a network of cracks similar to those in the side passageway. "I think we'd better pick up our pace."

CHAPTER SEVENTY-SEVEN

Lily stood in front of the altar in the sanctuary, praying for a sign from the Mother Goddess when she felt the tremor under her sandals. A rapt smile came to her face. The goddess had heard her voice. She was shaking the earth deep in the Labyrinth to signal eagerness for the sacrifice.

Lily gazed down on the lovely face of Kalliste who lay in a fetal position on the sacrificial table between the sacral horns. Her arms and legs were trussed with rope and she was heavily drugged. Lily's heart welled with happiness as she thought back to the first sacrifice she had attended so many years before.

She and the other young priestesses were standing in a grove of trees around the victim, a lamb that lay on a platform in much the same position as Kalliste. This was long before the High Priestess became the withered crone in the Paris sanitarium. She was in her eighties, but her pale, translucent skin was still tight against her cheekbones.

Lily remembered the flash of sunlight on the dagger blade, the last pitiful bleat and the bright river of crimson against white wool. With blood dripping from the dagger, the crone had looked up from her work to gauge the reactions of the young girls. Some had covered their eyes. Others stood with mouths open in shock. The crone's blue eyes had fastened on Lily, whose face showed neither fear nor loathing, but rather cold interest. She had smiled, and from that moment, Lily had been groomed as her successor.

The High Priestess was dead, but she would never die. Her spirit had merged with all the high priestesses before her to be reborn in the great goddess Potnia, the Lady of the Labyrinth. Potnia, herself, was a combination of all the Minoan deities—the Snake Goddess, the Goddess of the Earth and the mistress of the animals, Britomartis.

By impersonating the goddess, Lily would *become* the goddess in an epiphany that gave her complete control over the Way of the Axe. Once she had made the transformation, she would speak with the voice of the goddess. There would be no hesitation when she ordered the priestesses to tear Salazar to pieces. The Mother Goddess would be pleased with the double sacrifice and shower the faithful with good fortune. The success of the operation in the United States would be ensured. Lily would take control of Auroch Industries and expand her power around the globe.

She looked up at the mummy of the High Priestess sitting on its throne. Under the influence of the opiates she had taken to prepare for the ceremony, she imagined that the leathery features of her predecessor's face once again glowed with health and life. This was not a four-thousand-year-old pile of withered flesh and brittle bones. She saw the lips widen in a smile. The voice of the long-dead priestess filled her head.

She must die.

Lily heard the piping of the flutes. Once Salazar brought in the rhyton the ceremony would begin.

Soon, Mother. Very soon.

CHAPTER SEVENTY-EIGHT

Chad tried to fight off the drug that had dug its talons into his brain, but the hallucinatory effect was powerful. Luckily, it was short-lived. The dancing flowers that had whirled around him transformed back into the hard-faced priestesses, although their colorful robes still glowed as if they were on fire.

The flutes and the lyres started up again. The priestesses began to chant in the weird language. The music was less frenzied, more like a funeral dirge, which didn't make Chad feel any better.

The procession filed through the open door and into a great hall. Chad gripped the bull's head close to his chest as if it could ward off the evil that seemed to surround him. The chant echoed off the ceilings and walls of the vast room. His eyes darted right and left, taking in the colonnades of red columns that ran along the walls. He stored the layout in his brain so he wouldn't have to think about it when it was time to make his move.

The parade marched further into the room, passing between the biers. The procession continued to the far end of the hall and stopped in front of an altar made of black basalt. Rising from the altar was a horn-shaped sculpture. Framed by the horns was a mummified body that sat in a throne-like chair. On either side of the mummy was a stone pillar with a bronze-bladed double axe sticking out of it.

Chad only glanced at the hideous dead face before his eye was drawn to the figure lying on the altar itself. Kalliste was bound hand and foot, like a piece of meat ready to be carved up. Chad knew exactly who was going to do the carving; the tall, glassy-eyed woman in the flounced skirt who stood off to the side of the altar holding a long-bladed bronze dagger in her hand. She was staring at him.

The music had stopped. Everyone seemed to be expecting something. He saw the woman wrinkle her brow and thought maybe she had seen through his disguise. He realized his behavior was raising suspicion. He snapped out of his daze. Recalling Salazar's instructions, he placed the rhyton next to Kalliste's head, then stepped aside. The woman smiled and turned to address the others in the procession. She spoke in the unknown language. He didn't understand a word, but judging from the glittering eyes of the priestesses and the evil grins of the dog-handlers something bad was about to go down.

He glanced at the unconscious form on the altar. He couldn't let these creeps hurt Kalliste. Screw Salazar. He reached into the pocket. His fingers found the remote control, gave the knob a twist with his thumb and forefinger, and he waited for the right moment to press the button three times.

CHAPTER SEVENTY-NINE

After escaping the Minotaur's lair, Hawkins and Calvin followed the map to a stairwell that took them up three levels. Their ears still rang from the missile explosion and they relied on hand signals to communicate.

The passageways at the upper level were narrower and better lit than the depths of the Labyrinth. They navigated the warren of corridors at a fast trot, heading in the general direction of a large chamber marked with the snake symbol. The map showed that the big space had entryways on the front and back. The front entrance opened onto an antechamber and a wide flight of stairs. Hawkins decided that the stairway area might be busy with comings and goings, choosing to use the back door to gain entrance.

He edged around the corner. The corridor was unguarded. He and Calvin dashed to a double-door made of wood held together with metal straps, and tried the latch. The door was locked. On their missions in Afghanistan, Hawkins and Calvin had developed their own sign language to cover unique situations.

Hawkins pointed to the lock, then to his forehead like the Scarecrow in *The Wizard of Oz*.

Any idea how to do this?

Calvin made a cranking motion with his hands.

We drill it.

Calvin extracted a battery-operated drill from his pack and

quickly drilled a circle of holes around the lock. Hawkins drove his rifle butt into the serrated section of wood; it fell inside.

He forced the door with a shoulder slam. The entryway opened onto a corridor that ran left and right. A strange piping music filled the air. He pointed to his ear. Calvin nodded.

"Yeah, my hearing's come back too. Maybe we should split up."

Hawkins said, "Let's do a recon, then decide."

Hawkins made a random choice and headed off to the left. They sprinted along the corridor which made a right angle turn into the shadows of the colonnade, and ducked behind a thick column. The vantage point gave them a side view of a stone altar surmounted by horn-shaped sculptures similar to those Hawkins had seen at Knossos.

As he peered around the column, he noticed the spider-web of cracks, like those in the walls of the lower level where Calvin had spiked the bull robot. A building inspector would condemn this dump in a second.

Calvin, who was looking through a pair of binoculars, murmured, "This is a freaking freak show."

He handed the glasses over. In the torch light Hawkins saw several women dressed in long ruffled skirts and wearing round, flat-topped hats. A bald, blue-headed man—who could have been a brother of the attacker he'd killed on Spinalonga—was holding a tether attached to the same animal pictured in the photo Lily had shown him.

Another man stepped forward from the crowd toward the altar. His head was shaven but unpainted. Hawkins recognized Salazar from his photo and watched him place a dark object on the altar where Kalliste was curled up.

As soon as Salazar stepped aside, a woman who wore a taller hat than the others came forward to take his place. Holding a dagger at her waist, she slowly pivoted her body. She wore a long, multi-colored robe pulled back to display her breasts.

The woman turned in his direction and paused. Hawkins recognized Lily even though her face was covered with heavy make-up. Her eyes were shut tight and her lips were moving. She turned again and stopped. Hawkins surmised that she was offering the knife to the points of the compass. Her lips were moving.

No time to lose.

"We need those tear gas grenades pronto," he said.

Calvin dug out the canisters and handed one to Hawkins, who mentally kicked himself for not putting Calvin in place on the other side of the room. Even a delay of seconds could cost Kalliste her life.

"You're faster than I am with this bum leg. Get to the other side. Give me a single laser flash. I'll do one flash back to let you know I saw the signal. Count to fifteen. We'll toss the grenades and move in. Take out anyone in your way. We grab Kalliste and go."

Calvin took off at a speed Hawkins could never reach with his patched-together leg bones. Seconds later, as Lily made another quarter turn and stopped, a pinpoint of light blinked almost exactly across from where he stood.

Hawkins bit down on the air cartridge mouthpiece and began the countdown.

Lily had completed her 360-degree turn. She lifted the dagger above Kalliste. Hawkins tossed the grenade. In his haste, he made a bad throw. The grenade hit the floor around ten feet from where Lily was standing and skittered toward the blue-headed man.

The dog monster saw the spinning canister coming his way and lunged away from the threatening object, jerking the leash out of blue-head's grip.

A grenade arced in from Calvin's position. His aim was better, and the hissing canister slid into the crowd. The women in the long gowns scattered in flight amid a chorus of shrieks.

Hawkins slipped his CAR-15 off his shoulder and moved out from behind the column. He walked with cool deliberation toward the altar. Blue-head had seen him approaching and had his rifle at his waist. But before he could squeeze the trigger, he launched into a coughing fit from the gas rising around him. Hawkins snapped off a shot. The bullet caught the man in the chest. He dropped his weapon and crumpled to the floor.

Hawkins continued past the twitching body through the billowing gray clouds of gas. Lily was coughing violently, but when she saw him coming toward her she struggled to bring the dagger back over the altar.

Hawkins aimed the carbine. "Drop the knife, Lily."

She got her coughing under control and stared at him with watery eyes that still managed to blaze with fury.

In a surprisingly clear voice, she said, "I am not Lily. I am Potnia."

"Don't care who you are. Drop the damned knife."

Her hands tightened on the hilt of the dagger. Hawkins would have killed her if Lily hadn't been distracted by the arrival of a second blue-head. He had been on the other side of the crowd where Hawkins hadn't seen him. He, too, was without his dog monster.

Hawkins had no time to move his aim from Lily to the new target. But as the blue-head brought his gun to his shoulder, preparing to cut Hawkins in half with a quick blast, the attacker's body stiffened. The rifle fell from his fingers and he pitched forward onto his weapon.

Hawkins heard a voice yell, "Hoo-yah!"

Calvin stepped from the gas cloud, lowered his carbine and stuck the air tank regulator back into his mouth. Hawkins went to give him a thumb's up, but he faced a new threat. Lily had turned her attention from Kalliste. She staggered toward Hawkins, one hand holding the dagger above her head, and screamed in an unknown tongue. Her face was a mask of fury.

Her drug-induced frenzy was no match for tear gas. She got into a coughing fit and dropped the dagger so she could place her hands over her mouth. Still coughing, she whirled around and disappeared behind the gas cloud.

Hawkins signaled Calvin to keep watch and went over to the altar. Kalliste had inhaled tear gas and was coughing convulsively in her slumber. He shouldered his CAR-15 and lifted her in both arms. As he turned away from the altar, he heard Calvin shout:

"Hawk. Watch your back."

A figure appeared out of the gas cloud, holding the lapel of his robe against his face as a makeshift gas mask. He uncovered his face for a second to see where he was going. Hawkins immediately recognized him from the material Molly had sent him.

Salazar.

Calvin had removed his air tank to warn Hawkins. He raised

his carbine to shoot but when he got a whiff of gas and started coughing. The moment's delay gave Salazar a second to shout: "Hawkins. Don't shoot! It's me. Chad."

Hawkins hesitated. Salazar spoke again, this time in an English accent.

"For godsakes, guv'nor, lower that blasted gun."

Hawkins yanked the mouthpiece from between his teeth. "What the hell are you doing here?"

"I'll explain later. I know the way out of this dump. Follow me."

He covered his face again and pointed. Hawkins lifted Kalliste onto his shoulder. With Calvin taking up the rear, they followed their unlikely savior.

The tear gas had done its job. No one stood in their way as they raced between the rows of mummified priestesses to the chamber door, through the antechamber, then up the stairs. They stepped into the Tripartite Shrine and were headed for the exit when they heard angry voices coming from ahead.

Salazar had been pacing back and forth in the courtyard outside the entrance to the Tripartite Shrine, waiting impatiently for the explosion Leonidas was supposed to trigger with the remote control. What he got instead was an explosion of disheveled priestesses. They burst through the door of the shrine and fell on the ground where they gasped for air, or vomited, or both.

He grabbed a priestess by the arm and ordered her to tell him what had happened, but she couldn't give him a coherent answer. He turned to Bruno.

"Take the men inside and find out what's going on. If you come upon that fool Leonidas, shoot him."

Bruno summoned the other guards and they plunged through the entrance and raced through the shrine to the stairway leading down to the Maze. He paused for a second at the top of the stairs when he inhaled a breath of tear gas, but the mask hiding most of his face filtered out some of the irritants in the gas. He and his men were well paid for their dirty work. And when Salazar gave an order, it was wise to obey.

He told his men to follow him into the Maze.

Chad had been leading the way out of the shrine when he heard Bruno shouting. He herded Hawkins and his friends into the shadows of an alcove. Bruno and his men passed, and they were on the move again. Chad paused to peer out the entrance door, but saw only the stricken gang of priestesses. He motioned for the others to follow him.

Still holding Kalliste in his arms, Hawkins looked around the courtyard for an avenue of escape. His eye fell on the Auroch helicopter.

"Did you come in on that chopper?" he asked Chad.

"Yeah. It's Salazar's personal chariot. You know how to fly one of those things?"

"I don't, but my partner does."

"I'll warm up the engines. You follow," Calvin said.

He tossed his carbine to Chad and raced toward the helicopter. He moved fast, even burdened with his gear bag. Hawkins followed with Chad behind him. He stopped when he heard Kalliste groan. She was waking up but was still too groggy to walk on her own. He was about to start off again when he heard a mellifluous voice say, "You're not leaving the party so soon, are you, Mr. Hawkins?"

He turned and saw Salazar holding an automatic rifle pointed at his double. Chad dropped his gun and raised his hands in the air. Hawkins looked from one Salazar to the other. Chad had done an amazing make-up job.

"I'm afraid so," Hawkins said. "Things are getting too confusing at this party."

"Then let me un-confuse you. I'm the real Viktor Salazar. I've seen your photo. It's such a pleasure to meet you in person at last."

"Can't say the feeling is mutual, Salazar. What's a big businessman like you doing with this gang of looney-toons?"

"My family has served the Way of the Axe for centuries, but that arrangement will soon end."

"You're handing in your resignation?"

"In a manner of speaking. I'm throwing off the yoke that has bound the Salazars for centuries. There are matters far more important than these fools realize with their costumes and their thirst for blood. I'm talking about power and influence on a global scale. Soon to be mine alone. Lily and her minions are the past. Auroch is the *future*. Tell your friend to return from the helicopter."

Calvin had started the chopper's engines. As the rotors spun in preparation for take-off, he glanced out the cockpit window and saw Salazar holding a gun on Hawkins and Chad. There was no alternative. He got out of the helicopter and walked back to join the party.

Salazar watched Calvin approach, hands held high.

"Your friend shows good judgment," he said. "You wouldn't have made it very far. The castle's defenses are automated. The pilot has to activate a signal to disable the drone. We have unfinished business to take care of, Leonidas. You disobeyed my orders."

"You fired Leonidas, Mr. Salazar. My name is Chad."

"I don't care what you call yourself now. You never pushed the button on the remote."

"You mean *this* remote?"

He unwrapped his fingers from around the ear-piece, which he had palmed before raising his hands. He had given the button two punches. He pressed the button one more time. He wasn't sure what it would accomplish, but he hoped it would distract Salazar long enough for him to make a grab for his gun before Bruno and the goons arrived.

The priestess sanctuary had up-to-date ventilation and temperature control systems to prevent the mummies from further deterioration and the gas was quickly sucked out of the chamber. The security guards who'd been searching the Maze for Kalliste had heard the commotion in the sanctuary and came running back to the chamber. They saw the dead bodies of the Prior and gathered protectively around Lily, who stood in front of the altar, staring up at the mummy of the High Priestess.

The drugs had worn off and she saw the priestess not as a beautiful hallucination, but as she was, a horror of dehydrated flesh. But she still heard the voices calling from the dark caves of Sumer that had spawned the perverted religion and the secret society that came to call itself the Way of the Axe.

The voices in her head chanted over and over again.

She must die. She must die.

"Potnia."

She turned at the new chorus of voices that had called her name. The priestesses had returned to the sanctuary. Their gowns were soiled and their make-up smeared all over their faces, but their eyes still burned with fanaticism.

She smiled. "Welcome back, sisters."

She must die.

Lily understood why she had brought down the displeasure of the Mother Goddess. The offering had been insufficient. She wanted more blood than Kalliste could provide.

Lily would purge Auroch of those who opposed her, reward the ones who came to her side and launch a campaign like none before to slake the goddess' thirst. The Inquisition would be child's play by comparison.

She picked up the bull's head rhyton and held it to her breast.

She must die.

A second later Chad triggered the remote. The explosion vaporized Lily and pieces of the bull's head ripped into the priestesses and the security guards clustered closely around her.

The shock wave knocked over the flaming braziers setting the altar boughs on fire, swept aside the pillars holding the double-edged axes and slammed into the colonnade. A shower of red-hot clay fragments rained down on the rows of mummies. Within seconds, the Old Ones had burst into flames.

CHAPTER EIGHTY

Those in the courtyard heard the explosion as a muffled *whump* coming from below the Tripartite Shrine. The ground shook. A couple of sacral horn decorations fell off the roof. A metal support holding the camouflage canopy buckled. The covering over the shrine listed at an odd angle.

Salazar realized what had happened. He raised his rifle to shoot Chad, but stopped with his finger on the trigger. From the corner of his eye he had seen two gray blurs racing toward him across the courtyard. He reached instinctively for the double-axe medallion that normally hung around his neck, and realized he had given it to Chad to wear. He swiveled and let off a burst of gunfire. The fusillade missed the speeding Daemons by yards.

Salazar threw his weapon at the creatures in a failed attempt to divert them and began to run for the helicopter. He had only gone a dozen feet when the first Daemon bowled him over like a tenpin and brought its massive jaws down on his throat. The second monster dove in, fighting to be in on the feast.

The monsters were half-mad from the stinging gas when they saw the group standing near the shrine. They had been trained to focus on those not wearing a medallion, carrying a weapon or on the run, and Salazar qualified as a target.

Hawkins looked away from the disgusting sight and loped for the helicopter with Calvin by his side. Chad, who had retrieved his weapon, again took up the rear. They made it to the helicopter. Calvin got in and leaned out to pull Kalliste through the door.

"Climb in and we'll be on our way," he said.

"We can't go yet." Hawkins told Calvin what Salazar had said about the automatic launch of the drone.

"No problem," Calvin said. "I brought some bug spray."

He slipped the gear bag off his shoulder and extracted the Spike missile and its launcher which he aimed at the metal insect sitting on its staging. There was a whoosh as the missile flew from the launcher and the drone exploded in a ball of yellow and red flames. He threw the launcher away and climbed into the helicopter.

Startled by the explosion, the Demons turned away from their feast and ran back into the shrine.

"I thought that was gator repellent," Hawkins said.

"Pest's a pest."

His hands went to the controls. Within seconds, they were airborne. Calvin flew the chopper straight up, and when he had gained a few hundred feet of altitude, he hovered over the canopy.

Another support had buckled, and the camouflage cover had split apart, producing an odd optical illusion. Where only the courtyard had been visible before, there were now glimpses of the shrine's towers. Smoke bellowed from the entrance.

"That slimy bastard," Chad fumed. "The damned thing was a bomb."

"What are you talking about?" Hawkins said.

"It was a jug shaped like the head of a bull. Salazar called it a rhyton but it was full of explosives. He ordered me to carry it into the sanctuary. Gave me a remote that I was supposed to press when the ceremony began. He said it would send a signal to break up the ceremony, but what he really wanted was to blow me and everybody else up."

Hawkins went to reply, but he stopped to stare at the Tripartite Shrine. The towers had collapsed and were disappearing into the earth. He remembered the foundation cracks he had seen throughout the Maze. The columns supporting the roof must have crumbled from the force of the explosion. The weight of the shrine was too much for the ceiling to bear. The remnants of the shrine would plunge to the deepest depths of the Labyrinth.

"Like I told Salazar," he said, "I've seen all I want to see. Let's go home."

Calvin nodded and put the helicopter on a course away from the castle.

Abby was sitting in the cockpit waiting for Matt to call in on the radio when she saw the helicopter approaching. She had disobeyed his orders to leave if he and Calvin didn't call in. The deadline was an hour past, and the radio had been silent. Something had happened. That could only mean one thing. Matt was dead.

Tears welled in her eyes. It was probably too late to escape the oncoming aircraft, but she didn't care. She grabbed a spare CAR-15, stepped out of the cockpit and aimed, thinking that it was funny that the aircraft running lights were on and that it was turning side-to, offering an easy target.

Screw it, she thought. She was about to set her sights on the Auroch bull horns logo on the fuselage of the chopper, now only a couple of hundred feet away, when an arm waved at her from the helicopter window. A familiar voice came over the radio.

"Hoo-yah, Abby."

She lowered the weapon, and with the widest smile possible on her face, waved back at Hawkins.

CHAPTER EIGHTY-ONE

Molly was ecstatic when Hawkins called and said all were safe after rescuing Kalliste.

He told her how he and Calvin had infiltrated the castle maze through the water system, and with the help of someone named Chad, had stopped a bunch of crazy cultists from murdering Kalliste. A deep frown came to her chubby face at the news Salazar was dead.

"How'd he die?" she asked.

"Um. A couple of monster dogs tore him to pieces."

"Serious?"

"Serious."

"Hah," she said. "It would have gone a lot worse if I got a hold of him."

Hawkins chuckled. "I'm sure that's true, Molly."

"Dang. Guess it's over," she said.

"I wish I could be sure. Members of the Way of the Axe are scattered around the world. Salazar and Lily are dead. But as long as Auroch Industries is in business, the possibility remains that they could rekindle this whole sick thing. Salazar talked about power on a global scale. He said he was not looking to the past, but toward the future."

"Is that what he said? *Future?*"

"Yes."

"Maybe I can do something about that," Molly said.

She hung up before Hawkins could say another word. She wanted to pull her thoughts together. She went down the list in her head.

Salazar learns about the fusion process and becomes a generous supporter of the new energy source, even though it would put Auroch out of business. He puts money into an organization called FUTR. He sends an explosives expert to Cambridge where a formal announcement will be made of the new process at MIT, along with a demonstration of how it works.

An explosion kills the scientists who have developed fusion and casts doubt in the eye of the unsophisticated public over the future of science that created it. It was the way Auroch had always dealt with rivals.

Molly looked at her digital watch. The start of the energy forum was minutes away.

She called up a map of the MIT campus onto her computer screen. Big place. She had to narrow it down.

She got into the files she had downloaded from the phone retrieved from the attacker she was calling the "bird man." He had visited the campus several times, but kept coming back to the same point.

Kresge Auditorium.

She looked at a photo of the Saarinen-designed auditorium. Its distinctive rounded roof was an eighth of a sphere, made of reinforced thin shell concrete, with sheer glass curtain walls. The demonstration would be held in the concert hall of Kresge. A bomb blast would have devastating impact, testing the spirit of 'Boston Strong,' the motto that described the city's resilience after the Marathon terrorist attack.

She thought about what Hawkins had told her, that Salazar got someone to smuggle a bomb into the Maze. Guys like Salazar don't change their spots. He would do the same thing in this case. The bomb could be any innocent-looking object.

The speeches would come first, then the demonstration. The speakers stood at a podium. Good place to stash a bomb.

She went back over the credit card records of the bird man

and saw the charge for the rental truck and another for a sign painter. Using an untraceable phone, she called the sign painting company, said she had seen the job they had done. Using the bird man's name, Sutherland said that she wanted something similar for her food truck.

"Cain't remember the exact wording."

They checked their records, and said, "Acme Office Supply."

Not very imaginative. "Thanks," she said. "I'll be calling you."

The bomb would have to be triggered at the precise moment during the demonstration. With the bird man dead, that wouldn't happen. Something nagged at her. She went back to the credit card and saw that the bird man charged two dinners and lunches on several occasions. He had an accomplice.

They had kept the truck under rental. She guessed that the accomplice could sit in the truck watching the broadcast on his tablet; at the correct time, he'd make a telephone call that would trigger the bomb. She hoped the speakers would be long-winded. In the meantime she tapped away at her keyboard. Her fingers were a blur. Sweat poured down her forehead and into her eyes.

She kept an ear open to the TV volume and heard that the professor had ended his speech.

She glanced at the TV screen. The speaker had stepped away from the podium.

He smiled broadly, and said, "Now I will turn this over to my colleagues to demonstrate a discovery that will revolutionize the delivery of non-polluting cheap energy to the farthest reaches of the globe."

She punched the keyboard one more time. The television screen flickered and went dark. She had hacked the Cambridge power grid and stopped the demonstration in its tracks. She knew she had only bought some time. She had to get the auditorium evacuated and the bomb disabled. She looked up a number and called it.

A man answered. "Bomb squad."

"You'd better clear out Kresge Auditorium in a big hurry and get your bomb-sniffing dogs to the podium before the lights come back on."

"Are you saying there's a bomb at MIT?"

"Yup. Bomber's going to trigger an explosion from an Acme Office Supply Truck. Keep an eye out for him."

"May I have your name, please?"

She paused, smiled, and before she hung up, said,

"The name is Gowdy."

EPILOGUE

Two weeks later

As soon as Hawkins returned to Woods Hole he picked up the pieces of his life. His first task was to reacquaint himself with Quisset. Uncle Snowy had spoiled the dog, but when Hawkins came by to take her home she jumped right into his truck and snuggled against him.

He was biking every day. Spending time at home surrounded by his collection of antique dive gear. Spain was all a blur. The flight back to Cadiz. Chad disappearing at the airport. The trip to the hospital where Kalliste was diagnosed as dehydrated but otherwise in good shape. The ocean glider project was on track and the pay-off was making its way to his bank account. It might just cover the deductible the insurance company wanted him to pay for *Falstaff*'s loss, but it was good to be back in the rhythm he'd become accustomed to.

He hadn't heard a whisper from Kalliste since they'd said goodbye in Spain, so he was pleased when the padded envelope arrived in his mail with her Santorini address on the outside. Inside the envelope was a plastic baggie containing a coin and a note. The coin appeared to be made of gold and was irregular around the edge. Pictured in relief on one side was the profile of a man. The flip side had the image of a dove.

The note said: *Skype me anytime.*

With Quisset at his heels, he climbed the stairs to his upstairs office, connected to the Skype function of his computer, and clicked on Kalliste's address. Her smiling face appeared almost instantly. She looked rested and happy.

"How wonderful to see you, Matt! Sorry I didn't contact you earlier. I've been hard at work on my lexicon of Linear A."

"No apology needed, Kalliste. You must have a pile of work to do."

"I'm putting in twelve-hour work days and loving every minute. This will be an on-going project for years to come. The computer translation program has accelerated my work tremendously. The writer, luckily, wrote in simple declarative sentences, using a tightly spaced script, so there's a lot of information. I have deciphered the scroll and confirmed that it was written by the second in command to King Minos."

"The mysterious Minotaur?"

"He was in the thick of things. He confirms that the Theran eruption here on Santorini sparked a civil war between the king and the High Priestess and her brother. Rather than offer his only child for sacrifice as the priestess demanded, he ordered his commander to take the girl to safety."

"Which is how they landed in Spain."

"They were heading to Egypt but the priestess was catching up, so they sailed to Spain hoping to throw her off. The priestess followed. There was a sea battle. His ship, the one we dove on, sunk, but he escaped in a sailboat. He made landfall, married the girl's nanny, and they went into hiding. The king's daughter married and had children, of which I am a descendant."

"It's fortunate for both of us that the girl survived. Otherwise we never would have met."

"That's sweet of you, Matt. It's also lucky the Minotaur kept a journal at the order of the king. The scroll was passed down from generation to generation. By the time my grandfather had it, there was no one left in the family who knew how to read Linear A."

"Any indication when the Salazars entered the picture?"

"Minotaur said that the ship with the High Priestess and her brother-consort was damaged but made it to shore. The Salazars helped them take over the Minoan mining colony that grew into Auroch Industries, allowing them to keep the sacrificial ritual intact. The Minoans and the Salazars had a symbiotic relationship that lasted centuries."

"Apparently that relationship wore thin."

"It was bound to. The Salazars were used as enforcers. My guess is that some family members were allowed into the inner sanctum only after male mutilation, which rendered them neutered."

"Salazar didn't strike me as an old tabby cat."

"He wanted the reward for his sacrifice, which was complete control of Auroch. He may have wanted revenge as well."

"How did Minotaur know the layout of the Maze that was on the scroll?"

"He sent spies all over Europe to keep an eye on the priestess and her gang. Some of them helped build the Maze that would later form the foundation of the castle."

Hawkins thought back to the flawed construction that he'd seen in the Labyrinth. "Maybe the Minotaur's men supplied the lousy concrete that brought it down."

"We'll never know, but it would be sweet to learn that the Minotaur was responsible for the collapse of the Maze."

"Any indication what happened to Minotaur?"

"Nothing in the scroll. But I recalled a strange mound on my grandfather's vineyard. I was warned to stay away from it. Grandfather said there were ghosts. It's approximately the size and shape of a Minoan burial chamber. The Minotaur said he wanted to be returned to Crete after his death. Maybe he got his wish. And maybe the scroll came with him. I think my Papou knew more about what was under the mound than he let on."

"The Minotaur's tomb would be a fantastic discovery."

"I won't be the one to make it. Minotaur deserves a peaceful rest for his devotion to the man whose profile is on the coin I sent you."

"I suspected it was ol' King Minos. Thanks for the present. Where did you find it?"

"Remember the reference in the scroll to more than one treasure? The king's daughter was the first. The Minotaur left directions to the second treasure. The coin was part of it."

"You're making my head spin, Kalliste. You found an actual treasure?"

"I will say no more than this. I have exorcised parts of the scroll that deal with the second treasure from my translation."

"I don't understand, Kalliste. Why do that?"

"My country is in dire financial straits. People would gladly plunder their heritage to make up for their own foolishness. I must admit to plunder myself, thus the coin, but if you tell anyone where you got it, I'll deny it. Call it partial payment for all your help, Matt. Hope we will work together again."

"I'm sure we will, Kalliste. Good luck."

She smiled once more and the Skype connection was gone.

Hawkins was staring off into space, trying to absorb the enormity of what Kalliste had told him, when he heard Abby call from the first floor. He tucked the note and the coin into a drawer and locked it, then went downstairs. Abby was standing in the foyer holding a sea bag. She was dressed in shorts and a T-shirt and cap with 'Navy' on it.

"First Mate Abby reporting. Ready to go?" she said.

"Aye-aye, mate. Snowy gassed up the yacht for us."

They got into the pick-up truck with Quisset, drove to Eel Pond and rowed out to the *Osprey*. The Water Street drawbridge was raised and they cruised out to the harbor on a course for Martha's Vineyard where they would stay the night before heading to Nantucket. When he'd extended the weekend invitation, he said it wasn't the Greek Islands cruise she'd asked for.

"Just promise me that guys with blue heads won't be chasing us all over the place. Ugh. Do you think those crazies are done for good?"

"There's a good chance. Auroch Industries has gone under. The company was the financial support for the Way of the Axe. The bomb-sniffing dogs found the explosives and the cops rolled up Salazar's triggerman. The fusion discovery announced at MIT has a long way to go, but it's another nail in the coffin holding the Auroch corpse."

"I hope so. What's new from Calvin and Molly?"

"Calvin has decided to return to field work. Worried that he's losing his edge. Molly's back into bird photography. She sent me a photo of a Golden eagle sitting on a nest. She seemed quite happy. Said she will enjoy being a grandmother."

"What on earth did she mean?"

He shrugged. "Who knows? This is Molly we're talking about."

The weather was superb, with fair winds, blue cloudless skies and temperatures in the high seventies. They sat on the beach at Katama and walked the cobblestoned streets of Nantucket. At night they became reacquainted with each other's bodies. After a passionate few days on the high seas, they chugged back to Woods Hole tanned, tired and happy. As usual, their relationship had fallen into an affectionate limbo.

"Where do we go from here?" Abby asked, as Hawkins tied up to the mooring.

"Anywhere you want to go. North to Maine. South to Florida."

"That's not what I meant, Hawkins."

"I know what you meant. I was trying in my clumsy male way to avoid discussion of a commitment."

She sighed. "That's progress, I guess. In other words, we're still on but not really."

"I think it's more than that, Abby."

She threw her arms around him and gave him a long kiss. "Keep in touch, Matt."

"I will. That's a promise."

"Good. Now promise you will call immediately the next time you get into trouble."

"You have my word."

She smiled. "In that case, I hope you get into trouble very soon."

Hawkins missed Abby from the moment she left. He buried himself in work, and rather than go home to his big, lonely house after leaving his harbor side office that night, he walked across the fog-shrouded street to the Captain Kidd. He joined his team from the ocean glider project and talked about working together again. He stayed after the others had left and was sitting under the mural of the pirates, wondering whether to have another beer, when the waitress came over with a foaming mug.

She pointed to the bar. An older man who had thick, white hair and a matching beard waved at him, then slipped off his stool and came over. He was wearing jeans and a T-shirt that read, *Hunley*, with a picture of the Civil War submarine that had been recovered from Charleston harbor.

Hawkins lifted the mug. "Thanks for the brewski."

"My pleasure," he said with a twinkle in his blue eyes. "You looked like a guy in need of a drink."

"What brings you to Woods Hole?" Hawkins thought that with his windburn complexion the man looked like someone who spent time on the sea. "Business with WHOI or the Marine Biological Lab?"

"Neither. Met a guy from here in my travels. Thought I'd check out the place. Nice little burg. Kinda like the fog. Now if you'll excuse me, I've got to get going."

As he headed for the door, Hawkins called out, "What was the guy's name? Maybe I know him."

The man turned and broke into a big grin. "I think it was Hawkins. Matt Hawkins," he said, and stepped through the doorway.

Hawkins stared at the door and started to rise from his chair only to settle back for another sip of beer. His new friend would have disappeared into the fog by the time he got there. The damp weather had affected his bum leg, but even without the limp, Chad or Leonidas or whoever he was now would have disappeared.

As anyone knows who has tried, it's impossible to catch a will-o'-the-wisp.

ABOUT THE AUTHOR

My fiction-writing career owes it start to the bad navigation of an 18th century pirate. For it was in 1717 that a ship, the *Whydah* went aground, reportedly carrying a fabulous treasure. In the 1980s, three salvage groups went head-to-head, competing to find the wreck. I was working for a newspaper covering the treasure hunt. The controversy over the salvage got hot at times and I thought there might be a book based on the story.

I developed my own detective, an ex-cop, diver, fisherman, and PI named Aristotle "Soc" Socarides. He was more philosophical than hard-boiled. Making his first appearance in "Cool Blue Tomb," the book won the Shamus award for Best Paperback novel. After many years in the newspaper business, I turned to writing fiction and churned out five more books in the series.

Clive Cussler blurbed: "There can be no better mystery writer in America than Paul Kemprecos."

Despite the accolades, the *Soc* series lingered in mid-list hell. By the time I finished my last book, I was thinking about another career that might make me more money, like working in a 7-11.

Several months after the release of "Bluefin Blues," Clive called and said a spin-off from the *Dirk Pitt* series was in the works. It would be called the *NUMA Files* and he wondered if I would be interested in tackling the job.

I took on the writing of "Serpent" which brought into being

Kurt Austin and the NUMA Special Assignments Team. Austin had some carry-over from Soc, and another team member, Paul Trout, had been born on Cape Cod. The book made *The New York Times* bestseller list, as did every one of seven *NUMA Files* that followed, including "Polar Shift," which bumped "The DaVinci Code" for first place.

After eight *NUMA Files* I went back to writing solo. I wrote an adventure book entitled, "The Emerald Scepter," which introduced a new hero, Matinicus "Matt" Hawkins. I have been working on the re-release of my Soc series in digital and print, and in 2013, responding to numerous requests, I brought Soc back again in a seventh *Socarides* book entitled, "Grey Lady." After that book I wrote a sequel to the first Matt Hawkins book, entitled "The Minoan Cipher," and I'm working on an eighth *Soc* book which I'm calling "Shark Bait." My wife Christi and I live on Cape Cod where she works as a financial advisor. We live in a circa 1865 farmhouse with two cats. We have three children and seven granddaughters.

To learn more about Paul Kemprecos, check out his website at http://www.paulkemprecos.com.

78597175R00218

Made in the USA
Columbia, SC
18 October 2017